NIGHT LIFE

NIGHT LIFE

DAVID C. TAYLOR

A TOM DOHERTY ASSOCIATES BOOK
NEW YORK

NIGHT LIFE

Copyright © 2015 by David C. Taylor

A Forge Book
Published by Tom Doherty Associates, LLC
175 Fifth Avenue
New York, NY 10010

www.tor-forge.com

Forge® is a registered trademark of Tom Doherty Associates, LLC.

The Library of Congress Cataloging-in-Publication Data is available upon request.

ISBN 978-0-7653-7483-7 (hardcover)
ISBN 978-1-4668-4343-1 (e-book)

Forge books may be purchased for educational, business, or promotional use. For information on bulk purchases, please contact the Macmillan Corporate and Premium Sales Department at 1-800-221-7945, extension 5442, or write to special markets@macmillan.com.

First Edition: March 2015

Printed in the United States of America

0 9 8 7 6 5 4 3 2 1

For Priscilla, Susannah, and Jennifer, with love

ACKNOWLEDGMENTS

My thanks to my agent, Lisa Gallagher, for her diligence, her encouragement, and her smart, concise, and provocative comments on the manuscript; to Tom Doherty, Bob Gleason, Linda Quinton, Kelly Quinn, and the kind people at Forge for their enthusiasm and for deftly guiding me through uncharted waters; to Cynthia Merman for her precise, stylish copyediting.

To my writer friends who encourage through word and example: Jeffrey Lewis, George Semler, Alex Beam, Henry Rosenbaum, Carlos Davis, Beth Gutcheon, and Tony Fingleton; and special thanks to my brother, Michael, who first led me astray down to the bright lights of Times Square, the pool halls, and the pinball parlors.

Toda la vida es sueño,
y los sueños, sueños son.

—Pedro Calderón de la Barca,
Life Is a Dream

NIGHT LIFE

PROLOGUE

New Year's Eve 1953. A good year, 1953, all in all. That shit head Stalin is finally dead. And those Commie spies, the Rosenbergs, went to the hot squat at Sing Sing. The Korean War is over, though maybe that didn't work out as well as it should have. But it's over. The CIA kicked the Red son of a bitch Mosaddegh out of Iran and put the shah back on the throne where he belonged. That showed the Russkis not to screw around in the Middle East. Sure, the Dow is below three hundred at 280.9, down twelve and half points from the beginning of the year, but everyone knows that's going to change. America, the arsenal of democracy, a beacon of freedom to the world, is the richest, most powerful country on the planet. 1954 is going to be great. Forget The Bomb. Forget the Red menace. Tonight New York is electric with the joy of all that is sure to come. It is good to be alive.

Especially if you have a good job, money in your pocket, and a great-looking woman on your arm, and the three young men walking west on 50th Street had all of that and more. They had been at P.J. Clarke's and had taken on just enough champagne to be sure the world was made for their pleasure. They were headed for Times Square for the New Year's Eve lights and the crowds and the fun of it. They were doing the New Yorker's zigzag—down a block, over a block, down a block, over a block, jaywalking, dodging cars, never stopping—and their latest zag took them along the north side of the Waldorf-Astoria. The lights of Park Avenue glittered ahead of them. The cold air reddened their cheeks and pinched their fingers, but the men walked with their coats open, because who gives a damn about the cold; they were impervious, invulnerable. A black Cadillac limousine idled at the side entrance to the Waldorf, exhaust drifting from its tailpipe, and the thought that went through the minds of the three young men when they saw it was, *Someday, man, someday.*

Two men in dark overcoats and fedoras came out of the hotel. One opened the back door of the limo, and the other took up a position next to him to block the sidewalk, and the young people had to stop, which was not what they had in mind, not them, not tonight, and one of the men, recently back from a business trip to London, said, in his best Brit accent, "I say, my good man. You are stopping the Sutton Place Rangers from their appointed rounds. Kindly step aside." He grinned and took a step forward as the others laughed at his daring. *Good old Pete, always had something up his sleeve.*

Overcoat put a hand to Pete's chest and stopped him. "Step back." His voice was cold and he added a short, abrupt shove for emphasis, and good old Pete stumbled back and almost fell.

"Hey, wait a minute. What the hell?"

The man ignored him, because a uniformed doorman opened the side door to the Waldorf, and a party of five people hurried out toward the limousine. There was a woman in their midst. Her head was covered with a scarf. A red dress showed under her open mink coat. She wobbled on high heels. The men around her were laughing at something as they came out the door. The one who helped her into the car was movie star handsome, in his twenties, wearing a fawn-colored Chesterfield coat with a collar of chocolate velvet. His blond head was hatless, and the lights made his hair shine like gold. He put a hand under the woman's elbow, and as she bent to enter the limousine, the scarf pulled back to show a glimpse of a heavy, powdered pouched face, and the hem of her dress rode high enough to reveal thick legs, and then she was gone, and the young men scrambled in after her. The man holding the door and the blocker went back toward the hotel. The limo pulled away.

"What an ugly broad," good old Pete said with perfect timing so the man who had pushed him had to have heard it as he went back into the hotel. Pete's friends all laughed, and the small, dark cloud of the encounter was blown away by the laughter, and they went on toward Times Square and the New Year, and all it would bring.

1

Orso stamped his feet in the snow and watched the all-night drugstore up the block on Sixth Avenue. "He ain't coming. I told you. Only a mongoloid hits five in a row. He wised up." Orso was well over six feet tall and weighed more than two hundred pounds and had the round, well-fleshed face of a sensualist.

"Give it a chance. He always hits around midnight. It's quarter to." Cassidy was an impatient man who was trying to teach himself how to wait. He was shorter than his partner, broad shouldered and strong, but whip thin as if the motor running inside consumed everything as it entered.

"New Year's Eve. We should be in a warm bar someplace, not freezing our asses off waiting for some stickup guy who ain't going to show," Orso said. "Guy's got half a brain he's over at Dempsey's getting plastered waiting till next year to go back to work."

"If he had half a brain he wouldn't be robbing all-night drugstores one after the other right up Sixth Avenue."

Orso lit a cigarette and cupped it in his hand so the glow was hidden from the street. "Did you hear about Gavrilich?"

"Hear what?" Cassidy leaned against the brick wall of the alley and watched the snow filter down past the streetlights. He wore a sheepskin jacket and boots against the weather, and the gun in his pocket was cold through his thin leather glove.

"Canned. Cleaned out his desk this morning. Eighteen years on the job, no severance, no pension. Turn in your badge, your gun, and sayonara. The shooflies got him. Loyalty clause, or whatever the hell they're calling it. Turns out he joined some group a few years ago, now it's on the attorney general's list, a Commie-front organization. Only reason he joined was there were a lot of women in it, he figured he'd get laid."

"Well, he's fucked now."

"Politics. Stay away from that crap. If I can't eat it, drink it, wear it, or fuck it, I'm not interested." A core philosophy Cassidy had heard from Orso before. He wished his own view of life were as straight a line. That's what we do, isn't it? Try to keep it simple, control the chaos, keep the lines straight. Did it ever work?

The traffic was light on the avenue, and the car tires hissed in the wet. Somewhere a group of drunks sang "Should old acquaintance be forgot . . ." loud and off-key. Cassidy looked east along the block to the neon sign for the Cortland Hotel, its colors muted by the falling snow.

Orso followed his look. "You threw him out the window." Orso flicked a hand at the hotel.

"Yeah." He flinched from the memory and felt his heart race the way it had that morning when he woke from the dream, months ago, but still vivid.

• • •

In the dream, a woman screamed. In the dream, Cassidy and a man he knew— who was he? who was he?—walked together toward an open window, face-to- face, chest-to-chest, as if in a dance, and then the man disappeared with a cry. Cassidy awoke that morning with his heart pounding, and the unease from the dream stayed with him through the day.

It had been Indian summer then, the briefest of seasons, one he loved, the last soft days of the year, elegiac in their echo of the summer past and yet promising that spring would come after the dark cold days of winter. Kids played stickball and ringolevio in the streets until called inside for dinner. People sat on their stoops and fire escapes—the men in T-shirts, the women in cotton dresses—and listened to radios propped on windowsills, Guy Lombardo's band, or Count Basie over at Birdland, or to *The Lone Ranger, Broadway Is My Beat,* or *Inner Sanctum.* "Who knows what evil lurks in the hearts of men? The Shadow knows."

That afternoon Cassidy was on the corner of Sixth Avenue, not far from where he stood now, tearing the cellophane off a fresh pack of Lucky Strikes and thinking how lucky he was to have been born in this city, that when it worked, it worked better than anyplace.

He heard a woman scream and turned toward the sound. He waited but did not hear it again. It could have been anything, a mouse across a kitchen floor, a cockroach in a drink, a cold hand up a skirt. He lit a cigarette and started east along the block. Ahead of him May Stiles burst out of the lobby door of the Cortland Hotel. She spotted Cassidy and came at him in a stumbling run on high heels and grabbed him by the arm. "Cassidy, there's a guy upstairs beating the hell out of one of my girls. Do something."

Another scream.

"Will you do something, for christ's sake? He's hurting her bad."

"Do you have a key to her room?"

"A key? Yeah. A key. Sure." She scrabbled around in her big purse and fumbled him a hotel room key.

"Wait in the lobby."

Cassidy listened outside the room on the third floor and heard a grunt of effort and the smack of a fist on flesh, and "Bitch," muffled by the door. He slipped the key into the lock and turned it slowly while he eased the knob. The latch freed with a click and the door opened. The room smelled of gin, cigar smoke, and burning meat. The bed was torn apart, blanket and sheets dragging. A naked woman huddled on the floor near a knocked-over chair. Her legs were bent awkwardly, and one arm was raised to ward off the man who stooped over her. He was naked, bowlegged, and big gutted with a mange of hair across his shoulders. He held an iron in one hand. The cord ran to a socket under the open window.

"You work for me. You don't work for that bitch. You work for me, got it? What? You didn't think I'd find you? The fuck I wouldn't." He pressed the iron down on her thigh and her scream almost covered the sizzle of the burn.

"Hey," Cassidy said.

The man turned. His chest was matted with hair, and his belly hung down like a sack. He looked at Cassidy without surprise. "What the fuck do you want?"

"Get your clothes on, Franklin. Get out of here."

"Hey, fuck you, Cassidy. I'm on the job." The woman sobbed until she ran out of breath. She crawled to the overturned chair maybe with the thought of getting under it to hide.

Cassidy could smell her burned flesh. "You're on the job?" He could feel the rage rising. "You're on the job? What the hell do you mean? This is the job?"

"Get the fuck out of here." Franklin put the iron down on the table, and smoke curled up around it. He took a step toward a chair against the wall where his clothes were draped; a holstered gun was threaded on his pants belt. "I'm going to teach you a hard lesson, you uptown punk."

Cassidy moved to block him.

Franklin threw a punch. Cassidy slipped it and slammed Franklin's arm as it went by. The momentum turned him, and Cassidy hit him twice in the kidneys and his breath whistled out. Cassidy punched him in the neck and he sagged. Franklin put his hand on the table to hold himself up. "You fuck. I'm going to kill you, you fuck."

"Not today." Cassidy grabbed two handfuls of the man's gut, squeezed hard, and lifted. Franklin came up on his toes whinnying in pain and hammering at Cassidy's head and shoulders. He tiptoed backward as Cassidy lifted and pushed, and they went toward the open window as if in a dance. The backs of Franklin's legs hit the windowsill. Then Cassidy threw him out, and he went with a cry.

When he dreamed of the man falling, he did not know it was going to be a cop.

He had had dreams like that since childhood, dreams in which he was both asleep and awake. They let him rise toward waking but held him below the surface, trapped in the dream and aware of it. Days, weeks, or months later he would be somewhere in the city, and he would recognize that this was what he had dreamed, this street, that person; the snatch of conversation as two people left a room; that opening door with that woman behind it; that man with the two black dogs, who smiled at him like a shark. The dreams were random. Sometimes they came true, sometimes they did not but just disappeared to wherever dreams go. He tried to find markers in them that would allow him to separate them from normal dreams, but he could not. He had assumed that everyone had dreams like that, until he talked to Brian about them, and his older brother looked at him and said, "Are you nuts?" and told him about déjà vu. But these dreams weren't that. They were something else.

He did not know they were prophetic until he dreamed of his mother's death.

• • •

"A cop," Orso said. He flicked his cigarette away to hiss in the snow.

"A pimp."

"Yeah. Okay. But Franklin's also a cop."

"Exactly my point." Cassidy's breath escaped like smoke. "You want to be a pimp, be a pimp. You want to be a cop, be a cop. Pick a side and stick with it."

"You can't throw a cop out a window. They're going to stack your ass in a corner and take turns pissing on it."

"They're not going to do anything. They didn't even call a disciplinary board. Why? Because what the hell are they going to find out? That a Vice Squad lieutenant was running whores and got thrown out a window when another cop caught him torturing one of those whores? They don't want to touch it. So they transfer me out of Vice and pretend it never happened."

"They don't get you for that, they'll get you for something else. That's how it works."

"Never happen. You know why? Because my heart is pure."

"Your heart may be pure, but your mind is fucked-up is what it is."

"Hey," Cassidy said, and jerked his chin up the block. A man in a bomber jacket and cloth cap walked past the window of the drugstore and slowed to look in. "Casing it."

"Or checking to see if they've got his brand of hemorrhoid cream."

"See if he goes by again."

The man walked past the drugstore and then stopped in the unlighted doorway of a closed shop and surveyed the street. A man and a woman walked past him arm in arm, and after they were gone, he stepped out of the doorway and strolled to the drugstore and stopped to look in the window as if searching for a product.

"Waiting for the customers to get out of there," Cassidy said.

First an elderly man left. He wore a long, dark coat and fur hat with earmuffs and carried a small white paper bag, and then three young men and three young women followed. Their voices, full of cheer, carried to the two cops in the alley. "Ugly broad," one of the women said, and they all laughed. One of the men scooped snow from a parked car and threw it at the others, and the six of them went down the block, laughing and calling, in a running snowball fight.

The man in the bomber jacket looked around casually to make sure no one was approaching, pulled his hat low over his eyes, put his right hand in the pocket of his jacket, and went in.

"Here we go," Orso said. They crossed the sidewalk and went along outside the line of parked cars and ducked down behind a Hudson Hornet opposite the drugstore.

"Damn," Orso said. "Fucking snow. Thirty bucks' worth of brand-new Florsheims ruined. The radio said no snow tonight, and I bought it."

Cassidy watched the man in the bomber jacket. He had stopped to leaf through a magazine from the wire rack just inside the door, but now he moved back to where the white-haired pharmacist stood behind the counter in a white coat. The pharmacist looked up and resettled his glasses with the tip of one finger. The man pointed to something in the case, and when the pharmacist bent to look at it, the man pulled his pistol and touched it to the pharmacist's head. The pharmacist's hands shot into the air and his shoulders hunched. The man shouted something that did not escape the glass of the window, and the pharmacist put his hands down. The robber looked over his shoulder to see if anyone had seen the dumb show and then turned back and jabbed his gun at the pharmacist and moved him over behind the big cash register.

"I think I'm going to shoot the son of a bitch when he comes out just for the shoes," Orso said. "You back me up?"

"Absolutely. Shoot him. Self-defense."

"I'll go north. We'll box him." Orso moved along the line of cars until he was past the drugstore, and Cassidy went south and squatted behind a DeSoto coupe. The pharmacist put the money from the register in a white paper bag, and when he was done, the robber hit him on the head with the gun barrel. He did not go down, but even at that distance Cassidy could see the blood begin to stain his white hair. The old man put one hand to the wound and held the other up to plead. The robber hit him twice like driving a nail, and the pharmacist folded out of sight behind the counter. Shit, he didn't have to do that, Cassidy thought. He had the money. He didn't have to hit the old guy. Why'd he do that?

The stickup man paused just inside the glass door and checked the street. When he came out, the gun was back in the pocket of his jacket and he carried the paper sack holding the money. He turned north. Cassidy did not know which car hid Orso until his partner stepped onto the sidewalk behind the robber. "Police, asshole. Hold it."

The man took off running. He tried to pull the pistol from his pocket, but it caught on the cloth, jerked from his hand, and skittered away across the pavement. Orso went after him, but his new shoes betrayed him. One foot went out from under. He slid wildly for a moment, then went down. Cassidy glanced at him as he ran by. Orso was pushing himself up from the snow. "Goddamn it! Go get him. I'll get the gun."

The robber turned east on 53rd Street. A man walking his dog shouted at him as he ran past. Cassidy had his gun in his hand, but there were people on the street. He put the gun away.

He gained when the thief skidded as he ran out into the traffic on Fifth Avenue. Horns blared at both of them. The cap flew off the man's head as he reached the east side of the avenue. Down the block people leaving the Stork Club crowded the sidewalk. The robber dodged for the street. Cassidy caught him and slammed him against a Cadillac limousine double-parked and idling. The bag of money flew from the man's hand. Someone on the sidewalk said, "Hey, what's going on?" Cassidy grabbed the struggling man's hair and jammed his face into the limousine hood to calm him. He yanked him around by the shoulder and elbowed him in the mouth, and then hit him under the rib cage. *That was for the pharmacist, an old man doing a job. He gave you the money, goddamn it. You didn't have to hit him.* The thief sagged with a groan.

Someone pulled on Cassidy's sleeve. He brushed him away without looking. "I'm working here." He hit the robber again. An old bull named McGinley had taken him out for a drink when he first put on the uniform and told him, "When you catch one of the fuckers in the act, beat the shit out of him. He may beat you in court. Witnesses might not show, might lie. Someone could pull strings to cut him loose. Maybe he jumps bail. But you beat the crap out of him, every time he looks in the mirror, sees that broken nose, he's going to know." Cassidy let go and the thief curled himself around his pain in the gutter. The hand came back to pull hard at his sleeve. He turned.

A young man faced him, young except for his eyes, which were pale, heavy lidded, and as old as the bottom of the sea. "What do you think you're doing?" the man demanded. Rubberneckers crowded the sidewalk behind him.

"Back off, bud. Police business." He was calm now. His anger was a switchblade. It flew out fast and bright and sharp, and then it folded away again, gone until the next time. How long had it been there? Since the war, certainly.

"Back off? You don't tell me what to do." The man's dead eyes were always moving, never settling on Cassidy. "That's my car. Get that man away from my car. I have to go." The chauffeur had gotten out of the driver's side and now stood uncertainly in the street.

"In a minute."

Orso came through the crowd. He was breathing hard, and there was a rip in the knee of his pants.

"Tony, he dropped the loot. I don't know where the hell it went."

"Right," Orso said.

The man was impatient. "Thompson, move the car. We have to go now." The chauffeur looked to Cassidy nervously.

"A couple of minutes, we'll be out of your way." He turned back to pat the robber down for other weapons. There was movement behind the tinted windows of the limo, and he could sense there were a number of people in the car, but the smoked glass blurred their faces.

"No. Now." The man grabbed his arm again.

"Back off or I'll run you," Cassidy said.

"Do you know who I am?" The young man asked.

"No," Cassidy said. He clicked handcuffs on the robber and spun him to the pavement.

"Hey," the robber complained. "I'm in the snow down here. You're ruining my trousers." Cassidy kicked him lightly to quiet him.

"I'm Roy Cohn." He waited for the impact on Cassidy.

"Happy New Year, Mr. Cohen."

"Not Cohen." Tight with anger. "Cohn. Roy Cohn."

"Okay. Well, give my congratulations to Mr. and Mrs. Cohn, and I hope they're as happy with the result as I am." He smiled into the man's anger and leaned against the fender while he lit a cigarette. He kept a foot on the stickup man's head to hold him.

Orso stepped around Cohn. He held the paper bag of loot. "The doorman had it. He was keeping it dry for us under his coat. A concerned citizen."

"What's your name?" Cohn's face was stiff with rage, and for a moment those dead eyes held on Cassidy.

"Cassidy. Detective Michael Cassidy." He jerked the stickup man to his feet and pushed him toward the sidewalk, and Cohn had to step aside.

"You're going to hear from me," Cohn said.

"Always a pleasure to hear from a citizen, Mr. Cohen."

Cohn started to say something, then wrenched open the door to the limousine and scrambled in. Before he slammed the door, Cassidy saw that the car held four or five men surrounding a heavy-set woman in a red dress.

Cassidy walked the stickup man to Fifth Avenue and sat him on the curb at the corner. The man spat blood into the snow between his feet.

Orso unlocked a call box and ordered a squad car to come pick up the prisoner. He offered Cassidy a cigarette, took one for himself, and lit them both with his Zippo. "Hey, you really didn't know who he was?"

"Cohn? Yeah, sure. He's Senator Joe McCarthy's rottweiler, his lawyer on the what? The Senate Subcommittee for Investigations, something like that. They're going to save us from the Communist menace. Going to root out the Commies in all walks of life. Last I heard they were saying maybe Eisenhower's a Commie. Cohn's the one who's always whispering in Mc-Carthy's ear or drilling into some poor witness. 'Detective Orso, are you trying to tell this committee that you had no knowledge that the Italian Ravioli League was a Communist front? You're an idiot if you think we don't know of your Commie affiliations. How dare you come before this committee and lie about your attempts to overthrow the U.S. government!' He's that guy."

"Not someone to screw with, I hear."

"Fuck him. What's he going to do to me?" The limousine pulled up to wait for the light. Cohn, a ghost behind the smoky side window, looked at Cassidy. The light changed, and the car turned north on Fifth.

The stickup man threw up in the gutter. Orso nudged him with his shoe. "I don't think this guy's looking at a happy new year," Orso said.

2

March. Cold rain and dark days. Winter still pressed at the city's back. Spring was a distant hope.

Cassidy listened.

"It was blood, you could tell, you know what I mean? Knew it right away, blood. Come right through the kitchen wall up at the top there, up in the corner over the stove. She's yelling, 'It's a miracle. It's a miracle.' I'm telling her, shut up. It ain't no miracle. It's blood from upstairs. Don't never marry someone with religion. She'll drive you nuts." Donovan wore an Eisenhower jacket with no shirt underneath and army-issue trousers. His bare feet were stuck into untied shoes. He was unshaven, and his belly tested the jacket's buttons.

"It could've been. It could've been a miracle, blood through a wall. Like them tears at Lourdes the little girls saw. The Virgin, and that . . . the stigmatism. It could've been." His wife's hair was dyed an unlikely orange, and her hands clutched each other and were never still.

"She wants to call the priest, Father Dunbar over there to St. Mary's. Call him, I says, but it's blood from upstairs, like when the commode overflowed. I'm going up."

"He ain't afraid of nothing. He was in the war, Iwo Jima, Okinawa, all them. Killed a lot of Japs. Ain't afraid of nothing." She rubbed her hands down the front of the apron that covered a yellow-and-green-patterned housedress. Fuzzy pink slippers shaped like bunnies muffled her feet.

"Was the door open?" From where they stood on the landing, Cassidy could see through to the bathroom and the dead man.

"Nah. It was locked." Donovan dug a ring of keys from his pocket. "I've got the key, see. I'm the super. I hear the radio playing. I knock. No answer. I figure they can't hear me over the radio, so I knock again, loud. No answer. I'm banging pretty good but nobody's coming, so finally I think, what the hell. I open the door, and I seen him dead over there."

"You could tell he was dead?" Cassidy asked.

"I walked over and took a look. I've seen dead men before. He was dead."

"He was in the war. He's seen a lot of dead men in the war." She touched her husband on the shoulder, and he turned and gave her a wink.

"Did you touch anything?"

"No."

"Besides the doorknob," Cassidy said mildly.

"Yeah, right. The doorknob. I didn't want to go in, but I thought I ought to see, see if he needs help or something, but he's dead, so I go out and find the beat cop having a pop up to the Chinaman's and bring him back."

"Okay. Thank you, Mr. Donovan."

"Yeah. You're welcome. Don't mention it."

"I'll come talk to you in a while, if you'll just wait in your apartment."

"Sure." They took one last look, and then Donovan put a solicitous hand under his wife's elbow and eased her down the stairs.

Cassidy nodded to the uniformed cop waiting by the window and then went to the open bathroom doorway and looked at the dead man. He was tied to a wooden armchair with brown electrical cord. His shirt had been cut or ripped off him and lay in rags near the chair. A towel was loosely knotted around his throat. There was blood on the towel and blood on his mouth. A gag. He had been tortured. There were dark wounds on his chest and neck where something had torn out chunks of flesh. One nipple was gone. Cassidy saw the bloodstained pliers in the sink. There was a military-style hairbrush next to the pliers in the sink and another one on the floor. Blood from the wounds had soaked the man's suit pants and then pooled under the chair. It ran thick and bright down the black-and-white tiles to the corner behind the toilet where the tiles were broken. The room smelled like a slaughterhouse.

A year of combat, eight years on the Force, and the viciousness men offered each other still surprised him. When was he going to learn? Or maybe that was something you should never learn.

The man's blond head was tilted back and to the side, and even dead he was movie star handsome except for the agony, softened by death but still etched on his face. His eyes were lightless, as dull as stones. Whoever had killed him had robbed him of everything he was and everything he might have been. What had he done to attract such savagery? Maybe it wasn't something he had done but something he knew.

Cassidy turned back into the living room. The furniture crowded it as if bought with a grander space in mind. There was a white carpet, a black sofa with matching armchair and hassock, and an ebony-and-glass coffee table within reach of the sofa. A brushed-aluminum lamp like something off an airplane swooped over the sofa on a long flexible stalk. There were framed prints on the wall that Cassidy recognized as Degas's dancers. A black-and-red Chinese lacquered cabinet held liquor bottles and a siphon. A fawn Chesterfield coat with a chocolate brown velvet collar had been hung on a coatrack near the door. A suit coat that matched the bloodstained trousers in the bathroom was draped on the back of a chair.

Six glasses, one plate, one fork, one knife, one spoon, one cup, and one saucer were in the drying rack in the narrow galley kitchen. Cassidy recognized it from his own kitchen as a bachelor's array. When he was home, the dead man drank more than he ate, and he mostly ate alone. A brown paper bag on the counter next to the small refrigerator showed dark where something inside was thawing. Cassidy looked in and found two baking potatoes, a box of frozen peas, and a package wrapped in white paper with *sirloin* scrawled on it with a butcher's pencil. When Cassidy poked it with his finger, he found it cold. He could feel the uniformed cop's eyes on him, but he ignored him and went into the bedroom.

The window was wide open. Rain puddled on the floor. Cassidy crossed and looked out. The fire escape led up to the roof and down to the alley next to the building. There was a broken flowerpot on the landing outside the window where someone might have kicked it scrambling out. Cassidy turned back into the room.

A fake fur throw covered the double bed. There was another white carpet on the floor. A dark green leather armchair with a side table and reading lamp next to it took up one corner. A low, wide ebony bureau, topped by a large mirror, was against the wall opposite the window. Cassidy raised his eyes and caught his reflection in the glass. Unruly black hair, dark eyes bloodshot from lack of sleep, angular face with winter-pale skin stretched over bones that threatened to break through. *Who the hell are you, and why do you keep looking at me that way?*

A wooden tray on the bureau top held a collection of matchbooks. Cassidy flicked through them: the Copa, "21," El Morocco, the Stork Club,

Jimmy Ryan's, and some of the other clubs on Swing Street. A photograph in a silver frame showed the dead man on a beach, arms lifted toward the bright sky, muscles taut and defined, hair blowing, smiling, a good-looking young man in a bathing suit caught in a moment of joy. The closet held four suits, five sports coats, slacks on spring-loaded hangers that held them by their cuffs, a rack of ties, four snap-brim fedoras on the shelf above, gray, dark gray, black, and brown, one straw hat in hopes of summer, and a half dozen pairs of shoes on the floor. He looked at the labels in the suits—Paul Stuart. The man was a dandy, liked clothes, and could afford them. So why was he living in a Hell's Kitchen walk-up?

He turned back into the living room to the uniformed cop shifting nervously near the window. He was a big man made bigger by his blue wool overcoat with the brass buttons. His hat was on the radiator near the window and his white hair was matted down. "Scalabrine, right?"

"Yeah. Right. Hey, look, Detective, I wasn't drinking. Donovan's busting my balls 'cause I've been after him about leaving his garbage cans on the curb. Lazy bastard. They're out there three, four days. I just stopped into the Chinaman's to buy a pack of smokes."

"Did you call the meat wagon?"

"Yeah."

Cassidy looked around the room. The top was up on the big Motorola radio-phonograph near the bar and the green light on the dial glowed. "Was the radio on when you came in?"

"Yeah. Loud. I turned it down."

Cassidy turned the volume up and Benny Goodman's clarinet swung "Puttin' on the Ritz" out into the room. "Louder than that?"

"Yeah."

Cassidy turned the radio off. He looked out the window and saw the van from Bellevue pull up and park next to a fire hydrant. "The wagon's here. When they come up, I want you to go canvass the rest of the apartments, see who's here. See if anyone noticed anything, screaming, somebody coming or going."

"Sure, I can do that." Scalabrine had been on the force long enough to know how to handle detectives, but not this Cassidy guy. He wasn't a big man, maybe five ten or eleven, a hundred sixty-five pounds. He wore expensive clothes, not the cheap suits most bulls waded around in. He looked like a fucking wolf. The guys in the house said he wasn't like the rest of them. Different, they said, maybe 'cause he was a rich man's son. Smart, unpredictable. Some said he didn't seem to give a shit, and others said he cared too much, that he couldn't step back. Some said he was this, some said that, but they all ended up with "different," whatever the hell that meant. It meant he threw Franklin out a window. Threw another cop out a fucking window. What was that about? Well, tonight it was about keeping your mouth shut and your eyes open, Scal, yes, sir, no, sir, three bags full, sir, and hope he forgets you exist. Fucking Donovan, he didn't have to mention the Chinaman's.

"I'll be back," Cassidy said and went downstairs to the Donovan apartment. It smelled of boiled cabbage, furniture polish, and baking bread.

"Nah. Didn't hear a thing," Donovan said. "We had the radio going, me and Mae, listening to Joe McCarthy take some of them Reds over the jumps." The room was furnished with worn and shabby pieces. Pictures of saints cut from magazines hung on the walls in five-and-dime frames. A red blanket covered the sagging sofa where Donovan sat. His bare feet were up on a low coffee table already burdened by a large prewar radio in a heavy wood case.

"Did you hear anything when you went up and knocked on the door?"

"The radio, like I said."

"Nothing else? Nobody moving around?"

"Nope."

"How long were you out there before you opened the door?"

"I don't know. A minute or two. I wanted to give him time, in case he didn't hear me at first. Then I figured, blood, hell he might be hurt. That's when I opened up." He took his feet off the table. "You want a beer or something?"

"No, thanks."

"I'm going to get me one." He heaved up and Cassidy followed him into the narrow kitchen where Mae Donovan pulled a crusty loaf from the oven and put it on a rack to cool and then slipped a baking sheet with a round dough in its place and closed the oven door. She brushed sweat-damp hair back from her forehead, leaving a smear of flour and smiled at Cassidy. "There's the blood." She pointed to a corner of the ceiling. The stain was already darkening to brown against the yellowing plaster. "I don't know how we get the stain out. How do we get the stain out, Ralphie?"

"Don't worry about the stain. I'll take care of the stain." He stooped to pull a Schaefer from the Kelvinator and popped the cap off with a church key that dangled on a string from the upper hinge.

"How? Blood and all. It don't come out easy."

"For me to know and you to find out." He grinned at Cassidy in male conspiracy and drank half the beer without coming up for air.

"Mrs. Donovan, did you hear anything, a scream, a yell?"

"No. We was listening to McCarthy going after them Reds, you know? We had it turned up pretty loud, 'cause I was in the kitchen and wanted to hear. Do you think he'll get them out of government and the Army and all? There seem to be an awful lot of them."

"I didn't fight a war so that these Commie sons of bitches can come in and take over." Donovan burped. "Root 'em out, says I. Send 'em back where they came from. This ain't their country."

"Did you hear music from up there? Apparently he was playing the radio too. Maybe you heard him turn it on." The killer used the radio to cover the torture screams. If they had heard it turn on, Cassidy would have a time frame.

"Nope. Didn't hear a thing." He looked to his wife for support, and she shrugged and shook her head.

"What can you tell me about him?"

"Ingram? Not much."

"Is that his name?"

"Yeah. Ingram. Moved in during the summer. Works nights, I think. Coming and going at all hours. Who knows? Scraping by when he first got here. Missed the rent a couple of times. Had to talk to him, a little heart-to-heart. Then he must've caught something, 'cause back in the fall the rent starts arriving like clockwork first of the month. Pays what he owes. Bunch of new furniture comes in."

"A nice-looking boy," Mae offered. "Always polite. Says, 'Good morning, Mrs. Donovan. How are you?' Helped me carry things a couple of times."

"Friends? Visitors?"

They looked at each other. "Nah," Donovan said. "Not that I know of. I don't spy on the tenants, you know? Live and let live, long as they don't cause trouble."

"You said you had to use your keys to open the apartment door. Was the dead bolt locked?"

"Nah. Just the latch."

Cassidy gave Donovan one of his cards. "If you think of anything, call me."

"Cassidy, huh? So where're you from in the Ould Sod? A lot of Cassidys down around Donegal."

"If I'm not there, leave a message. I'll get back to you."

He went back upstairs. *The sod of Donegal. Not too many of his Cassidys
down around there.* His father's name had been Tomas Kasnavietski when
he fled the border area between Russia and Poland as a fifteen-year-old
to avoid dying in the tsar's army. The story he told his children was that
he had worked his way south, sleeping in the woods, or in haystacks and
barns when he was lucky, working when he could, stealing when he had
to, avoiding farm dogs and Cossack patrols, until he washed up in Odessa.
He stowed away on a Black Sea tramp freighter, was caught, beaten, and
thrown off in Istanbul. He survived on the waterfront for six months, thiev-
ing and robbing, and then stowed away on another freighter, bound, he
was told, for New York, where he had it on good authority, the streets
were paved with gold. Having no idea of geography, he had only brought
food for a week. He was discovered ten days out, as the ship cleared the
Straits of Gibraltar, when he worked his way out of the hold where he had
hidden to try to steal food from the galley. The captain proved to be a
man with a generous heart. Instead of throwing him overboard, he put
him to work. The ship was bound not for New York but for Quebec City,
Canada, where Tomas Kasnavietski jumped ship into a winter as iron
hard as any he had left behind in Poland. He crossed the border into
Vermont through an evergreen forest knee-deep in snow, and hopped a
freight train south.

A year after he left home, he disappeared into the polyglot slums of New
York, where the streets proved to be paved with cobblestones and horseshit.
Thomas Cassidy had seemed the perfect American name to his ear, an era-
sure of the past, a fiction on which to build a bright American future. It
was a story his children had gleaned over the years in bits and pieces. Sometimes their father threw a fragment in passing; sometimes, the dinner wine
working with the after-dinner bourbon, he spun the stories out to his
children sitting near the fire in the darkened library, while his wife, Joan,
went to another room to read. To young Michael Cassidy, it had seemed an
incredibly romantic adventure, one that he could never match. As a man he
understood that it had not been romance but a fight for survival reimagined
from a position of comfort and safety.

Cassidy went back into Ingram's apartment. The body had been strapped to a gurney for the trip to the morgue, and Cassidy had to step aside to let the morgue team maneuver out the door. Al Skinner, the lead tech, was crouched in the living room. He had pulled up a corner of the white carpet and was examining the underside.

"Find something?" Cassidy asked.

"Hey, Cassidy, how're you doing? Nah. I was just checking. You see this carpet? You know what it cost? There's a place over on Twenty-ninth and Third under the el there, ABC Carpets. You know that place? Best deal in town. I was in with the wife a couple of weeks back, I saw one just like this. You know what it went for? Four hundred and fifty bucks. You turn your back, I'm going to slide this thing out of here." Skinner grinned and stood up. He was a spider of a man, dark and wiry, with lank brown hair and bright blue eyes.

"What've you got for me?" Cassidy tapped a Lucky Strike down on his thumbnail and lit it with his Zippo. He offered one to Skinner, who shook his head.

"Stuff'll kill you."

"What won't?"

"Multiple tearing wounds to the torso and abdomen consistent with the pliers we found in the sink. Right now, I've got no cause of death. None of the wounds killed him. There's a lot of blood, but he didn't bleed out." He handed a manila envelope to Cassidy, who dug in it and found the dead man's wallet. Gold letters stamped on the leather showed it was from T. Anthony, an expensive leather shop on Madison Avenue. "A hundred seventy-five bucks in cash. Almost two weeks at my salary. Finders keepers, but I'll split it with you, 'cause I've got a generous heart."

There was an expired New Jersey driver's license in the wallet with an address in Englewood. According to the license, Alexander Ingram was twenty-four years old. Cassidy wrote down the address, and when he slid the license back in, he found another card. "Huh."

"What? Did I miss a couple of hundred?"

"An Equity card."

"What's that?

"Actors' union."

Cassidy shook the envelope out on the coffee table to see what else Ingram's pockets had held. Loose change, a blue silk handkerchief, a gold penknife, a ring of keys, a gold Ronson cigarette lighter, an alligator-skin cigarette case holding six Chesterfields and a hand-rolled tucked to one side. He took it out and sniffed it. "Reefer." He dropped it back in the envelope. "Anything else?" he asked Skinner.

"Not till I get him on the table. Where's your partner? He owes me ten bucks on the Yankees game."

"In court. Testifying."

"I don't suppose you want to settle up for him? No? Okay." Skinner gathered up Ingram's belongings and left.

Scalabrine was waiting for Cassidy on the landing. "Nothing. Nobody heard nothing. The apartment right above is empty. There's an old lady across the hall wouldn't hear a gun go off you stuck it in her ear."

"Okay. Tape and seal the place when Crime Scene is finished. Then get a couple more men and canvass the area. I want to know if anyone saw somebody use the fire escape from this apartment, or saw someone come out of the alley down there."

"Sure. Uh, Detective, are you going to say anything about my being in the Chinaman's?"

"No."

"Thanks."

• • •

Cassidy found Skinner downstairs on the sidewalk watching the attendants slide the gurney into the van. Rubberneckers clustered on the neighboring stoops. There were not many. Dead bodies were not rare in Hell's Kitchen, and the cold March drizzle was discouraging. The streetlights were on and the rain-slick pavement glistened.

"You'd think winter'd give us a break," Skinner said. "Sally wants to go upstate to look at antique stores on Saturday. I told her, it snows, she's on her own, I'm not leaving the apartment."

"Call me tomorrow after the cut."

"Tomorrow? I've got six stiffs and a floater-bloater waiting. I'm understaffed, and the new guys they hired must've learned anatomy in an auto body shop."

Cassidy took a ten-dollar bill from his pocket and showed it to Skinner, who looked around quickly to see if anyone was watching.

"You know, Cassidy, you can get arrested for bribery."

"Not in this town."

Skinner snaked the ten from his hand and slipped it in his pocket. "Give me a couple of days. I'll call you. Hey, and tell Orso I want my sawbuck."

Cassidy flicked his cigarette into the gutter and turned east to Broadway.

The drizzle softened to mist that muted the blare of the neon. Cassidy nodded to Charley One Leg, shrouded in a black wool coat that dragged on the pavement as he leaned on his crutch and hawked tickets for the second-floor dance hall on the corner of 50th. It was early, and only three sailors on leave, their romantic optimism fueled by cheap booze, took a chance and climbed the stairs past the framed photos, glossy head shots with white smiles, the hair just so, taken when the women waiting above were young, optimistic, still sure that their break was just around the corner, the next audition, the next open call.

A bearded man in a white robe stood on a milk crate at the corner of 49th and tried to interest the hurrying people in the fast-approaching end of the world. The clatter and bong of pinball machines and the whoops of players at the shooting games rattled out the open door of the arcade on 47th. Just past it was a discount store that had been GOING OUT OF BUSINE$$$$ for six years. It sold cheap portable radios, Japanese cameras, World War II surplus equipment, and knives that couldn't hold an edge AT ROCK BOTTOM PRICE$$$$$. Four punks sneered at passersby as they leaned against the window of a Pokerino parlor under a tinny speaker that crooned Perry Como, the collars of their leather jackets turned up, cigarettes dangling from the corners of their mouths, pompadoured hair slicked back to ducktails, pegged jeans tucked into engineer boots. They looked at Cassidy with cold eyes as if deciding whether to eat him. He measured them in return and smiled, and they turned away with elaborate indifference. Past them, three jittery dopers with jumpy eyes and neck tendons like wires were chopping open Benzedrine inhalers on the glass of a pinball machine just inside the door. Nighttime on Broadway— the Stem, as the denizens called it—and everybody was having a good time. Jesus, he loved it.

The sidewalk was crowded. Out-of-towners moved slowly, eyes raised toward the Planters sign in the Square that poured endless neon peanuts from its bag and the Camel cigarette man who blew five-foot smoke rings from the billboard on the Claridge hotel. Impatient New Yorkers, immune to the scene, jostled them in their rush to get wherever it was they were rushing to. Cassidy walked fast, a New Yorker's pace. He slipped through gaps, turned his shoulders to slide past gawkers, still playing the game from his childhood of going as quickly as possible without touching anyone, a skill, Gwen said when he told her about it, that he brought into his personal life.

Tony Orso stepped out of an Orange Julius halfway down the block carrying a cup of juice in one hand and a rolled newspaper in the other. He saw Cassidy and drank the juice while he waited for him. He wore a white nylon shirt, a short, wide orange-and-green tie, and scuffed shoes, with what he called his testifying suit, a cheap off-the-rack number from Robert Hall that he wore only when he went to court. Three years before, dressed as he usually dressed, he had testified as the arresting officer of a bunco artist posing as a priest who had bilked people out of thousands of dollars. The jury acquitted the man, and Orso learned later that some of the jurors, noting the elegance of his clothes, decided that he dressed too well to be an honest cop and that they could not trust the testimony of someone so obviously corrupt against the word of a man of God. From then on, he wore his testifying suit.

"How'd it go?" Cassidy asked.

"Twenty to life. Sayonara, baby. Couldn't have happened to a nicer guy." Orso crushed the paper cup and tossed it in a trash can. "I hear you caught one."

Cassidy told him about Ingram.

"Tortured, huh? What do you think the guy was after?"

"No idea. We'll start checking in the morning, friends, family, whatever. Someone's going to know something. He had a beef with a business partner. Someone thinks he stole something and wanted it back. You know how it goes. Somebody gets a half-smart idea and a couple of days later he's explaining to us that he didn't mean to hurt him, it just got out of hand."

"What're you doing now? You want to go get loaded? I always work better with a hangover."

"I'm meeting my brother and sister for dinner at Sardi's."

"I'll walk a ways with you." They walked south. "You tell that sister of yours she wants to give up the Park Avenue life and move to a walk-up in Bed-Stuy, I'm the man for her."

"I don't see how she can turn down that offer."

"Not if she's smart. Ah, shit. Look at that," Orso said.

Down the block, a man talked earnestly to a young woman who leaned her back against a drugstore window. She wore a gingham dress with a full skirt supported by can-can petticoats, a fuzzy pink angora sweater, and pumps with two-inch heels. Her blond hair was held in place by a black velvet band. She looked like a girl on the way to the prom or the grange hall dance and might as well have worn a sign saying *Just off the bus.* The man had one hand up on the glass by her head and leaned in to talk to her with practiced intimacy. He was a good-looking slick in black trousers pegged tight at the ankles above pointed half boots, a dark yellow one-button roll jacket, a green shirt open at the collar, and a stingy-brim porkpie hat with a bright red feather in the hatband. He smoked through a black cigarette holder clenched in his teeth. His black hair was combed to a ducktail. He leaned in close to say something to the girl's ear, and then pulled back and laughed and put his free hand on her arm and rubbed it up and down. She watched him with the fascination of a mouse held by a cobra's weave.

Orso said, "Hey, Flea, what's happening?" The man started to turn from the girl with a startled expression, and then Orso slapped him on the back with the rolled newspaper in what looked to anyone nearby like a friendly gesture. Pain washed Flea's face, and his knees buckled. Orso turned him away from the girl with an arm around his shoulder and slapped him on the chest with the paper and said, "Let's you and me have a little talk," and moved him to the curb.

The girl looked scared.

"It's all right, Miss," Cassidy said, and showed her his badge. "What's your name?"

"Juney Gilmore. What's going on? What happened? Did we do something wrong? I was leaning on the window. Is that okay? I'm sorry."

"No, no. That's okay. Everything's fine. My partner just had something to say to Flea. How long have you been in town? Do you mind my asking?"

"I've been here a week. I'm staying at the Barbizon. Do you know the Barbizon? It's really swell." The Barbizon was a hotel for single women on East 63rd and no men were allowed above the first floor. "I've got a job starting on Monday. Secretary in a law firm on Lexington. Stickney & Decker?"

"How'd you meet Flea?"

At the curb, Orso still held the man with an arm around his shoulders, and Flea was bobbing his head in agreement with whatever Orso said.

"Flea? Is that his name? He said his name was Steve." She was beginning to relax. "It was real clumsy of me, I guess. I was walking and looking up at that sign with the man blowing smoke rings, and I bumped right into him and almost knocked him down. But he was real nice about it."

"I'm sure he was." Bump into a tourist who was not paying attention. Lift his wallet, or, if you were Flea, start a conversation and see if it took you where you wanted to go. "Flea's a pimp, miss."

"What?" She looked over wide-eyed to where Flea and Orso talked.

"A pimp. He uses women to . . ."

"You think I don't know what a pimp is? I know what a pimp is. Just because I don't come from New York doesn't mean I don't know things."

"Flea specializes in young women new to the city."

She looked over again, and Cassidy wondered whether he saw more curiosity than fear in her face.

Orso put his face close to Flea's and said something hard, and then he slapped Flea on the chest again with the newspaper and turned him loose. Flea walked away without looking back, hunched over with his arms hugging his chest as if holding something in.

The newspaper Orso carried wrapped a lead pipe. He always carried a rolled newspaper when he walked the Stem, and the paper always held the pipe. Some people, like Flea, Orso said, just needed a little extra encouragement to do the right thing.

"Miss Gilmore is staying at the Barbizon before she starts a job next week," Cassidy told Orso. "Juney, this is Detective Orso."

"How do you do." She offered a white-gloved hand.

Orso took it and held it. "How about we put you in a cab. You'll be back at the hotel in ten minutes, safe and sound."

She took her hand back, and her face set. "I'm not a child."

"No, I can tell. You certainly are not a child. But still . . ."

"You sound like my parents. The big, bad city. I can take care of myself."

"Of course you can." Orso looked over at Cassidy with a raised eyebrow. Cassidy shrugged.

"I have places I want to go and things I want to see, and when I'm done, I'll go back to the hotel. I'm going to the Automat for dinner."

"That's a good choice," Orso said, who would never go through its doors. "Just be careful."

"I don't have to be careful. I'm twenty-three years old." She recovered some of the politeness her parents had drummed into her. "But thank you both for helping me. I'm sure I would have been fine, but thank you anyway." She nodded to them and went off down the street. Innocent. Full of possibilities. A magnet for guys like Flea. How long would the innocence last?

"You can't save them all," Cassidy said.

"Yeah. Fuck it."

"Come have a drink at Sardi's."

"Nah. I'm going to stay out here and fight crime awhile longer. I'll see you tomorrow." He tapped Cassidy lightly on the shoulder with the paper-wrapped pipe and headed south toward Times Square.

• • •

Cassidy crossed 45th and went down Shubert Alley through the pack of theatergoers, women in fur coats, men in tweeds and wool, as they crowded the doors to the Shubert buzzing with anticipation of Cole Porter's *Can-Can*. He dodged two slow-moving taxis on 44th Street and went into Sardi's and surrendered his hat and coat to the hatcheck girl. Sardi's had been the theater community's clubhouse for more than thirty years. Cartoons by Alex Gard of actors, directors, producers, and other Broadway luminaries lined the walls. The Tony Awards had been invented at Sardi's, and the yearly announcements of the nominees and winners from the Broadway shows took place there. The upstairs room was where Cassidy's father hosted opening night parties for the plays he produced. The cast, crew, investors, and friends waited for the publicist to deliver the first editions of the newspapers with the evening's reviews. If the reviews were good, the party went on till dawn. If they were bad, people left quickly as if fleeing contagion.

Vincent Sardi Jr. stood by the bar, head bent to listen to a waiter's complaint, smoothing his mustache with his thumb. He put a hand on the waiter's arm to stop him for a moment and said, "They're already here, Michael."

His brother and sister were in their usual booth along the wall near the middle of the dining room, their drinks half finished in front of them. Cassidy slid onto the banquette at the unoccupied place where a martini waited.

"In this ever-changing world, the one thing we can count on is that Michael will be late," Leah said. "One more minute and I was going to drink that myself to keep it from getting warm."

"Glad I could save you from that sacrifice." He drank some of the martini, cold, clear, astringent, and felt things loosen inside him. "You look beautiful, as always. That too is immutable." Two years younger, she had his black hair, but smooth and glossy like a raven's wing, and his pale skin tight over the bones of her face, but with the angle and edge softened to give her a startling beauty that made men and women stare.

"What about me?" Brian said over his raised glass of scotch. "I was voted the handsomest child two years in a row at the Presbyterian Church School." Their older brother was a big man with a barrel chest, a big square head, and a broad, cheerful face.

"You are without equal."

"I get that. I get that. Damned with faint praise. I know an actor, when he goes backstage to see a friend who just stunk up the joint, says, 'Good is not the word.' I get it. You, by the way, look like crap."

"Ah, family. You can always count on the kindness."

"Do you ever get any sleep?" The question of a man with an orderly life.

"Not much."

Brian was clearly his father's son. The Alex Gard caricature of Thomas Cassidy that hung on the wall above the booth could have been of Brian. It was as if the genetic material of the mother and father had been isolated and passed on intact, the father's to Brian, the mother's to Michael and Leah. The three of them clinked glasses and smiled at each other. They met here once a month, and while spouses and lovers were invited, they rarely came.

"It's a club, just the three of you, and no one else gets to join," Gwen had said. "You finish each other's sentences. You laugh at jokes no one else gets. You say things and suddenly the three of you are nodding and chuckling and saying, 'Yes. Right. Has to be,' or something like that, and nobody else at the table has a clue." It was one of those nights when she was picking through his crimes in no particular order of severity.

• • •

"Tortured with pliers," Brian said, and winced.

The waiter slipped in to pour Leah more wine. They talked of other things while they ate, of the McCarthy subcommittee hearings going on then, the new plays on Broadway, and the prospects of the new musical their father was producing that was now in rehearsal, but finally they had come to this.

"A fawn Chesterfield," Leah said. "Where the hell did he get a fawn Chesterfield?"

"Paul Stuart," Cassidy said. He pushed his plate back and lit a cigarette.

"You looked."

"I did," Cassidy said. "I'm a detective. Clues are my business." He waggled his eyebrows at her.

"Defective detective."

"Not the point, is it?" Brian said. "The coat, I mean. It seems to me the point is the torture. Was the guy hiding something, or did someone just hate him?"

"Of course the torture is the point," Leah said.

"What about the coat, though?" Cassidy asked.

"I don't get it. Come on, Sherlock. Give," Brian said.

"Was his coat wet?" Leah asked. "Were his shoes?"

"Yes."

"He'd just come in."

"I think so." Cassidy waited for her to go on.

"What else? There's something else. Have you told us everything?" She chewed her bottom lip and studied him for clues with dark eyes that mirrored his own. He loved her intensity even when it blew her up, or blew up the people around her, which it sometimes did.

"Everything I noticed," he said.

"He bought a sirloin steak, two potatoes, and a box of peas, dinner for two."

"Right."

"So who was the guy with the pliers? The dinner guest?"

"I think so."

"And he wanted something Chesterfield had, or knew."

"His name was Ingram. Alex Ingram."

"Do you think Ingram told him?"

"I would have."

"And nobody heard anything?"

"He had him gagged. I think he'd do something to him and only take the gag out if he thought Ingram was going to answer."

"Jesus, you two. Can we change the subject to something slightly less morbid?"

. . .

"Have you gone by rehearsal?" Brian asked while the hatcheck girl retrieved his coat and hat.

"I haven't had time."

"When was the last time you saw him?"

"Maybe a month ago."

"He's your father."

"I see him."

"Not enough." Brian saw his brother's face and held up his hands. "All right, all right. Look, I've got to be down in Washington starting next week, and then I'll be back and forth, so maybe you could pick up some of the slack."

"Washington?"

"We're going to televise the Army-McCarthy hearings. I'm going down to D.C. to set it up. The boss thinks people will want to see them, and we've got to do something different. CBS and NBC are killing us." Brian produced a news show for ABC, the upstart television network.

"Like watching paint dry."

"McCarthy's the most dangerous man in America. He doesn't believe in anything, no matter what he says. He's like a nasty boy torturing a cat. There's no purpose to it but the pleasure he gets by inflicting pain. From the very beginning this whole business of finding Communists in government has been crap. Do you know how many lives he's ruined by accusing people of being Communists? Hundreds. Do you know how many Communists have been successfully prosecuted since he started? None. Zero. Now he's out to wreck the army, and all because that little shit Cohn couldn't get an officer's commission for his friend Schine."

"Roy Cohn?"

"Yeah. Why? You know him?"

"I ran into him once. He didn't like the way I was doing my job."

"He's been running around with this guy David Schine, a rich kid from California. Schine got called for the draft. Cohn tried to get him out of it, and when that didn't work he tried to pressure the army into making Schine an officer. The army said no. Schine's a private out at Fort Dix, and Cohn's using McCarthy and the committee to get revenge by investigating the

RESULTS TODAY : THE PRESS, MOVIES, COLLEGES, ETC ARE ALL LEFT WING SOCIALISTS OUT TO GET THE U.S.A. NOT SUPPORT IT!

NIGHT LIFE ⋯ 41

army." Brian took his coat and hat from the girl. "Thanks, honey." He put fifty cents in her bowl, shrugged into the coat, and turned to clasp Cassidy's hand. "Anyway, I have to be back and forth to Washington, and I'd really appreciate it if you'd look in on Dad."

"Okay." He would do it, because it would please Brian. "Love to Marcy," Cassidy said.

"Absolutely. And to Gwen." He saw Cassidy's face. "Uh-oh."

Cassidy shrugged.

"When?"

"Last week."

"You want to talk about it? I can stay."

"Nothing to talk about. She discovered she didn't like me much anymore, and she left." How do you explain the end of something you thought was going to last?

"Ah, jesus." He hugged Cassidy, as if to offer another ration of comfort. "I'm sorry."

"Yeah. Me too." As if that covered it.

A quick flash of her, turning to see him as he walked into the Oak Bar at the Plaza to meet her for drinks, blond hair cut short, a bright smile, happy to see him, eager. His heart would lift. A kiss, quickly broken by her, her Midwestern upbringing making her leery of public displays of affection. Early in the affair when it was full of light.

He watched through the glass door as his brother went out, impatient to get home to his wife and two daughters. Brian hailed a taxi and got in without looking back.

Cassidy stood up from the table when Leah returned from the powder room. "Brian left."

"Wife and kids. The happiest man I know. Did he talk to you about Dad?"

"How'd you know?"

"He asked me if you'd seen him lately. I said I didn't know. He got that serious look on his face, the one he gets when he's going to do something he thinks will make us one big, happy family."

"We aren't?"

"I don't know. Yeah, I guess we are. As happy as any other. Are you going to go to a rehearsal?"

"I guess so."

"Good. That'll make him happy."

"Brian?"

"Dad, stupid."

"Yeah, right."

"It will, because you, sweetie, are the favorite."

"You're the favorite, if he has one. Or Brian. I'm tail-end Charlie."

"Uh-huh." She smiled at her brother's denseness.

"Want to walk over to the Street, listen to some jazz? Tatum's playing at Jimmy Ryan's." He was not ready to face an empty apartment.

"Not tonight. Put me in a taxi, okay?"

The night had cleared. The streets were still wet, and the neon signs were gashes of color the wet street threw back in broken reflections. Cassidy waved down a Checker and opened the door. Leah hugged him. As he started to let go, she held on. "I want to talk to you. I need some advice." Her voice was muffled against his chest.

"Sure." Uh-oh. Where had she gone off the rails this time?

"Maybe next week. I have to think. I have to make a decision."

"About what?" Maybe it was nothing. Maybe she couldn't decide what to buy their father for his birthday. Sure.

She pulled back to look up at him. "Uh-uh. You have to buy me lunch to get the dirt. Some dive where all you cops and hoods hang out."

"Where we stir our coffee with our guns. Everything okay with Mark?"

"Mark is great, but Mark is in Delaware talking to DuPont. Mark is in love with polyvinyl chloride."

"I didn't know that little Greek strumpet was still around."

"Strumpet. Ha ha. Plastics, dummy. Mark is bullish on plastics. He's going to be even richer." She put a hand against his cheek. "I love you, Michael. I wish you took better care of yourself."

"I love you too. Call me when you want to have lunch."

He watched the taxi drive away. His sister had always run with scissors, and he knew that one of the reasons he had left home was to miss the moment when she tripped.

• • •

He joined the army the day after his eighteenth birthday, with a young man's illusions that war was an adventure to run toward. A year of combat across France and Germany taught him a harsher reality. There were days of cold and hunger and wet, hours of fear, moments of horror, endless seconds of real terror. He learned that in the hottest times something inside him stayed cool, that he could go forward when other men would not.

In April of 1945, the war was winding down. Spring came as it did every year no matter what men did to each other, and spring brought hope the way it brought flowers out of the dead land, hope for survival, hope for an end to this. Cassidy and his squad came to Flossenbürg concentration camp in April. Human skeletons in striped rags clung to the wire and stared at them with huge uncomprehending eyes. The camp gate was open, and all the prisoners had to do was step forward, but no one came out. It was as if the freedom offered was too great a prize to test. One of them—A man? A woman? Impossible to tell—stretched a bony hand toward them, and then slowly collapsed to the spring mud and died. The man standing next to Cassidy, a big blond BAR gunner from Nebraska named Gordon, began to cry.

He had dreamed of this moment months before while lying in a hospital bed recovering from shrapnel wounds. He had pushed the dream aside, dismissed it as the product of drugs, fear, and pain, but now they were here in front of him, human skeletons hanging on the wire, just as he had seen them in the dream, the one on the ground, Gordon crying. He had not had a dream like that since his mother's death, and he had thought that he was through with them, that the agony of that day had burned them out of him. But they were back, occasional, elusive, unsettling.

• • •

Cassidy shipped stateside two months after VE-Day. Demobilized and back in New York, nothing fit, not the old clothes, the old attitudes, the old friends, the old haunts. The war lit anger in him that he could not extinguish. His father offered him a job at his theatrical production company, but Cassidy knew that was wrong, and when Tom Cassidy said he would give him a stake in any business he wanted, there was nothing that he did want. Brian, recently demobilized as a major from the Army Signal Corps in Washington, was at work at ABC and offered to find him a job there, and gave him a rueful smile and a pat on the shoulder when he said no, thank you.

The first year home was a blur of bars and booze, of women whose names he could not remember when he woke up next to them, of early-morning escapes with his shoes in his hand from apartments he did not recognize out to the quiet, empty gray dawn streets and the surprise of where he was in the city. Days were passed in recovery and anticipation of darkness and bright lights, ice rattling in a glass, and boozy laughter. How could he tell it was morning if he didn't have a hangover?

Leah watched him without comment and then asked, "Are you ever going to be like you were?"

He said, "No. I don't think so."

"Well, that's not all bad. You were kind of a pain in the ass sometimes." Which made him laugh. "And you're kind of a pain in the ass now. When are you going to snap out of it?"

"I don't know."

"Do it soon, will you?"

He enrolled at Columbia but dropped out after six months, unable to find traction.

One day he walked by the police station-house on 67th Street, saw the recruiting poster, went in, and signed up.

At dinner that night, when he announced it, his brother said, "That's wonderful, Mike. The city needs more people like you, people who are willing to take some responsibility."

Leah said, "Cool. Will you teach me to shoot?"

His father, rigid with anger, said, "I did not raise my son to be a Cossack," and left the table.

His mother, of course, was dead.

3

The driver's license and Social Security card in the man's wallet said his name was Edmond Fraker. He had been Edmond Fraker for a couple of months now and was getting used to it. If they caught him, the name would trace back to a dead end, giving his employers deniability. Not that he would get caught. It had never happened, no reason to think it would that night. Still, get cocky, get hit. The war had taught him that. He took the knife from his pocket, flicked the blade open with the snap of his wrist, and slit the police tape on Ingram's apartment door. The dead bolt was unlocked, so he slid the blade into the gap between the door and jamb, found the latch tongue, and eased it back. A moment later he stood inside with his back against the closed door. He listened for a while. No doors opened in the hall. No curious neighbors. No shouts of alarm. He turned on his penlight and shaded the narrow beam with his hand, and used it to avoid furniture as he crossed to the windows and pulled down the blinds. When he crossed back, he glanced through the open door to the bathroom, and his light picked up the dark blood on the tiles. He wedged a straight-backed chair under the front doorknob just in case. It would hold for a few seconds. Not that he expected anyone, but he thought of himself as a careful man. He pulled on thin medical gloves and started his search. Fraker savored assignments like this, a nighttime creep, clandestine, solo.

During the war he discovered night was his territory. Where most feared the darkness, he welcomed it, no, loved it, felt more alive in it than he did in the day. He slipped the knife from his pocket again and flicked the blade open, five inches of Solingen steel, both sides edged and honed, the aluminum haft solid in his hand, the surface pebbled for grip. He had taken it off a Waffen SS sergeant an hour after the parachute jump that had put him behind enemy lines in France in the days before D-Day. Clouds wisping across the moon. The fading engines of the drop plane. The hum of wind through the shrouds and the flap and rustle of the canopy above him as he fell, heart racing, toward a darkness pricked by the flames of marker fires lit by French partisans in the field below. The wind took him away from there, and he watched the markers disappear. When he landed, no one answered the cricket click of the toy noisemaker he had been given for signaling. He was alone, and he liked it.

He moved west by compass through the dark woods searching for the river that would lead him to the village of St. Pierre and the backup rendezvous. Sometimes he heard the snap of gunfire and once the deeper cough of a machine gun and the crump of a grenade, but it was always in the distance. He stopped at the edge of the woods and looked across a field toward the dark line of the hedgerow at the other side, the grass damp under his knee. More than two hundred yards of open ground, nowhere to hide, and the full moon turning the new spring grass to silver. The night was warm. A light breeze rustled the leaves of the trees behind him and the air smelled of new-turned earth. The hedgerow at the far side was a dark mystery. It could hold a hundred men . . . or none. One way to find out. Step out and see what happens. All right, then. Go. He started to rise, and he heard the snick of metal on metal no more than twenty feet from where he crouched. The man moved and Fraker saw him. He too was at the edge of the trees looking out at the open ground. One of his? One of theirs? Theirs. The coal scuttle helmet silhouetted against the paleness of the haystack behind him answered that, so Fraker shot him twice with the silenced pistol he'd been issued. Near the dead man's hand was the knife and the piece of garlic sausage he had been about to eat. The snick of the blade opening was the noise that betrayed him, his bad luck and Fraker's good, and he had carried the knife as a charm ever since. He had discovered its wonderful efficiency at everything from opening letters to slipping between a man's ribs to puncture his heart. Trust the Krauts to get something like that right.

Fraker pulled a cushion from Ingram's sofa, slit it open, and felt inside for anything hidden there.

• • •

Jimmy Ryan's was packed with people who had come to hear Art Tatum play.

"Just finishing the set, Michael. I can get you a table. Second set's in an hour."

"I won't go in, Hank," Cassidy said. "I'll hang here till he's done." Hank Dixon, thin and gangling as a stork, punched him on the shoulder with a bony fist and ambled into the main room as Cassidy leaned against the bar. The bartender held up a bottle of whiskey, and when Cassidy nodded, slid him a tumbler of Jack Daniel's over ice. From where he stood he could see the piano and Art Tatum in the baby spot. His face was wet with sweat but expressionless. His body was still, his fingers flat on the keyboard as he drove "Tiger Rag" out so fast it swept you up and carried you, and you wanted to slow it down, stop the rush so you could figure out how it was happening. But no, just let it take you. Go with it. The last cadenza ran the keyboard, and then, bang, it was done. Tatum stood and took a big pull from the glass of whiskey waiting on the piano. A waiter said something to him. Tatum put his hand on the man's shoulder and let him lead him in his blindness back through the room and out the door without acknowledging the applause. Cassidy left a buck for the bartender and went out onto 52nd Street.

Swing Street. Get into any cab in New York when he was a kid and say, take me to the Street, and the cabbie would drop you here on 52nd between Fifth and Sixth. He had started coming down to the jazz clubs when he was fifteen and had discovered that he could sneak out of the house on 66th with impunity. The housekeeper, who was supposed to ride herd on him and Brian and Leah, would be oblivious, cocooned in sleep from the pint of rye she used to blunt the end of her day. Their parents, Tom and Joan, were out most nights. He would be at the theater if he had a play on, or who knows where if he did not. She was a regular on the charity ball circuit, usually escorted by a tall, elegant man named Drew who worked in publishing, dressed beautifully, danced well, could be amusing on almost any subject, and whom she referred to as her "walker," a term, Cassidy learned later, that described a New York "extra man" who could be counted on to escort women to parties their husbands refused to attend and yet had no instinct or desire to threaten the marital peace.

Even in daylight, Tom and Joan were distracted parents. Tom had been orphaned early and assumed that Joan, being a woman, had inherited all the necessary skills for bringing up children. She had been raised an only child by two chilly WASPs who thought that affection, like capital, should be doled out only in extraordinary situations. Joan assumed that as long as her children were fed, clothed, and educated, and had a dry place to sleep, they were fine. Tom and Joan were charming, funny, kind in their fashion, but on the whole, their children might as well have been brought up by wolves. Brian became the voice of reason among the three of them, and Michael and Leah ran wild. When Michael began sneaking out at night, Brian tried to hold him in by pointing out all the risks and the punishments that awaited his getting caught, not understanding that risk was part of the attraction. Leah wanted to come along, but he wouldn't let her. He was navigating unknown territory, and she was hitting adolescence at full speed, and would, he was sure, crash the enterprise before he found what he was looking for. Whatever that was.

It was 1941, a couple of months before Pearl Harbor. He was in the Three Deuces to hear Erroll Garner and had promised Brian he would be home by midnight. At eleven thirty Charlie Parker showed up to sit in, and a little later Billie Holiday came in through the kitchen and leaned on the piano smoking, doing nothing for a while until Garner led her into "Easy Living" and she started to sing. Jesus. Billie Holiday.

Cassidy was drinking scotch and soda; he'd discovered that the bartenders did not care how old he was as long as he had the money, as long as he didn't play the fool. The cold glass, the clink of ice, the bite of scotch made him what? Cool, on top, in control, out of the constricted orbit of his daily life. The liquor and the music freed him from whoever the hell he was during the day, from whoever the hell anyone else thought he was supposed to be. The night, the booze, and the music jazzed his blood, and he was flying. Holiday stopped at the end of "Long Gone Blues" as if awakening from a dream, touched Garner on the shoulder and Bird on the cheek, and left the way she had come.

Two o'clock in the morning. School tomorrow. How did it get to be two o'clock in the morning? The musicians got up for a break. Cassidy pushed his way through the crowd toward the door and then stopped in the shadows among the tables when he saw his father at the bar. He was with a group of four people who were laughing at something he said, and unless she had turned into a twenty-five-year-old blonde, his mother was not the woman with her hand in his father's pants pocket. He could tell they were theater people. Their clothes were tailored beyond the edge of fashion, hair longer than most, laughter louder, gestures and faces animated to reach the back of the house. So, what now? Out through the kitchen the way Billie Holiday had gone, catch a cab, home in ten minutes, and no one the wiser. Wait a minute. Wait a minute. Stick it to him. See the surprise. See the guilt. The whiskey daring him.

"Michael. Hey, what are you doing here? Did you hear Holiday? Is she the best? Have you ever heard anything like that? She tears my heart out. Half the time I don't know if to laugh or cry. Here, meet people. This is my son, Michael." A proprietary arm thrown over his shoulders to turn him to the group.

Handshakes and smiles. Mischa, with an accent like his father's but much thicker, "The greatest set designer on Broadway. Wait till you see."

His father's testimony knew only superlatives.

Kitty, tall and languid and underwhelmed by fifteen-year-old boys, "I've never known costumes like this woman makes. They tell the story themselves. Every part comes alive the moment the actors put on their costumes. Magic." Brandon, who held his hand a little too long and looked at him in a way that made him uncomfortable, "The best choreographer I've ever worked with, and you know I've worked with some of the giants. The best." And Cory, the blonde, "A brilliant actress. Brilliant. You're going to hear from her for years to come," who hugged him, breasts pressed against his chest, and said, "Oh, my God, he is so cute," so that things churned in him and he could feel his face go red.

"Do you want a drink?" his father asked. And then, "Hey, wait a minute. Don't you have school tomorrow? Aren't you supposed to be in bed?"

His father put him in a taxi. "Better not tell your mother. She'll worry if she knows you're out at night." A compact of discretion he agreed to by silence.

• • •

Cassidy flicked the cigarette away and went out from under the awning at Jimmy Ryan's. The Three Deuces where he had listened to Billie Holiday was gone, replaced by a girly show and watered booze. Most of the jazz clubs had folded in the years since the war, done in by television, they said. He raised his hand, and a Checker pulled to the curb. He got in and gave the cabbie his address on Bank Street.

The liquor made him sleepy. He took off his hat, put his feet up on the jump seat, and leaned his head back. His eyes closed, and he drifted between waking and sleep, where images of the day blur toward dreams. *The walk up the stairs of the Hell's Kitchen tenement. The woman with orange hair. The dead man in the chair, head back, mouth gaping. And then he was in the bathroom looking at him, not really there, but in a dream and knowing he was dreaming. There was someone else there in the dream in the apartment with him and the dead man, but when he turned, there was no one, just a sense of someone present behind a light. He stepped toward the light, because he knew if he could just take a step through that light, he would see him. If he could see him, then he would know. Know what? Only that if he could see him he would know something he needed to know. He moved toward the light.*

A car horn blared in the dream, an echo of the horn blaring outside in the street, and the cab braked hard and jarred Cassidy awake.

"Asshole," the cabbie offered out his window to a turning sedan.

It was just a dream, the product of whiskey and fatigue. It meant nothing.

"I've changed my mind. Take me to Three Twenty-six West Fifty-third."

• • •

Cassidy saw that the police seal on Ingram's door had been sliced by something sharp. Somebody had gone in. Was he still there? He pushed his coat and jacket aside and took the .38 from where it hung under his left arm. The doorknob turned in his hand. He pushed. The door opened an inch and then came up against something hard.

All right, Cassidy thought, he's in there. He's got a chair wedged up under the knob. Go down to the Donovans'. Wake them up. Use the phone. Get backup. Sure, and the guy's out the window and down the fire escape. Does he have a gun? Maybe. Would he use it? Why else would he have one? Chances were he was the man who'd killed Ingram. What had he come back for? Go in and ask him. This is what they pay you for. He stepped back and stamped one foot hard against the door. It gave. He stamped again, something broke on the other side, and he hit the door with his shoulder and went into the dark apartment fast and low. He felt movement to one side, and something hard slammed into his arm, then hit him again in the back with enough force to whistle breath from him. His hand went numb, and the gun fell away. He stumbled and crashed into a piece of furniture. The coffee table. The door bounced back, but something kept it from closing, and the man who hit him was silhouetted against the narrow band of dim light from the hall.

Got to stop him, Cassidy thought, but the man was not leaving. He was coming for him. Cassidy felt for the gun with his good hand, but he could not find it. He got to his knees, and the coffee table dug into his back. He dragged it around and shoved it at the man, who yelped when it hit him in the shins. Cassidy felt the sofa and used it to help him stand. His right side felt weak from the two blows. Whatever the son of a bitch hit him with hurt and he did not want to be hit again. The apartment was dark. He listened for his attacker but the carpet was thick and he heard nothing but the thud of his pulse in his ears. What was the setup in the apartment? The big sofa. The chair. The bar next to the record player against the wall behind the sofa. He put his hand out and stepped sideways. Nothing. He stepped again. His hand touched a bottle. He tucked it under his bad arm, picked up another. He listened, but the man had gone still, no movement, no sound of breathing. Who would move first? Cassidy tossed one of the bottles away from him. It hit the rug with a thump and did not break, but he heard the whisper of a shoe on the rug as the man turned to the sound. Cassidy grabbed the second bottle with his good hand and took two quick steps toward the sound, toward a solider dark in the darkness. He heard the snick of metal on metal, and as he raised the bottle, something burned across his ribs that made him hiss in pain. He brought the bottle down hard, and the man grunted, thudded back against the wall, and bounced forward. Metal skittered on the bottle. A knife, the guy had a knife. Christ, not a knife. Cassidy stepped back. He tried to remember the room. He knew the sofa was near, felt it with his leg, and moved around the end of it. The man came forward, not worrying about noise now. He bumped into the sofa and hesitated and then came on. Cassidy retreated. His side felt wet and warm, and he knew he was bleeding, but he couldn't tell how badly he was hurt. Feeling was coming into his right hand, and he shifted the bottle and put his left hand out, hoping to find the doorway to the bedroom. The door to the bedroom was opposite the open front door. If he could get in there, the attacker would be silhouetted in the opening, and for a moment Cassidy would have the advantage. He touched the doorframe. The door was open. He slipped in and stopped a few feet inside and waited. How bad was the cut? He could feel the blood soaking his clothes. He clamped his arm against his side to slow the bleeding. He heard the slither of cloth against the wall in the living room and gripped the neck of the bottle tighter. The dark form of the man filled the doorway. Cassidy raised the bottle.

A light stabbed out and blinded him. The son of a bitch had a flashlight. The man was unidentifiable behind the beam. *The dream in the taxi.*

The man behind the light. Who was he? Cassidy threw himself sideways. He kicked out and caught a leg, and the man stumbled back. The light pitched wildly around the room, and then the man steadied, and the light pinned Cassidy again as he got to his feet. The man came forward, and Cassidy could see the light glint off the blade. Jesus. He didn't want to get cut again. He had a quick flash of Detective Brennan cut by a Puerto Rican hophead with a box cutter the night they raided a dope den on Tenth, Brennan's cheek slashed open, his teeth and tongue visible in the wound.

Cassidy had lost the bottle. He retreated, one hand groping behind him for something he could use as a weapon, a lamp, an ashtray, a chair, anything. The knife flicked at him, driving him back. His legs hit the foot of the bed, and he stumbled and fell backward and scrambled across the mattress and fell to the floor. The light and the knife came after him. His leg banged against the bureau. The light showed him how trapped he was. The man was between him and the door. Cassidy could retreat into the corner, or he could go back across the bed. He snatched up a pillow. If he could tangle the knife, he'd have a chance. He stepped into the corner and waited for the man. The light and knife came on backed by the dark shape of the man who held them.

"What the hell's going on here?" The lights went on in the living room. Donovan, the super, stood inside the front door, holding a baseball bat.

The man turned quickly and the knife disappeared. He went toward Donovan with one hand up as if to stop traffic, the other was in the pocket of his coat. "Hold it. Hold it," the man said with some urgency. "We've got a problem here."

"Watch out," Cassidy yelled.

Donovan shifted the bat, confused. "What problem? Who the hell are you?" The man's authority made him hesitate, and then the man's hand came out of his pocket and he hit Donovan between the eyes with a leather-covered sap and Donovan dropped as if his strings had been cut. Cassidy saw the man pick up a shopping bag waiting by the door, and then he was gone.

4

Morning sun through the skylight woke Cassidy. His right arm was stiff, and his back ached from the blackjack, and when he moved, pain pulled a hot line across his side where the emergency room doctor had stitched the cut. He went into the bathroom and ran cold water on his head to drive away the pain pills' dullness. Gwen had left a nearly empty tube of tooth-paste on the sink. He picked it up to throw it out, then put it back and went barefoot into the living room. The apartment was on the top floor of an old warehouse building in Greenwich Village far west on Bank Street. The building had been bought at the end of the war by a visionary who thought that if he created large, open apartments, people would give up the expensive warrens they lived in uptown and come to the Village to pay the same amount for more space. He had renovated the top floor for himself before going bankrupt, and Cassidy had bought it from the new owner with money his mother left him. The new owner cut up the rest of the building into rental apartments, and the street floor held an ever-changing series of small businesses that began in optimism and ended in unpaid bills, sheriffs' notices, and nighttime decamps.

The ceiling of Cassidy's big living room was twelve feet high, and two of the walls were exposed brick. The four tall windows at the end looked out over the roofs of the piers along West Street to the river and the New Jersey cliffs beyond. In the evenings Gwen would stand there with a drink and watch the ships head downriver to the sea, the lights of their super-structures bright above their dark hulls, and she, raised in a landlocked state, would make up stories about their cargoes, their crews, and their destinations.

The apartment was emptier without her, though in her last weeks it had been overcrowded with the two of them maneuvering through silences, trying not to abrade. There was evidence of her wherever he looked, her presence in her flower arrangement now dying in a vase on the black walnut counter that divided the kitchen from the living area, her absence in the colorful batik now missing from the back of the sofa, her clothes gone from the closet in the bedroom. Her imprint was still in the chair at the end of the plain pine table near the windows where she read scripts and marked her lines with a red pencil. So far he had avoided sitting there.

She had come from a warm, stable family, three generations of farmers on the same land. She was the one who had broken loose to come to New York, to discover the world. She thought of herself as a rebel, but what she really wanted was the same stability and order that she grew up with, but in a different wrapping. She had thought Cassidy would give it to her, and for a while he had thought that he could, that he wanted to, but from the beginning he knew somewhere inside him he would not. She cried easily out of happiness as well as sadness, and wore her emotions close to the surface, while his were buried so deep they'd need, she said, dynamite for the excavation. Except anger. He could tap anger. Gwen was a believer in a place for everything, in straight lines and squared corners, but now his disorder was slowly overwhelming her neatness, like a jungle taking back a cleared field.

• • •

New York was at its best that morning, clean from the rain, bright and fresh. Women in their spring dresses were heartbreakingly beautiful, full of promise, released from the prison of winter. People walked with light steps, and cabbies forgot to blow their horns. A good day to be alive.

The air in the Bellevue morgue was heavy with chemicals and the smell of corrupting flesh. There were two bodies on gurneys in the hall. The first was an old man, gray in death, with sunken cheeks and a nose like a blade, his mouth open to reveal a few long, yellow teeth. The other was a young Hispanic woman. Her slashed throat gaped, her eyes were wide as if in surprise at what had happened to her.

Cassidy found Skinner leaning against the big green multicompartmented cooler in which they stored the random body parts that often turned up in the city: legs, torsos, arms, an occasional head without a body. Skinner was eating a liverwurst sandwich and drinking a Coke he kept cool in one of the smaller compartments.

"You look like shit, Cassidy. What happened to you?"

"Let's go take a look at Ingram."

"We can't." Skinner rewrapped half his sandwich in waxed paper, pounded the cap on the half-drunk Coke with the heel of his hand, slid his lunch into the cooler, and closed the door.

"Why not?" Cassidy lit a cigarette against the chemical taste that was coating the back of his throat.

"He's not here."

By law, violent death in the city delivered the body to the Bellevue morgue for autopsy. "Where is he?"

"I don't know. Don't look at me like that. I don't know. A couple of guys showed up and took him away."

"A couple of guys? Just like that? Excuse me, Mr. Skinner, you got an extra stiff lying around we could use for the day?"

"No. Not just like that. What do you think? They had the authority."

"What authority?"

"They had a guy with them from the district attorney's office. Piccardi. One of the assistant DAs. You've seen him around. Funny-looking mouth, wet lips."

"Who were the guys?"

"I don't know. Guys you don't argue with."

"Did they show you credentials?"

"They didn't show me anything. Piccardi was their credential." He tossed it off, but Cassidy could see he didn't like it, didn't like someone coming into his place and changing the order of things.

"They sign the body out?"

"Yeah. Of course."

"Show me."

The two signatures scrawled in the ledger could have spelled liverwurst. Skinner described the two men, one tall, thin, sallow, the other big, red faced, overweight, both of them wearing business suits. "Like accountants or something, but not. You know what I mean?"

"Did you do the cut?"

Skinner was uncomfortable. "Look, I'm not even supposed to be talking to you. They said, don't talk to anyone. Anybody asks, you don't know anything. That's what they said."

"Al."

"Uh-uh. These were not guys to screw with."

Cassidy took his wallet out. Skinner looked away. "Ah, Jesus, come on, Cassidy." Cassidy took out a ten, then another, then another. "Shit. Okay. You didn't hear anything from me."

"I was never here."

Skinner took the money. "I did the cut before they showed up. There was a contusion at the back of the head. A sap, a piece of pipe, something heavy. That's probably what put him down so the guy could tie him up. You saw the wounds from the pliers, but the guy died of a myocardial infarction."

"A heart attack?"

"Yup."

"No shit?"

"No shit. Weird in a young guy like that, but you never know what stress'll do. Someone starts going at you with pliers, things pop. You can't imagine the kind of pain this guy endured. At one point, he bit through his tongue."

"So the guy who did it didn't get what he wanted."

"How do you figure?"

"He was still working on him when the heart attack killed him, so Ingram never gave it up. Whatever it is, it's still out there."

"What is it?"

"I don't know."

• • •

At midday the squad room was quiet.

"What are you doing?"

The man looked up from searching Cassidy's desk. A second man pushed away from where he had been leaning on Orso's desk and said, "Detective Cassidy?" while the first man opened another drawer.

Cassidy went around the second man and slammed the drawer, and the first man barely got his hand clear and jumped back and said, "Hey," in a surprised voice. Both were dressed in dark suits, white shirts, and striped ties. The one at Cassidy's desk was twenty pounds overweight and had bought his suit when he wasn't. His face was flushed and his dark hair was cut short and receded from his forehead. The second man was tall and thin with sallow skin and dirty blond hair cut in a flattop. They looked like accountants, but they weren't.

"I'm Carl Susdorf," the thin one said. "Paul Cherry over there. We're with the FBI." He offered a leather case with a badge and ID. They had the easy arrogance of men with power, men who were used to being deferred to and feared.

Cassidy snapped the case out of Susdorf's hand and sailed it across the room with a flick of his wrist. "I don't give a shit who you are. You've got no business in my desk."

"Got something to hide, Detective?" Cherry asked. He was still raw about the slammed drawer. Susdorf went to retrieve his badge.

"Pictures of your sister from when I worked Vice."

Cherry's face went redder and he took a step forward, but stopped, his body clenched like a fist. "Oh, yeah, smart guy? You don't even begin to know the shit that could fall on you."

"G-men." Cassidy made a kid's noise like a submachine gun. "Take that, Johnny Dillinger." He laughed. "Get the fuck out of here."

Cherry stepped toward him, but Susdorf put a hand on his arm to check him. "It's okay. He's right, Paul. We should have waited till he got here."

The door to the lieutenant's office opened and Lieutenant Tanner stood in the doorway in his shirtsleeves. "Cassidy, step in here."

The two Feds followed him in.

Tanner was as bald as an egg and had the battered and thickened face of an unskilled boxer. Behind his desk he looked like a big man with the shoulders and chest of a heavyweight, but when he stood he showed the legs of a bantam, so he looked top-heavy and in danger of toppling. He retrieved a half-smoked cigar from the ashtray and got it smoldering again with a kitchen match struck on the desktop.

"Sit down, Detective," Susdorf said. There were three chairs arranged in front of the lieutenant's desk. He indicated the one in the middle.

Cassidy walked to the window and rested his butt on the sill.

Susdorf pulled one of the chairs around to face Cassidy and sat. Cherry leaned against the wall near the door.

"They want to ask you some questions about the other night," Tanner said.

Susdorf took a leather-covered notebook from his pocket and made a show of looking through it while Cassidy waited, amused. He had used the same interrogation techniques himself, the middle chair to make the suspect feel hemmed in, the long wait while notes were read, details of the case checked, all meant to unsettle him, make him eager to talk. He lit a Lucky and scratched the stitches under his shirt.

Susdorf closed the notebook and tapped it on his knee. "Do you love your country, Michael? You don't mind if I call you Michael, do you? Do you love your country?" He was as earnest as a preacher.

Jesus, Cassidy thought, and did not answer.

"I'm pretty sure you do." He gestured with the notebook. "A decorated war hero. D-Day. The Bulge. I envy you that. My duties with the Bureau kept me stateside." He smiled at Cassidy, inviting a response.

"Yeah, we had a ball," Cassidy said. "Good times. All blondes, French wines, and feather beds."

Tanner, a Marine captain who had survived Saipan and Okinawa, snorted.

Susdorf laughed uneasily, knowing something had flown by him. "Let's talk about Alexander Ingram." He checked his notebook again and then looked up expectantly at Cassidy.

Cassidy waited him out.

"Did you search the apartment?"

"I looked around. When I first got there. Searched it? No."

Susdorf waited for him to go on. He did not. "Did you find anything? Anything out of the ordinary?"

"Aside from the dead body in the bathroom, no."

"But you went back."

"Yes."

"Why?"

"Something bothered me."

"What was that?"

"I don't know. Instinct. Hunch. Whatever you want to call it." He certainly wasn't going to talk to them about a dream in the back of a taxi.

"Were you looking for something in particular?"

"No."

"Then how would you have known if you found it?"

"Because it would have been hidden."

Cherry snorted in disgust.

"The man who attacked you was already there, right?"

"Yes. He had cut the crime scene tape and slipped the lock."

"Why didn't you call for backup? You could have sealed the building and trapped him in there."

"I didn't know he was still in there until I tried the door and it ran up against a chair he'd stuck under the knob. Then he knew I was outside. If I'd left, he would've taken off."

"The super had a phone downstairs. You could have had him call it in while you watched the front."

"There was a fire escape the guy could've used. Or he could've gone up and over the roofs. It was my call. I made the one I thought was best."

"Yeah, that worked out real well," Cherry said.

Susdorf put up a hand to check his partner. "We're all on the same side here, Michael. We're all trying to get to the bottom of something. You said this man who attacked you had been searching the apartment."

"That's what it looked like when the lights were on. He'd cut open some of the cushions. He'd tossed the kitchen. He hadn't gotten to the bedroom yet."

"Yes, the bedroom. Nothing there as far as we could tell."

"You searched it too."

"Yes."

"What were you looking for?"

"That's not germane to this conversation. Now, the man who left, the one who assaulted you, did you get a look at him?"

"I saw him from the back when he went out."

"Describe him."

"Five ten. A hundred sixty pounds. Athletic build. Dark hair cut short. Black trousers, black windbreaker, black rubber-soled shoes. I didn't see his face. I think he was wearing gloves."

"Was he carrying anything?"

"It seems to me he grabbed a shopping bag as he went out the door. One of those big paper ones like you get from a department store. It was on the floor near the door and he grabbed it as he went."

The two Feds exchanged a look. That bothered them.

"And after he left, you're sure you didn't look around and find anything?"

"Like what?"

"I'm asking you."

"I didn't look. I didn't find anything."

Susdorf looked at Cassidy to see if he could spot a lie, and then nodded. "All right."

"Let me ask you something," Cassidy said.

"Go right ahead." He smiled, happy to help.

"Why is a New York homicide federal business?"

"We have an overriding interest in Ingram's death. It pertains to matters outside the jurisdiction of the New York Police Department."

"Ingram was tortured. What was his killer looking for? What did you search the apartment for?"

"I'm afraid I can't answer that. That part of the investigation is a federal matter, not a local one. I can't tell you anything more. Sorry."

"Even though we're on the same side, all trying to get to the bottom of something? What is it we're trying to get to the bottom of if it's not murder?"

Having his own words thrown back did not bother Susdorf. "It's a matter of national security. I'm sure you're aware, Michael, that we are at war with people who are trying to destroy America. It's an undeclared war, but a war nevertheless, and in a war like this some rules have to be set aside."

"Alexander Ingram was a Commie agent?"

"He was a person of interest to us on a matter of national security. That's all I'm going to say. We're asking for the cooperation of the New York Police Department in this matter. We expect you to investigate in the normal manner, but we require that you keep us informed of all developments in the case. I cannot emphasize enough that there are matters here beyond the scope of your department." He put his notebook away and stood up and put several of his business cards on Tanner's desk.

"That's it?"

"That's it. You report daily. You tell us what you've turned up no matter how insignificant it might seem to you. Are we clear?"

"Clear."

Cherry grinned at Cassidy and opened the door. The two of them went out into the squad room.

"So?"

"So what?" Tanner said.

"As long as the Feebles are happy, we're happy?"

"I got a call from a guy who got a call from a guy who got a call from a guy. Cooperate. Give them what they want. The word from on high."

"They don't care about the killing. They're looking for something they think Ingram had."

"If you find it, give it to them. You don't want to push on this. You're hanging by a thread. One wrong move and you're out of the department. This is not the time to be sticking your head up. There are plenty of guys who want to see you fall for what you did to Franklin."

"Screw Franklin. He deserved what he got."

"Do what the Feds want. Don't argue. Don't make waves. Now get out of here."

Tanner had no malice toward Cassidy, but whatever idealism had led him to be a cop had been ground out of him by the realities of the job. Now he was a man who watched his back, avoided conflict, and looked to retirement. He respected Cassidy and would not harm him if he could avoid it, but he would not go out of his way to protect him when he stepped over the line.

5

As Cassidy pushed through the theater doors, he could hear the rehearsal pianist banging the keys of the upright and the shuffle and stomp of a chorus line going through a bit. The lights were up onstage, but the seats were in darkness. Small lamps on bendable stalks clipped to the backs of seats in front of the fifth row allowed the director and his assistants to take notes on the rehearsal. The chorus line, eight men and eight women in leotards, leg warmers, old sweatshirts, and sweaters, shuffled their steps as the piano banged to a stop. Cassidy could see that the finish was ragged and half the chorus ended off the beat.

"Boys and girls. Boys and girls. That was the button. You don't hit the button, you don't get the applause. It's a triple rhythm, three steps to two beats of the music. You've all done it before. All right, take a break. Back in five." The dance captain, Marco, waved them away. He was a trim man in his thirties wearing black tights and a blue sweatshirt with the sleeves cut off. His hair was longer than the close-cut fashion of the day.

He ignored the stairs and leapt off the stage and started toward the cluster of people in the fifth row. "Sorry, everybody. The new boy's just a little off, and everyone's a bit thrown. We'll do it again after the company meeting. We'll get it." And then he saw Cassidy. "Michael!" He bounded up the aisle, jumped on Cassidy, and wrapped his legs around Cassidy's waist with his arms around his neck. "You missed me. You couldn't stay away. You've decided you can't live without me."

"All of the above," Cassidy said. "I need to talk to you."

"Honey, you can do anything you want to me."

Jesus Christ, Cassidy thought, the theater. Different rules, different customs. When you are a child, everything that is part of your parents' lives is your norm. Only later did he realize how different the world he had grown up in was from the world outside it. He carried Marco down the aisle as if it were perfectly normal to have a man cling to him like a limpet to where the group sat in the fifth row. "All right, down, boy." Marco disengaged.

A tall, silver-haired man in a well-tailored suit rose at the end of the row. "Hello, Albert," Cassidy greeted him.

"Michael. How nice to see you." He offered his deep, resonant voice and his large, soft hand. Albert London was called the best stage actor in America. He was elegant, graceful, and dignified, and a dedicated womanizer who married often. He could occasionally be persuaded to direct a play, and everyone said Tom Cassidy was lucky to get him for *Now and Forever,* but luck was only part of it. London needed the work to pay his multiple alimonies. "Everybody, you know Tom's son Michael, don't you?"

Murmurs of greeting.

"Tom went over to the office to make some calls, Michael. I could have someone call over for him."

"That's all right. I'll see him later." He was relieved his father was not there, and troubled by his relief. "If you don't need Marco for a few minutes, I have to talk to him."

They went to the male dancers' dressing room with its long row of mirrors above dressing tables littered with hairbrushes and combs, full ashtrays, boxes of Kleenex, its familiar smell of face powder, cold cream, makeup, and sweat. The theater had been Cassidy's playground, the cast and crew his babysitters.

"Alex Ingram?" Marco took a deep drag on a thin black cigarette and waved the smoke away from his face. "That bitch is why I'm breaking in a new boy three weeks before previews. He missed rehearsal again a couple of days ago. That's one time too many." He snapped his fingers. "He's gone. There are plenty of boys out there dying to work."

"He was in this show?" Cassidy had come to talk to Marco because Marco knew all the gypsies, but he had not expected that. "Tell me about him."

"A good dancer. Classically trained. You can tell someone who's come out of a good ballet school. He'd be better if he understood the value of real work. Lazy. A little flamboyant, the extra gesture, the head toss, hands flying, too much hip. He wants to be the boy in the chorus everybody's watching. You have to hold him down sometimes." He blew more smoke and then looked at Cassidy sharply. "Why do you care about a Broadway gypsy?"

"He's dead."

"Dead? How?"

"Someone killed him."

Marco's face paled. "Oh, my sweet Mary, and here I am being a bitch about him. When? How?"

"In his apartment sometime two days ago. Late afternoon."

"Well, he should have come to rehearsal. He wouldn't have been home then, would he?" Then he slapped himself gently on the cheek. "Oooh, Marco. Nasty."

"When was the last time you saw him?"

"He came by to say he couldn't make rehearsal. So I fired him. A couple of days ago? I guess that was the day he was killed."

"How'd he take that?"

"As if he couldn't care less. Told me to take a flying fuck at the moon. Said he didn't need a crappy little hoofing gig."

"What's a gypsy doing walking away from a job? Didn't he need the money?"

"I don't know. He said the next time I saw him he'd be rolling in it."

"How was that going to happen?"

"It wasn't from working as a room service waiter at the Waldorf. That's what he did between gigs." Marco thought for a moment. "You know, that's funny. Alex was one of those guys who always tapped you for five or ten between paydays. Not lately, and when I stop to think, his wardrobe went way uptown."

"Who were his friends? Who do I talk to?"

"Oh, God, I don't know. Did Alex have friends? If he did I certainly wasn't one of them. He could be charming as hell when he wanted something from you, but the moment he got it, he was gone. Let me ask around."

"Women?"

"Could be. He hit from both sides of the plate. He was a very ambitious boy; he'd fuck anybody or anything to get ahead. Beautiful to look at, sunny exterior, but one cold bitch underneath."

"Where did he hang out?"

"Oh, you know, the places. The Village. Bird Alley. You know Bird Alley, Michael?"

"Yeah."

"Oh, yeah. You were in Vice. I forgot about your sordid past."

A dancer stuck his head around the doorjamb. "Marco, do you mind? I want to get something out of my locker."

"Go ahead, Victor."

The dancer was taller than most, dark haired, and with high cheekbones and a cast to his eyes that hinted at Asian blood. He smiled at Cassidy with even white teeth. "I'll only be a second."

"If you think of anything else, friends, people he owed money, anything, give me a call."

"Of course." Marco stubbed his cigarette out and got up. "You look like shit, Michael. You should take better care of yourself." He touched Cassidy on the arm and left.

The dancer named Victor lit a cigarette from a pack in his locker and was now rummaging for something else. Cassidy got up and headed for the door and then stopped. I'm getting too stupid to do this job, he thought. "Did Alex Ingram have a locker?"

"Alex? Sure. Why?"

"Which one?"

"That one." Victor nodded at a locker across the aisle. It was held shut by a cheap padlock. Cassidy wrenched at it, but it wasn't that cheap. He found a screwdriver among a scatter of tools on a table, worked it into the lock hasp and levered.

"Hey, what are you doing? You shouldn't be doing that." Victor looked alarmed.

"I'm a cop."

"Oh." Victor stepped back. "A cop? What did Alex do?"

"He got killed."

"Oh, no." Victor sat down heavily on a bench in front of one of the makeup tables. "When?"

"A couple of days ago."

"Jesus." The cigarette burned unnoticed between his fingers.

"Were you friends?"

"Friends?" As if the question startled him. "Well, you know, a drink after rehearsal, that kind of thing. I didn't really know him all that well. But, I mean, you see a guy every day, you don't think about him getting killed. Who did it?"

"We don't know yet."

The lock gave with a snap. Cassidy worked it off and opened the door.

Rehearsal clothes, leg warmers, an old gray wool scarf hung on the hooks. A couple of pairs of dance slippers and some used socks tangled on the floor. Glossy head shots of Ingram were taped to the inside of the door. There was a shelf at the top that held a tin of aspirin, a jar of Bengay, and a small bottle of Listerine. It was too high for Cassidy to reach to the back. He looked for something to stand on. Victor turned to stub out his cigarette to show that he was not watching.

A stagehand appeared at the door. "Victor, company meeting. They need you now."

Cassidy waited until Victor left and then dragged a chair to the locker, got up, and reached in. He found a crumpled cotton T-shirt, and when he pushed it aside he felt something taped to the back wall. He scratched the tape loose, pulled out a small, stiff buff-colored envelope and got down from the chair. The return address was for a photographer on Lexington Avenue. Red string wound around two cardboard buttons sealed the flap. The envelope held only a fifty-cent piece. Cassidy examined the coin, then found a fifty-cent piece in his pocket and compared them. They were identical. There was nothing to indicate why Ingram would have hidden his, but he had hidden it for some reason. Was this what Ingram had been tortured for? It seemed unlikely. Cassidy flipped it in the air, caught it, sealed it back in the envelope, and went out.

• • •

The company gathered on the lighted stage with the anxious looks of schoolchildren in detention. They talked quietly among themselves. Some smoked. A couple of the dancers tried out steps together. They all were avoiding a heavy balding man in a dark suit who stood at a wooden table sorting a sheaf of papers he had taken from his briefcase. He handed them to an assistant director who distributed one to each of the company. Three people dropped theirs as if they were reluctant to grasp them. Some read the handout. Others waited for the man to speak.

He rapped on the table for silence and when the murmuring stopped, held up one of the papers. "This is a standard loyalty oath. I'm going to read it to you. After I've read it, you can sign your copies and bring them to me here." He fished glasses from the breast pocket of his jacket and put them on, cleared his throat, and read: "'I hereby swear that I have not and will not lend my aid, support, advice, counsel, or influence to the Communist party or any other affiliated party or organization that espouses

WHAT'S WRONG WITH THIS?

the overthrow of the United States Government.'" He took off his glasses and tucked them away. "There are some pens on the table for those who do not have one. Please return the pen after you use it." The murmuring started again. Someone said, "Ah, shit," and was quickly shushed. People shuffled forward to sign.

AND WHY NOT?

"Excuse me, but why should we sign?" The man who asked was an older actor named Simon Clay who had, Cassidy remembered, been in at least four of his father's productions and usually played the loyal male servant, or the older, suave uncle, the judge, or the father's best friend. He had a narrow, patrician face and thick silver hair.

The man with the papers looked at him. "Why wouldn't you sign? You're a loyal American, aren't you?"

"We were hired to act and dance and sing. It's none of your business what we think politically." He looked around for support. A couple of people nodded but did not speak. Other cast members avoided his eyes.

"What's your name?" *OVERTHROW THE USA?*

"Simon Clay."

"The man made a note. "Do you have something to hide, Mr. Clay?"

"That's not the point."

"Loyal Americans, people who have nothing to hide, have no reason not to sign."

"It's not right." *ARE YOU NUTS?*

An actress in a green-and-yellow sundress said, "Just sign it, Simon. It doesn't matter," and then leafed through her script to distance herself. *IT DOES*

"What happens if we don't?" Simon insisted. "Do we lose our jobs?"

"That's up to the producer. He'd certainly be within his rights to wonder whether you're a real American and if you belong in the show."

"Christ." For a moment Clay seemed unsure of what to do next, but he could feel the weight of the company's eyes, and after a moment he went to the table, angrily scrawled his signature, and then jerked upright and stalked out of sight. *YOU ARE NOT ASKED IF YOU ARE A*

Cassidy passed Albert London, who stood in the shadows near the doors *DEM OR REP* smoking and watching the people onstage sign their loyalty oaths. London shrugged in embarrassment as Cassidy went by. "Dangerous times, Michael. Sad and dangerous times." *I OVERTHROW THE USA*

Cassidy pushed through the doors and out into the brightness of the lobby. He stopped to light a cigarette and the street door opened, and his father came in followed by his wife, Megan, a striking blonde, a former

BECAUSE THEY 'THINK' THEY HAVE A RIGHT TO OVERTHROW THE COUNTRY.

dancer who at thirty-four still went to the barre every day and still moved with a dancer's grace.

"Michael." Tom Cassidy did not hide his delight. He was a big man with big emotions, and he hugged his son hard. He missed Cassidy's wince of pain, but Megan did not. Megan missed little.

"Dad." He put one arm around his father's broad back in return and looked past him to where Megan watched the two of them with no expression. "Megan."

"Hello, Michael." No smile, just an appraising look.

"What are you doing here?" his father asked. "Did you watch rehearsal? How far have they gotten? Did you see the eleven o'clock number? You have to see the eleven o'clock. It's terrific. It's going to stop the show." He listened at the door. "What are they doing in there? I go away for five minutes and they stop working."

"They're signing loyalty oaths."

"Oh, that." He saw Cassidy's look. "What?"

"Nothing." But the tension between the two of them was already there.

The father heard the accusation in his son's voice. "Some of the investors asked for it. They want to be sure we're working with the right kind of people. They want to be comfortable. What am I supposed to say? They sign and go on about their business. It doesn't mean a thing." *YES IT DOES YOU FOOL!*

"If it doesn't mean a thing, why ask them to do it?"

"Everybody's doing it. What's the big deal?"

"If they don't sign, do they lose their jobs?"

"Nobody's going to lose his job. I know everyone in there. They'll sign."

"Did you sign one?"

"Me? Why should I sign one? I'm a loyal American."

"How do we know that unless you sign?"

Megan tried to intercede. "Michael, stop it. Tom, please. Michael, let it go."

"Michael, what the hell's wrong with you?"

"What else are we going to have to sign about? That we're not thieves, or murderers? Maybe that we're not liars. Or we're not Democrats, or not Republicans." *NO! JUST THAT YOU ARE NOT GOING TO OVERTHROW THE U.S. GOVERNMENT*

Megan banged back outside so she would not have to listen.

"I'm a businessman. I'm trying to produce a play, that's all. Do you know how hard it is to produce a play? It's damn hard. Is it bullshit? Sure it's bullshit, but my investors want it. Everybody's doing it. It doesn't mean

NIGHT LIFE ··· 69

anything. Why do you always fight me? I say black, you say white. I say high, you say low. You might be wrong, you know."

"I've got to go."

"Okay." His father started toward the doors to the theater, then stopped and turned back. "Just come in for a few minutes. I'll get them to run the number. You tell me what you think."

Cassidy recognized the peace offering. He tried to push his anger down, but he could still feel its heat. *Go now, before it gets worse.* "I can't. I'm on the job."

"Oh, well, okay. Another time." He smiled, but Cassidy knew he was disappointed. He went into the theater, and Cassidy opened the big glass door and went out.

Megan stood under the marquee smoking a cigarette. "That went well," she said.

"Yeah."

"It doesn't have to be a fight every time you see him."

"I don't want it either, but goddamn it."

"Stop being so angry at him."

"Sure, Mom."

She blew smoke toward the marquee and studied him. "When are you going to stop giving me this crap? Is there a statute of limitations?"

"I don't know." He was always surprised at how direct she was. He would admire it if he let himself.

"I make your father happy. We have a good time together. I'm not a gold digger. I'm sorry about what happened with your mother, but that's not about me."

"We're not going to talk about that."

"We've been married six years. I'm here to stay. You have to get used to it." She spoke without heat, simple statements of fact. "Your father doesn't know why you're angry at him. He doesn't know why you don't come around. He makes excuses for you. You're working hard. You're working nights. But it makes him sad."

"I doubt it."

"Sometimes, Michael, you can be a real asshole."

He had no answer to that.

She flipped the cigarette to the gutter where it landed in sparks and went into the theater.

He walked south as the evening fell and the lights came on in the city.

He watched the people leaving work and hurrying toward home, eager for what and who waited there, and he wondered where they found that ease. He could never remember it in his own home. Not that it had been a battleground when they were growing up, but there was always a low current of tension generated by two people living together who had completely opposite expectations of life. They did fight, and the fights were explosive, but they made up with the same intensity, and for a while the air would be clear like after the passing of a thunderstorm.

His father's world was the theater, a business that kept him out late, caused him to travel, involved him, as Cassidy had learned, with other women who offered him something his wife did not. He expected to come home to a perfect American household, a loving wife and three happy, handsome, bright children, the house neat and clean, the laundry done, dinner on the table, whenever he chose to appear. When he left in the morning it was as if in his mind the family remained behind unchanging, locked in amber, until his return. It was not, Cassidy eventually understood, malice or indifference on his father's part. It was just an inability to consider what happened outside his immediate orbit. He had come from so little and had gained so much, had come so far and was so happy with where he had arrived, that he could not believe that anyone who had not had that struggle could be unhappy. He was an instinctive optimist, and if he was happy, everyone was happy. How could it be otherwise? He viewed the world through the crack in his own forehead and assumed that everyone saw what he saw.

What he did not see was his wife's drift, and when he did notice it, he assumed it would be fixed by Dr. Valentine and his vitamin B_{12} shots, or by a week in Bermuda, or a trip to Paris. Joan asked for a divorce thinking it would shock him into paying attention, and he agreed to it, thinking he had no right to refuse her. It was one of her many miscalculations about him. Her first had been the idea that he had been sent to save her from a life of middle-class boredom when it was precisely that middle-class regularity he wanted as a sign of his success.

Her last miscalculation happened one night when Cassidy was sixteen.

Brian was in the navy by then, finishing his officer's training. Leah had gone skiing with the family of a friend from school. Cassidy spent the day with his friend Mal Brown and would not be home, if his pattern held true, until after his eleven o'clock curfew. The housekeeper had gone to see her sister in New Jersey.

Joan made an appointment with Tom, Cassidy learned, for three in the afternoon to discuss the divorce, and Tom swore that he would be there on time. She called him again at the theater to make sure. He assured her he had not forgotten. She took him at his word, which was the next miscalculation. A set malfunctioned, or maybe an actress, or maybe he lost track of time, it was never clear, but he missed the appointment. Cassidy got into an argument with Mal, and so he came home early.

Early was too late.

When he entered the house, it was quiet. His mother's black mink coat was on the upholstered bench in the front hall, dropped there with the perfect understanding that someone else would hang it up in the closet.

When he saw the coat, he knew that he had dreamed this moment weeks before. He wanted to turn and go, but he could not. In the dream he had been awake and yet in the dream at the same time, as if watching from just outside himself. He had been in this hall. He had gone upstairs, drawn against his will toward some fearful thing that he knew but could not see.

Cassidy, filled with dread, went upstairs calling his mother's name.

No answer.

As in the dream, he moved slowly, as if he were underwater.

He went down the hall to the master bedroom. The door was open. He knocked on the frame and called again. "Mum?"

No answer.

He did not want to go in. He thumped his head against the wall hoping that would wake him, but he was awake, caught in what he knew was to come, as surely as if he had lived it before. He stepped into the room. She was in bed, leaning back propped against a bank of pillows, and though she looked like she was asleep, he knew she was not.

Later he understood that she had arranged herself for her husband, hair and makeup perfect, peach-colored peignoir that he had always loved. See what you're losing? See what you could still have? The clock had been turned on the bedside table so she could see it easily, and the empty bottle of pills was next to an empty glass of water.

She was cool to his touch.

He later understood what she had planned. She would take the pills. Tom, arriving at three, would find her and save her, and they would live happily ever after.

For reasons he still did not understand, Cassidy moved the clock to the bureau where it could not be seen from the bed, and in doing so changed

WHAT ?

what his mother had done from an act of optimism to one of despair, and
in some ways he let his father off the hook, because Tom Cassidy never
suspected Joan's calibrations, never knew that by being on time he could
have changed death into life. The coroner's estimate of her time of death
was imprecise, which allowed Tom Cassidy to believe that she had killed
herself early in the afternoon so that he would find her dead when he came
at three. He did not understand that she meant to seduce him. He assumed
that she had killed herself to punish him and had arranged for him to find
her body.

Her death pulled the family together for a time. Brian, always responsible beyond his years, grew up overnight. He took compassionate leave
and organized the funeral with the help of Tom's lawyer, Harry Gould.
He oversaw the distribution of their mother's belongings to friends and
family. Then he went back to the navy.

Tom Cassidy's reaction was stunned incomprehension. Why? What had
caused it? A man so full of life could not understand how someone would
voluntarily end hers. He thought she wanted the divorce. He was going
to give it to her because she wanted it. She was getting what she asked for.
He asked questions of his children over and over again, but they had no
answers for him. For days he refused to leave the house. He wandered
the rooms in his bathrobe as if he might stumble on the answer in some
dark corner. He did not eat. He did not shave. He sat for hours in the easy
chair in their bedroom. Then one day, someone called from the theater
with a problem only he could solve. He went down to see about it and went
back again the next day, and then the next. For a while he came home
every night for dinner. After a month he missed one or two a week, and
soon after that Leah and Cassidy ate alone five nights out of seven.

What do you do when the props are knocked out from under your life?
What do you do when you lose someone you thought would always be
there? Grief blindsided him. He found himself standing on a corner of
Madison Avenue waiting for a bus and weeping while people shied away
from him. He would hear something that made him laugh and think, *I
have to call her and tell her,* and then the thought would drift away with the
realization that there would never be another call.

One night he tried to tell Leah about the dream.

"What do you mean, you dreamed it? You dreamed she killed herself?"
She looked at him with horror.

"I didn't know what I was dreaming. It was one of those nightmares that I couldn't get out of. I was awake and still in the nightmare, and I could see her in her bed. When I walked into the house that day and saw her coat on the floor, I was back in the dream. I knew what she would look like in the bed. I knew."

"Bullshit, bullshit, bullshit, bullshit. Stop it. I don't want to know. You didn't dream it."

"I didn't know what it meant. That's what I'm trying to tell you. I dreamt it, but I didn't know what it meant. If I had known, I could have done something."

"No. No. Stop it." She put her hands over her ears.

Leah went away to boarding school, and for a few months Cassidy and his father drifted around each other in the house on 66th Street. Then he joined the army.

6

"Do you recognize him?"

The man behind the counter took the photograph of Alex Ingram that Cassidy had found in the backstage locker and tipped it toward the light. "No, I don't think so." He looked again. "No." He turned the photo over and looked at the back, then put it down on the counter and took off his glasses and shook his head. "This is not my work. I don't use this paper. It's cheap. You see how it curls at the edges. And look. This is a portrait, a head shot as it is called, for an actor, yes?" His accent was faint, his constructions formal, those of a second language. "See, here, see the glare on the cheekbone, how the eye is too darkly shadowed? This is badly lighted. No subtlety. Not my work." He seemed offended by the sloppiness.

"Can you tell who took it?"

"No. I don't know. There are many photographic shops in New York. Often a shop stamps the name and address on the back of such a photograph, as advertisement, but this one has not."

The camera store was on the ground floor of an office building on Lexington Avenue between 38th and 39th Streets. Before going in, Cassidy had paused in front of the window. The display box inside was draped in thick blue cloth to set off the framed photographs of smiling brides in white dresses, and businessmen, dignified and upright in dark wood chairs, challenging the camera. Cassidy could see that care had been taken with the lighting so that the portraits drew the eye of anyone who paused to look.

The man behind the counter said his name was Rudi Apfel. He was in his late forties, Cassidy thought. His long fingers were stained with developing fluid. His dark tweed jacket was buttoned over a starched white shirt, and he wore a navy tie patterned with small dark red sea horses.

He was about middle height, wore horn-rimmed glasses, had an open, pleasant face, and if you passed him on the street you would never remark or remember him.

"What about this envelope?" Cassidy handed him the envelope from Ingram's locker. The fifty-cent piece was in his pocket.

Apfel examined it. "Yes, this mine. You see the address."

"Do you have any idea what was in it?"

"Negatives, I assume. This is what I use these envelopes for. If someone wants negatives, I give them in an envelope like this."

"You don't remember giving this guy an envelope of negatives?"

"No. I'm sorry. It may not seem so today, but I have a busy shop. I cannot remember everyone. I could have given this a year ago. Who would remember?" He shrugged. "If you have the negatives, I could look. Perhaps this will make me remember. I am better about pictures than I am about people, I'm sorry to say. So, let us look at the negatives. Shall we?"

Cassidy put the envelope back in his pocket. "Thank you for your trouble."

"Not at all. If there is anything I can do, I would be happy to help. I am sorry the man was killed. We live in a savage time, Detective Cassidy."

"Yes, we do." Cassidy pocketed the photo of Ingram.

"If I do remember something, is there a way I can reach you?"

Cassidy found a business card that held the precinct's and his home phone numbers.

Apfel looked it over, smiled, and nodded, and tucked it away in his shirt pocket. "And now, Detective, perhaps you would sit for a moment and let me take your picture. You have a very interesting face. There is something, and I do not mean in any way to be rude, wonderfully melancholy there."

"Melancholy?" Cassidy laughed.

"Ah. I'm sorry. I do not mean that you are sad in any way. That would be presumptuous of me. No, no. I sense a melancholy absorbed over generations." He laughed and opened his hands in a gesture of apology. "I'm sorry. I'm Russian. This is how we think. No. How we feel. What we know. Some of us carry the sadness of generations, some the joy. Do you have Russian blood, Detective?"

"Who knows?"

"No matter. In America it is enough to be American. So, the photograph." He reached under the counter and retrieved a large Speed

Graphic camera like the ones police department photographers used at crime scenes.

"No, thank you."

"Five minutes. No more. Then you will have something wonderful. For your wife? Girlfriend? Someone at home who will be pleased to have it." He smiled as if to apologize for his insistence.

"No one this week."

"No? A good-looking young man like you?"

Cassidy hailed a cab on Lexington. What was it about Apfel that pricked him? The accent, maybe, so like his father's. Or just the frustration of a dead end on the envelope found in Ingram's locker? As he closed the door to the cab, he glanced back at the store. Apfel watched him from the counter and raised a hand in good-bye.

• • •

Fraker cut a piece of toast, a piece of fried egg, and a piece of sausage, stabbed them with his fork, and poked them into his mouth.

"You didn't find anything?" Crofoot asked. He was a compact man with a narrow face and nervous, muscular hands that drummed fingers on the table. He had ginger-colored hair and eyebrows above pale blue eyes. He wore a hairy three-piece tweed suit that would not have been out of place on an English country weekend, and he watched Fraker eat as if he had not seen the act before.

"I don't think so. You'll have to decide. It's all there. Every piece of paper, every photo in the place I could grab before the guy showed up, but nothing like you described, and nothing you might call hidden." He pointed his fork at the paper shopping bag that bulged on the windowsill. "Of course, I was interrupted before I really had time to toss the place. I could go back, tear it apart."

"Maybe," Crofoot said as he pawed through the shopping bag's contents.

They were in a booth in the rear of a diner on Gansevoort Street in the meatpacking district of Greenwich Village west near the river. Three long-distance truckers were at a table near the door banging on the Yankees. Could that fucking Whitey Ford win more than the seventeen games he won last year? Allie Reynolds and Johnny Sain were over the hill at thirty-seven and thirty-six. Management should trade them before their arms fell off. That kid Mantle looks okay, but he ain't gonna make us forget

Joe DiMaggio unless he hits more than the twenty-one home runs he had in fifty-three. Two meat cutters in wool caps and long white coats stained with drying blood sat elbow to elbow at the counter and ate an early lunch without talking.

Crofoot pushed the shopping bag away. He had not found what he was looking for, and the disappointment showed. "What about the two men? Are you sure they can't identify you?" he asked. He had an accent that was neither English nor American but somewhere in between.

"Not a chance. The one who came in first, the one with a gun, it was dark, and then when the lights came on, I was facing away from him, headed out. The other one, I had my hand in front of my face, sapped him down before he knew what the hell was going on." Fraker forked in another mouthful of food.

"What is that? The dark thing? Do you mind my asking?"

"Blood sausage," Fraker said around the food. "Best place in the city." He waved his fork at the diner. "The slaughterhouses are just across the street. You want the blood fresh."

"Ah," Crofoot said, meaning *How disgusting*. "The one with the gun was a cop named Cassidy. He works out of Midtown South. We're trying to get a handle on him."

"How do you know?" He saw Crofoot's look of amusement. "Yeah, yeah, yeah. Okay. You guys know everything."

"Not everything. What was he doing back there in the middle of the night?"

"I don't know. He didn't say anything. He just came in hard." Fraker signaled the waitress for refills on their coffees.

"We don't like it. We don't like him going back. Why would he go back unless he was looking for something? We're thinking maybe he's connected to the other guys."

"Could be. They've got long arms."

"Ingram was tortured. Who would have done that?"

"Maybe the other guys."

"Yes. Possibly. Not their style, though they're capable of it, I guess. Still, very impatient. Easier to offer money. Ingram liked money. That was clear," Crofoot said.

"You want me to do something about him, the cop?"

"No. Keep looking. I'll deal with the cop. You have another name, don't you? Speak to him. Maybe he'll give you more."

"How far can I go when I *speak* to him?"

"You'll have to use your own discretion, but this cannot come back to us."

• • •

On Sunday Cassidy woke to rain rattling the windows. Gray clouds scudded low over the steel-colored river. His side felt better, and the blackjack bruise was going yellow and was less tender to the touch. He spent the morning trying to paper over the hole Gwen had left. He threw out the dead flowers, moved the chair where she used to read to another angle, threw out her toothpaste, rearranged his clothes in the bedroom closet to fill the gap where her clothes had hung, and redistributed things in the bureau. He stacked the old scripts she had left and the old issues of *Variety* and tied them in bundles to put out with the trash. He found a hat with a long green feather, part of her costume from an industrial show she had done in January, and put it on a high shelf in the coat closet in case she called for it, though he knew she never would.

By midafternoon he felt raw and trapped. The rain had eased to drizzle. He put on a slicker and a Giants baseball cap and went out. An apartment on the floor below him had been vacant for months, but now there were boxes piled outside the open door and he had to step over a guitar case to get by.

He walked to the White Horse on Hudson. Two couples in blue jeans and plaid wool shirts played poker at one of the tables in the back room while at another, three bearded men argued about Theodore Roethke's "The Waking." Was it a true villanelle? Whatever the hell that was.

Cassidy took a table near the window in the quiet front room and had a hamburger and a beer while he read a copy of the *Journal-American* someone had left on the sill. John Foster Dulles warned against the growing Communist influence in South America. There were three cease-fire violations between North and South Korean troops along the 38th parallel. Senator Joseph McCarthy denounced both NBC and CBS for refusing to give him air time to answer an attack by former Democratic presidential candidate Adlai Stevenson. He called the networks' actions "completely immoral, arrogant, and dishonest." Cassidy laughed and the bartender asked, "What've you got there, Mike, the comics?"

"Yeah, something like that."

"That *Maggie and Jiggs* cracks me up."

Cassidy paid his bill and walked home slowly through the rain. The weather suited his mood.

There were fewer boxes outside the open door on the fourth floor, and the guitar case was gone. "Hey, you." He was already past the door, but he turned back. A young woman was standing inside the apartment with her hands on her hips. "Give me a hand." Not really a question, not quite a command. She was tall and rangy, nearly as tall as he was, and her dark red hair was cropped to short curls. High cheekbones, a wide, sensual mouth. She wore canvas sneakers that had once been white, blue jeans, and a faded green flannel shirt.

"Sure." He hung his wet slicker and hat on the stair rail in the hall and went in. She had moved to the end of a big green sofa that had seen better days.

"The bastards I hired dumped the stuff and took off when I was in the can. I want to move this over under the window." Her voice was smoke and whiskey.

"Okay." He went to the other end of the sofa and bent for a grip.

"Bad back, weak heart, hernia?"

"No. But I tend to weep uncontrollably in moments of stress."

"Not going to be a problem here. You ready?"

"On three. One, two, three." The sofa was heavy, but he refused to show the strain. Pride, a beautiful woman. They dropped it with a thump under the window that looked out on West Street.

She stepped away and pushed her hair from her forehead with the back of her wrist. "A little farther this way." He pushed. A judicious look. "Too far." He pulled. Another look. "Okay."

He tapped a Lucky from his pack and lit it, and she took it out of his mouth before he got the first drag and put it between her lips. "You live upstairs?" She blew smoke at the ceiling.

"Yes. Michael Cassidy." He lit another cigarette for himself.

"You tap-dance, Michael? Learning to play the bongos, any early-morning roller skating?"

"No. I occasionally howl at the moon."

"Won't bother me. I work nights."

"What's your name?"

"Dylan."

"Dylan what?"

She looked him over carefully. "Thanks for the help, Michael," and turned away to rip tape sealing one of the boxes. A dismissal. He waited for a moment, but there was no more, so he left and went upstairs.

God, she was good-looking. Were her eyes green or blue? Green.

The Bl

the el. T

walk. The

eyes adjust

someone had

room to break i

sex dancing, a la

a raid on a queer bai

zens that deviance wou

the men past the arch at t

together in the awkward poses o

o'clock, and the place was filling up wit

buildings. They wore suits and ties and buttoned-down

wingtips, the gray flannel uniform of the day. Camouflage. It w

being queer in America. Maybe in the arts you could get away w

but otherwise you had to live a clandestine life and present a false fr

the world. If you were found out, it would destroy you. You woul

everything, job, friends, family. It was worse than being a Commu

Cassidy walked to the end of the bar to pull the bartender away

the drinkers farther down.

"Help you?" the bartender asked. He kept his tone and attitude

tral in case Cassidy had wandered in by mistake looking for a drin

nothing else. He was a big man with a round, ruddy face, sloping s

ders, and big, rough hands that had seen a lot of hard work.

"Let me have a Knick."

"Knick it is." He went away and came back with the bottle of bee

e

ιex

.isp.

badge out,

five minutes

.p the block to

κ to your clients.

.p. No names. I'm

...ie, in case they have to ask?"

... .ie change and a business card on the bar and went

... rumbled by overhead.

ordered a bowl of soup and a sandwich to appease the waitress and

.m quickly. After an hour he was about to give up and leave when a

.ame in, looked around for a moment, and then came over to the

He walked herky-jerky like a robot needing oil. He was gray pal-

bone thin, hollow cheeked, with eyes sunk deep in their sockets. He

.ell over six feet tall and couldn't have weighed more than a hundred

.rty pounds. He carried a black fedora in one hand. His black suit

.oose on him, and his shirt collar was sizes too big.

.u Cassidy?"

.s."

.folded himself onto the bench opposite and rested his hands on the table. They were big, knob knuckled, hard boned, and the first two fingers of his right hand were stained yellow-brown with nicotine. He slipped a pack of Camels from an inside pocket, shook loose a cigarette, and lit it with a kitchen match scratched on the underside of the table, inhaled, blew out a plume of smoke, and then coughed into his fist. He watched Cassidy while he did, and Cassidy watched back. The man didn't look like anyone who might have been dancing in the back room of the Parrot, but you never knew.

"You got a beef with the Parrot?" His voice was as dry as sand.

"No. No beef."

The waitress came over, but the man shook his head and she went away. "Cassidy. You're the guy threw a guy out the window."

Cassidy nodded. The man was tapped in to what went on in the department.

"Like Griff said, Friday's the day. You want to change that, you've got to talk to someone. You don't just show up."

"I'm not working Vice anymore. I'm not carrying the bag for anyone. I'm not interested in your arrangements. I told Griff I just want to know about a guy who used to hang out there."

"It's a fairy bar, right? You know who owns the joint?"

"I know."

"There's a problem, we take care of it. We don't need anything, what? Like official."

"Alexander Ingram. He used to drink there and a couple of other places like it. Bird Alley. Someone killed him. If he had friends, I want to talk to them."

"That's it?"

"That's it."

The man stood up. "I hear anything, I'll call you." Cassidy offered him a card, but he waved it away. "You ain't hard to find."

• • •

There was a new name in the fourth-floor mailbox slot in Cassidy's lobby. McCue. The woman's name was Dylan McCue. The door to her apartment was closed and the boxes were gone from the hall.

When he opened the door to his apartment, the lights were already on. Chairs were upended, covers ripped from sofa cushions, books pulled from the bookcases. A man was bent over the open drawer of a table near the window. As he started to turn in surprise, Cassidy pulled the pistol from under his arm. A hand clamped his wrist.

"Take it easy, Cassidy."

Susdorf stood next to him. Past him Cherry waited with his gun in his hand and a grin on his face.

"Search warrant," Susdorf said. With his other hand he took papers from his inside pocket and offered them to Cassidy. "Put the gun up."

Cassidy jerked his arm away and holstered the gun.

"Keep going, Bob." The man near the window went back to his search.

"What is this? What are you looking for?"

"The warrant specifies documents and/or objects pertaining to a case of threat to national security. If you don't have them, you don't need to know. If you have them, you already know and I don't have to tell you."

Another man came out of the bedroom. "Done in there. Nothing."

Cassidy went into the kitchen and found a bottle of bourbon. The kitchen was a chaos of spilled canisters and overturned drawers. Broken glass crunched underfoot. He poured a drink and tried to hold down his rage.

"I told you I didn't find anything in Ingram's apartment."

"We asked around. People say you're a little too independent for your own good. That appears to be true. I told you to keep us informed of your investigation. You have not done that. So I thought we better come down here and take a look around."

Maybe there was some truth in that, but Cassidy knew the real reason for the search was to show him that they were powerful and he was not, and that enraged him more. For a moment he savored the giddy pleasure of shooting one or two of them, but then he let reality intrude.

Ten minutes later they were gone.

He swept up the broken glass in the kitchen. He righted the canisters and brushed their spills into the trash can. Ice cream melted in the sink. Someone had probed the container for anything hidden. He ran hot water to wash it away.

Someone knocked on the door. They were back. What had they forgotten? He went to answer it with his fist knotted. At least he would have the satisfaction of punching one of them in the mouth.

He opened it and found Dylan McCue in the hall. She had a glass in her hand. "Hey, neighbor, can I borrow a cup of gin? And maybe some ice?" She stepped past him into the apartment. "Whoa. You have got to fire your cleaning lady."

Cassidy took the glass from her hand and went into the kitchen. "Come on in."

"What happened, a burglar?"

"No."

He levered cubes from an ice tray into her glass, took a bottle of gin from under a cupboard, and put it next to the glass on the counter. "Tonic?"

"Vermouth?"

He found a bottle of vermouth, picked up a lemon from the floor and a knife from near the stove and put them next to the gin. "Help yourself."

She made her drink and stirred it with her finger. "Aren't you going to call the cops?"

"I am the cops."

"Come on." She reached over and opened his jacket and saw the gun under his arm. "Huh. Never would've guessed. I would've said ball player, maybe, or teacher." She studied him for a moment. "No, not teacher. You'd spook the kids." She looked around. "So who were they and what were they after?"

"I don't know what they were after, but they were FBI agents." He liked her lack of surprise and concern and wondered what she had been through that taught her that calm.

"FBI? Really? Have you been a bad boy?"

"Not in any way that should interest them. I'm working a murder. They think the man who was killed might have had something that got him killed. They were just making sure I hadn't taken it home for safekeeping."

"What is it?"

"I have no idea."

"Who's the dead guy?"

"A Broadway gypsy name Ingram."

"A Broadway gypsy? What's that?"

"A guy or girl who sings and dances in the chorus of Broadway shows."

"Why does the FBI care about a chorus boy?"

"I don't know."

"The FBI is cops. You're a cop. Cops don't talk to cops?"

"Only when it suits them. Like everyone else, cops protect their turf.

If they don't think I have to know what this is about, they are not going to tell me. Do you know what a check valve is?"

"No. What?"

"It's a valve plumbers put in a pipe so that the water can only flow in one direction. The Feds are like that with information. They want it to come to them. They're not interested in sending it back the other way."

She studied him. "So you really don't know what they were looking for? Or if you do, you're not going to tell me. The secrets of men. Don't tell the women."

"No. I really don't know."

She finished her drink and put the glass on the counter. "Do you want some help cleaning up? Hey, don't look so surprised. It's the neighborly thing to do."

"In New York?"

"I'll start in here. How do you want the books put back?"

"Alphabetized by author."

"Don't push your luck. And I get dinner afterward. I haven't eaten yet."

"Deal."

She turned away, and when she crouched by the bookcase, her shirt pulled up from her jeans and he could see smooth skin of her back and the top of the cleft of her butt.

• • •

Only three tables at Minetta Tavern were occupied, but the bar crowd was two deep, loud, and mostly men, and most of them turned to look at Dylan when they came in. Cassidy knew it had happened to her many times, because she walked through them without concern, as if it was her due, as if it did not matter.

Cassidy watched Dylan attack her steak.

"Do you want a bite?" She offered a piece speared on her fork.

"No, thanks. But I do admire the way you eat."

"My mother always said I ate like I was afraid someone was going to steal my plate."

"Brothers and sisters?"

"You mean stealing the food? No. No brothers, no sisters. She just meant the way I went at it. Like I had to get it done as fast as possible. "Impatience. Dylan, slow down." That's what she used to say all the time. I never learned how." She raked her fingers through her copper hair and smiled so open and free that he wanted to reach across the table to her.

"Do you see her much?"

"She's dead. Cancer."

"I'm sorry."

"Thanks. I was eleven when she died. I don't remember a time when she wasn't sick."

"That must have been tough."

She shook her head. "I was a kid. When you're a kid, what you have is all you know. Hard? Easy? That doesn't enter into it. It just was." She drank some wine. "You ask a lot of questions. How much do you want to know?"

"Enough to get started." Where did that come from?

She smiled at him. "That's it, isn't it? Enough to get started. Who the hell knows what happens after that? What about you? Family?"

"An older brother, a younger sister, a father."

"Mother?"

"She's dead."

"How?"

"An accident." He let it go at that. There was too much to explain.

"I'm sorry."

The waiter brought another bourbon and he drank it while she finished. She pushed her plate back and poured the last of the red wine from the half bottle she ordered with the steak. She took a sip while she watched him from across the table with steady green eyes. "You know what I like about you, Michael Cassidy? You don't talk all the time. Most men spend the first hour puffing up their feathers and singing their song. You just let it go."

She reached across the table to take a cigarette from the pack next to his plate. He took her hand and turned it over and back. There were little flecks of white scar scattered on both sides, heavier on the back up into the forearm. "Where'd these come from?"

She looked at her hands, turning them to the light. "Welding. No matter how careful you are, you burn yourself."

"Welding?" He could not keep the surprise out of his voice.

"I know, I know. Girls don't weld. Dad told me I should find a skill that would let me work no matter where I went. He had in mind typing and shorthand. That's what girls did, but I never wanted to do what everyone else did. Or maybe I just didn't like doing what was expected or what I was told. I wanted to learn how to make things, how to fix things. Dad was struggling after Mom died. He didn't know what to do with me, so he pretty much let me do what I wanted. There was an old welder in town who thought it was funny to teach a girl. Now I work whenever I want. I go into a place to ask for a job, all the guys laugh and spit and do that thing that men do when they shift their balls around, and then they ask me to do something they think is really hard, no girl can do, and I do it better than any of them can, and I have a job. Every time."

He had never met a woman who talked the way she did, straight out with no filters, as if she did not give a damn about what other people thought, as if she had given up the customs of reticence that kept people in check.

"Where are you working now?"

"A place south of Houston Street."

"You said you work nights."

"I do, but it's not like a regular job. I do the work pretty much on my own time." She drank some more wine. "So what are you going to do about your gypsy killer? Are you going to just let the FBI handle it?"

"The FBI's better at recovering stolen cars than they are at solving a homicide. I'll work it. The killer will be someone Ingram knew. He'll have made some mistakes. Someone will have seen him with blood on his clothes. Someone will remember seeing them together or know that they were supposed to have dinner that night. Ninety-nine times out of a hundred I'm looking for someone who did something stupid on the spur of the moment and now is scrambling to cover his tracks."

"That's how it works?"

"Ninety-nine times out of a hundred."

He paid the bill and they left, followed by the envious eyes of the men at the bar.

• • •

On the sidewalk she said, "Come on," and turned south.

"Where are we going?"

"Do you always have to know first?"

"No."

"Then come on."

She put an arm through his. The easy intimacy surprised and pleased him. Who was this woman and where had she been all his life? *Don't get ahead of yourself. Don't count on things. You've learned that by now.*

She drew him south along the crowded, brightly lighted streets of the Village and across the broad divide of Houston Street and into the dark grid of unpopulated streets that lay south of Houston. Here there were blocks of six- and seven-story industrial buildings that had been put up in the mid- and late-nineteenth century when materials and labor were cheap, when modern industry was starting to boom, and the men who rode its wave had a muscular pride in the structures that held their businesses. Now their elaborate cast-iron fronts peeled paint, and the windows were black with grime. They held sweatshops and light manufacturing, and at that time of night the streets were empty except for a few delivery trucks.

Dylan keyed open the door to a building on Prince Street and they went into a wide entry hall. She found a light switch whose dim bulb barely contradicted the dark. She pulled the big door and gate of an industrial elevator shut behind them and they rode up. She pushed the doors open and they stepped out into the top floor. Big windows on two sides let in enough city light for Cassidy to tell that they were in a cavernous space. Dylan moved away from him in the dark, and a moment later bright lights came on in fixtures in the high ceiling.

The room had been a manufacturing space and it ran a hundred feet by forty. A scarred wooden counter ran the length of the room under the windows on the north side. It was littered with pieces of metal and wood, stretched canvases, rolls of paper, broken easels, paintbrushes, boxes of colored chalk, hammers of different sizes, metal cutting shears, chisels, and tools Cassidy could not identify. There were six small anvils of varying sizes screwed to the counter and three bigger anvils were bolted to blocks of wood on the floor.

"What's that?" He pointed to a big metal pot set on three feet of firebrick. There was a door in the front with a heavy glass window, and tubes ran out of it to tall, green gas cylinders against the wall.

"A forge."

Cassidy walked around a sculpture in the middle of the floor. It was a tangle of metal rods and spikes higher than his head and six feet in diameter, and trapped deep inside was a bronze piece that might have been a heart or a bird or a fist, depending on your slant. An easel near it held a charcoal sketch of the sculpture and next to that another easel held a meticulous diagram for the intricate placement of the metal rods. A big welding rig stood nearby, the acetylene and oxygen tanks side by side on a dolly. Tubes ran from the tanks to a welding gun hanging on the dolly handle.

"Carlos Ribera, Cuban modernist," Cassidy said and looked to Dylan for confirmation.

She was taking protective leather chaps and a heavy cotton jacket with leather sleeves from hooks near the elevator, and she looked over at him in surprise.

"I read about him in the *Times* a couple of months ago when the Museum of Modern Art had one of his pieces—*Explosion #4*. Out in the sculpture garden near the Rodin. I like it."

"You're kidding. A cop who likes modern art."

"Hey, don't get me wrong. I still like to give a prisoner the third degree, but a man's got to spend his graft someplace. Why not on art? Besides, a museum is a great place to pick up women using the two basic approaches. One is to act dumb and get her to tell you about the painting she's looking at. Or play it the other way and offer her some wildly esoteric explanation of what the artist was up to. I tend to go with the first. There's less heavy lifting."

She offered him a Bronx cheer. "I've got to go to work. You can watch or go home. Whatever you want."

He heard it as a challenge. "I'll stick around for a while."

She smiled and turned away from him and studied the sketch and the diagram next to it while she pulled on leather gloves. Her concentration was so intense that he ceased to exist. When she had seen what she needed to see, she lowered the helmet's faceplate and turned the valve that sent acetylene to the torch. Gas hissed. She hit a striker near the torch nozzle and flame popped. She adjusted the valve until the flame stopped smoking and then let in oxygen from the second valve until the flame turned from yellow to blue and developed defined edges. She selected a bent piece of metal from an old kitchen table nearby, checked it against the diagram, laid it into a gap in the sculpture, and dipped the flame to the join. Cassidy admired the way she worked. Her movements were precise and economical. She checked the diagram before setting in a new piece and checked again before the weld took and adjusted it if she felt it was off. The flame hissed. Sparks showered from the welds. The room smelled of burned metal. He could not tell if she ever looked at him through the thick glass plate on the helmet, but he did not think so. The work engaged her completely. What would it be like to be with someone who was that focused?

He roamed the studio. There was a kitchen in one corner. The sink was full of dirty dishes. A pot of green soup scummed over on the stove. The icebox rattled and groaned. The walls were wood-paneled to eight feet and then gave way to exposed brick. Paintings and drawings of all sizes were pinned to the paneling. There were oils, pen-and-ink drawings, delicate watercolors, and bold canvases slashed with color, and it was clear that many artists were represented. There were also charcoal and chalk sketches of sculptures already made or planned for the future, and Ribera's strokes seemed to have been applied to the paper in a fury.

Cassidy pushed open a door near the elevator and found a windowless bedroom. He turned on the light. There was a king-size box spring and mattress on the floor, its top sheet and blankets kicked aside. Clothes were piled on a chair in the corner and hung from hooks in the wall. A painting hung on the wall opposite the bed. As Cassidy moved to see it more clearly, the elevator rumbled down the shaft. The painting was a life-size nude of a young woman. She stood on a tropical shore and was partly turned from the observer, hip cocked, one foot pointed to test the water that licked the edge of the beach, both hands lifted to tie back her black hair with a red ribbon. The figure was so realistic that Cassidy thought he might be looking at a large photograph, but when he was close he could see the brushstrokes in the paint.

The elevator rumbled up.

She was a Latina and her body was the color of dark honey. From her smile she understood that a man was watching her, a man who wanted her, the painter and whoever saw the painting.

The elevator doors clashed open.

When Cassidy stepped into the main room, the man closing the elevator doors turned and looked at him and then raised his eyebrows in mock surprise and said, "Who the hell are you, and what are you doing in my house?" He was a big man, bull thick through the chest and shoulders. He had a heavy, big-featured face and a mass of wild thick gray hair that sprang from his head in tangled curls.

"Michael Cassidy. I followed her here. I'm hoping she'll keep me." He nodded toward Dylan, who was bent over the sculpture oblivious of all else.

"Hell, yes. An ass to follow anywhere," he said in a thick Cuban accent.

He carried a brown paper shopping bag in the crook of one arm, and when he moved, the bottles inside rattled. "I told her after I hired her that we should become lovers, but she laughed and said no. Laughed at me. At Ribera. Can you imagine?" He laughed. "Come on, let's have a drink. I told her that in a week with me she would learn more about being with a man, more about being a woman, than she could learn in a year with any other man. She laughed again. Said no. Again." He shrugged at the foolishness of women. He put the sack down on the counter near the icebox and pulled bottles out with a flourish like rabbits from a hat. "With most women, 'no' is just the beginning of the dance. With Dylan, no means no. Yes means yes. Very unusual woman. Do like tequila?" He held up a bottle of pale amber liquor. It carried no label.

"I do."

"*Bueno, hombre,* you are going to have something wonderful." He found two glasses on a shelf above the sink and wiped them with a towel of dubious cleanliness. He pulled the cork from the bottle. "I have a friend who smuggles this in from Mexico. You cannot buy it here. It comes from the highlands above the town of Tequila in Jalisco where the big blue agaves grow. The soil there is very red, and the blue agaves grow very big and the tequila they make from them has a delicate sweetness. This is *añejo,* which means old. They age it in wood casks to make it smooth. Taste." He shoved a full glass at Cassidy and raised his own glass. "*Amor y pesos,* love and money. What else is there?" He answered his own question. "Art. Of course, art." He drank the tequila quickly and banged his glass on the counter.

Cassidy drank his. The liquor was smooth with just enough bite, and the taste was vegetal rather than grain.

"Good?"

"Yes."

"Another." He poured two more, and they drank. "You were in the bedroom looking at Carmen."

"Yes. Beautiful."

"Do you know why I painted her?"

"Why?"

"Because of the critics. They said I was an abstractionist, because I had to be, because I could not draw. So I did that to show them what fools they were. And I was in love. In love and worried about what the critics thought. The problems of a young man. What do you do, Michael Cassidy?"

"I'm a cop."

"Ah, the ultimate critic. 'Stop or I'll shoot.'" He laughed and drank again. "I hate cops. They guard the towers of the monsters who rule over the people. Without the cops, the towers would fall and the monsters would be crushed."

"Without cops there'd be someone standing over you with a gun taking your wallet with the other hand."

"Always the same argument. But who protects the people from their protectors?"

"I do."

Ribera peered at him. "Hmm, a good-hearted Fascist? Well, maybe there is one. Me, I'm a Marxist-anarchist. Not a Communist, mind you. Fuck the Communists. The dictatorship of the proletariat is just another dictatorship. I believe in the central tenet of Marx: from each according to his ability, to each according to his need, because I have extraordinary ability and extraordinary needs." He turned away abruptly and went to examine Dylan's work.

Cassidy liked him and liked his liquor.

Dylan saw Ribera approach. She straightened from the last weld, turned off the torch, and took off the helmet. Her face shone with sweat. She peeled off the gloves and ran her fingers through her matted hair and shook her head hard.

Ribera looked closely at the work she had finished and then stepped back to look at the whole. He scrubbed his face with his hand as if to wipe out what he had seen and then looked again. "It's wrong."

"I checked the diagram and the sketch. It's what you drew there."

"I don't give a shit what's there. It's wrong. It's wrong. Can't you see it? Can't you feel it? Goddamn it, I knew it. I knew it was wrong, but I did not listen to the voice. I did not pay attention. I just went ahead, because I am an arrogant shit who does not learn. Fuck!" He whirled, saw a sledgehammer leaning against the table, and picked it up and swung it hard into the sculpture. The head struck with a clang, and some of the new welds broke. Pieces of metal flew like shrapnel. Ribera swung the hammer up and drove it into the sculpture again, and again, smashing welds, breaking pieces loose, bending others.

The fury flamed out. He dropped the hammer and stepped back, his shirt dark with sweat, his chest pumping, and assessed the damage and took one last deep breath and let it out. "All right. There." He looked at

Cassidy and Dylan standing together. "There is no creation without destruction. Now we start again. Go home, Dylan. I'm going to get drunk." The streets were deserted except for an occasional taxi or delivery truck pulled by its headlights through the night.

[handwritten in margin: WRONG THIS STATEMENT IS JUST DUMB.]

"What did you think of him?"

"Too wishy-washy for me. He's soft. I like men with strong opinions."

"Hey." She punched him on the arm. "He's a genius."

"He wouldn't argue with you on that."

"Why are men so prickly with each other? They always swell up when they first meet."

"Women. Women confuse us. They make us act strangely."

"Why is it always our fault?"

"I don't know. God's design, joker that he is. No, I like him. I like his liquor. I like what he makes. I like his taste in welders."

"Okay, then."

They walked home through the warm evening, and after a couple of silent blocks she slipped an arm through his. He felt a surge of pleasure, the giddiness, hope, and confusion of a teenager on a first date, and he wondered at that.

He followed her up the stairs. Bless the man who invented tight blue jeans. Ribera was right, an ass to follow anywhere. She stopped in front of her door and turned to look at him with big eyes and a smile tugging the corners of her mouth, and he wondered if she could hear his thoughts. They looked at each other for a moment without saying anything, and then both leaned in at the same time and met in the middle. He put his hands on her waist and pulled her in, and her arms went around his neck and the length of her body pressed against him and he could feel himself rising against her.

She pushed away from him, breathing hard. "No. Too fast."

"No." His heart raced. He tried to pull her back to him, but she put her hand on his chest and held him off while she searched his face.

"I do what I want," she said.

"All right."

"Nobody makes me do anything I don't want to do. I do what I want. Do you understand?"

She was telling him something important, something beyond this moment, but he missed her meaning. "Sure. It's okay." God, he wanted her.

"Nobody."

"No."

She looked at him one more time as if to be sure of something, and what she saw must have satisfied her, because she came back against him, pressing into him, and kissed him. They broke, and he took her hand and they went up bumping hips in the narrow staircase. He fumbled the key into the lock with one hand, unwilling to let go of her with the other. They went to the bedroom without speaking. He stripped off his jacket and threw it and his gun rig on a chair and went to her and unbuttoned her shirt while she unbuttoned his. He unsnapped her bra and cupped her breasts while she unbuckled his belt. She hooked her thumbs in her waistband and pushed off her jeans and panties in one motion while he kicked the rest of his clothes to the floor. They went to the bed. He ran his hands over her and she bucked up against them. He kissed her nipples and went down and tasted her and when he went into her she rose against him.

When he woke in the morning, his arm was over her waist, and they were pressed together like spoons. He could feel himself get hard against her, and she murmured something and shifted so he could slip into her and then pushed back against him and he held on tight while she moved.

Afterward he lay on his stomach with his head pillowed on his arms, and she sat cross-legged next to him and traced the scars on his back with a finger. "What did this?" His back was ridged as if scourged by whips.

"Shrapnel."

She waited. "Is that all you're going to tell me?"

"Outside Bastogne. We were pinned down in the snow. A guy named Markowitz got hit. He was out in a forward listening post. He couldn't make it back alone, so I went out to get him. They dropped a shell near us before we made it back. He got most of it. It killed him. What was left did that to me."

"That's it?"

"Yeah." He wasn't going to tell her about Markowitz's screaming, or about the prayer litany that ran through his own mind when he went out to get him, the prayer they all shared: "Not me. Please, not me. Not me."

She leaned down and kissed his back. "Lucky you. Lucky me."

When he got out of the shower, she was gone from the bedroom. He got dressed and found her drinking coffee leaning against the black walnut counter that separated the kitchen from the living room. She was wearing one of his shirts, which just reached her thighs.

"What are you smiling at?"

"You. You're beautiful."

"Ah, well. Okay. Thank you." She kissed him lightly on the mouth and she tasted of coffee.

There was another cup on the counter waiting for him.

"It's black. I didn't know how you like it."

"Black's fine." He drank some and lit a cigarette.

"It's only the beginning of what I don't know."

"What do you want me to tell you?"

"Nothing more now. I don't have to know it all at once. Do you?" She searched his face the way she had the night before on the landing in front of his door.

"No."

She smiled. "We'll explore. Okay? Little by little."

•   •   •

As he walked toward the subway, he suppressed the urge to skip. How could this have happened? Who was she? Where the hell did she come from to suddenly appear in his life like a miracle? Is this what he had always been waiting for? It felt like it. No, it felt like something he'd heard rumor of but never expected to find. No warning. Just suddenly there. Wait. Don't get ahead of yourself. When you come back in the evening, she could be gone.

8

Cassidy agreed to meet Leah at Carmine's on Mott Street. While he waited
for the light, he pulled the envelope from his inside pocket and took out
the fifty-cent piece he found in Ingram's locker and examined it again in
the sunlight. Nothing. It was just a coin. Fifty cents. A couple of hot dogs.
A short ride in a cab. Is this what the FBI was looking for? Why? There
must be a reason, or Ingram wouldn't have hidden it. He flipped it in the
air, caught it, and put it back in the envelope, and thought about where he
could hide it.

Leah was waiting at a table against the brick wall at the back of the long
room of wooden tables covered with red-and-white-checked tablecloths.
Three hoods in sharkskin suits were drinking espresso at the bar. They
made him as a cop when he came in, and as he went back toward Leah,
they scooped their change and started to leave until the bartender leaned
over and said something in a low voice, and they settled back on their stools.

"Hi."

"Hi, yourself," she said as he leaned over to kiss her. She smiled brightly,
but he could tell she was nervous. She fiddled with her glass of red wine,
drank some of it, and then started to speak but stopped when the owner
arrived with menus.

"How're you doing, Mike?"

"I'm okay, Aldo. How are you?"

"Good. Good. Leo's getting out in a week. Good behavior and all. Best
thing that ever happened to him. He's coming to work for me. A year from
now, it all works out, I'll make him a partner."

"Is that going to be okay?"

"Yeah. I really think it is. And what am I going to do? He's my brother.

I've got to try to make it right." He put the menus down. "I'll give you a couple of minutes."

"What was that about?" Leah asked.

"I busted his brother on an armed robbery charge about five years ago. Leo was a hophead. They put him away for five to eight. Apparently he cleaned up, found Jesus. Aldo thinks I did the family a favor."

"And those guys at the bar?"

Cassidy glanced over. "I don't know them personally, but at least one of them works for Joey Adonis. You know who he is?"

"A gangster. I read the papers. Isn't he a friend of Uncle Frank's?"

"I wouldn't call him a friend. A business associate."

They ordered.

Leah rolled the stem of her glass between her fingers. "Did you ever, in your wildest dreams, think you'd be here?"

"Lunch at Carmine's?"

"Don't be dense. A cop. Gangsters who know you. Are you carrying a gun?"

"Yes."

"Carrying a gun."

"My wildest dreams? No."

"What, then?"

"I don't know."

"Come on."

"For a while, pitching for the Yankees. Then the greatest jazz pianist in the world."

"What? You can't even play the piano. You hated piano lessons. You used to hide when Miss Schoenfeld came to the house."

"Dreams aren't about what you can do. They're dreams."

"Jazz pianist, wow."

"What about you?"

"I kind of wanted to be a lumberjack for a while when I was about nine. I didn't know what one did, but it sounded cool. Then a movie star. Standard stuff. Then when you joined up and went to war, I wanted to be Margaret Bourke-White, or someone. A war correspondent or photographer. I'd find you and take pictures of you doing heroic stuff."

"You wouldn't have used much film. What about now?"

Her eyes darkened. She looked away for a moment and then looked back. "Now I just want to be peaceful."

The waiter brought food, and they ate in silence. When the coffee came, Cassidy pulled out his gun and stirred the sugar in with the end of the barrel. Leah laughed. "Thanks. Perfect."

"What's up?"

The laughter fled. "I'm pregnant."

"Hey, great. Congratulations. That's wonderful. Mark must be really happy."

Her face was like stone. "He doesn't know."

"Why not?"

"It's not his." She threw it away with a casual voice and then looked up to meet his eyes, braced.

"What the hell?"

"I don't know. It happened, okay?"

"Jesus, Leah . . ."

"Don't. Just don't."

"Does this mean you and Mark . . . ?"

"No. It's not like that. It's so stupid. I love him. And I know he loves me. I just . . . I don't know."

"And this other guy?"

"Nothing. Nobody. Just a thing for a minute." Serious eyes, clenched jaw.

"Does he know?"

"No. No. Of course not." Pleading. "I know, I know. I just don't want to talk about it. Don't lecture me, okay?"

"No. I won't."

"Don't you ever just want to tear it all down, smash it up?"

"Sure. Yeah. I do."

"What makes us like that? Why can't we just be happy with what we have?"

He reached out to cover her hand on the checked tablecloth. "How can I help?"

"I want to get rid of it."

"Right. Sure. Okay. Look, it's illegal. It's dangerous." Playing for time. "Are you sure you've thought this through? You could have the baby. No one's going to know."

"I'm going to know. And Mark's going to know. I don't know how, but he's going to know. I can't do that to him."

"Then why the hell did you—"

"Don't." She cut him off. "I did something I shouldn't have done. I made a mistake. I'm not going to pay for it for the rest of my life. I'm not going to make some child pay for it. I'm not going to make Mark pay for it. Do you think I haven't thought this over? I have to do it now, before it's something I can really feel. If you won't help me, I'll do it on my own."

"No. Don't do that. You don't know what kind of butchers girls end up with. Don't run off on this."

"I thought, maybe, you could go to Uncle Frank and get a name. He must know someone."

"No. Not Frank. He'd be the last one. You've heard him talk. Mother Church this, Mother Church that. Family and church, nothing more important. I'll find someone. It's going to be all right. Leave it to me."

"Don't tell Brian. It'll just make him worry. You know what he's like. He wants everything to be smooth, everything to be perfect. And he'd want to fix it, and he wouldn't know how."

"I won't tell him."

"Not like you. Nothing bothers you."

Is that how she saw him? How could she think that was true?

9

Dylan slipped the latch on Cassidy's apartment with a stiff piece of celluloid and went in. Shouldn't a cop have a better lock? Maybe he didn't have anything worth protecting. She leaned her back against the door and studied the big room. What she wanted would not be hidden in an obvious place and not in a place where the FBI agents would have found it. Be smart about this. Where would it be? For a moment she thought about leaving, about not doing this to him, but she knew that wasn't an option. Do it. Just do it. It has to be done. She would save the bedroom till last. The bedroom seemed a greater betrayal.

She pushed away from the door and moved into the room and began to search.

10

Cassidy stood behind the iron gate that guarded the front desk of the flop-house from the lobby and looked at the five men who sat on the worn so-fas near the barred windows that gave out on Tompkins Square while Orso talked to the manager. The men were sharing a quart bottle of Ballantine Ale and unlikely ideas on how to get rich quick. One of the men, a wiry terrier in army surplus khakis and a denim jacket, was the leader, and all the others deferred to him. His face was thin and knobby, and when he drank from the bottle his prominent Adam's apple bobbed up and down.

The manager pointed to him. "Jerry Scanlon. He was here when In-gram was boarding. Hey, Jerry, these guys want to ask you a couple of questions."

Scanlon made them for cops. "I didn't do it, officers. I was home with me mum all that night." The other men on the sofas laughed. Jerry sa-luted his audience with the bottle.

"Do you remember Alex Ingram?" Orso asked.

"Alex Ingram? Sure. Lived down the hall from me."

"What can you tell us about him?"

"What's it worth to you?"

"The thanks of a grateful citizenry."

"More than that, boyo. *Nam et ipsa scientia potestas est.*" He grinned and winked at his friends.

"What the hell?" Orso said, and looked to Cassidy for an explanation. Cassidy shrugged.

"Knowledge is power itself, boyo," Scanlon translated. "And surely power draws money like flies to honey." He laughed at his own wit and saluted them with the big green bottle.

"Jesus christ, an educated bum."

"Not a bum, my friend, a hoddie. A man of skill and courage."

"Five bucks," Cassidy said. "If it's worth anything."

"The money first."

"No."

"Okay, then. You look like an honest man, for a cop. And when you hear it, you'll probably pay me ten." He took the last of the bottle and reached into a paper bag at his feet to extract a new one and passed it to the man sitting next to him to open it. "Alex Ingram. Much too good for a place like this, according to him. The kind of fella who thinks his shit don't stink. Never a good word to anybody." The bottle came back to him and he took a slug.

"Not worth a dime so far. We've heard that from everyone we've talked to."

"Give it time. A story builds. So one day I'm over at Washington Square playing speed chess, and I seen him on the corner of Fifth, waiting like. Then a limousine as long as my dick pulls up, and in it he gets, and off it goes. So I think, well then, a limousine. Maybe you can pay me back the dollar I lent you in a moment of weakness, young Alex. So the next time I sees him, I mentions it. Wrong, he says. Not me. No limo. No Fifth Avenue, and no dollar. The lying shit. So, I think, well okay. Then a week later I'm carrying a hod of facing bricks on a building we're doing on the Upper East Side where the swells live. I'm up six floors on the scaffold and I look over, and there, big as life, in the window across the street is Alex Ingram, buck naked and dancing around with his willy flopping." He stopped and looked expectantly at Orso and Cassidy.

"What do you mean, dancing?" Cassidy asked.

"Dancing. You know, twirling and leaping, and jumping with the arms spread out. Ballet, you ignorant flatfoot. But naked. Never seen that before."

"You're sure it was Ingram?"

"Of course I'm bloody sure. And when I mentioned it to him a couple of days later, he says I tell anyone, he'll kill me. And I think he means it. The next day he's gone. Never seen him since, clothed or bare ass."

Cassidy passed him five dollars. "Worth every penny whether it's true or not."

"True as true can be. On the heads of my unborn children who are still in my dick."

"Where was the building?"

"Sixty-fourth between Park and Lexington. We was facing a building on the south side. He was on the north. One of them fancy buildings with the doorman outside in his uniform, brass buttons and all, the last one before Lex. Sixth floor."

"Did you see anyone else? Anyone go by the window?"

"Nope. Not a soul."

Cassidy and Orso walked three blocks and went into the dim, religious light and smell of spilled beer and sawdust of McSorley's for a cold one. The bartender drew them a couple of pints of ale and refused payment.

"I could have used you a half hour ago, officers. I had to throw a damn woman out, she wouldn't take no for an answer. I told her straight out, no women allowed, but she's bitching she wants a beer. Said it was her right. Can you imagine? Her right? What the hell's with that? McSorley's is a men's joint. It's always been a men's joint. It's always going to be a men's joint. I told her it was my right not to serve no damn split-tail, and if she didn't leave on her own, I'd assist. Came out from behind the bar, and she skedaddled." He carried his outrage down to the other end of the bar to share it with the men drinking there.

"Do you believe him?" Orso took a long pull on his beer.

"Dancing naked? Hell of an imagination if he made it up. I'd like to know who he was dancing for."

"Faggot stuff. Jesus."

"What, you've never danced naked with a woman?"

"I'm kind of shy. I'm still working up to that. What do you favor, the fox-trot?"

They had talked to chorus gypsies, dance masters, casting directors, rooming house inmates, secretaries at Actors Equity, and they had learned the same thing from all of them and little else. Ingram was described as a charming little shit, an ambitious little shit, a greedy little shit, and variations on the theme. . Nobody admitted to knowing more about him than that.

"I'm going to call the Feds."

"Why waste the nickel?"

"I want to know whose apartment he was dancing in. If you and I go up there and ask who lives there, they'll tell us to get lost, come back with a court order. We'll let the Feds carry the weight."

He took his beer mug back to the phone booth near the men's room and put it on the shelf while he found Susdorf's card. He put a nickel in the phone and dialed, told the secretary who he was and who he wanted, and waited until Susdorf came on the line.

"Why do you want to know who lives there?"

"Ingram was seen there in an apartment on the sixth floor. We'd like to know who he visited. Everything else is a dead end so far."

"I'll get back to you."

"Do you want another?" Orso asked when he returned to the bar.

"No, thanks. I'm going home. I've got a date."

"Dylan?"

"Yeah."

"Every night this week. What is this?"

"I don't know exactly, but it sure as hell is something."

• • •

Cassidy knocked on Dylan's door and lit a cigarette while he waited for her to answer. The sound of her approaching footsteps made him smile in anticipation. She opened the door and kissed him lightly on the mouth and took the cigarette from him and took a drag.

"You look beat."

"Nothing a shower and a drink won't fix. Are we going to have dinner?"

"Sure."

"Do you have to work afterward?"

"No. I have to go to Ribera's, but not to work. He's having a party and he wants me to be there."

"A party."

She heard his unspoken question. She hesitated. "Do you want to go?"

He read the hesitation. "Not if you don't want me to."

"No, no. I just didn't know if you'd want to. You should come." He read something in her face. Reluctance?

"Third wheel?"

"No, no. Half of New York will be there. You should come."

He could tell she was holding something back. "Do I have time for a shower?"

"Sure. I'll come up and drink your liquor."

He went upstairs and left the door cracked so Dylan could get in. Something about the apartment was different. Something had changed, something was out of place. He stood in the living room and studied it, but he could not put his finger on what bothered him. It was probably something left over from the FBI search, that feeling of invasion. He shook it off and went to shower and change. When he came back, Dylan was lying on the sofa with a drink. Dylan offered her glass, and he took a sip of her martini.

The phone rang. "Hey, how are you?"

He listened.

"No, I can't. Not tonight."

He listened.

"I can't. I'm busy. I don't know about tomorrow. Maybe. Dad, I would if I could, but I can't tell you for sure."

He took another sip of Dylan's drink.

"I'm not trying to avoid anything. I'm just trying to do the work I have to do." He could hear the exasperation in his own voice. "You don't need my help on this. No. You don't. Okay. Okay. I'll get there when I can. Yeah. Sure. I promise."

He banged the phone down.

"Your father?"

"Yes."

"Do you always fight?"

"Only when we talk."

• • •

Four Cadillac limousines, bulbous and black, gleaming under the streetlamps, waited in front of Ribera's building. The doors to one were open and swing music played from the radio. The four chauffeurs gathered there to smoke and talk. Dylan wore a blue silk shirt and a long steel-gray skirt of some light material that molded to her long legs as she walked, and they turned to watch her as she and Cassidy went into the building.

They rode up in the elevator with three businessmen and their dates, who clung to their arms and looked at them adoringly and laughed at the things the men said. An adventure to deepest, darkest downtown. Artists, Bohemia. The men signaled their readiness for the wildness of the night by loosening their ties, hunching their shoulders like Bogart with a gun, holding their cigarettes between thumb and forefinger, and squinting against the smoke when they took tough little puffs.

The din of the party swelled into the elevator before it stopped and the old man running it clashed open the gates. The businessmen and their girls stampeded out with cries of delight into the seethe of people crowding the loft. The long counter under the window was now massed with bottles of beer, booze, and wine, glasses half full, full, empty, and broken, platters of food, clean and used plates and cutlery. The air was dense with cigarette smoke and loud with the trilling laughter of women, the shouts of men, and the occasional crystal break of glass. A record player near the elevator competed with a quartet at the back of the room near the forge, where three couples danced the mambo. Ribera spotted Dylan over the heads of the crowd. He smiled and waved. Then he saw Cassidy and his face clouded and he bulled his way through the people toward them, and as he went, people touched him on the shoulders and arms and spoke to him, eager for his attention, but they could not deflect him. By the time he got to them, he was smiling again. He lifted Dylan in a hug and kissed her on both cheeks. "I was afraid you weren't coming."

"Here I am."

He turned to Cassidy and looked him over. "So, you got a taste, and you could not stay away." He threw a heavy arm across Cassidy's shoulders. "I'm glad you're here," though his expression when he first saw Cassidy made that a lie. "But I must ask you for a favor. Tonight you are not a cop. You are at my party. You are Michael Cassidy or anyone else you want to be, but you are not a cop. Nobody does anything wrong here. There are no laws. All is allowed. Well, if you see someone killing someone, please step in, but other than that. Agreed?"

"Agreed."

"You are in Cuba tonight. Things are different in Cuba. We are people of great appetites and little shame. Not like you northern people who pretend these things don't exist, who hold them in, hold them tight." He minced around in a circle with his shoulders bowed and his hands covering his groin.

Cassidy laughed. He liked this man. *why? WHAT IS THERE TO LIKE?*

"Now, I must take Dylan for a little while. Get yourself a drink and something to eat. Go flirt with the pretty girls. Give them some excitement."

"Don't forget who you came with," Dylan said.

Ribera laughed, clapped Cassidy on the back, and led her into the crowd.

Cassidy found a reasonably clean glass on the counter and filled it with ice from a large steel bowl and bourbon from a half-full bottle of Jack

Daniel's. The autumn burning-leaf smell of reefer was heavy near the bar. This was probably the reason for Ribera's discomfort when he saw Cassidy with Dylan. Nothing like a few arrests for drug possession to put a damper on a party.

A woman in a long unadorned black dress stood on the counter, her bare feet among the dishes, and swayed to a rhythm only she could feel. Her hair was thick and black, her face hard and angular as if cut from stone. Her eyes were closed, and her arms and hands moved as if underwater. Men and women stood watching her with the fascination of people witnessing an accident. She reached down and took the hem of her dress and slowly lifted it over her head and flung it out into the crowd. Underneath she was naked, and her body was pale and white. The watchers burst into applause. New York, greedy for everything, money, power, art, pleasure, diversion, desperate to taste it before it slipped away.

He recognized faces in the crowd, two state senators, a congressman, a city councilman, a retired general. There were well-dressed men and women from uptown who looked like they were rubbed with old money every morning until they achieved a perfect glow, people he had seen at the parties his father gave for investors in his shows, elaborate confections, as much as theater party, usually thrown onstage in the set when the current play had a night off. The backstage lights would be up, the doors to the dressing rooms ajar, the makeup mirrors lighted, the jars of creams, cakes of mascara, wigs, false eyelashes, and boxes of blush and rouge scattered in front of them as if the actors had just left or were about to sit down to prepare for the evening's show. It gave the partygoers the feeling they had lifted the curtain, had been let in on the mystery. Everyone arrived a little stiff, the conversation too loud, laughter too bright. Booze flowed, and the stiffness warmed away. Actresses, actors, chorus boys and girls flirted with stockbrokers and investment bankers, East Side housewives, and magazine publishers, and people who arrived alone did not always go home alone.

When he was sixteen, he had been taken in hand at one of those parties by the second-lead actress of a drawing room comedy about mistaken identity, a lost will, an adoption that no one knew about. She was in her early thirties and clever enough to allow him to believe that he was the instigator. She reeled him in, pushed him back, reeled him in again, sent him for drinks, laughed at his jokes, stroked him like a cat, and eventually took him back to her apartment on West 74th Street and deftly relieved him of his clothes, his virginity, and many of the misconceptions sixteen-year-old boys have about women, including the one held sacrosanct in school locker room bull sessions, that women did not like to do it, unless they were sluts, and that they had to be tricked into bed. For the rest of the night, after that first explosive tumble, she taught him what she liked, that pace and rhythm were more important that speed, and that things could be done with the tongue, fingers, and even toes that he had never imagined. In the morning she had sent him away, and when he asked when he could see her again, she smiled a bit sadly and said she would phone, and never did. He consoled himself with the bitter, cutting things he would say to her when he saw her again, things that would wound her and make her understand how much she had lost, but he never did see her again, and eventually he understood what she had given him.

He looked for Dylan but could not find her. He could see Ribera, half a head taller than most, but she was not in the group of people around him. Wait, who was that? A glimpse of a familiar face. Where had he seen him before? Black hair, high cheekbones. Where? There he was again, and this time Cassidy caught his eye just before the man recognized him and turned away.

"Victor." The man was hunched over to light his cigarette as if there were a high wind in the loft. "Victor Amado, right?" In tight black pants and a fitted black silk shirt that clung to his dancer's body. He looked at Cassidy and pretended to struggle to remember him. Cassidy watched him work it. "You're the cop. The one at the rehearsal."

"Michael Cassidy."

"Right. How are you? I didn't expect to see . . . I mean . . ." He brushed away whatever he meant.

"You didn't expect to see a cop here."

"Yeah. I guess." Amado laughed and looked around for an excuse to escape.

"I'm not a cop tonight. I'm just a guy at a party."

"Uh-huh. Okay. Great. Good to see you. Listen, um, I'm going to go get a drink." He nodded to Cassidy and turned and pushed his way to the bar.

People are nervous around cops. Everyone is guilty of something. Cassidy was used to it, but Amado's discomfort was stronger than that.

"What's going on, Victor?" Amado started and slopped gin on the bar.

"What do you mean?"

"I've been asking around about Ingram, checking with people who lived where he lived, people he worked with, no one seems to have liked him much. How about you?"

"I didn't know him very well. Like I told you, we went out for a drink a couple of times. That was it."

"Victor, I talked to the other people in the chorus. I spoke to Marco. He said you and Ingram had worked together before. He said you came to the first dance audition together."

Amado looked around to see if anyone was paying attention to them. "I can't talk to you."

"You're going to have to talk to me. I'm investigating a murder. You knew the dead man."

"I can't talk here." He looked around again. "I can't."

"Why not?"

"I just can't. I don't want to get involved."

"Involved in what?"

"Look, leave me alone, okay? Just leave me alone."

He was scared of something and Cassidy realized there was no use pushing now. "All right. Here's my card. You call me." He slipped it into Amado's hand. "If you don't call me, I'll pick you up and take you down to the house. If I do that, people will know. If you want to do this quietly, call me."

Amado looked like he was going to say something else, but instead he turned and pushed into the crowd.

Amado would never call him. And he certainly wasn't going to talk to him here. He would have to go to him. Tomorrow would be time enough. Cassidy picked up a bottle of Jack Daniel's from the counter. Did he want more? He poured an inch in his glass and added a few melting cubes. A hand touched his arm.

"I know you." Roy Cohn looked at him with his dead eyes. His gray suit jacket was buttoned. His tie was tight to his collar. His smile was a smirk. "You're the cop from New Year's Eve."

"Ah, Mr. Cohen. How nice to see you."

"You see this guy, David? I told you about him. The wiseass cop." The remark was thrown to a pleasant-looking blond man who stood nearby swaying under the load of liquor he had taken aboard. Cassidy recognized him from the newspapers as David Schine, the son of a California hotel mogul who had worked as an unpaid assistant on McCarthy's subcommit-

tee before the army drafted him, the cause, according to Brian, for Mc-
Carthy going after the army. "Detective Michael Cassidy. I've been doing
some research on you. I've been looking into you. I've been checking
around."

"Did you find out I was Stalin's love child, or is my secret still safe?"

"You're a violent man, Detective Cassidy. I saw that on New Year's Eve
when you beat that man in front of the Stork. Violent men think of the
moment, not of the long term. Violence is temporary and ineffectual. Violence is bullshit. You know what I like? I like power. Power endures."
He flicked the ash from his cigarette and it sprinkled a cheese plate on the
counter.

Cassidy realized Cohn was drunk too. Tightly controlled but drunk,
and full of boozy certainty.

"You treated me like shit that night, like I was nobody. You were the
cop with the gun and the fuck-you attitude. Well, *you're* nobody. I checked.
You're nobody, and your father's nobody, and I'm the guy who's a friend
of Director Hoover and of Senator McCarthy. I call judges, senators, con-
gressmen, and they take my calls immediately. I've had lunch with the
president."

Cohn was leaning in to make his point. His voice was not loud, but
people shied away, and the three of them stood apart in the crowded
room, isolated by the force field of Cohn's malevolence.

"Do you know how the world works? The world works on the Favor
Bank. You do something for someone, you build up credit. You don't draw
on it till you need it. Just keep doing the favors, putting money in the Favor
Bank. Comes a time, you're a rich man. You, you fuck, have nothing in the
bank. You're a fucking pauper. Nobody owes you anything. I checked."

"Ah, but I am rich in other ways, in the warmth of my friendships and
the strength of my loves." Cassidy blew smoke toward Cohn's angry face.

"Wiseass. You're in for a surprise, wiseass. I've got something that's
going to knock you on your ass."

"And a nice ass it is." Dylan was at his side and she hooked her arm
through his and smiled at Cohn.

"Who are you?" Cohn asked.

"You first," Dylan said.

Cohn pointed a finger like a gun at Cassidy and pulled the trigger. Then
he turned away and said, "Come on, David," and led Schine into the pack
of people.

"Having fun?" Dylan asked.

"Not a bit."

"Let's go home."

The ranting of a drunk. He put Cohn out of his mind.

11

The taxi dropped Cassidy in Times Square so he could walk the last blocks to the station house, a few minutes of privacy before the day truly started, a few minutes to savor the city while it was still waking. Times Square was quiet, empty of tourists. The street-cleaning crews had been through, and the trash was gone from the gutters that still ran with trickles of water. The asphalt was wet and gleaming in the sun that slanted down the street canyons from the east. The Camels man blew his smoke rings, and the peanuts fell endlessly from the Planters bag, but the neon was off, and the few people on the sidewalks were New Yorkers on their way to work.

He ate breakfast in a diner on 46th Street and read the *Daily News* someone had discarded. Senator McCarthy denounced the Democratic Party as "the party of communism, betrayal, and treason." J. Edgar Hoover, in a speech in Virginia, said that America was at war with ruthless communism, and that in times of war such as these the people are best protected by removing some of the restrictions that hampered police in their pursuit of the enemy. The age-old cry of a man with power, *Give me more.*

U.S.A, LOST IN 2018.

2019 HE WAS RIGHT. DEMOCRATIC/SOCIALISTS IN CONGRESS, NEW YORK GOV. "AMERICA WAS NEVER GREAT." LAW MAKERS FOLLOWING MARX.

"Mr. Holden, you say this guy has robbed you before."

"Yeah."

"And you're sure it's the same guy?"

"Yeah, I'm sure." Holden flicked his cigarette toward the ashtray on Cassidy's desk, and missed. He was a stocky man in his midforties with a five o'clock shadow that was dark an hour before its appointed time.

"How many times?"

"With this one, three."

"And you've never reported it before?"

"No."

"Why not?"

"I don't know." He shrugged.

"Tell me what happened today." Holden was not telling Cassidy everything, but he knew they would get to it.

"I'm in the store alone. The delivery guy's out making a run, a case of scotch down to the Shuberts. I'm restocking the shelves. I go to the storeroom for a case of Jim Beam. When I come back, the guy's at the front counter. He's got the mask on and the gun, and he tells me to empty the register."

"What kind of mask?"

"You know, like a bandana up over his nose, like a stagecoach robber on *The Lone Ranger* or something, and a hat pulled down. So I give him the money, and he goes. And I think, well, okay, fuck it. Three times. Enough. And I come down here."

"He had a mask on. He had a hat pulled down. Mr. Holden, how can you be so sure it was the same guy?"

"It was the same guy."

"How do you know?"

"'Cause I know. I just know." Holden twisted nervously in his seat, suddenly reluctant.

"Okay. But *how* do you know?"

"'Cause I know him. All right?"

"You know him personally."

"Yeah. Personally."

"Through the mask and everything?"

"Yeah. Fucking guy's got a snake tattoo comes out under his watchband. Every time he comes in, he's got his left hand in his pocket so I won't see it. Gun in the right. I empty the register, hand him the bag, out comes the left hand to take the bag. The fucking snake. Stupid bastard."

The phone on Cassidy's desk rang.

"So we're looking for a man with a snake tattoo on his left wrist."

The phone rang again.

"No. You're looking for Jerry Wood."

Cassidy picked up the phone and said, "Cassidy, here. Yeah, Susdorf, hold on. I'll be back to you in a minute."

"You know the stickup guy's name?"

"Yeah, I know his name. He's my fucking brother-in-law."

• • •

The big circular bar at Toots Shor's was packed three deep. Saloon noise—the laughter, the shouted talk, the rattle of ice in glasses—and saloon smoke always lifted Cassidy. He and Orso shouldered to a place at the bar and Al, the bartender, brought him a heavy pour of Jack Daniel's and Orso a martini without asking. You did not go to Toots Shor's for the food. You could get a decent steak and baked potato, a lobster, a chop, or oysters if you wanted them, but Toots Shor's was a watering hole. You came to Shor's to drink. A couple of pops on the way home from the office, or after dinner at a restaurant with clients, then to Toots's to round out the evening. It was a place for sportswriters and reporters, for Hemingway, Ruark, and other literary boozers, for Yankees and Giants when the teams were playing home games, for fighters from the Garden a few blocks over, for actors and wiseguys, and for businessmen who had surrendered to the nine-to-five but were still trying to hold on to some part of who they had planned to be in their dangerous hours. Women were allowed, but if a man showed up with his wife too many times, the frost was obvious and he had a hard time getting served. Showgirls, models, secretaries got some slack, but it was a man's world.

Orso lifted his martini carefully and took a pull. "God, I love that first pop at the end of the day." He took another sip. "So the stickup man's the guy's brother-in-law, and he doesn't want the wife to know he fingered him." Tony Orso in four months' salary of black lightweight wool suit, cream-colored silk shirt with a dark green and silver tie, black hair slicked, face freshly shaved and talced by the barber at the Park Sheraton, fingernails gleaming from the evening manicure, as sleek as a seal and smelling of bay rum.

"Right."

"Why doesn't he just smack the guy a couple of times and take the money back?"

"The wife thinks the brother can do no wrong. He's afraid she'll take his side. If it comes to it, he thinks she'll walk."

"Here's your hat. What's your hurry?"

"He's in love with her."

"Well, good luck with that. What does he want you to do?"

"Figure out some way to brace the brother-in-law as if I got the information somewhere else."

"Have you figured it out?"

"Not yet."

"What did the FBI want?"

"Susdorf says he went to the building on Sixty-fourth where the guy says he saw Ingram dancing. He says there's nothing to it. He checked it out, top to bottom, whatever the hell that means, and it's a dead end. No reason for us to bother."

"They're playing us."

"Yes."

"Why?"

"I don't know."

"Why'd you go back to Ingram's apartment?"

"I just had a feeling." He had never talked to Orso about the dreams. "I think the guy who did Ingram was someone he knew, someone he trusted."

"How do you figure?"

"Ingram bought a pound of steak, two potatoes, a box of frozen peas. Someone was coming for dinner. He didn't put the food in the icebox, so he was planning to cook it and eat it with the guy, but he never got the chance. There's no sign of struggle in the living room. I think he came home with someone, took off his coat and hung it up to dry, put the food on the counter, and then, he's a vain guy, he goes into the bathroom to brush his hair, first thing. He wasn't scared of whoever the other person was. He turns his back on him to brush his hair. *Whack.* The guy hits him over the head and knocks him out. When he wakes up, he's tied to the chair, and the fun begins."

Orso drank half his martini. "Screw it. The Feds claim it, they can have it. They want us to do their work for them? Screw them. There's plenty of crime in New York for us to worry about. Let's go talk to Mr. Holden's brother-in-law. We do this Ingram thing on the side when we're not doing something else." He saw the look on Cassidy's face. "Okay, what am I missing?"

"I don't know. There's the guy who tortured Ingram. There's the guy searching the apartment when I went back. Is that the same guy? Maybe.

Maybe not. And the Feds are very interested in whether I found anything hidden in the place. Why else search my apartment?"

"What's that about?"

"I don't know. Why are so many people interested in a chorus line dancer? And how did this gypsy go from a guy who couldn't pay his rent on time to buying new furniture and dressing out of Paul Stuart?" He took a pull on his drink.

"Tell me."

"Blackmail."

"Fairies."

"Yeah."

"Who?"

"Someone with a lot to lose. A wife, family, a position of some sort, maybe a big job, political. I don't know. We keep pulling on the string, he'll show up."

"So why does the FBI care? Blackmail's not federal."

"I don't know. Hoover's files, maybe. They say he's got dirt on everybody in Washington. Maybe this is new dirt on someone he wants to influence."

"You think the files exist?"

"My brother says people in Washington are sure they do. The story goes that when Ike was elected, he was going to bring in someone new to run the FBI. Hoover went to see him in the White House. He had a file with him. They were alone for an hour, no aides, no witnesses. Ike kept him on, said he was a great American, said he was essential to the continued excellent operation of the Bureau."

"So Ingram had something on some guy who Hoover wants in his files. The guy goes to have a little chat with Ingram. It gets out of hand. Hoover knows about the something. He wants it too, but he's late. Ingram's dead. The blackmail material is in the wind."

"Why not?"

"What do we care? A couple of fairies."

"Yeah. Fairies, wops, niggers, yids, hunkies, gooks."

"Hey, hey. Easy. I'm on your side."

"They're all somebody's son, somebody's brother, somebody's friend. A guy gets killed, we're not supposed to decide whether he deserved it. We're supposed to find the guy who did it."

"Okay. You figure anything out, point me at it, and I'll go tear it up."
He drained his martini. "I've got to go. I've got a date. Go home and rest.
You look like hell. Oh, hey, Franklin's back. He's off medical leave and
he doesn't like you much. I don't know if he has the balls for it, but he
might want a piece of you. Watch your back." He slapped Cassidy on the
shoulder, put a couple of bucks on the bar to cover the drinks, and pushed
his way out through the crowd.

• • •

Al brought him another bourbon. Cassidy savored the smoke and bite of
the whiskey. The FBI was trying to limit what he learned about Ingram.
If he found something that pointed him toward the killer, they would
take it away from him. Did he care? He didn't like being told what to do,
and he didn't like being played.

Something hard prodded his side. "Stick 'em up, copper." He flinched
and touched the gun under his jacket and then saw Mal Brown, an investment banker with Brown Brothers Harriman, former classmate, onetime
pursuer of his sister Leah. His tie was down, his top shirt button undone,
his suit coat open. His hair was mussed and he had one arm around a young
woman. His free hand held a fountain pen stuck in Cassidy's side like a
gun. "Hey, Mike, have you met Rhonda? Rhonda works for the *New York
Post,* so be careful. Anything you say will be read at breakfast tomorrow.
Rhonda, this is Mike. Mike's got a real gun, honey. You ought to ask him
if you can see his gun." He was just drunk enough to believe that anything he thought of was a good idea.

"Hello, Rhonda." She was tall and slim, with a narrow face made
striking by huge dark eyes. She wore a tailored suit that did not hide large
breasts and narrow hips, and long, long legs, and she wore a chic black
hat with a dashing red feather and a couple of inches of veil that hung
toward her eyes, not to conceal them but to draw attention to them.

"I've seen his gun. He showed it to me once or twice. You were supposed to call me, Michael."

"Uh-oh," Mal said.

"I did call. You weren't home."

"Liar. I have one of those new answering services just in case someone
who promises to call, calls, you rat." She did not appear angry.

"I'll let you two fight it out," Mal said. "I'm going to go tell Red Smith what he doesn't know about baseball." Smith, the *Herald Tribune*'s sports columnist, was at his usual post at table number 1.

"I'm sure he'll get a kick out of that," Rhonda said.

"Bet your ass." Mal tacked away through the crowd.

Rhonda watched Cassidy coolly.

"I thought you'd given up married men."

"Yeah, well, what are you going to do? Old habits are hard to break. Besides, the good men are either taken or gun-shy. My mother keeps saying, Find a nice Jewish doctor, Rhonda, but I guess I'm looking in the wrong places. Why don't nice Jewish doctors hang out in saloons? Are you going to buy me a drink?"

"Sure. What do you want?"

"A rusty nail. Can we get it at a table? I've been on my feet all day."

• • •

They took a table in a corner away from the noise of the bar, and the waiter went off to get their drinks. Rhonda took off her hat and shook her black hair free. She leaned forward to accept a light for her cigarette, and then leaned back against the banquette's red leather and turned so she could study Cassidy. "How's the crime business?"

"Quiet. We've got New York pretty much cleaned up."

"Yeah. I haven't been mugged in a week." The waiter brought drinks and went away. "How come we didn't make it long term, Michael? I thought we were good together."

"I don't know. My fault, probably. What do you think?"

"I think definitely your fault. You're kind, sweet sometimes, smart, sexy, but you do not let anyone in. You're impenetrable. I never really knew what you felt, if you felt anything at all, or if you were just faking it."

Cassidy tasted his drink and held up the glass. "Is this the right thing to be drinking with abuse?"

Rhonda laughed. "And you could make me laugh, but it was a way of holding me off. You need someone to break through all that. Do you think it's going to be the girl I saw you with at Carlos Ribera's the other night?"

"You were there?"

"Yes. Who is she?"

"A woman who lives in my building."

"That's all I get?"

"I don't know much more. I just met her. She just moved in. She works for Ribera helping him build his sculptures. What were you doing there?"

"It's part of my expanded beat: interesting social events, the people who go, the things they say and do. The kind of stories that are every girl reporter's dream. Pretty soon they'll even let me cross the street by myself, and then who knows, maybe I'll get to do a story on why the mayor likes golden retrievers over poodles."

"What do you want to do?"

"I want to do real stories, stories that count. I want them to look at me and say she's a good reporter, not she's a good reporter for a woman. I want the same thing any man wants. I want to be allowed to do the job I can do."

"Why Ribera? Nothing else going on that night in the city?"

"Oh, no. Carlos Ribera is a hot property these days. He gives great parties. He's one of those oversized personalities New Yorkers love. And he is rumored to be a Communist, but he's kind of a safe Communist, because he's an artist. Artists can get away with stuff."

"Anarchist, not Communist. At least that's what he told me."

"Sure. And how many people at his party could define the difference? He's perfect for the uptown slummers who want to rub shoulders with the real people but don't want anything to rub off. So they all come, politicians, the Union Club hotshots, the society dames, the military brass, the artists and actors, the millionaire bohemians, and if they don't all go home to their own beds, so much the better."

"There was a dancer there, a guy from my father's show."

"Sure. What's a party without pretty boys and pretty girls?" She raised her empty glass to the waiter.

"Do you want to do something for me?"

"What?"

"Find out who lives in a building on East Sixty-fourth Street."

"Why?"

"It's part of a case I'm working." That sobered her. She waited for him to go on. "I can't tell you about it now, but if it breaks, I'll give you the story first."

"Why don't you go to the building and ask yourself? You've got a badge."

"Sure. And they've got lawyers. I thought that if you went, maybe said you were interested in an apartment there—"

She interrupted. "Don't tell me how to do my job, Mike."

"Right."

"What building?"

"I don't know the number. East Sixty-fourth, the last one on the north side before Lex. I want to know who has apartments facing Sixty-fourth Street from the fourth floor through the eighth." Just in case the hod carrier had miscounted the floor of the apartment where Alex Ingram danced naked.

"And I get the exclusive."

"You get it when I can tell it."

"Pinkie swear."

"Jesus, come on, Rhonda."

She stuck out her hand with her pinkie sticking up. He hooked it with his, and she pumped their hands up and down three times and grinned at him. "Nobody who grew up in the city would dare break a pinkie swear."

The waiter delivered the drink she had ordered, but she ignored it. "Anything else I can do?"

"No."

"Don't jerk me around on this, Michael. I need this."

"Okay."

She got up. "Tell Mal he's on his own. I'm going home." She turned away and then thought of something and came back.

"I'm sorry about your father. I hope it works out. Half the time those guys are just fishing."

"What about my father?"

"You don't know?"

"Know what? Come on, Rhonda."

"It was just coming in on the wires when I left the paper. The McCarthy subcommittee's subpoenaed him to testify."

"Testify about what?"

"Maybe communism in the theater business. I don't know. You really didn't know?"

"No."

12

The Senate Permanent Subcommittee on Investigations met on the eleventh floor in the Federal Courthouse at Foley Square. Cassidy showed his badge to the guard at the door and went to stand against the back wall. It was a large wood-paneled room. The windows were heavily curtained, but the room was brightly lit to accommodate the photographers and movie news cameras.

Members of the subcommittee sat behind a hedge of microphones at a long table that faced another long table where those called would sit to face their inquisitors. Aides leaned over the shoulders of the committee members and pointed out crucial passages in papers the august men shuffled importantly for the cameras. Senator McCarthy sat at the table's middle. He had the heavy, florid face of a drinker, and even at ten in the morning his beard was dark. His dark, thinning hair was oiled to his skull, and his suit was rumpled. Roy Cohn sat at his shoulder and looked out over the crowd with his heavy lidded, empty eyes.

The subpoenaed huddled with their lawyers. There were few allies and supporters in evidence. Who knew how a friend's toxic history might corrode your life? Better to stand clear.

Privileged spectators filled the seats in the gallery. There was the smell of blood in the air, and the crowd in the room was charged with excitement, like people waiting for a cockfight or an execution.

Tom Cassidy sat at the long table. His lawyer, Harry Gould, five feet three inches tall in his handmade shoes with built-in lifts, a bespoke suit, thick black rims on his glasses, and a head as bald and smooth as an egg, was next to him. Harry Gould never met a deal he couldn't make, never met an angle he couldn't turn to his client's advantage, but he hadn't been in a courtroom in twenty years, and bringing a show business lawyer to a McCarthy committee hearing was like bringing Tinker Bell to a street brawl.

"Stop worrying," Tom had told Cassidy when they spoke on the phone the night before. "Harry's just coming to make sure I don't say something stupid. If he has to, he'll step in and clear it up. You know, set them straight. This is America. I've done nothing wrong, so I've got nothing to worry about."

Tom saw his son at the back of the room. He waved and smiled, and made a big wide-armed gesture that said, *Hey, here we are,* as if being called in front of a Senate subcommittee was arrival at a longed-for goal. And maybe it was for him, the immigrant boy. Cassidy remembered the talks with his father at the head of the dinner table, beaming down at his American family while his mother, Joan, her ancestors American for two hundred years, sipped bourbon and picked at her food and said nothing. "America," his father would say, "the greatest country in the world. You can be anything here, anything you want, and no one can stop you. Look at me. I come from nothing."

Brian, Michael, and Leah would roll their eyes at each other. *Here we go again.*

"From nothing, from less than nothing, and look at me now." A sweep of the arm took in the dining room with its candlesticks, silver, crystal, and heavy china, serving plates with too much food, the American children, the American wife, the town house, and all beyond. "If I had stayed, I would have been a peasant picking at the fields, hungry, cold, poor, condemned by where I was born. Here you can be anything, anything. Freedom. Democracy. The greatest country in the world. Don't laugh. Don't laugh at this. You'll learn I'm right."

"Do you swear to tell the truth, the whole truth, and nothing but the truth?"

"Yes, I do."

"Sit down. Your name is Thomas R. Cassidy?" McCarthy occasionally glanced at papers on the desk in front of him.

"Yes."

"Please tell us what the *R* stands for, Mr. Cassidy."

"Nothing. I just wanted a middle initial."

There was laughter in the room. McCarthy grinned at the unexpected result of his question.

"You live at Fifty Central Park South?"

"Yes."

"Please identify the man sitting to your left."

"Harold Gould. Mr. Gould is my attorney."

McCarthy looked to Cohn, who leaned forward and said in a flat voice, "Mr. Gould, you may sit with your client. You may consult with him, but you are not to participate in any other manner in the hearing. You are not to ask questions; you are not to cross-examine; you are not to make objections; you are not to argue. You may remain under these conditions. If you do not adhere to these conditions, you will be removed. Do you understand?"

Gould flushed to the top of his bald skull. He was not used to being treated with such dismissive arrogance, but he nodded and said, "I understand."

McCarthy loved asking questions, because when he did, all eyes were on him. His pace was slow, his voice low and measured, and he had a habit of repeating a phrase to give the question gravity. "Mr. Cassidy, where are you from?"

"Like I told you, Central Park South."

"Born, Mr. Cassidy. Where were you born? Please tell us where you were born."

"I was born in a little town called Lvosk. Not even a town, really. Like a village."

"And what country was this village in, Mr. Cassidy? Please tell us the country."

"Well, sometimes Poland, sometimes Russia. Depending. Right there the border kept moving back and forth depending on who was stronger, Russia or Poland."

"Yes, Russia. Communist Russia."

"Not then. Not when I was born. I left there in 1915, and it was still the tsar then."

"And what is your real name?"

"That's my real name."

"Cassidy?" He said it in a way that made the word a lie. "What name were you born with?"

"Kasnavietski. Tomas Kasnavietski."

"Do you correspond with anyone from Lvosk, Mr. Kasnavietski?"

"I legally changed my name to Cassidy in 1928. I don't know anybody in Lvosk anymore."

"In Russia. Do you correspond with anyone in Russia? Please do not split hairs with me, Mr. Kasnavietski. Please do not prevaricate."

Tom Cassidy shifted in his seat and rubbed his face, something he did, Cassidy knew, when he was under pressure. "Sure. I've got some cousins there. I send them things. Clothes, money. Things are tough for them over there, the war and all."

"Isn't it true, Mr. Kasnavietski, that the *cousins*"—again the word made a lie—"that the *cousins* live in Moscow, the seat of power of the Communist regime?" He pronounced the word "commonest." "And that one of the cousins to whom you send money is a member of that regime's secret police?"

Harry Gould leaned in to say something to Tom Cassidy, but he shook him off. "No it's not. It's not true."

McCarthy held up a manila envelope. "I have here, Mr. Kasnavietski, a sworn affidavit that states that your cousin is a captain in the MVD, the Communist secret police."

"No, no. He's like a traffic cop. That's what he is, a traffic cop."

"I can only state the hard facts, and the hard fact is that he is a member of the secret police."

Tom Cassidy half rose from his chair. Two guards pushed away from the wall behind the committee table in case he made a rush, but all he did was hold out a hand and say, "I'd like to see that."

"No, sir. You will not see it. I will not give up the source of this information." McCarthy was playing to the cameras. "I will not put in jeopardy the life of the brave American who testified to these facts. I will never give up the names of those courageous men and women in government who risk everything to bring these matters to light."

"I thought in America if you were accused of something you got to see your accuser. I want to know who said this stuff about me."

"You dare, sir, to come in here and talk to me about America? I am trying to protect the America your cousin and men like him are trying to tear down. I will not aid them by exposing the name of the patriot who gave me this information. I will not risk the lives of the brave men and women who step out of the shadows to help our fight to keep America safe. No, sir, you will not see the names."

Tom Cassidy sank back into his seat.

McCarthy was not finished. "Mr. Kasnavietski . . ."

"My name is Cassidy." It was a weak protest.

". . . are you now or have you ever been a member of the Communist Party or an organization affiliated with the Communist Party?"

"No. I have not, and I am not. Never. I'm a Republican, for Christ's sake. I voted for Dewey. I voted for Eisenhower."

McCarthy picked up a sheaf of papers and held them high, playing to the audience. "I have in my hand the membership rolls of the American Theatre Alliance, an organization that has been deemed by the attorney general's office to be an affiliate of the American Communist Party—"

"Now wait a minute," Tom Cassidy said, outraged. "I was a member of the alliance in 1935, and I can assure you it had nothing to do with the Communist Party, and furthermore—"

McCarthy bulldozed him down. "I will not wait a minute. We do not have time to wait a minute while people like you continue to support the very enemies who are trying to destroy us."

"I was a member for six months in 1935, and—"

McCarthy bulled over him again. "So you admit to membership in a Communist affiliate. Very well. Let's move on. Mr. Kasnavietski, when you applied to become a citizen of this great country, you swore on your application that you had never been arrested, never convicted of a crime. Was that a true statement of fact?"

Cassidy saw Harry Gould put his hand on his father's arm. The two men leaned together to confer in whispers. His father straightened and ran a hand over his hair to settle himself. "Mr. Chairman, under the protection of the Fifth Amendment, I respectfully decline to answer that question on the grounds that it might incriminate me." He leaned back in his chair as if braced for a storm.

What the hell? Cassidy wondered. *What was this?*

McCarthy flung his hands up in disgust. "Once again we have before us a man who hides behind the very Constitution he seeks to destroy. Another Fifth Amendment traitor. However, Mr. Kasnavietski, you do not have to answer that question. I will answer the question." He put his hand out, and Roy Cohn gave him a sheaf of papers, which McCarthy held above his head and shook so the papers rattled. "I have in my hand an arrest report from the Syracuse, New York, Police Department. It states that on April 28, 1926, a man going under the name of Tom Kasner was arrested for illegally transporting liquor. That he, and six other men, were arrested while driving trucks full of illegal liquor that had been smuggled across the border from Canada. The fingerprints of said Tom Kasner match the fingerprints you submitted when you illegally applied for citizenship in this great country. The photograph is clearly you. What do you have to say now, sir?"

"I was a kid. I . . ." It was barely a murmur.

"What? We did not hear you. Speak up."

"Nothing. I have nothing to say."

Cassidy had never heard his father sound defeated before.

"Well, I have something to say. We do not need your kind in this country. Fortunately we have laws that allow us to get rid of people like you. The Immigration Department will take you into custody today, and procedures for deportation will begin immediately. We will, Mr. Kasnavietski, ship you back to Russia, a country you seem to like more than ours."

The applause reddened McCarthy's face with pride.

Tom Cassidy struggled to his feet. "Why are you doing this to me?" The applause died so people could hear. "Why? I love this country. Why are you doing this?"

McCarthy did not reply. He picked up his briefcase and left the room, but Roy Cohn looked up at Cassidy at the back of the room and pointed a finger like a gun, and he understood that everything that had happened here was on him, that it had all started with his confrontation with Cohn on New Year's Eve outside the Stork Club. Cohn nodded as if to confirm the thought, then turned and followed McCarthy out of the room.

Two immigration officers converged on Tom Cassidy. Each took an arm and moved him toward a side door. Cassidy pushed through the crowd to intercept them. The two officers leaned on Tom Cassidy when he tried to stop to speak to his son. "Keep moving," one of them said.

Cassidy showed them his badge. "He's my father."

The bigger of the two men blocked Cassidy's path. "I'm sorry, but my orders are no one speaks to him." The other officer urged Tom Cassidy toward the door.

"I'm a cop. I need a minute with him."

"Sorry. No can do." The man was braced in case Cassidy tried to go through him.

Just before the door, Tom Cassidy shouted over his shoulder, "Call Frank. Get hold of Frank." Then he was gone.

• • •

The family met at Tom Cassidy's apartment in the St. Moritz on Central Park South. It was a big apartment on the thirty-fourth floor, and the windows of its living room, master bedroom, and study gave out on a view of Central Park. At night the park was a dark rectangle threaded with lights and bounded by the walls of lighted buildings along Fifth Avenue and Central Park West.

The living room was furnished with comfortable chairs and sofas. Some were pieces Cassidy remembered from his childhood and the house on 66th Street, some Megan had bought. There were large, colorful abstract paintings on the walls. A corner bookshelf prominently displayed leather-bound scripts from the plays that had made the apartment possible. Even the flops were there, because, as Tom would explain, even though there may have been some mistakes in casting them, or in their direction, or maybe the critics didn't know what the hell they were talking about, they were all good plays. They had to be good plays because Tom Cassidy had agreed to produce them.

Megan stood looking out the window. One leg was slightly bent and the instep of that bare foot rested above the calf of the other leg, the unconscious stance of a dancer. When she turned to say hello to Michael, he could see that she had been crying. "Make yourself a drink, Michael."

Leah sat in an armchair near the fireplace. She looked angry. Her husband, Mark, sat on the arm of the chair with a hand on her shoulder as if to keep her from launching.

"Mike, how are you?" He stood and offered a hand. He was a former college hockey player, still solid and compact, with an air of easy competence and calm, the perfect complement to Leah. He had a square head, thinning blond hair, and an open face and manner that invited confidence. He had made a great deal of money very quickly after college with the same apparent effortlessness with which he'd scored on the ice. People were already talking about his political future.

Cassidy leaned down to kiss Leah and she offered him a tight smile.

Brian came away from where he leaned against the mantel to hug Cassidy. "I caught the first train from D.C. after you called. What the hell?" He looked stunned.

"Yeah. I don't know. We'll figure it out." What would they figure out? How they were going to go up against the McCarthy subcommittee?

How could their father have a bootlegger past they had never heard of? That's what we do. We talk of what we like to remember, and we push away the rest as if it never happened. Why would his father be different?

"A drink."

As they crossed to the bar built into the wall and concealed behind cabinet doors, Cassidy saw Harry Gould talking quietly on a phone in Tom Cassidy's den, a room of tall bookcases and leather chairs. Framed posters from Cassidy's plays hung on the walls. Gould nodded and held up a finger indicating he'd only be a minute.

"Bourbon?" Brian asked.

"I'm going to make a martini. Do you want one?"

"Sure."

Harry Gould came out of the den and shook hands with Cassidy. "Michael, I'm sorry. I've never been so badly used in all my years as a lawyer. The arrogance of those people. We'll get him out. It's still the rule of law in this country."

Gould took a stance at the fireplace. His head barely reached the height of the mantel where Brian had easily rested his arm. He took off his glasses and polished them with a handkerchief and put them back on, an old courtroom trick that quieted the action and made everyone turn to him.

"As you all know, Tom was arrested this afternoon by Immigration Department officers on the charge that he lied on his application for citizenship thirty years ago. This is a minor technicality, and it is unusual for them to use it to pursue deportation for someone who has been as productive and well known a citizen as Tom has been. I'm sure that when we have our day in court, the outcome will be in our favor."

"Harry," Brian said, "I spoke with some people at the network, and they say there are cases where the proceedings don't come to court, that the decision is made on camera."

"Yes, it does happen, but it is very unusual. Almost never."

"But it could happen. He could be deported without trial."

"It is highly unlikely. We're going to get a good lawyer for him. The best. Someone who specializes in immigration cases."

"Who?" Brian asked.

"I'm still working on that."

Cassidy could hear the evasion. "Harry, how many immigration lawyers have you called?"

Gould looked uncomfortable. "Six."

"They turned you down."

"Yes."

"Why?"

"They're all carrying heavy caseloads, and they don't feel they can devote the time and effort necessary." He said it like a recitation.

"They've been warned off, haven't they?"

"It's possible. I'd prefer not to think that. There's a general reluctance to take on these cases at the moment. No one wants to be tarred by the same brush. The mood of the times."

Megan had moved from the window. She stood clutching the back of a chair hard enough to whiten her knuckles. "He did something thirty years ago. Why do they care now?"

"Mike, do you have any ideas?" Mark had been watching him, and now everyone looked at him.

"Last New Year's Eve my partner and I arrested an armed robber. He stuck up a pharmacy over on Sixth, fractured the pharmacist's skull, and took off. Orso and I ran him down in front of the Stork Club. There was a guy there who took exception to what we were doing. We were blocking his car. It was inconvenient for him. He wanted us out of his way."

"Who?" Brian asked.

"Roy Cohn."

Gould scrubbed his bald head with the flat of his hand. "Did Cohn know who you were?"

"Yes."

Brian said, "What happened? He pushed and you pushed back, right? You don't have to rise to every challenge."

"I was doing my job."

"Cohn's a powerful man. Do you think he engineered this?" Gould asked.

"I know he did."

"He had Dad arrested just to get back at you?" Brian asked.

"Yes."

"Shit." Leah sprang up from under Mark's hand. "I want a drink." She crossed to the bar and banged bottles around angrily.

"Harry, how much time do we have?" Megan asked.

"I don't know. I suppose if Cohn wants he can move Tom to the top of the list."

"Tom has spoken out against Russia many times. He's given money to anticommunist causes. Doesn't that count for something?"

"If it comes down to a matter of law, the law says that if you lie on your application for citizenship, they can revoke it and deport you. And, of course, if he is deported they'll . . ." Gould stopped abruptly.

Megan finished his thought. "If he's deported, the Russians will know that he's worked against them. They'll kill him. That's what they do with their enemies."

For a time no one spoke.

"We'll find a lawyer," Brian soothed. "There has to be someone with the courage to take this on. Mark, you know people in politics, people who don't agree with what Cohn and McCarthy are doing. I'll talk to people in the news business. If we get this out in front of people, shine some light on it, it may slow them down. Harry, you've got to find us that lawyer. We'll get an injunction. We'll—"

"Talk. It's just talk." Leah banged her glass on the table and it shattered. "Michael, you started this with Cohn. You got Dad into it. Do something."

13

Cassidy stood back as a woman in a white mink coat came out of the Co-
pacabana. He and the doorman watched in admiration as she stilted up
60th Street on impossibly high heels. He went in and nodded to the bartender and stopped near the maître d's desk at the entrance to the dining
room. It was after eight and the big room was three-quarters filled with
men in tuxedos and women in evening dresses and jewelry listening to
Harry Belafonte in his early set in front of a small orchestra. The cigarette girl was making a delivery to a table near the door. She saw Cassidy
and winked and then bent over just enough so the man buying cigarettes
could appreciate the view down her top. She thanked him for the tip and
then swayed toward Cassidy. She was dressed as an island beauty, a flow-
ered sarong around her hips, and fake fruit held in her hair by a bright
bandana. Her lips were glossy and as red as blood. "Hi, Michael. Long
time, no see."

"How are you, Francie?"

"I'm as good as they get. And I'm off at midnight."

Jules Podell, the manager, appeared at Cassidy's elbow. Podell was a
sleepy-eyed thug in an expensive tuxedo. "Francie, there's a guy on table
six trying to get your attention."

"I'm going, I'm going. Can't a girl stop to say hello to a friend?"

She winked and at Cassidy and went away on high heels following her
tray of smokes.

"What do you think of the coon?" Podell pointed at Belafonte on the
bandstand.

"I like him."

"Yeah. I wasn't sure. First one we let play here, you know. He brings in a good crowd. And he's not one of them real dark ones, so I said what the hell."

"You're a real humanitarian, Julie."

"Yeah? You think so?" Missing the irony. "How about that?"

Harry Belafonte, tan and impossibly handsome, finished singing about a banana boat in a voice like syrup and went off to strong applause. The band swung a little light music out, and a handful of couples got up to dance.

"You been sick, Michael? You don't look so hot." Podell's eyes never stopped moving as he monitored the club. He snapped fingers at a passing waiter. "Water on twelve. And fifteen's waiting on the check. Hop it."

"Is Frank here?"

"At his table."

Until the televised investigations by the Kefauver Committee on organized crime in 1950, Frank Costello had lived in the shadows. He was known only to people who needed to know him, who required his services, or who had something he wanted. Television changed that. He had been subpoenaed to appear before the committee and had agreed to testify on the condition that his face would not be shown on camera, but that dam did not hold, and soon he was known to millions of Americans. The newspapers called him "the Prime Minister of the Underworld," a grandiose title that was almost accurate.

Cassidy knew his story. Costello's mother had fled the poverty of Calabria when Frank was five and he grew up in New York where opportunity abounded, where like-minded men could come together to prosper. Jail for eleven months in 1915 was a small price to pay for his introduction to Lucky Luciano and his crew, men of vision who provided New Yorkers with services they wanted but could not legally obtain. Luciano ran the muscle to keep competitors in line. Costello showed a talent for greasing the intersection between their businesses and the legitimate world. If a politician needed money in his war chest, if a businessman was having trouble with a union that did not appreciate the problems of his thin profit margin, if a judge was embarrassed by a woman who mistook his intentions, if a developer found it difficult to get the right permits from City Hall, Frank Costello could mediate. He developed a reputation as a discreet, forceful, efficient man you could trust to get things done in an increasingly difficult world.

Two men got up from the table next to Costello's and blocked Cassidy as he approached. They could have been brothers. Both were dark and agate eyed with lumpy faces that had been hit hard a few times. Their dark business suits could not hide what they were, gun muscle to watch Costello's back. They recognized Cassidy. "Give him a minute, Detective Cassidy, okay?" the bigger one said. Lou and Franco. Franco and Lou. Interchangeable parts. There'd been a couple of guys like them near Costello for as long as Cassidy could remember.

Cassidy recognized the man sitting next to Costello, the shock of white hair, the square jaw and strong nose, a face made for the news cameras. He was leaning in, talking fast, selling. He tapped Costello's wrist for emphasis and Costello pulled his arm back. He did not like to be touched. The man slipped a thick envelope from his inside pocket and slid it out on the table. Costello palmed it and put it in his pocket without counting the contents. The big man stood up, shook hands, and turned to go.

"Good evening, Senator. How're you doing?" Cassidy said.

"Great, great." Mistaking Cassidy for a constituent, he shook his hand and massaged his shoulder. "Great to see you again." As he headed for the door, he stopped at several tables to dispense charm to the voters.

Costello got up and hugged Cassidy, and Cassidy smelled the familiar lime cologne and talcum powder from Costello's daily shave at the Biltmore, a smell from his childhood when Costello was regularly in the Cassidy home. Costello had a long, rounded face with a prominent nose and thinning dark hair brushed back from his forehead. His eyes were black, small, cold, hard. They were also, Cassidy knew, capable of sentimental weeping over songs of childhood, the sad end of romantic movies, a fallen sparrow. He wore a well-tailored dark suit in a muted windowpane pattern, a white shirt with a starched collar, and a dark red tie with blue diamonds. He looked like a successful Italian importer or manufacturer, a middle-class businessman doing well enough to afford some of the simpler luxuries: an apartment on Central Park West, vacations to Florida, a mistress in a small apartment on West 90th, the occasional visit to Tiffany to pick up a little something for the wife.

"It's good to see you, Michael. It's been too long. You should come by the apartment, see Loretta. She misses you." He lit a cigarette and blew smoke at the ceiling.

"How are you, Uncle Frank?"

"I'm okay. But no more of that Uncle Frank stuff. It was fine when you were kids. Now it makes me feel old."

After Cassidy joined the cops, he asked his father how he came to be friends with one of New York's biggest hoods, and Tom waved the question away. "We've been friends since a long time. Since when I first got here. He was the guy who showed me the ropes. I was a raggedy-ass kid on the streets. No English, not a clue. He took me up. He's been a good friend." No further explanation, but there was clearly more or his father would not have thought of Costello first when he got in a jam.

"You look like hell. You eat? You getting any sleep? Here, eat something." He pushed a platter of egg rolls and spareribs toward Cassidy. "Let me get you some wonton soup. Best Chinese in the city. Better than anything you get down in Chinktown. It takes an Italian in the kitchen to make good food."

"No, thanks. I'm not hungry."

"You should take better care of yourself. You don't have your health, you don't have nothing." A man who had taken health from a lot of people. "You want a drink?" Costello asked.

"Why not?"

Costello raised his hand, and a waiter jumped to take their order. When he went away, Costello slapped the newspaper he had been reading. "McCarthy's going too far. Commies are one thing, but you don't want to hit the army, not with Eisenhower in the White House." He tossed the paper down, and McCarthy looked up from the front page with his bad boy's grin. "He's going to get it in the neck, you wait and see. I just wish he could take that Kefauver bastard down with him." Costello was still smarting from his raking over the coals at the Kefauver hearings. "Fucking hypocrites. Every one of them's got his hand out. I'll tell you something, Michael. It doesn't take much to buy a politician. Just like the Automat. You keep pushing the nickels in till what you want comes out." He laughed.

The waiter put a Jack Daniel's on the rocks in front of Cassidy and a rye and soda in front of Costello and retreated.

Cassidy told Costello about his father's arrest.

"Ah, hell. I told him."

"Told him what?"

"I told him don't go on that run. That was Owney Madden's run, and he was a cheap mick. Back then we'd pick up the booze coming over from Canada in these little towns on the lake, Lake Erie, put it in trucks and run it down to the city. You ever been up there? Beautiful country. Farms and forests. A lot of streams, wilderness, I don't know what. Pretty much all the roads run down around Syracuse, so we had a deal with the

Syracuse cops. Never had a problem. Owney thinks maybe he can run a few loads through without paying. But everybody up there, the guys who unload the boats, the guys who load the trucks, the cops, they're all related, so the cops know the booze is coming, and they hit 'em. Your father's riding lead truck, and they got him. I sent a guy up there who knew his way around and got him out, but I guess it stayed on the record."

"I never knew this. I never knew he worked that side." What else didn't he know? His father rarely talked about his past. All he cared about was today and the future.

"Why would he tell you? That's his business. Anyway, that's where he got the money to get into the theater business, from the booze business. He got out early. He knew what he wanted, and when he had the dough to do it, he quit. A means to an end, like they say."

"Terrific."

"What? I've got to tell you how the world works? It was something he did for a while, and then he stopped. Look at him now, a successful guy, rich, completely legit." His voice full of admiration.

"Can you help with this thing?"

"It's immigration, so that's a little different, but I've got a guy. He'll talk to some people, find out who's the judge. If it's a judge we know, we'll be okay, we'll get him out on bail. We'll see. It depends on how hard they're going after him. It could be we might need some leverage. First we get him out. One thing at a time."

Cassidy felt a surge of relief. "Thanks, Frank."

"Hey, come on." Costello brushed the gratitude away. "You want another drink?"

"No, thanks. I've got to go."

"Before you do, let's talk about something else." Costello's manner changed. He was harder, cooler. "You were in one of our places over on Third Avenue the other day asking about a guy named Ingram, Alex Ingram."

"That's right." It did not surprise him that the information got back to Costello.

"Someone popped him, is what I hear."

"What's your interest?"

Costello ignored the question. "You were first on the scene."

"There was a uniform there before me."

"Yeah, yeah, Scalabrine. He doesn't know nothing. What do you know?"

"Not much. He was tortured. He was dead." Cassidy was wary. Where was this going?

"Yeah, that's what I heard. You think they got what they were after?"

"I don't know. What's it to you?"

Costello considered his answer. "I met him."

"You met him? Why?"

"He had something he wanted to sell. He hung around some of the places we own, and he seemed to know what's what. He put out the word. I had a guy go talk to him, check him out. He wouldn't show the guy much, but it looked like it might be legit, so I set up a meeting."

"What was he selling?" He watched Costello calculate how much he should tell.

"Photographs."

"Blackmail?"

"Leverage."

That word again. "Leverage to do what? Who was the leverage going to move?"

"You don't have to know that."

"Photographs. Did he take them?"

"Did he take them? I don't know. I just know he had them."

"How many?"

"He said five. He only showed one."

"What's in the photographs?"

"Uh-uh. If you find them, you'll know right away you've got the right ones. If you don't find them, it's best you don't know. I want you on this. Find them. My guys are good at some things, but you've got to point them at it. I need someone who thinks. You're going to do this thing for me, Michael, and I'm going to do this thing for you. Right?" No mention of old friendships. Just the deal. Costello watched him, waiting for his response.

"Why didn't you buy them right then?"

"I would've, but he was being cagey. He had other buyers. He was looking for the best deal. Who could blame him? You take what the market gives you."

"Who were the other buyers?"

"I don't know."

"How many were there?"

"I don't know that either. I got the feeling there were a couple more out there, but he didn't say. So are we going to do this?"

"Okay." As neutral as he could make it.

Costello nodded, apparently satisfied.

Cassidy got up and left as Harry Belafonte came back on and sang about "man smart, woman smarter," a thought that made men in the audience laugh and women smile secretly.

Cassidy stopped outside the club to light a cigarette. A big Packard limousine pulled to the curb. The chauffeur jumped out and hurried to open the passenger door. The first man out was Joe McCarthy. He stumbled as he exited, and the chauffeur was quick to hand him upright. Roy Cohn followed and stood deferentially near the open door. A tall man got out, and Cassidy recognized him from newspaper pictures as Clyde Tolson, number-two man at the Bureau. Cohn reached back in to offer a hand to J. Edgar Hoover, but Hoover ignored it. Hoover was short and broad with the face of a bulldog. He wore a pinstriped suit designed to minimize his bulk, and Cassidy could see that it was custom tailored. McCarthy led them toward the club entrance, turning to talk to Hoover as they went. Tolson walked at Hoover's shoulder. Cohn, looking for an opening, darted around the group like a terrier and settled for clapping Tolson on the back as the doorman opened the big door to the club. People on the sidewalk recognized Hoover and applauded. Hoover acknowledged the applause with a modest wave and led his party into the club.

Cassidy smiled when he heard one of the men on the sidewalk say, "Greatest living American. They should make him president. I'd vote for him in a minute. Only honest man in Washington." Cops knew different. Cops knew the FBI Office of Public Affairs worked overtime to puff and polish the reputation of the director and the associate director. According to planted news reports, Hoover and Tolson were always on duty. They never took a vacation, never rested in their efforts to keep America from harm. They were in California together in the spring to inspect the San Diego office, and it was only coincidence that the racing season opened at the Del Mar track during those weeks. They inspected the Miami office when, by chance, Hialeah opened, and it was coincidence again that they were often in New York on FBI business when there was a big-time fight at the Polo Grounds, a home series at Yankee Stadium, or the running of the Belmont Stakes.

They stayed at the best hotels, and management learned not to present a bill. They did not pick up restaurant checks. They did not pay for tickets. Puffed up with their own self-regard, they sailed along, sure that the myths they had created were the reality.

• • •

Cassidy knocked on Dylan's door, but there was no answer. Disappointed, he went upstairs and made a sandwich and got a beer from the icebox and ate at the table in front of the window looking out at the lights of the night-time river traffic moving upstream with the tide, and the lighted buildings across the New Jersey shore. He washed his dishes and left them in the drying rack by the sink. He poured bourbon over ice and put an old Brunswick label seventy-eight recording of Red Nichols and His Five Pennies on the big RCA combination record player–radio and reminded himself to look into the new "hi-fi" equipment Tommy, the clerk at Liberty Music, had been raving about. Tommy swore that stereo was the coming thing.

He settled into the chair at the window with his feet on the sill and drank the whiskey and listened to the music. Jimmy Dorsey on alto sax and clarinet. Small-band Dixieland, improvisation, and tight group playing. Very progressive thirty years ago but considered old hat now by people who had to be on the cutting edge. Cassidy still loved it.

He flipped the record when he got up to make himself another drink. The bourbon dulled him and let him drift. Alexander Ingram, a Broadway gypsy tortured to death in a crappy apartment furnished with stuff he shouldn't have been able to afford. Why did the FBI care about the case? Who was the guy who cut Cassidy? And now Costello. Leverage, Costello said. Everyone was after something Ingram had. Photographs. Photographs of who or what? Who did the leverage move? Was it enough to get his father out of immigration jail? What was the cost and who would pay it?

Cassidy finished the drink and went to bed. He lay in the dark and listened for footsteps on the stairs but fell asleep before he heard them.

He did not dream.

When he woke in the morning, Dylan was asleep next to him.

• • •

"I have to go."

Cassidy turned from the window. Dylan was at the counter finishing a cup of coffee. She was dressed in jeans and a work shirt, and a canvas bag of tools was on a stool next to her.

"What time is it?"

"A little after eight. I have to go over to Brooklyn and buy some supplies."

"I've got to go too." He finished the coffee in his mug and carried it to the kitchen.

"What's wrong?"

"What?"

"You haven't said three words since you got up. You've been staring out the window for fifteen minutes. Something's wrong. I've got time if you want to talk about it."

"Nothing. It's okay."

"Come on, Michael. Don't shut me out."

"I'm sorry. Sure. You're right." He told her about his father's arrest, about Cohn and New Year's Eve, about Frank Costello.

"That's why Cohn was such a shit at Ribera's that night."

"Yes. He must have already known about my father's arrest up in Saratoga. They'd already done the research. He was just waiting to spring it on me."

"Just because you were rude to him."

"What's the point of having power if you can't use it to kick someone in the balls?"

"What are the photographs? What do they show?"

"I don't know. Somebody doing something he shouldn't to somebody. Costello saw one, but he wouldn't tell me what was in it."

"And Costello said Ingram had them, but you didn't find any, did you, when you searched his apartment?"

"No."

She stared out the window for a while with a troubled look on her face.

"What's bothering you?"

For a moment she looked startled, as if he had caught her at something. "Nothing." Her face cleared, and she smiled. "I was just thinking what a strange job you have. What are you going to do about your father?"

"I'm going to get him out."

"How?"

"I don't know. Maybe if I find the photographs I'll have some leverage. He's in there because of me. He's my father. I have to do something."

She kissed him and held his face so she could look at him. "You're a good man."

14

"What can you tell me about Roy Cohn?" Cassidy asked.

"Hi, Rhonda. How are you? Gee, you look great. Did you do something to your hair? It looks wonderful."

They were leaning on a wall looking down into the Rockefeller Center skating rink where a few diehards circled on ice turning mushy in the springtime sun.

"You do. You look great. Your hair looks wonderful, but I don't think it's that. Something else? Have you lost weight?"

"Nice try, but too late."

"I'm not *trying*. I'm telling the truth."

"Nice try again."

He offered her a cigarette to cover the moment, but she waved the pack away. He lit one for himself, shielding the Zippo from the wind that gusted from the river to the west. Rhonda tracked an elderly couple dancing on the ice to the music from the tinny loudspeakers. The dance ended with a twirl, and then he kissed her on the cheek.

"What's wrong with me?" Rhonda watched the couple glide to the boards to rest.

"Nothing," he said, but she was not listening to him, but to herself.

"I just want to be with someone. Is that wrong? Just to be with someone who likes you, someone you like?"

"No."

"Why's it so damn hard? What do I do? Why do they always run?" Her eyes were full of tears. He put his arm around her, and she turned into him and rested her forehead on his chest. He patted her back helplessly and looked out over her head to the skaters and smoked his cigarette until she pushed back. She turned her head away from him until she had gathered herself.

"Okay. Roy Cohn." In a businesslike voice. "What do you want to know?"

"What've you got?"

"He's smart as hell. He graduated from Columbia Law School at twenty. He had to wait till he was twenty-one before he was allowed to take the Bar. His old man is Judge Albert Cohn. The word is the old man pulled strings to get him a job with the U.S. attorney, Irv Saypol. They say Cohn's good in court. He prosecuted the American Communist Party leadership under the Smith Act and sent them away. He was on the team that prosecuted the Rosenbergs and sent them to the electric chair at Sing Sing. If you want, I can get you a clip file on him from the paper."

"Just tell me what you know."

"He's ambitious as hell and well connected. He's very conservative politically. He has a lot of reporters in his address book. Walter Winchell thinks he sits on the right hand of God. Anything Cohn leaks to him goes right in the column without checking."

"What's not in the research book?"

"What's this all about, Mike?"

"He's the one who sicced McCarthy's committee on my father. I want to know who I'm up against."

She heard the half-truth, the minor evasion, examined him for a moment, and then decided to let it go. "They say Hoover recommended Cohn to McCarthy. I'd like to know that for sure, but I can't get a confirmation."

"What else?"

"He sucks up to the guys above him and steps on the ones below. He's a vengeful shit. You don't want to cross him."

"Too late for that. What else?"

Rhonda hesitated.

"What?"

"It's rumor." She had a good reporter's distaste for the unconfirmed story.

"Tell me anyway."

"He and his pal David Schine took a junket through Europe last year. Did you read anything about that?"

"An inspection tour of the embassy libraries or something."

"U.S. Information Agency libraries. They were going to make sure Karl Marx and Lenin weren't on the shelves. They had thirty thousand books removed, almost as efficient as the Nazis in that department. Dashiell Hammett, W.E.B. Du Bois, who probably was a Commie, Steinbeck, Thoreau, Melville."

"The white whale was a Red?"

"First-class hotels, the best food and wine, drunk every night, and all on the government checkbook."

"So?"

"Adjoining rooms in the hotels. Easy access back and forth."

"Come on. What are you saying?"

"I'm not saying anything. I'm just telling you."

"Schine and Cohn?"

"Schine, I don't know. People say no, but Cohn? Yes, maybe Cohn."

"Really?"

"The word is there are some places down in Washington where he goes. You know those places, bars without too many women. Hell, you worked Vice."

"Do you think Hoover knows? Do you think he knew when he sent him to McCarthy?"

"Hoover knows everything. A lot of people in Washington hate the man. A lot of people would like to see him go, but no one makes a move. Too many people have too much to hide, and he's got it on the record. Even if he doesn't have the files, it's enough that everyone thinks he does. The power lies in the fear."

"Yes."

"I've got to go."

"Thanks, Rhonda."

"Sure." She turned away, took a step and then turned. "If you ever tell anyone I went all girly on you, Michael Cassidy, I will have your guts for garters."

15

"Cassidy, Orso, my office, please." Tanner left the door open and went back to his desk.

Orso raised his eyebrows. Cassidy shrugged. They carried their coffee mugs with them and went in.

"Don't bother to sit. This'll be short. You're off the Ingram case."

"Why?" Cassidy asked.

" 'Cause I got a call from a guy, who got a call from a guy, who got a call from a guy who said you're off."

"Who's taking the case?"

"Bonner and Newly. That, too, is the word from on high."

"The Pig and the Nig?" Orso protested. "They can't carry our water."

"Doesn't it bother you that the Feds are telling us what to do?" Cassidy asked.

"A lot of things bother me. Traffic. My wife's cooking. My daughter's boyfriend, what the fucking mechanic's charging to fix the Chevy, the crap my kid listens to, calls it music, but what the hell, I've got to live with it, so I live with it. Give everything you've got so far to Bonner and Newly. Now get out of here. Go fight crime."

• • •

Alfie Bonner and Clive Newly, the Pig and the Nig, as they were known, though never to their faces. Try that one in front of Bonner, and you would lose teeth. He did not mind what you called him, but he tolerated no disrespect for his partner, and Cassidy liked him for that. Bonner was an old-fashioned street cop who had been working the Stem for more than twenty years. He knew every punk, grifter, con man, pickpocket, stickup artist who preyed on the people drawn to the bright lights of Broadway and Times Square. He believed in back alley blackjack justice, and more than one punk left the city nursing broken bones. Wops, chinks, hunkies, dagos, niggers, spics—his disdain was democratic, and nobody could figure out how Newly escaped it.

Their desks were pushed together so they faced each other near the stairs, because Bonner liked to be first out the door when a call came in. From ten feet away Cassidy could smell his perfume of whiskey and cheap cigars.

"The wop and Park Avenue."

"Good to see you too, Bonner."

Bonner was built like a bulldozer, five nine, two hundred and ten pounds, square, low to the ground, indestructible. His head was a block with mismatched eyes, one blue, one hazel, a small nose, a thick-lipped mouth, and fine white hair buzzed short. He had the look of someone who had been slapped together from spare parts. He had put in his twenty more than five years ago, but everyone knew Alfie Bonner would be a cop till something or someone killed him.

Clive Newly was a tall, thin Negro with salt-and-pepper hair and a long face that rarely changed expression, a mask of calm. Who knew what it covered? Being a Negro was hard enough, being a Negro cop was harder. What were you to your people, an ally or an enemy? Newly, who lived with prejudice, hated nobody as far as Cassidy could tell, and he went about his business quietly and dispassionately.

"How're you doing, Detective Newly?"

"I'm fine, Detective Cassidy. How are you?" A low voice as smooth as honey. Newly had been in uniform for eleven years before his luck happened. Until then it was understood that he might make sergeant but would go no further, the quota for black officers in the higher grades being filled. On a fine July day the year after Pearl Harbor, he was walking a beat in the Bronx and stopped at a grocery store where the owner was good for a cold Coke and a pack of smokes. He found two Puerto Rican punks pistol-whipping the owner while a third cleaned out the cash register. When the gunfire stopped, two of the punks were dead and the third was down and screaming for his mother. Newly took a bullet in the arm and one in the side. It was an election year, and the councilman for the district was in a close race, and there was a suspicion that the blacks of the district would be the margin of victory. A smart young aide persuaded the councilman to declare Newly a hero and to push through his promotion to detective. The councilman won by eighty-three votes.

"What've you got for us?" Bonner asked.

"Nothing. We were just getting started."

"Nothing? What do you mean, nothing?"

"Nothing. Alexander Ingram, twenty-four years old. Tortured. Dead. We don't even know where he worked. We were just getting started. You want to know more, check with the Feebles. They yanked his body out of the morgue. We don't even have a cause of death."

Orso covered his surprise.

"How can you not know the cause of death?" Bonner asked.

"The Feds pulled the body from Bellevue. They put a clamp on Skinner. He's not giving anything."

"So get out of here, you useless fucks."

• • •

"What was that about?" Orso asked.

A diner on Ninth. The place was empty except for the counterman, who was at the other end reading the *Daily News*.

"I can't drop the case, and I need a head start over Bonner and Newly on it." He told Orso about his meeting with Frank Costello.

"He didn't tell you what the photos are?"

"No. They have to be of someone powerful enough that Costello thinks he can use him. And the Feds want to control the same guy."

"What does Costello want?"

"If he gets them, he's got a legit guy in power who can run interference for him."

"Is that a good thing?"

"He can get my father out. He's got more grease than anyone else in town."

"That's it? You find the photos, Costello gets your old man out. You like that deal?"

"It's all I've got. When it comes down to it, I don't give a shit about what Costello wants. I don't give a shit about what Hoover wants. My father's locked up because of something I did. That's on me. I have to make that right."

"Okay. Whatever you want to do, we'll do. But the Pig and the Nig aren't stupid. They know how to work a case. It won't take them long to figure out you're still working it too. And it won't take them long to catch up."

• • •

The Waldorf-Astoria took up the entire block between Park and Lexington Avenues and 49th and 50th Streets. Finished in 1931, it was considered by many to be New York's most elegant hotel. It was, at times, home to General Douglas MacArthur, President Herbert Hoover, the Duke and Duchess of Windsor, Cole Porter, and Bugsy Siegel, the hood who invented Las Vegas. President Roosevelt, it was said, used to pull his private railroad car into a little-used siding beneath the hotel. His armor-plated Pierce-Arrow would rise by elevator to 49th Street, exit through polished brass doors, make a sharp right-hand turn, enter the hotel garage, and stop in front of the elevators, sparing the crippled president the embarrassment of riding his wheelchair in public.

A concierge in a starched collar and a dark uniform with discreet gold trim sneered politely at Cassidy's badge but passed him off across the thick carpet to an assistant manager in an elegant office who sneered less politely at his badge but passed him off to a bellboy who led him without comment across the lobby, down the marble hall past the expensive shops, through an unmarked door, down one metal staircase and then another, along a corridor crammed with service trolleys, past the open doors of a steamy kitchen of shouting cooks and clanging pots to a red-painted door on which was stenciled in black letters SORINO. The bellboy knocked once and waited. A voice inside said, "Come." The bellboy put his hand on the knob and looked at Cassidy expectantly, palmed the quarter Cassidy handed him, and opened the door. Cassidy went in.

The office was small and windowless. There was an old wooden desk near the back wall. Two of the walls were lined with unpainted wood shelves that held loose-leaf binders. A big corkboard on the wall to the right of the desk was covered with charts and lists. The desk was piled with papers. The man sitting behind it wrote quickly with a fountain pen, stabbed a period, put the paper to one side, pulled another in front of him and wrote again. "Yes?" He did not look up. He was in his late thirties, Cassidy guessed, and his black hair was oiled and so neatly combed the part looked cut by a razor. He was narrow shouldered and soft looking, and he wore a blue-and-white-striped shirt with red arm garters to keep his cuffs from smearing the ink when he wrote. His jacket, a peculiar mustard color, hung on a clothes tree behind him. He stabbed another period, stacked the paper left, pulled another in front, held the pen poised, and looked up at Cassidy. "Yes?" Impatiently.

"Mr. Sorino, I want to talk to you about one of your employees."

"Yes?" He began to write again. "Which employee?"

"Alex Ingram."

Sorino kept writing. "He is not an employee at this hotel."

"But he was."

"But he isn't."

Cassidy dropped a business card in front of Sorino. Sorino stopped writing and looked up. "What did he do?"

"Someone killed him."

"Couldn't have happened to a nicer guy, the prick." Sorino capped his pen and leaned back in his chair.

"Why prick?"

"Have you ever worked in a first-class hotel, Mr."—he looked down at the card—"Cassidy?"

"No."

"The Waldorf-Astoria is a first-class hotel. Everyone thinks people come for the rooms, for the bar, for the restaurant, and while they do come for those things, they would not come at all if the service weren't excellent. A first-class hotel is made by first-class service. Few people understand that. I do. When he wanted to be, Alex Ingram was a first-class waiter. He was attractive, efficient, personable. The guests liked him. However, he had a tendency to do as he pleased when he pleased. It did not matter to him that he inconvenienced others. The last time was one time too many."

"When was that?"

"He was scheduled to work last New Year's Eve, a very important night, as you can imagine. A night where there are many private parties, where service is of paramount importance, and where, I might add, there is a good deal of money to be made in tips. He pestered me for months to put him on. I did. He did not show up. He did not call. You can't imagine the trouble that caused. When he came by the next week to pick up his pay, I told him to clear out his locker."

"Did he?"

"What?"

"Clear out his locker."

"I have no idea."

There was nothing in the locker but a crumpled room service order sheet with nothing on it and a soiled white waiter's jacket with empty pockets.

"I need to talk to someone he worked with, someone who might have known him well."

Sorino sighed, another burden added to the load he carried through his busy day. "If you must. I'll check the work roster and see who's here."

• • •

"He was a prick. What can I tell you?" Fred Bandy voted with the majority while he arranged lunch on a room service cart in the kitchen in the subbasement below the Waldorf Towers. He was a round, cheerful man with the broken veins and red nose of dedicated drinker. "Not always. When he first got the job here, he was all sweetness and cream. Help you out anytime but full of questions. How do you do this? Where do you put that? Who's who? What's what? He started out as a breakfast waiter in the hotel, but he figured out quick that the money was in serving the Towers. Pretty soon he was sucking up to the right people and got transferred over. Man, he liked going into those big apartments. All that money. Once he said to me, 'Someday, Bandy, I'm going to live here.' I laughed, but you could tell he was serious." Bandy rearranged the parsley that garnished the roast chicken.

"What do you know about him outside of work?" The smell of food reminded Cassidy that he had not eaten since breakfast.

"Nothing. He wasn't a guy who went out and had a couple of beers. He had other things to do, but don't ask me what they were. I don't know." Bandy filled the water glasses.

"When did you see him last?"

"New Year's Eve." He went to a glass-fronted refrigerator and removed a bud vase holding three dark red roses. He put it on the cart and rearranged the stems to please his eye.

"Sorino said he fired him because he didn't show up New Year's Eve."

"He showed up. He just didn't show up to work." He patted his pockets until he found a box of matches that he put at the ready by the two silver candlesticks. "I was serving the Vanderlin apartment on thirty-three. Nice people. Sugar money from Cuba. Always here New Year's. I was taking the cart down the hall, the elevator stops to let some people out, and there he is, bold as brass, standing in the guest elevator, dressed to the nines. Tuxedo, patent leather shoes, the full rig, a Chesterfield coat. Very nice. I remember thinking, where the hell did he get that?"

"Fawn colored? Brown collar?"

"That's the one. He looks right through me like I'm not even there. The doors close. Off he goes."

"Do you know where he was going?"

"Thirty-four and up, 'cause I was on thirty-three, and he was going up. I asked the other waiters who were working parties above me. No one saw him."

"Was he alone in the elevator? Was he with someone?"

Bandy checked the ice bucket to make sure it was full. "There were a couple of other guys, maybe three. Young guys. Same age. Full rig too. He was talking to one of them when he saw me, so maybe they were together."

"What did they look like? Can you give me a description?"

"Nah. I don't know. I mean, I was stunned. I was looking at Ingram like, what the hell? The others, I never really saw them. Just that they were there." He folded a white towel over his arm. "Listen, I've got to get this upstairs while it's hot."

"Thanks. If you think of anything else, call me."

"Sure." Bandy tucked Cassidy's card in his pocket. He closed the big chrome warming dome over the food and wheeled the cart into the service elevator.

Sorino, pen poised above paper, was not happy to see Cassidy back and was even less happy with his request. "A list of who occupied the apartments in the Towers on New Year's Eve? I don't think so."

"Just above the thirty-third floor."

"Detective Cassidy, I don't think you appreciate what you're asking. The Waldorf Towers are quite distinct from the hotel. Many of the apartments are rented on a yearly basis. There are people who have lived in the Towers for years. Most of them are rich. Many of them are public figures. General Douglas MacArthur is a guest. One of the reasons they come here is for the privacy. Even if I had such a list, I could not give it to you without permission from the manager."

"What information did Ingram give you when he applied for the job here?"

"He filled out the standard form."

"May I see that?"

Sorino hesitated.

"The man's dead. It's a little late to be delicate about his privacy."

"Of course."

There was nothing on the form he did not know. The home address listed was the one in New Jersey that had been on his driver's license. Cassidy folded the form and put it in his pocket, thanked Sorino, and left.

• • •

The Waldorf Towers manager was an affable man in a cutaway coat and striped trousers. His office was furnished with antiques, including a large partners' desk with an inlaid top of dark green leather that held a telephone whose ring was so muted it sounded like an apology. "I'd like to help you, Detective, but there is no way that I can give you such a list without a court order. I'm so terribly sorry." He was so sincere Cassidy almost believed him.

• • •

The precinct house was worn shabby by the rub of misery that came through its doors. The late-afternoon sun barely penetrated, and the dim white bulbs in the overhead fixtures weakly contested the gloom. Two men were handcuffed to the opposite end rails of the big wooden bench just inside the precinct doors. Both were bleeding from head wounds, and one of them kept snuffling blood back up his broken nose. The ignored each other while a uniformed cop explained their situation to the desk sergeant. Cassidy went by them and up the stairs.

Newly stopped Cassidy as he walked toward his desk. "Someone called you three times this afternoon. He didn't leave a name. He said he'd call back at five." He checked his watch. "A couple of minutes."

"Thank you."

"You're welcome."

Cassidy hung his jacket on his chair, pulled the phone where he could reach it, and put his feet up on the desk. Half the calls that came in were anonymous, and most of them started with *I don't want to get anyone in trouble, but* . . . If it wasn't about trouble, why were they calling the cops? He lit a cigarette and tossed the pack onto the desk. What was Ingram doing at the Waldorf on New Year's Eve? A guy who loved money gave up the richest night of the year to go to a party? Everybody remarked that

Ingram was money hungry, so the party was going to be more valuable in some way. How did that work?

The phone rang.

"Cassidy."

"Detective?"

"Yeah." Someone played a piano in the background, and he could hear people talking away from the phone. "Hello?"

"This is Victor Amado. I don't know if you remember me."

"I remember." The rehearsal piano at the theater. "Thank you for calling, Victor." Alfie Bonner came out of the toilet zipping his fly.

"Look, I don't know whether I should be talking to you at all. I just don't know."

"You knew Alex better than you said."

A long silence. "Yes."

"What did he have that made someone torture him?"

Another long silence. "I can't talk about that." Cassidy could hear the fear in his voice.

"Okay. What do you want to talk about?"

Bonner stopped at Cassidy's desk.

"Hold on a second. Don't go away." Cassidy put the phone against his shoulder and nodded to Bonner.

"Are you still working Ingram?" Bonner asked.

"No."

"Who's on the line?"

"My girlfriend."

Bonner grinned and made a kissing noise, did a jerk-off motion, and moved on.

"Are you still there?"

"Yes. They're calling us back. Break's over. I've got to go."

"Victor, do you have any idea why Ingram was killed?"

"I can't talk about it on the phone."

"I can be at the theater in ten minutes."

"No, don't. We're in rehearsal. I can't. Not here."

He could feel Amado slipping away. "This is a murder investigation, Victor. I'm coming over."

"No, please. There are too many people."

"After rehearsal."

"I don't know."

"I'll meet you wherever you want. We'll talk. You tell me whatever you want. And I can keep you out of it." The reassuring lie.

"I don't know. Jesus. I live in the Village on Christopher Street."

"Great. Perfect. I'm on Bank." He held his breath.

Silence. "Do you know the White Horse? I usually stop there for a drink on the way home."

"The White Horse. What time?"

"Nine?"

"I'll see you there." He hung up and let out a breath. Landed him. Maybe.

• • •

Cassidy bought eggs, coffee, and bread for breakfast at the Italian grocery store on 12th and walked west toward his apartment as darkness fell and the sky turned dark blue over the river. The breeze off the water smelled of salt, and it stirred scraps of paper in the gutters. Cassidy thought about Dylan and hoped she was home. There was enough time before he met Amado to have dinner somewhere in the Village, or maybe they'd go to Chinatown to the place off Canal on Mercer he liked. Did she like Chinese food? There was so much about her he did not know. A man stood outside the phone booth on the corner of Washington. As he went by, the man stepped into the booth and made a call.

There were three bills and a postcard from Peter Burchard, an army friend, in his mailbox. He stuffed the bills in his pocket and read the postcard as he went upstairs. Burchard was coming to New York on business in a month and hoped they could get together. The light on the card dimmed as he left the third floor, and he looked up to see that the bulb was out on the landing in front of Dylan's apartment. Glass crunched underfoot. The light was out in the hall above too. Cassidy stopped and listened. A board creaked. It was an old building and it groaned and spoke as the weather changed. Not unusual. Still. He smelled cigarette smoke and something else. What was that? He shifted the groceries to his left hand and touched the gun under his arm. A noise turned him, and then the men came down from above in a rush. He got the gun out, but he lost it when they hit him, and it clattered down the stairwell. He slashed back an elbow and felt it connect, heard a grunt. Someone grabbed him from behind, and he slammed his head back into the man's face and felt the hold loosen. He jabbed fingers at a face and felt something wet and heard a shriek, but there were too many of them, and he went down under their weight. He could feel hot breath on his face, and the smell of whiskey. He tried to get his back against the wall, but someone grabbed his legs and pulled him back to the center of the landing and then lay on his legs and pinned them. Men grabbed his arms and all he could do was buck and heave, but he could not shake them off. They beat him efficiently with fists and feet, grunting with the effort. Some part of him warned that if they did not stop soon, they would beat him to death, but there was nothing he could do, and he started to slip away.

"Hey! What the hell's going on out here?" Dylan McCue stood in her open door with a three-foot-long piece of steel rebar in her hand.

Someone leaned close and said, "Franklin says hello." A parting kick to his back. And then they were gone.

The last thing he remembered was wondering why Dylan dripped water on him when she crouched down to say, "You're going to be all right. Hold on. Don't move. Just hold on. I'll call an ambulance."

16

Fucking Amado pissed him off. Fraker picked him up outside the theater after rehearsal and trailed him to a greasy spoon on Eighth Avenue and watched him eat fried crap washed down with Coca-Cola. The man clearly had no respect for food and didn't give a damn what he put in his body. He would eat anything. What the hell was wrong with him? He was a dancer. That was like being an athlete. You had to take care of yourself. He followed him to the Village, thinking he would go home and Fraker could get on with it, but no, Amado went into the White Horse on Hudson and ordered some drink with fruit in it and took a table near the door. Fraker took a stand at the end of the bar and nursed a beer for half an hour.

After nine o'clock, Amado started checking his watch every couple of minutes. Clearly he was meeting someone who was late. Fraker didn't like that. He wanted to get this done, and another guy in the mix would cancel it for the night. The bartender asked him for the third time if he wanted another, so he ordered a refill that he didn't want, and that pissed him off too. He left it half finished and went out and watched Amado from the street. Amado gave up at ten, and Fraker tailed him home and then broke into a panel truck parked among other panel trucks in a vacant lot off Christopher Street and watched Amado's building until everyone settled in for the night. An occasional taxi went by, but it was late and there was little traffic. After midnight the waiters and cooks left the restaurant on the corner and walked east toward the subway station at West 4th carrying brown bags of leftover food and talking softly in Spanish.

Fraker waited for the street to quiet. It did not bother him to wait. He liked the solitude and the quiet rehearsal of the action to come. He knew

Amado was in an apartment on the sixth floor, and he knew the questions he had to ask, and that was all he needed to know. For Fraker it was never "why" but only "how" the job was done. He had no curiosity. The work paid well and was often interesting, and there were side benefits that suited him.

The lights in the building went off one by one except for one window on the third floor.

A man walked his dog past the truck and never saw Fraker waiting in the dark. The dog stopped to examine a tire, found it acceptable, and lifted his leg. The man yawned and tugged the dog away from the interesting smells. They walked back up the block and turned the corner. Fraker waited a few minutes and then got out and crossed the street. The light in the third-floor apartment stayed on, but there had been no movement past the window for over two hours, and he decided it was a lamp left on all night by someone timid about the dark.

The lock on the outer door was broken, and he slipped the lobby door latch with his knife blade and went up the worn stairs, walking close to the wall so they would not creak. The stairwell was dim from low-watt bulbs that saved the landlord money and it smelled of old frying oil from the coffee shop next door. He paused on the third floor and listened, but there was no sound behind the door to the lighted apartment, so he went on. The bulb on the landing of the top floor had burned out and he used his penlight to examine the two locks on the door. They were no better than the lock on the front door. He held the penlight in his teeth and worked his picks until the tumblers clicked. He eased the doorknob until the tongue left the receiver and then pushed gently. The door gave inward for a couple of inches and then stopped with a muted metal clank. A security bar, one end socketed in the door, the other in a metal plate on the floor. Step back. Reassess.

The fire door to the roof opened with a squeal. He stopped and waited. No doors opened below. No one yelled. He stepped out and waited until his eyes adjusted and he could see the vent pipes that stuck up through the tar, dark on dark, shin breakers. Three shirts and four pairs of pants danced on a clothesline in the breeze off the river. The skyscrapers sparkled in the night city, but to Fraker light was an enemy. He moved carefully from the doorway past the clothes on the line to the broad coping and the top of the fire escape that dropped along the rear of the building to the alley. A slow and deliberate check. No lights in the building opposite. No sleepless wanderers on the roofs nearby. He grabbed the rusted railings and swung to the iron steps and went down.

Trust a man with two locks and a security bar to leave his bedroom window open for air. Fraker crouched to look in over the sill. He could make out the bulk of the bed against the far wall of the dark room. The man in the bed breathed with a long steady rhythm. In . . . out . . . in . . . out.

A breath ended in a snort and rattle. For a moment there was silence, and then the rhythm began again. Fraker slipped through the open window, straightened, and took a step to the side so he wouldn't be silhouetted if Amado woke. He waited there for a moment to assess.

The lingering scent of cologne.

The tick of the clock on the bedside table, its numbers and hands glowing yellow-green.

The warmth of the room, and the man's steady breathing, which matched Fraker's own.

Complicity.

What was going to happen here offered an intimacy that made Fraker's cock stir. He took a step toward the bed. A floorboard creaked under him and the man in the bed shifted and groaned, turned over on his back, and flung an arm across his chest. Fraker waited until he settled again and then crossed to the bed. He bent close and the wash of city light showed him Amado in repose, as peaceful as a child. Fraker took the knife from his pocket and let the blade out. He pinched the sleeping man's nose closed between thumb and forefinger and covered his mouth with his palm. For a moment nothing happened. Then Amado bucked against his hand, trying to draw breath. Fraker touched the point of his knife to Amado's throat and looked down into his terrified eyes. "Don't worry. Everything's going to be all right," he lied.

17

Cassidy awoke to pulsing pain and a drugged stupor.

"You're lucky," the young doctor said. He had a shock of straw-colored hair, big hands that were gentle as they probed, and he loped around the bed with a forward lean as if walking into a strong wind. "A few cracked ribs. Some bruises that are going to be wonderfully colorful. A concussion. Heavy contusions around the kidney area. We're going to keep you with us a few days, make sure you're not passing blood."

There was nothing Cassidy could do. It was out of his hands. He let himself drift away on the painkillers.

When he awoke again, Dylan was sitting by the bed reading. She looked up when he moved. "Hey, look who's back." She marked her place. "How do you feel?"

"Great. Never better."

"Atta boy."

"Thank you."

"For what?"

"I was almost finished when you came out."

"What are friends for?" She had just gotten out of the shower when she heard the fight in the hall. That explained the dripping he remembered as he went under. "I thought it was kids fighting on the landing or something. Who were they?"

"I don't know."

"All right, don't tell me." But he could tell that she did not like the dismissal.

"They were cops." He wanted her to know. He told her about Franklin.

"Good for you." She leaned down and brushed a kiss across his lips. "You lead an interesting life, Cassidy. One week the FBI tears your place apart. The next a bunch of your fellow cops beat you up in your own building. Are you sure you're on the side of the law?"

"Am I sure the law's on my side?"

"I'm glad I was there."

"I am too."

"Are they going to come back?" She was anxious, and she put a hand on his arm. "I mean, what if they do?"

"They won't be back. They gave me their message."

"And what are you going to do about them? I mean once you're better."

"Nothing. It ends now." Maybe that was the truth. Maybe it was just the way it should be, but he wasn't going to think about that now.

"It didn't have anything to do with what the FBI was looking for?"

"No."

"You're sure?"

"I'm sure."

"How are you doing on that one? Did you figure out where the photographs might be?"

"No."

"Nothing?"

"Nothing. Dead ends." He did not want to talk about it.

He knew he was shutting her out, and that she did not like it, but after a moment her face cleared. "I have to go, but I'll come back. I'll bring Ribera. He wants to come cheer you up."

She started to go, but he took her hand and tugged her back. She bent down and kissed again just as Leah entered the room.

"Oops. Sorry. Bad timing. One of my specialties."

"That's okay. I was just leaving." A cool look at Leah and then down at Cassidy.

"My sister, Leah." The cool look warmed. "Leah, this is Dylan McCue, my downstairs neighbor, my rescuer. She came out of her apartment swinging a club, and the guys on me took off running."

The two women shook hands and looked each other over carefully. They liked what they saw.

"Thank you. I've gotten used to having him around."

"Is he usually this much trouble?"

"Yes."

They both laughed.

Cassidy, not for the first time, wondered at how quickly women could connect. They were without the big dog wariness with which men first approached each other.

"I'll leave you two alone." She left.

"Wow."

"Yeah, yeah."

"She's beautiful, Michael."

"Really? I hadn't noticed. I'll take a closer look when she comes back."

"You've noticed, and you've already taken a close look." Leah sat on the edge of the bed and examined him. "You look awful. Does it hurt much?"

"They're feeding me pills. It's not too bad."

"Do you know who they were?"

"Cops."

"Why?"

"A long story not worth the telling."

"Does it have anything to do with Dad?"

"No."

"Promise me."

"I promise. I got into something with some other cops. They didn't like what I did. This was their way of showing it. It's over now."

She took her cigarette case from her purse, selected a cigarette, tapped it down on the case, and lit it with a gold lighter. She watched Cassidy while she went through the ritual, and he could tell she was working up to something. She blew smoke at the ceiling. "I'm sorry about what I said the other night."

"What did you say?"

"That it was your fault that Dad is in trouble."

"I didn't need you to tell me that." He knew it was the wrong thing the moment it came out of his mouth.

"I'm trying to apologize for saying it." She stubbed her half-smoked cigarette out angrily. Leah did not like to be wrong and did not like to be called on it. "But if you hadn't pushed Cohn—"

"Hey."

She stopped.

"It'll work out. Don't worry about it."

"Don't do that. I'm not a child."

"Right. Sorry. I'm working on something. When it comes together, we'll have some leverage."

"What is it?"

"I can't tell you. It's part of the Ingram case. Just let me work it out."

"They can't send him back, can they? He's been here since he was a kid. He's an American citizen."

"They can do anything they want these days. It's the times we live in. We came out of the war thinking everything was going to be all right, and the next thing you know things are worse than ever. Russia. The bomb. Everyone's living with the idea that the world could blow up and we could all die tomorrow. People are scared. The guys like McCarthy and Cohn know that, and they know it works for them. If you scare people enough, they'll let you do anything you want as long as you promise it's for their protection."

She patted his hand. "Thanks. That cheered me up." She twisted her wedding ring, looked away, and then looked back. "Have you had a chance to . . . ? The problem I mentioned?"

"As soon as I get out."

"Okay."

"Are you all right? Really?"

"I am. I'm fine. Really."

They had been trained early never to complain. It was part of their mother's legacy, the idea that if you saved the surface, you saved all. But it caused internal bleeding.

The nurse came in after Leah left and gave him a shot, and he drifted off.

In the dream he was on a dark street. The buildings were featureless, but it was someplace he walked often. He knew it but did not recognize it. He carried something heavy in one arm, but when he looked to see what it was, he could not see it. Something dreadful was about to happen. What was it? He was scared. Why was he scared? There was a deeper darkness ahead of him where something waited. He wanted to stop, but he kept walking. If he stopped, it wouldn't happen. What wouldn't? He did not know. Victor Amado stood on the sidewalk ahead of him and told him to go back. What was Amado doing here? Amado was dead. Wait. How could Amado be dead? This was a dream. Amado could be dead in a dream. Why was Amado telling him to go back? He kept walking. Amado disappeared. Now he was at the point of danger. Stop. Go back. Turn around. It's here. Turn around!

Cassidy awoke soaked with sweat. A dream. Just a dream. Don't worry. Victor Amado was dead in the dream, but he had spoken to him two days ago. What did that mean?

Dawn, and rain streaked the window.

• • •

The doctor probed Cassidy with stiff fingers. When Cassidy grunted or winced, the doctor nodded, murmured, "Uh-huh," as if something he suspected had been confirmed, and went on. He finished and stood leaning forward with his hands clasped behind his back. "I think we're doing very well here. If nothing changes, I don't see why we can't go home tomorrow. I was a bit worried about kidney function, but your urine's been clear, and that's a good sign."

"Doctor, have you ever heard of anyone having dreams that come true?"

"Dreams that come true. Like see the girl across the room, and then live happily ever after?"

"No. You dream of something, and then later it seems to happen the way you dreamed it."

"Hmm. No, no. Not part of my medical education. Maybe the psychs run across that. I don't know. Still, I believe we have no idea of the capabilities of the human brain. No idea at all. Is this something that has happened to you?"

"I was just wondering." The last thing he needed was to talk to a shrink. If the department heard about that, he'd be gone. All they needed was the excuse.

"Anything else bothering you?"

"I'm a little worried about the hydrogen bomb. And I think that television is ruining the jazz clubs in New York."

"Well, then." The doctor nodded to Orso, who was coming in the door, and loped out of the room.

Orso carried a box of chocolates tied with a red ribbon. "Schrafft's finest." He put the box on the bed. "You want me to open it?"

"Could I stop you?"

Orso grunted and ripped the cellophane off. He offered the open box. "The square ones are hard in the middle. The round ones are soft."

Cassidy ate one and then waved the box away. Orso ate two of each and put the box within reach.

"They worked you over pretty good. You look like crap."

"I feel like crap." Every time he moved, something hurt. His ribs punished him when he coughed. There was a bruise on his left thigh from knee to hip where someone had kicked him that ached even through the pills.

"So the word is it was all them fucking micks Franklin hangs with, big surprise. O'Brian, Allie Milliken, Ham Logan, he's got a broken nose, McGill, and that guy who's always hanging around with Franklin, the guy from Jones Beach?"

"Malachy?"

"Yeah, him. It looks like you got him a good one in the eye. He's out on medical leave." He ate two more chocolates. "It's not like they're trying to keep it a secret. What do you want to do?"

"Nothing."

"Nothing? Mike, you've got to do something. Those Irish pricks. You can't just let them roll over you."

"What would you do?"

"Kill one of them. Franklin, probably. He's got no family, and it all started with him. He's a shitball and he deserves to die."

"No."

"Easy to do. You go hang out someplace where a lot of people can see you, establish an alibi. Toots Shor's or someplace they know you. I've got a throw-down gun I took off a punk a couple of years ago. Untraceable. Franklin goes to that whorehouse on Eleventh once a week, gets his ashes hauled, gets loaded. He comes out, pop, pop, pop, he never knows what hit him, goes to Jesus with a smile on his face."

"No, thanks."

"You're sure?"

"I'm sure."

Orso shrugged at Cassidy's shortsightedness. "Okay. Anything you want? Anything I can get you?"

"My father's got a play in rehearsal at the Winter Garden. The dance captain's name is Marco Pinetti. He was going to come up with the names of who Ingram hung with. Stop by and see what he's got. When you're there, speak to a dancer named Victor Amado. Marco can point him out.

Tell him I'm sorry I missed the meeting. Tell him I still want to talk to him whenever, wherever."

"We're still working it?"

"Yes."

"Okay."

Cassidy woke in late afternoon from a dreamless sleep. The cadaverous gray man he had last seen in the diner near the Blue Parrot leaned against the wall by the door and smoked a cigarette. He wore the same black suit or its twin. He had taken off his black fedora, maybe in deference to the solemnity of the hospital.

"Come on in. Make yourself at home." Cassidy pushed himself up against the pillows with a groan and drank water from the glass on the bedside table.

"How're you doing?"

"Great. Never better"

"You look a little rough."

"Uh-huh."

"Frank wants to know whether this has anything to do with the thing he asked you to do." His gesture took in the hospital room and battered Cassidy.

"No, it doesn't. It's something else."

"Yeah, that's what I heard. Friends of the guy you threw out the window is what I heard."

He switched his hat to his cigarette hand and took a piece of paper torn from a notebook out of his jacket pocket. "Frank said I should talk to the bartender at the Parrot about this Ingram guy you was asking about, so I did. Griff came up with some names, guys this Ingram guy hung out with. Griff says this Ingram was a real hustler, always had his eye out for a way to make a buck. Guys went out with him, but mostly no one went back for seconds, if you get my drift. I don't know if it does you any good, but there it is."

He put the piece of paper on the bedside table and stepped back. "Frank says you need anything, you call me. My number's on the top. I've got one of those answering services. You tell the girl you want me to call. Leave a number."

"What's your name?"

The man thought for a moment and decided there was no danger in it. "Packer."

"Packard like the car or Packer like the cannibal?"

He smiled big yellow teeth, the first sign of animation. "The cannibal." His face closed up again. He settled his hat squarely on his head and went out.

Cassidy looked at the piece of paper he'd left. There were a dozen names on it written in pencil in block letters a child would make. Packer's telephone number was written in ink at the top of the page in tiny, precise script.

The doctor made evening rounds. He poked and prodded and grunted his satisfaction and told Cassidy, "One more day, I think. Just to be sure."

• • •

Dylan took him home in a taxi. The stairs tested his bruised thigh and made his cracked ribs ache, but when Dylan suggested they rest halfway up, he told her he felt fine. Pride.

"I bought a steak and some canned soup, in case you were hungry. I don't know what you like, so I bought some different kinds."

"Thank you."

"What are you going to do?"

"The doctor said take it easy. I guess I'll take it easy. Read a book. Look out the window. Listen to some jazz. Do you like jazz?"

"I don't know. I don't know anything about it." They were aware of each other in a way that made them awkward, as if they were starting fresh.

"We'll go listen to some." God, she was beautiful.

She smiled. "I'd like that. Your sister came by yesterday when you were asleep. She asked that you call her when you got home."

"Okay." The way she moved. The way she smiled.

"I like her."

"So do I." Like something wild. *Jesus, the next thing you know you'll be writing poetry.*

"Will you be all right?"

"I'm fine." *Tell her to stay.*

"I've got some things to do downstairs. If you need anything, just bang on the floor."

She crossed the room, wide shoulders, slim back, solid butt, and long, leggy stride. When she reached the door he stamped twice on the floor.

She turned and looked at him. "What took you so long?"

Tangled in each other and their clothes.

"Ow." His bruised shoulder against the doorjamb.

"Sorry."

"Uh." His thigh on the bedpost.

"Oops."

"Aaggh." He tripped on his pants and fell on the bed with her on top.

"Sorry."

"Take it easy. I'm a little sensitive down there."

"Jesus, I hope so."

When he woke in the morning, she was gone. She'd left a note in the kitchen saying she had gone to Ribera's to do some work. At the end it said, "Tonight?" He stood by the window with a cup of coffee and thought about her, about how it felt to push his fingers through in the tight curls of her hair, of the bold way she looked at him, the way she smelled of lightly scented soap, clean hair, and something that was hers alone, some dark, spiced fume.

18

"That guy Marco. He's a fairy, right?" Orso asked.

Christopher Street was crowded. Village whackos and weirdos, Orso called them, artists, poets, dancers, musicians, Bohemian New York, with a sprinkling of older people with foreign accents, string bags, and frumpy clothing who had washed up in the Village in the 1930s when they read the handwriting on the walls of Europe.

"Uh-huh. Actually, I think he'd fuck anything that would hold still for it. When did Amado quit showing up for rehearsal?" Cassidy lit a cigarette while they waited for a break in traffic.

"The day after you went in the hospital. A lot of fairies in the theater is what they tell me. I guess you must have known a few, growing up in it and all."

"Sure."

"They ever, you know, bother you?"

"No."

"I don't get these girly guys. What the hell's with them?" He flapped a limp wrist.

"That particular girly guy Marco jumped into France on D-Day with the 101st Airborne."

"No shit?"

"Of course he was wearing lace panties and a bra under his fatigues."

"Get out of here."

"He said if he was going to die, at least he'd go feeling sexy."

The entrance to the building was just off Greenwich Street. Half the bell pushes in the entry way lacked names. 6A showed Victor Amado in ornate script cut from a business card. Cassidy rang. No answer.

"Hey," Orso said. He pushed on the outer door and it swung open. They stepped into the vestibule of worn cracked linoleum, dim light from a single bulb, the smell of old frying oil from the coffee shop next door. A crappy lock held the inner door. "An invitation to burglary," Orso said as he examined it.

"What are they going to steal once they get in?"

• • •

They climbed through the cooking smells trapped in the stairwell, and the air got warmer and thicker as they ascended. In full summer the apartments would swelter, and in the winter they would be cold. But the rent was cheap.

When they reached the sixth floor, Orso leaned against the wall and tried to regain his breath while Cassidy rang Amado's bell.

"You could try eating less."

"Screw that. I could climb fewer stairs."

Cassidy rang again. "Not home. Maybe we should try later."

"And do these stairs again?" Orso leaned over and banged impatiently on the door. He tried the knob and then bent forward to examine the lock. "Hey."

Cassidy leaned to look. There were bright scratches in the brass of the two locks. "Someone forgot his keys."

"What do you think?"

"You're better at it than I am."

Orso took a roll of soft leather from his inside pocket removed three lock picks, and bent to the door for a minute. "Okay." Orso put the picks away. "Only the top was locked." He pushed open the door. A dangling security bar banged against the door. "Holy shit."

A wrecking crew had searched the apartment. Ripped cushions leaked stuffing. Tables lay upended. The searchers had pulled the carpet up and crumpled it on the eviscerated sofa. They had pulled every drawer out, torn every framed photograph from the wall, and smashed the frames to see if there was anything concealed behind the prints. Even some of the ceiling had been pulled down.

Their shoes crunched broken glass as they looked through the small apartment. The bedroom had been given the same fine attention as the living room. Someone had used a knife to hack open the padded headboard. Clothes littered the floor. The shoulders of some of the jackets had been cut open.

"So where's Victor Amado?"

The tiles in the bathroom were spattered with drops of drying blood, and flies buzzed at the crusted puddle in the tub. "Wherever he is, I'm going to bet he ain't happy," Orso said.

They went back into the living room, and Orso continued to the kitchen. Cassidy righted a coffee table and picked up some of the photos in their broken frames and laid them out on the surface. They were all of young men posed in bright light and cut by shadows, as if they were disappearing into the dark or stepping out into the light. Some were nudes. Some wore dancers' leotards. Art shots.

"Hey, Mike. You might want to step in here." Orso's voice was overly casual.

Victor Amado was in the refrigerator. He was naked. Whoever had crammed him in had broken one of his legs to make him fit. His chin was forced down on his chest and there was frost in his hair from the underside of the freezer unit.

"Check his hand." One hand was visible and Cassidy saw what Orso meant. There was blood under two of the fingernails all the way back to the lunule. "Someone had a knife or something up under there."

"What made you think to look?"

"I was hungry, figured I might find a snack. Is that Amado?"

"Yes."

• • •

The morgue attendants bitched while they worked to pry the body out of the Frigidaire. Rigor mortis and cold locked him in a curled position, and he lay lumpish on the stretcher like some ancient mummy coughed up by a glacier. A protruding knee bumped the door frame as they maneuvered into the hall. "Six flights. Shit. Why don't they ever die on the ground floor?"

"Don't expect much on time of death," Skinner said. "That icebox was set on high. He could've been in there for days. Blood in the tub is hard, a few days, anyway."

In the dream in the hospital, when Amado had stopped him on the night street, Cassidy had known he was dead. When had he dreamt that? Tuesday.

"I think he's been in there since Tuesday."

"What's that, a hunch?"

"Yes."

Skinner studied him for a moment to see if he was joking, and then shrugged. "Okay, Tuesday. I'll use that as a starting thought when I do the cut."

"Tomorrow?"

"Jesus, Cassidy, you're always in such a hurry. I'll give you a call when I get it done." Skinner followed his men downstairs.

· · ·

Orso bought an ice cream cone from a stand on Hudson while Cassidy made a call from a booth on the corner.

The phone was answered on the fourth ring. "Yes?"

"Frank Costello."

"Wrong number."

"Check anyway. Michael Cassidy calling." The man at the other end put the phone down hard and went away. Cassidy watched an old woman in a torn raincoat and the wreckage of an Easter bonnet pick through the garbage cans outside a bodega across Greenwich from his phone booth. She wore galoshes and heavy white kneesocks.

"Hold on."

"Michael, how are you?" Costello said.

"Fine. What's the progress on getting Dad out of lockup?"

"We're working on it. I hope to have good news soon. How are you doing on that matter we talked about?"

"I'm working on it too. There've been a couple of developments."

The old woman found something good and tucked it in a yellow shopping bag and then went back to foraging.

"Good. Well, let's hope we both have good news in the next few days. Call me whenever you want." He hung up.

The message was clear. Until Cassidy came up with something valuable to trade, his father would stay in jail.

Leverage.

Orso was leaning against a lamppost on the corner and licking his ice cream. "What do we do now?"

"Check with the building management, find out what you can about Amado: how long he's been there, who visits, any complaints. You know."

"What are you going to do?" A drip of ice cream started down the cone and he caught it with his tongue.

"I'm going to New Jersey."

"Jesus, Jersey? Well, better you than me." He took a last bite of ice cream and threw the cone in the gutter.

• • •

Cassidy rented a Ford from the taxi garage on Hudson Street and drove it up along the West Side Highway past the steamship piers and Riverside Park, and across the George Washington Bridge that soared over the river, and north to Englewood, New Jersey. He stopped at an Esso station and asked the man at the gas pump how to get to the address that Ingram had listed on his driver's license and on his job application at the Waldorf. It was warmer in Englewood than it had been in New York, so he took off his jacket and laid it over his gun and shoulder rig on the passenger seat. The man came back with the map and unfolded it on the hood of the car to trace the route to Linwood Street with a grease-grimed finger.

Linwood was a street of modest frame houses built before the war. There were small front lawns, and large, mature trees sprouted the lush new green of spring. The houses had short driveways that led back to one-car garages, and the cars parked in the drives were modest Fords and Chevvies. Most of them were three or four years old, but some were new. It was a solid blue-collar neighborhood, men with good jobs in the manufacturing plants, and stay-at-home moms. It was midafternoon. Cassidy drove slowly to spot the house numbers. School was out, and there were kids on bicycles on the sidewalks. On one block his approach scattered a group of boys playing baseball in the street. They coalesced behind him when he moved on.

Number 763 was a white house with green shutters and green trim. A covered porch shaded the front of the house and three red-painted cement steps led up to it. A five-year-old red Ford pickup was parked in the drive. There was another car past it covered with a tan tarp. Cassidy parked at the curb and went up the cement path that bisected the front lawn. It was cooler under the porch roof. Cassidy rang the doorbell. He heard shoes on hardwood, and then the front door opened and a man looked out at him through the screen door.

"Joseph Ingram?"

"Yup. But I've either got it, or I don't want it, 'cause if I wanted it, I'd have gotten it." He was a dark, cheerful man of about thirty-five, five foot ten or so and a hundred seventy pounds, little of it fat. He chewed an unlit pipe.

"I'm not selling anything."

"Well, then, what can I do for you, Mr. . . . ?"

"Cassidy." He showed him his badge and ID. "I'm sorry to bother you. I know this must be a hard time, but I need to talk to you about Alex Ingram."

"My brother?" He pushed out through the screen door, and Cassidy made room for him. Ingram walked to the edge of the porch and banged the ashes out of his pipe on the railing.

"Right. Alex."

"I know my brother's name. I just don't know what we're going to talk about, or why the New York cops care."

That seemed callous, but grief strikes people different ways. "I was the first detective on the scene. I don't know what they told you when they called . . ."

"Who? Who called?"

"Usually it's the watch lieutenant. It could have been somebody else, I guess." Cassidy had seen a number of relatives soon after a family member was killed, and none of them had reacted with Ingram's calm.

"Called about what?"

"Your brother's death."

"Why would the New York Police Department call me about my brother's death?" He was completely bewildered.

"Because he was killed in New York."

"Whoa, whoa, whoa. Let's back up here a little. He wasn't killed in New York."

"He wasn't?"

"Well, killed, I don't know about that. I guess you could say it. He drowned."

"Drowned?"

"Yeah. Someone left the neighbors' gate open. He got into the backyard." He gestured vaguely down the street. "Fell in the little swimming pool they had back then, one of those above-ground ones. You had to climb the ladder. He liked to climb. Drowned. Wasn't anybody's fault."

"When was back then?"

"Twenty-two years ago. He was two."

• • •

Cassidy spent the rest of the afternoon in the Englewood City Hall with a helpful clerk named Gladys Bochner, a good-looking, flirtatious woman in her thirties whose ring finger was marked by the pale band of a recently removed wedding ring. She helped him through the mystery of the filing system, and they discovered that Alexander Ingram had indeed died by drowning in June 1932. In September 1943, the Records Bureau received a request for a copy of Alexander Ingram's birth certificate.

"And you just send one off?" Cassidy asked.

"Sure. I mean, who wants someone's birth certificate except someone in the family? People need them for all kinds of things, estate problems, probate. You know."

"Is there a record of where the copy was sent?"

"There should be. Wait. Here, it wasn't sent anywhere. Someone picked it up in person and signed for it." She slid the paper to him and then leaned over his shoulder to point out the place on the form where a scrawled signature could have been Einstein or Lincoln and managed to press a large, soft breast against his arm. Her breath smelled of the peppermints she chewed from a roll on her desk.

"Do you like living in the city? I always thought I'd like it, but I could never get Carl, that's my ex, the louse, to move. Born in New Jersey, going to die in New Jersey, he'd say. Wish he had, it would've saved me the aggravation."

"Once someone's got a birth certificate, he can apply for a driver's license in that name, right?"

"Sure. A copy of his Social Security number, driver's license, whatever you need."

"Do you have those records here?"

"Uh-uh. Social Security's federal, driver's license is state. I've got a friend in records at the Motor Vehicle Commission. I could give her a call if you want."

"Ask her if anyone got a license in Ingram's name, and where it was sent if it was sent."

She pulled the phone over and dialed. "What did this guy do, rob a bank or something?"

"Nothing that exciting."

She dialed with a pencil to save her long red fingernail. "Hey, Doreen, Gladys. Hi, honey. What, Friday? Uh-uh, I can't. That's bowling night. I could go Thursday. I really want to see it. God, Brando. I mean, come on. Okay, Thursday. Listen, honey, can you do me a favor and look up a license? Alexander Ingram? There's this real cute guy here asked me, and I just can't say no." She winked at Cassidy. "Sure, I'll wait."

Alexander Ingram had applied for a New Jersey driver's license in November 1950 and had renewed it once. The address on both licenses was Joe Ingram's house on Linwood, but the mailing address was Box 1289 at the main post office in New York across from Penn Station.

Gladys waited until he had written down the information. "I get off at five. There's this Italian restaurant over on Palisades. It's pretty good. Maybe not New York good, but good." Gladys took a deep breath to show off her assets.

"I'd like to, but I can't. I'm with someone."

"Just my luck. I was with someone too, but he threw me back."

With someone. He thought about it on the drive back and knew it was true. Was someone with him?

• • •

He knocked on Dylan's door, and she opened it and said, "I'm glad you're back," and kissed him hard. He picked her up and she wrapped her legs around his waist, and he carried her to the bedroom. He pushed her up against the wall, holding her there with his weight and her legs around him and pulled her shirt out from her jeans and pushed his hands up under her shirt to her breasts. She bit his lip and then took his head in both her hands and pushed it back so she could look in his face. He did not know what she found there, but her eyes were bright, and then she drew him back and kissed him, her tongue deep in his mouth. She released her legs from his waist and they went toward the bed trying not to break the kiss. They undressed each other slowly to hold off the moment, to prolong the anticipation, but in the end impatience got him and he ripped the last three buttons from her shirt. When he went into her, one of them said, *Oh, God.* They would rest, and then one would reach for the other, a touch, a hand, a tongue, and they would go again until finally she rolled aside and laughed and said, no more, no more. I'm ruined. I'm so sore it's beginning to hurt. They lay together, pressing along the lengths of their bodies as their sweat cooled. Then they slept.

They woke hungry at two in the morning and walked to the Bickford's on Seventh Avenue and ordered ham and eggs. Dylan poured rum from the pint in her leather bag into their coffee. A couple of late-shift cabbies played gin rummy at one of the red Formica tables in the back while a

NIGHT LIFE ··· 175

third read the bulldog edition of the *Daily News*. A young drunk in a rum-pled tuxedo with wine stains on his ruffled shirt quietly sang Cole Porter songs to his date, a pretty girl in a dark blue silk dress who slept open-mouthed with her head cradled on her arms.

Cassidy told Dylan about his trip to New Jersey and his discovery that the real Alex Ingram had died more than twenty years ago.

"So somebody found out he was dead and stole his identity. Who would do that?"

"Somebody looking for a fresh start with a clean name. Maybe a guy with a record. Maybe somebody running from somebody else. I don't know."

"Do you have any idea of who he really was?"

"No."

"Wow. You're some detective."

"Hey." Mock outrage. "I did find out that he had his driver's license sent to a post office box here in the city."

"And?"

"I guess I better go see if there's anything in it."

"Like what?"

"I don't know. Maybe something that will give me a better idea of who Ingram really was."

"So you just kind of poke around hoping that something will fall into your lap to solve the case."

"You know, you could show a little more respect. I am one of New York's Finest."

"We're in trouble."

Dylan mopped the last of the egg yolk from her plate with a piece of toast, drank the last of her coffee, and took two cigarettes from his pack on the table. She lit one and gave it to him, and then lit the other for her-self. She blew smoke toward the ceiling and watched him. There was a question in her eyes.

"What?"

"Nothing. I just want to know you a little. Tell me something."

"What should I tell you?"

"Anything. I don't know anything, so you can tell me almost anything and I'll know more. Tell me what you were like as a boy."

"Oh, hell, I don't know. I was a boy. A pain in the ass. Impatient, will-ful, a wiseass."

"Why'd you become a cop?"

He told her about coming back from the war, about freewheeling, trying to find traction, out of sorts with everything he touched, and then seeing the recruiting poster and walking into the station house on 67th Street and signing up. She smoked another cigarette and watched him carefully while he told it.

"That's it? You joined out of boredom? Come on." She stubbed the cigarette out impatiently. "That's the story you tell everybody. I don't want the story you tell everybody. I want the story you tell me."

"I hate bullies." *Jesus, that sounds lame.*

She smiled and sat back. "I get that. Sure. I get that."

"Who protects the sheep from the wolves?"

"The guys who beat you up were cops."

"Hold it. Wait. Are you trying to tell me it's not all black and white?"

"Okay. Right."

"Quis custodiet ipsos custodes?"

"What's that, Latin?"

"Yes. It means 'Who watches the watchmen?'"

"Who does?"

"I do."

She touched his hand gently. "Why do men look so embarrassed when they talk about being good?"

• • •

New York streets are never empty, and there were a few people out as they walked home: shift workers coming or going, solitary serious drinkers tacking from one bar to the next, a horn player and a cellist carrying their instrument cases toward the 12th Street subway, an old woman walking three miniature poodles.

Dylan held his arm, and once when they stopped to let traffic clear, rubbed her head against his shoulder, and he did not want the night to end.

He stopped to light a cigarette and turned to shield the match from wind off the river and caught movement down the block out of the corner of his eye, but when he looked, there was no one there. He watched for a moment but saw nothing in the deep shadows of the doorways. When they went on, he had a prickly feeling on his back that someone watched them.

19

"What do you think?" Rhonda whispered.

A showroom at Henri Bendel on 57th Street. Thin, expensive women and a scattering of willowy men in well-cut suits perched on uncomfortable gilt chairs.

"I think I'd get paper cuts from her hips." The model turned and stalked back up the runway.

"Of the dress."

"I like the dress," Cassidy whispered back. A couple of people in the row looked at them in annoyance, as if they were talking in church.

"Coco Chanel. She actually makes clothes for women, rather than some weird semi-demi-male fantasy. I swear to God I'd wear only Chanel if I could afford it. Come on, let's get out of here. I have more than enough for my piece."

They walked up Fifth Avenue to The Plaza and took a table by the windows in the Oak Bar and ordered gin and tonics in a bow to spring. The trees in Central Park across 59th Street spread their new green leaves, and businessmen and -women from the buildings nearby carried bag lunches into the park.

"What did you get me into?" Rhonda leaned forward to accept a light for her cigarette.

"What happened?"

"I went to the place on Sixty-fourth Street and gave them some malarkey about an article I was doing on exclusive apartment buildings on the Upper East Side, and they politely told me to go to hell. So I found a janitor banging garbage cans around in the alley, and gave him twenty bucks, and he gave me the dirt. Mrs. Sculley on eleven tends to meet the delivery boys in her underwear. Mr. and Mrs. Fraser throw things at each other. The Samsons on three are two months behind in their rent. That kind of thing. And he gave me a list of apartments on four to eight facing the street." She slipped a piece of paper across to him. "And you owe me the twenty I gave him. I don't know what they're paying cops these days, but it's got to be more than what girl reporters get."

"Thanks." He handed her a twenty and she tucked it in her bag as the waiter left their drinks. "It's going to take more than thanks, because the next day I was paid a visit in the newsroom by a polite but arrogant young man in a crappy suit who wanted to know why I was asking questions about that particular apartment building. I gave him the same malarkey that I gave the building manager, but I don't think he believed me."

"Why not? I always thought you were an expert liar."

"Oooh, thank you. But flattery will get you nowhere. And by the way, the guy who came to see me, he's leaning against the bar. He's been there since we sat down."

Cassidy turned to look. One of the FBI agents who had searched his apartment was at the end of the bar near the door. As he watched, Susdorf came in and spoke to him and then crossed the room to their table and put his hands on the back of an empty chair.

"Miss Raskin, I'd like to speak to Detective Cassidy. Alone."

"I think I'll stay. Freedom of the press and all that. Besides, I haven't finished my drink."

Susdorf raised a hand, and the other FBI agent left the bar and came across the room toward their table. Rhonda sipped her drink and pretended to be calm. Cassidy lit a cigarette. Susdorf leaned his weight on his hands on the back of the chair and watched them without expression. The agent stopped at his shoulder. "Frank, arrest Miss Raskin, please."

"What charge?" Rhonda took another sip of her drink.

"Interfering with an FBI agent in performance of his duty."

"It'll never stick."

"You'll still spend the night downtown in the federal lockup."

Rhonda tried to gauge his seriousness. What she read made her put down her glass, pick up her purse, and stand. "Well, I'd love to be arrested by such a good-looking guy, but I've got work to do. Michael, give me a hug."

Cassidy stood and put his arms around her. She leaned in to kiss him and whispered, "Caldwell on the sixth floor was at Ribera's the other night." She pulled back, smiled at them, and said, "Bye, guys. Have fun."

Cassidy sat down again and took his cigarette out of the ashtray. He tasted his gin and tonic and outwaited Susdorf.

"Why'd you send her to that building? We already told you we checked it out. There's nothing there for you."

"What building?"

"The one on Sixty-fourth Street."

"I didn't send her there."

"Bullshit."

Cassidy shrugged. "I've known her a long time. We used to go out together. I bet you know that. I ran into her at Toots Shor's the other night. She said she was doing an article on upscale Upper East Side apartment buildings. We talked about getting together. Today we found the time."

"At a fashion show at Bendel's?"

"I like women. I like their clothes. You'd be amazed at how few men can talk to women about their clothes. You should take an interest. Your wife would appreciate it."

Susdorf's anger showed in his white knuckles on the chair back and bunching muscles in his jaw. "We're watching you, Cassidy."

"Thank you. It makes me feel safe in a dangerous world."

Susdorf jerked his hands off the chair, started to say something, thought better of it, and stalked away, followed by the agent Frank.

• • •

The doorman at the building on 64th said General Wilson Caldwell, of apartment 6B, was not home and probably would not be for a while. He had left with a suitcase two days ago.

A telephone call from the squad room to the Department of the Army told Cassidy that General Caldwell was commanding maneuvers in North Carolina. The information officer had no information as to when the general might be back in New York.

20

Three days of rain, and then the sun came out. Cassidy found May Stiles in her office, a booth in the coffee shop across the street from the Cortland Hotel. She was dressed in a gray linen business suit with red accents. Her makeup was perfect, and her blond hair was held back with tortoiseshell clips that matched her glasses. She looked like the middle-aged businesswoman she was, but there was little chance she would be mentioned in *Forbes* or *BusinessWeek*. A glass of iced tea sweated onto a folded napkin. There was a telephone at her elbow on the Formica tabletop. She held the receiver against her ear with her shoulder while she leafed through a small black notebook. Cassidy waited while she finished the call. "I'm sorry, Mr. Smith, Claudine isn't available today. She has classes. Lorette would be happy to accommodate you in the usual way." A cigarette bobbed at the corner of her mouth while she talked. She raised her eyebrows at Cassidy and offered the other side of the booth with a nod. Cassidy slid in. "How about Alana? She speaks of you very highly. Fine, then. Alana at two thirty. The usual arrangements." She cut off the call with her finger, then let the button up and dialed. "How're you doing, Cassidy?" Someone answered the phone. "Sweetie? That guy Smith. The one with the funny dick. Two thirty. Room six oh one. Key's at the desk." She hung up and made a note in her book, and then looked up at Cassidy. "What's up? I see that shit Franklin's back on the job. I wish you'd been on the sixth floor that night."

"I need a name, May."

"Sure. What do you fancy—blonde, brunette, redhead? You looking for a specialty, something a little out of the ordinary?" She sipped her iced tea and blew smoke at the window, where it curled against the pane.

"Who do you send your girls to if they get knocked up?"

She looked at him over her glasses. "Come on, Cassidy."

"It's not that, May. I'm out of Vice. I've got a friend who's in trouble."

She did not believe *friend*. "Jesus, don't you guys ever learn?" She made up her mind. "There's a guy I use. It'll cost you a couple of hundred. He only takes cash. You use my name."

"Is he good?"

"Yeah. He's a brilliant surgeon working out of an operating room at Doctors Hospital. What do you think? He's a guy who lost his license because he was writing prescriptions to himself, but he's clean and efficient, and he doesn't drink or toot during office hours. He's not some guy in a back room in Jersey City with a rusty hanger. I know maybe six guys in town who do abortions, and he's the best."

"Okay."

"You know, the world would be a much better place if men were born without dicks."

"You'd be out of business."

"It'd be worth it for the tranquillity."

• • •

Cassidy studied the Maxfield Parrish mural on the wall of the King Cole Bar of the St. Regis Hotel and sipped a Bloody Mary. Old King Cole didn't look particularly merry, but maybe Parrish had caught him on a bad day. There were only a few other midday drinkers, four businessmen at a table calling for another round, a solitary hunched over a martini at the end of the bar, and three out-of-town women surrounded by shopping bags, drinking mimosas and showing each other the loot from their store raids along Fifth Avenue. Leah arrived ten minutes late and slipped onto the stool next to him. She leaned to kiss him on the cheek and ordered a whiskey sour.

"Twee, tweedle dee."

"What?"

"That's the sound Old King Cole's fiddlers make in the rhyme."

"No wonder he looks so grumpy," she said. She had a knack for peeking into his thoughts.

"How are you?"

"I'm fine." She sipped her drink. "I went to see Dad."

"He didn't want you to go down there."

"Well, I wanted to, so I went. Jesus, what an awful place."

"How was he?"

"You haven't been down there yet?"

"No."

"Why not?"

"I just haven't had the time. I've been busy." He heard the thinness of the excuse.

"Michael, he's your father."

"I know, I know. I wanted to be able to tell him something when I went. I wanted to be able to give him something concrete to hold on to."

"Go soon. Don't worry about having something. Just go see him. He looks gray and tired. And scared. I don't think I've ever seen that before. Mark called a few people, but the moment they heard it was Cohn and McCarthy, they backed away. One guy said he couldn't afford to do business with Mark since his father-in-law was a Commie. This was someone we thought was a friend. He's eaten at our apartment."

"Frightened people."

"I'm one of them."

He started to reassure her, and then stopped. She hated meaningless phrases of comfort. She had a right to be scared.

The bartender slid her whiskey sour onto a coaster in front of her. She ate the cherry. "How's it going with Dylan?"

"Good, I think."

"You think?"

"I'm kind of in unknown territory here."

"Ah."

"What does that mean?"

"I always wondered what she'd be like, the one you finally fell for. I like her."

"Good."

"Just don't run away, okay? And don't drive her off. Play it out."

"I'll do my best."

"Do that." She leaned over and kissed him on the cheek.

"Leah, I've got that name you wanted."

Her smile dropped away. "Oh. Okay."

He put a piece of paper on the bar between them. It had the doctor's name and phone number and May Stiles's name for reference. Leah looked at it without touching it. "May says he's good, and I trust her."

"All right." She pulled the paper to her with a finger, folded it, and put it in her purse without reading it.

"Are you sure you want to do this?"

"Yes." Her voice was tight and low.

"I'll go with you."

"No." Sharply. Her eyes were fierce. "No, you won't."

"Someone has to go with you, Leah."

"Megan's going."

"You told Megan?" He was surprised.

"Yes. She's a friend of mine, Michael, no matter what you think."

He heard the rebuke.

"I need her."

"She'll tell Dad."

"No. She won't. I know what I'm doing, Michael."

"All right." He hoped she did. He wanted to protect her and had no idea how to do it. It was not the first time.

"It'll be all right, Michael. Really it will." As if he was the one who needed reassurance.

"I know. It'll be fine." Maybe he was.

21

In the evening, Cassidy and Dylan went to see a movie. They argued without heat about what to see. Cassidy refused war stories and cop films and opted for *River of No Return* with Robert Mitchum and Marilyn Monroe. Dylan wanted to see the musical *Seven Brides for Seven Brothers*, but the showtime was wrong, and in the end they walked across to the Loews and saw *Sabrina* with Humphrey Bogart, William Holden, and Audrey Hepburn, two rich brothers competing for the affection of a beautiful young woman who happened to be the daughter of their chauffeur. Democracy at work.

They came out of the movie into a misting rain. Cassidy bought an umbrella from a street vendor for a buck, and they walked to an Italian grocery on Bleecker Street and bought cheese and bread and salami and small hot pickled peppers and then walked home through the warm evening and the rain. Dylan held his arm and walked tight to him for the shelter of the umbrella. He was as happy as he had ever been.

"Do you have to work tonight?"

"No. Ribera's rethinking the project. That means a lot of yelling and banging things, slamming around. A lot of tequila. A lot of breakage. Better to stand clear."

"I'm glad."

She smiled at him and bumped his shoulder with her head. "Hey, what about you? Have you found anything more about who killed what's his name? Ingram?"

"Not much. We think he was blackmailing someone."

"And that person killed him?"

"A heart attack killed him. I think the guy was torturing him to find the blackmail material, and Ingram's heart popped before he did."

"What material?"

"Photographs."

"You told me that before, but of what?" She watched him intently.

"I don't know. Somebody doing something he shouldn't have been doing."

"Do you know who?"

"No. Somebody important. A lot of people want the photos, the FBI, Frank Costello, whoever tortured Ingram. Costello says they'd give him leverage, so whoever is in the photos has a lot of power, and whatever they show is something he can't afford to have out there."

"And you don't have any ideas or clues?"

They waited for a taxi to splash by and then quickly crossed Seventh Avenue. "I do have a clue, but I don't have a clue about what it means."

"What is it?"

"A fifty-cent piece. Ingram had it hidden in his locker backstage at the theater."

"A fifty-cent piece? What does that mean? How can that be important?"

"I don't know, but he thought it was important enough to hide."

"Maybe that's what they searched your apartment for."

"Maybe."

"May I see it?"

"I don't have it with me. It's hidden."

"Where?"

"I'm not going to tell you."

"Why not? Don't you trust me?"

"If it's what they killed Ingram for, it's dangerous information. I don't want you to have it."

She shook her head but said nothing, and they walked in silence.

"What are you thinking about?" he asked.

"The movie, how it all came out right in the end. I liked that. I'm a sucker for the happy ending. Did you like it?" she asked.

"Yes."

"But what?"

"I don't think she should have settled for either one of those guys. She would have done better if she'd gone into New York and gotten a job."

"That's not who she was. She didn't want a job. She wanted him. And the heart wants what it wants. There's nothing you can do about that. It's very romantic. She goes to Paris an ugly duckling and comes back a beautiful swan, and men fall at her feet."

"I hope she learned more in Paris than how to cook an omelet and where to buy clothes. Otherwise Paris was a waste."

"Jesus, men. She went to Paris a girl and came back a woman. Do you think that has something to do with omelets?"

"So the baron had his way with her?"

"Why do men always think that they have *their* way with women, as if women had no choice in the thing?"

• • •

They made love and then got up and made a picnic of what they had bought and ate it in the living room surrounded by every candle Dylan could find in the apartment.

"Who was she?"

"Who was who?"

"The woman who used to live here." Dylan sat on the sofa wearing one of his dress shirts. Her long legs were tucked under her, and she was eating ice cream from a bowl in her lap. "She left eyelash curlers in the bathroom, and a pack of Kotex."

"Her name is Gwen Morris. She's an actress."

"Did she live here a long time?"

"A couple of months."

"Why did she leave?"

"She found out she didn't like me as much as she thought she did."

"Hmm." She ate some ice cream. "Did you miss her when she left?" She licked the back of the spoon while she watched him.

"Sometimes."

"Sometimes?" Raised eyebrows.

"Hey, come on."

"I want to know."

"Not when she first left. We'd been arguing a lot, so when she first went, it was a relief. But then after a while, yes. Sometimes."

"Did you love her?"

"Dylan, what are you doing?"

"I'm just asking questions. You don't have to answer."

He got up and poured bourbon over ice in a tumbler.

"Did you love her?"

"I don't know. I thought I did for a while, but no."

"Did you tell her you loved her?"

"Come on. Stop it."

"Did you?"

"Yes, I did, I guess. Do we have to talk about this?"

"No." A couple of minutes later she asked, "Even though you didn't love her?"

"Yes."

"Why?"

"I don't know. Because she wanted to hear it. Because I thought it would make her happy."

"Oh, boy." She scraped the last of the ice cream from the bowl and watched him while she ate it.

He found it hard to breathe.

She stood with a flash of legs and carried her bowl past him and put it in the sink. She came back and stood next to his chair and tangled her fingers in his hair and pulled his head back so she could see his face. "Don't ever tell me that lie."

22

A cool, gray day with a lowering sky and dark clouds above the river. Late March weather, offering spring one day, taking it back the next.

The Immigration Department's detention center was a windowless block near the Brooklyn piers. The taxi let Cassidy off at the chain-link fence that isolated the center from the neighborhood. The guard in the gatehouse checked his ID and then let him through, and he walked the half block of open pavement through spitting rain to a gray metal door with a thick glass window that distorted the face of the guard inside.

They locked his gun and handcuffs in a cage behind the reception desk, and another guard in a gray uniform led him down a gray corridor to a gray interview room that held a wooden conference table scarred along the edges by cigarette burns, six wooden chairs, a gray metal wastebasket, four mismatched metal ashtrays, three of them full to overflowing. There was a framed photograph of President Eisenhower screwed into one wall next to a framed photograph of the flag raising at Iwo Jima. Cassidy lit a cigarette to add his smoke to the stale air and tried to see how many men strained to raise the flag on the rocky summit. Four? Maybe five. How many, he wondered, made it off that rock alive? On the opposite wall hung a framed copy of the Bill of Rights, a reminder to those about to be deported of what they would miss in their home countries.

Cassidy turned when the door opened. His father came in dressed in a green cotton jumpsuit that zippered from crotch to neck. His shoes had no laces, and he shuffled to keep them from falling off. Tom Cassidy's face lit up when he saw his son, and he opened his arms and said, "Hey, you're here. Great. Great," and stepped forward and hugged Cassidy and kissed him on both cheeks, a ritual left over from his father's childhood that had embarrassed the hell out of the schoolboy Cassidy. Over his father's shoulder, Cassidy could see the guard watching them with a peculiar expression. *Foreign men hugged. Americans did not.* The man shook his head and shut the door. His father pushed back and held his son at arm's length.

"How are you? Everything okay?" As if it was Cassidy who needed concern. "What's this? Where'd you get that?" He touched an abrasion on Cassidy's temple, a souvenir of a fist or shoe on the darkened stairway.

"Nothing. An occupational hazard. How are you, Dad?"

"I'm fine. Great. I've been in worse places. I spent a couple of weeks in a jail in Istanbul that makes this place look like the Waldorf. The food's not much, but that's okay. I've lost four pounds, and I could afford to lose them." He slapped his stomach. When he turned his head, Cassidy saw the bruise on the side of his face and dried blood on his ear.

"Dad, what happened?"

"Nothing."

"What happened? Who hit you?"

Tom Cassidy touched his ear. "Some asshole was going on about the country, America this and America that. I straightened him out."

"Jesus."

"What? He was saying things that weren't right. Better off in Russia. Just like Nazi Germany here. I couldn't let him get away with that crap."

"Just keep your head down, will you?"

"Sure. Don't worry about me." He took a cigarette out of the pack Cassidy had left on the table and bent to the light Cassidy held. "Have you talked to Frank?"

"Yes. He's got someone working on it."

"Okay, then. Good enough. That's what we need. Call Megan when you leave, tell her I'll be home in a couple of days. Stop her from worrying."

"Dad, it might not happen that fast."

"Hey, you don't know Frank. When he wants something, he gets it done. I want you to stop by rehearsal, let everyone know I'm okay. It would be good if you could stick around and watch the eleven o'clock number. I don't know if it's right. I like the song, but I don't know. It doesn't seem to fire. Go take a look. Tell me what you think."

"I wouldn't know what to look for."

"Sure you would. I always said you have a great eye for what works in the theater."

"Dad, saying it doesn't make it true."

"All right, all right. If you don't want to do it, don't."

"I'm working something hard, and it's important."

"More important than doing something for your father that'll take an hour? Come on. Is that too much to ask?"

"I'm working on getting you out of here."

"Frank'll get me out of here."

"Not unless I do something for him."

Thomas Cassidy read his tone. "You mean like a favor? Okay. That's how it works. You help your friends, they help you."

"He's Frank Costello. I'm a cop. How many favors can I do for a guy like that?"

"You're my son. Frank's never going to ask you to do something that'll hurt you." His father would see only what he wanted to see.

"I want you to think about something."

"Sure. What?"

"What if something goes wrong? What if Frank's guy can't do what he needs to do?"

"What are you talking about? Frank has this city in his pocket. People owe him. If he says he'll get me out, he'll get me out. This whole thing's a mistake. I'm an American citizen. I've led a good life here. I've done good, and I've done well. One lousy screw-up when I was a kid. They're going to look at that against all the other stuff, and it's going to be fine. Trust me. I know what I'm talking about."

Cassidy walked ten blocks in the cold spring rain before he found a cab. He gave the cabbie the precinct's address and settled back, grateful for the cab's heater. How could his father be so stubborn in his optimism? It was as if he could will the world to work the way he wanted it to work. What if Cassidy didn't find the photos? What if he found them and didn't turn them over to Costello? How many ways, large and small, do sons and fathers fail each other? When does it start and when does it end? One thing he knew, if he failed his father here, it would be terminal and he would have to live with that.

As they crossed the Brooklyn Bridge toward Manhattan, the skies let loose, and the rain fell in sheets.

23

"I'm getting pressure from higher up," Crofoot said. He flinched when Fraker stabbed a raw oyster with a small fork, put it in his mouth, and chewed. "Hoover's complained to the White House that we're running an operation here against our charter. The FBI gets domestic; we get foreign. It's not the way it should be. They're good at running down car thieves and the occasional bank robber, but this is way beyond their level. But Ike's got an open door for the old toad, anything he wants, God knows why. We have to get this done before the White House draws rein."

"Uh-huh." Fraker did not care about pressure from above. That was Crofoot's problem.

They were in the Oyster Bar under Grand Central Terminal. It was mid-afternoon, and the place was nearly empty. The hanging light globes made the arched tile ceiling shine. Two waiters gossiped near the kitchen door. A man in a suit read the *Journal-American* while he ate clam chowder and drank a beer at the other end of the bar. Fraker had checked him out when he first came in, soft hands, a wedding ring, horn-rimmed glasses, shoes with slippery leather soles, a businessman playing hooky from the office. No threat.

Fraker squeezed lemon juice onto another oyster, then picked it up with the fork and examined it. "You know how you can tell if they're really fresh? They kind of squinch up when you put the lemon juice on."

"Fascinating." Crofoot glanced away as Fraker ate. He knew Fraker sensed he was squeamish about food. It was why the son of a bitch always asked for meetings in restaurants. Crofoot couldn't seem to do anything about it, and he resented the loss of authority. "Amado. You didn't have to kill him."

"What the hell was I supposed to do with him at the end? Apologize? So sorry. Have a nice day." He stared at Crofoot.

"He was the only one besides Ingram we know about, and we were lucky that Ingram led us to him."

"I didn't kill him *before* I learned something. I killed him *after* I learned something. That's the way these things go."

"Tell me."

"There were four of them. Ingram, Amado, two others. He told me who, where, and when. Jesus, he was eager at the end. Ingram organized it. He had some guy who was willing to pay their monthly rent if they would make themselves available when he needed them, and bonuses when they performed."

"Who?"

"Amado never met him. The rent went straight to the landlord. The cash came in envelopes with no return. It was set up around September last year. They went out on a couple of calls. The first was a suite at the Plaza. Ingram took pictures then too. He had some special little camera, really small, that he could hide. They didn't know who the guy was, but Amado thought from what was said that he was military. Ingram knew him from somewhere else. Like they'd been together a few times before. The second party was in a private house. Amado was really drunk most of the time, but he thought one of the guys was a senator, maybe a congressman. There was another party he was pretty hazy on, a bunch of rich guys out in Cold Spring Harbor, and then the one you're hot for."

"What did Ingram tell him about the photos?"

"Not much, just that the photos paid their rent and the envelopes of cash. He got the idea with the last one that Ingram was double-crossing whoever set it up and was keeping the photos for himself. He said they were going to be worth a lot of money."

"Did he say where Ingram might have hidden them?"

"No, but he did say that cop, Cassidy, searched Ingram's locker at the theater."

"He had a locker? Jesus, why didn't we know that?"

"How the hell were we going to know it?"

"He didn't have any idea who was running Ingram?"

"No. He just knew that Ingram did it for someone, but now he was go-ing to screw him, go out on his own, make some real money."

Fraker stabbed another oyster and put it in his mouth.

Crofoot turned away so he wouldn't have to watch him chew. He was going to have to do something about Fraker when this was over.

24

Lieutenant Tanner came up the stairs and into the squad room. Uncharacteristically, he wore a suit and his tie was pulled up tight under his collar, and he looked more weary and harassed than a man should at ten in the morning. "Cassidy, Orso, in my office, please."

By the time they got there he had shed his jacket and was yanking his tie down and unbuttoning his collar. He dropped into his desk chair, pulled open a drawer, and put a quart of Irish whiskey on the desk. "Too early for you guys?"

"Not too early for me," Orso said.

"No, thanks."

Tanner found two shot glasses in the drawer, filled them, and slid one across to where Orso could reach it. He raised his glass in toast and drank half.

"Jesus, I feel like I've been nibbled to death by ducks. I get a call to show up at Centre Street, so I put on my suit, tighten my tie and my asshole, and present myself to the deputy chief's office for a reaming, not that I know what I'm getting reamed for, but what else do you go to Murtagh for? You guys know Chief Murtagh? If not, avoid the pleasure. So he's telling me what an asshole I am. A couple of the other deputy chiefs come in to watch the master at work, pick up a couple of pointers. Murtagh's telling me I can't even run a squad, much less a station house, 'cause I've got a couple of fucking guys running around doing what they please, even when they've been ordered to do something else. Which is you two and the Ingram case, which you've been told to drop. So do you do that? No, you don't. You find a dead guy, Amado, who's tied to Ingram. How the hell you do that if you've dropped the case, I don't know. You had a lead.

Okay, I get that, but you're supposed to pick up the phone, call Bonner and Newly. Do you? No. Why not? You can't find a phone?"

"Boss," Orso began.

"Uh-uh. No need to apologize. A good reaming saves me the cost of the colonoscopy my frigging doctor wants me to get. You will now do what you were always supposed to do. You will turn over all you've got to Detectives Bonner and Newly. You will be assigned other cases. There's plenty of crime out there to go around."

"Who complained to Murtagh?" Cassidy asked. "The Pig?"

"No. The Feds. What's the difference?"

Bonner and Newly were at their desks in the squad room. Bonner smoked a cigar that smelled like burning socks and Newly took notes while Cassidy talked about the Ingram case. Orso sat with his feet up on an empty desk nearby and made no comment while Cassidy told the detectives about Ingram's connection to Amado but not about the envelope with the coin he found in Ingram's locker, told about Ingram's work at the Waldorf, about his frequenting the bars on Bird Alley, but not about Costello's interest in the photos, talked about Ingram's false identity but not about the mailbox drop at the post office across the street from Penn Station.

"Thank you, Detective Cassidy," Newly said when he finished. "If you think of anything else, you'll let us know?"

"Of course."

• • •

Gottfried Properties was in a brownstone on Bleecker Street near Perry. Cassidy and Orso climbed the stairs to the third floor.

"They're good cops, Mike. They're going to find this place. They're going to know we've been here."

"You want to drop it, Tony, I'll understand. We could get fired for this, direct disobedience of an order."

"Ah, what the hell. I don't have to be a cop."

"What else would you do?"

"Fall back on my natural talents. Become a gigolo. You know, take rich women out to dinner and the theater, charm them with my savoir faire, take them home and screw their ears off, pick up the money off the dresser, and steal away into the night."

"Tough on the back after a while."

"You learn to pace yourself."

The Gottfried office was in a shotgun apartment, one room leading directly into another from front to back, and each room was crammed with piles of paper as if nothing that entered was ever removed. A middle-aged woman in a man's yellow cardigan sat at a scarred wooden desk in the front room and scratched a pencil through her tangle of brown hair while she talked on the phone. "It's a eighty a month, first and last and a security deposit. Yeah, right, refrigerator and stove. Okay, then. Bring me the signed lease and a check and I'll give you the keys. Bye." A burning cigarette bobbed in the corner of her mouth when she talked. She looked at Cassidy and Orso without surprise or interest. "Help you?"

He showed her his badge. "Bill Gottfried?"

"All the way back." She jerked a thumb over her shoulder and then picked up the phone, checked a list on a pad in front of her, and dialed.

Gottfried was at his desk, barricaded behind a drift of paper. The window behind him was opaque with years of grime. He was a big soft-looking man. He had a round, wide, big-mouthed face like a frog, black curly hair, and bright dark eyes behind black-rimmed glasses. He was dressed in a sweatshirt and blue jeans. He waved a hand in greeting and went on with his phone call.

"I don't give a shit what kind of problems you've got with what kind of suppliers. I've got six units standing empty costing me money while you screw around with plumbing you promised to have finished a month ago. You don't get this done by the end of the week, I'm calling in another guy I know to do it, and I'm not paying you a dime. The end of the week."

He slammed the phone down and stood up, smiling. "Contractors. You gotta be firm with them or they'll dick you." He offered his hand across the wall of paper. "Bill Gottfried. What do you need?"

"Victor Amado."

"Yeah, I figured that. You know I'm going to have to throw away that icebox. Brand-new a year ago. What about him?"

"Anything you can tell us. How long was he in the apartment? Did he ever have visitors, roommates? Any problems with the rent?"

"He's been in there since about September. The rent? No. The rent comes like clockwork the first of the month. Probably 'cause he doesn't pay it himself. It comes from a law office up in midtown."

"Is that unusual?"

"Nah, well, I don't know. I don't ask too many questions when the rent comes regular, but you get some where the tenant isn't paying, someone else is. Young women, actresses, and like that who've got some sugar daddy looking after them. Sons of rich guys down here trying to be artists. Like that."

"I need the address of the law office that paid Amado's rent."

"Sure. Hey, Betty." Gottfried's shout blew garlic across the desk. "Give these guys the address of that lawyer who paid Amado's rent."

● ● ●

The law offices of Fitcher, Freed, and Alamek were on the sixth floor of a ten-story building on Sixth Avenue just south of 38th Street. The elevator operator was a stooped and dusty man in a worn gray uniform two sizes too big. His thin gray hair was yellowed with age. He missed the landing four times, slamming the operator's handle back and forth, before he gave up, opened the gate, and growled "Watch your step" without much concern.

The pebbled-glass doors along the hall of cracked linoleum offered a chiropractor, two "painless" dentists, an advertising company, two mail-order firms, Sadie's Hats, Frank's Novelty Items, a glove maker, Goldfine's Foundation Garments for Women, a bail bondsman, and finally Fitcher, Freed, and Alamek.

A sturdy, middle-aged woman with hair dyed so black it absorbed light looked at Cassidy and Orso over horn-rimmed glasses shaped like cat's eyes from behind a wooden desk in the reception area. Her expression was wary, as if she had learned to expect little good to come through the door. Three men and a woman waited on hard wooden chairs along one wall.

Orso showed the woman his badge. "We want to talk to whoever sends rent down to Gottfried Properties for a Victor Amado."

"That would be Mr. Freed." She pushed a button on her intercom box and leaned toward it to speak. "Mr. Freed, there are two detectives to see you about the Gottfried Properties check."

There was silence. She keyed the intercom again. "Mr. Freed?"

After a moment, the box squawked back, "Send them in."

Two of the waiting men got up with their faces averted and went for the door. One of them said, "Tell him I'll be back." The other said nothing, and they hurried out.

The secretary indicated the right-hand office door behind her, and Orso and Cassidy went in.

"Eddie Freed, gentlemen. What can I do you for?" Freed leaned across the desk and offered them a glad hand and a smile wide enough to show the gold fillings in his molars. His thick dark hair was combed straight back and held down with something that made it look waxed. He had a long, narrow face dominated by a bony nose. He wore a black suit that had once been good but was beginning to shine at the elbows and lapels from too many dry cleanings, a light blue shirt with heavy gold cuff links, and a dark-green-and-black-striped tie held by a gold tiepin. When he sat down, the smile diminished but did not go away, and he twisted a gold ring on his left pinkie, an unconscious gesture of nervousness. He had the air of a man who had begun to slide and did not know how to stop it.

Orso and Cassidy took the chairs in front of the desk. "Tell us about Victor Amado," Cassidy said.

"Sure. What about him? What did he do? How can I help?" Freed broadened his smile to show he was eager to cooperate.

"Somebody killed him in his apartment over on Christopher Street."

"No. What happened, like a fight or something?"

"He was stabbed."

"Uh-huh." A man no longer surprised by the world's cruelties.

"The property manager says that the rent check comes from this office."

"That's right."

"How does that work?"

"Well, those are my instructions from my principal. I send the check at the end of every month so it arrives on the first of the next month. Ninety-seven dollars."

"Who's your principal?"

Freed licked his lips and raised his hands palms up to show he was hiding nothing. "I don't actually know. An envelope arrives. It's got the money in it. Ten bucks for me, eighty-seven for Gottfried. I write the check and send it on."

"Is there a return address on the envelope?"

"No."

"How'd he set it up?" Orso asked.

"I got a call. He told me what he wanted done, asked if I would do it."

"How do you get in touch with him if you have to?"

"I don't get in touch with him. I've got no way to do it. No return address. No phone number."

"You didn't think that was a little peculiar?"

"Sure. Of course I did, but I mean, what the hell? Ten bucks a month for writing a check. Nothing illegal. Who's going to turn that down? Right?"

"What was his voice like on the phone?"

"His voice? I don't know. A man's voice. Nothing to it. Like anybody else's."

"High? Low? New York? Alabama?"

"I don't know. It was awhile ago. I get a lot of calls." He was lying about something.

"Did you ever hear his voice again?"

"I told you. He only called once." Definitely lying.

"Mr. Freed," Cassidy said, "did you pay the rent for Alexander Ingram every month on the same basis?"

Orso looked at him in surprise. So did Freed.

"Before you decide to lie about that, let me tell you something. Someone murdered Victor Amado. The same guy probably murdered Alex Ingram. Whoever did it tortured them first. Now, did you pay his rent?"

"Alex Ingram? Over on West Fifty-third? Yes." He folded his hands on his desk and looked at Cassidy with as much eagerness as he could muster.

"The same deal? An envelope with money and then you wrote a check?"

"Yes."

"How many others were there?"

"Others?" He was a man who either had never learned to lie well or had lost the ability.

"Freed, how many more?"

He calculated for a moment and then gave up the idea of resistance. "Two more."

"And all the checks come from the same guy?"

Freed thought for a moment before answering reluctantly, "Yeah. Same guy."

"And you don't have any idea who he is."

"No."

"Who are the other two?"

Freed stretched his neck. "Okay, hold on here now a second. Now we're getting into attorney-client privilege, that kind of territory. You came in. You know the names of two of the men. Nothing I can do about it. You didn't get them from me. I can talk about them, but I just don't feel comfortable telling you the other two. I don't know if the client wants anyone to know."

"How about cop-attorney privilege?" Orso asked.

"What? Cop-attorney? What's that? I don't think I've ever heard . . ."

"It works like this. I've got the privilege of smacking you around until you give up the first name. Then I've got the privilege of smacking you around some more till you give up the second name." Orso moved toward the desk.

Freed shoved his chair back and lurched to his feet, one hand out as if that would slow Orso. "Wait a minute. Wait a minute. You can't do that."

"Sure I can." Orso slipped a sap from his pocket and slapped it into his hand so it made a meaty whack.

Freed stumbled over the tin trash basket by his desk. It boomed against the wall under the grimed window, and he saved himself from falling by grabbing the edge of the file cabinet. Orso kept coming. The grin on his face made him look deranged.

"Tony, hold on a second."

Orso stopped.

Freed had wedged himself into the corner between the filing cabinet and the window.

"Mr. Freed, you send checks to four guys. Two of them are dead. If another one dies, we're going to be right back here talking to you about accessory before and after. Can you carry that kind of weight?"

"Accessory? Hey, I'm a lawyer. I know what constitutes accessory. You'd never get the indictment."

"That's all right. We'll take you downtown and book you. Sometimes it takes a couple of days for an arraignment or bail hearing. People get lost in the system. I've known guys to spend a week while the paperwork catches up to them. We'll inform the Bar that you've been arrested. We might even have to padlock the office while we get a search warrant for relevant files."

Freed found courage from some memory of who he used to be. He straightened his suit while he looked from Orso to Cassidy with contempt. "You bastards. You pull this crap on me, because I'm a little guy. You wouldn't go into any of those white-shoe law firms up on Fifth Avenue and pull this, would you? I used to be in one of those firms. Cops would come hat in hand, yes, sir, no, sir, three bags full, sir. We'd make you sit out in the waiting room for half an hour minimum, and you never said a thing. So fuck you guys."

"Okay." Cassidy went to the desk and picked up the phone.

"What are you doing?" Freed asked.

"Calling the wagon to take you in."

"Wait a minute, wait a minute." Freed lost what courage he had found.

"I can't wait. Okay, we were assholes. But two men are dead, and two more might die soon. I need those names."

Freed put his hand on Cassidy's to stop him from dialing. "Cut it out. Cut it out. I'll give you the names. I'll give you the addresses. But that's it. I don't know who sends the money. I don't know where it comes from. I don't know anything else."

Freed wrote the information on a pad from his desk. Cassidy put it in his pocket. He gave Freed one of his business cards. "The guy who sent the checks might call you now that two of these guys are dead. If he does, if you think of anything else, you call me."

In the hall, Orso said, "How did you know Freed paid Ingram's rent?"

"I didn't. But Gottfried said that Amado's rent came like clockwork the first of the month. Donovan said the same thing about Ingram's. He didn't say Ingram paid, he said it came. I threw it out there and we got lucky." Maybe it was a triumph, but he remembered the sudden sheen of fear sweat on Freed's face. "Do you ever feel like an asshole leaning on a guy like that, a guy just trying to make a living?"

"Nope."

"He's right, you know. We never would have worked it that way in one of the big uptown firms."

"Hey, this is how the world works. Who are we to say different? Keep it simple for me, will you, Mike. Just keep it simple. We're the good guys looking for the bad guys. So what do you want to do?"

Cassidy looked at the names Freed had given him. "You take Stanley Fisher. I'll check out Perry Werth."

25

"General Caldwell?"

"Yes?" The general turned from the army green Cadillac limousine parked in front of the apartment building on 64th Street and watched Cassidy approach. Upright, trim, square jawed, silver hair at the temples, bars of decorations on his crisply ironed uniform, military and squared away from top to bottom.

Cassidy had seen him before. When? Where? He held out his badge. "May I talk to you for a minute?"

"Of course, Detective . . . ?"

"Cassidy. Michael Cassidy."

A stocky captain in gold-rimmed glasses, an aide to the general, hovered nearby. A corporal unloaded baggage from the open trunk of the Cadillac and piled it on a luggage cart held by the doorman.

"What can I do for you, Detective Cassidy?" No joking, no banter, none of the nervous reactions most people had to a cop. General Caldwell was used to command.

"I want to talk to you about Alex Ingram." WHEN DID HE GET THE PROMOTION?

"I don't believe I know Alex Ingram. Excuse me for a moment." He gestured to the captain. "Bradley, would you go with Sergeant Hennessey and show him where things go in the apartment?"

"Yes, sir."

General Caldwell took a silver cigarette case from his inside pocket and offered Cassidy a cigarette.

"No, thanks."

By the time he lit his cigarette, the two soldiers and his baggage had disappeared into the building, and the doorman had taken up station out of earshot. It had been deftly done, but Cassidy recognized that the general had stalled until there was no one to hear the conversation.

"Alex Ingram? No. I don't recognize the name."

Cassidy handed him one of the photographs he had taken from Ingram's locker. "Do you recognize him?"

Caldwell made a thing of studying the photograph. He handed it back. "No. I'm sorry," he said, with just the right note of regret. "What is this about?"

"He was murdered."

"That's too bad. A robbery?"

"No. We don't think so. He was tortured. We think he had something someone wanted."

"Well. I'm sorry, but why did you come to me?"

"We had some information that you might have known him."

"No. Maybe he was in one of my units, but I can't remember everyone. Alex Ingram, you say. I could have my aide check the records."

"No. He was never in the army."

"Well, then, I have no idea." He dropped his cigarette and carefully ground it out under his shoe. "Sorry I can't be of more help." He turned toward the building. Cassidy let him get a few steps away.

"How about Victor Amado? Do you know him?"

Caldwell stopped and turned. "Amado? Victor Amado? No. I'm sorry."

Cassidy held up a photograph of Amado, and Caldwell took a step closer. "Are you sure?"

"Quite sure."

"You were both at a party at Carlos Ribera's a couple of weeks ago."

Caldwell shrugged. "That may be. I've been to a number of Ribera's parties. They are always interesting evenings, in part because there are usually more than a hundred people there I would not otherwise meet. The social circles in the army tend to be rather tightly constricted. I find I need wider horizons sometimes."

"Did you meet Amado?"

"Not that I remember. Has he been killed too?"

"Yes, he has."

"I'm sorry to hear that. Now, Detective, if there is nothing else I can do for you . . . I'm running behind schedule."

"General Caldwell, are you married?"

Caldwell flushed. "What the hell business is that of yours?"

"Just curious."

"I'm divorced." Now his face had gone pale, and his jaw muscles jumped, the first sign of real tension, an overreaction to a simple question, simple, not innocent.

"Thank you. I know where to find you if I need you again."

Caldwell jerked around and marched into the building.

26

"Stanley Fisher has divine taste," Orso said. "Four ball in the corner."

The cue ball cut fine and kissed the four so it drove sideways, rattled against the pocket cushions, and then dropped. The cue ball spun back off the bottom rail and Orso sank the five in the side, and then the six in the far corner off a tricky bank.

"I'm glad to hear it." Cassidy used the tip of his cue to slide the counters on the wire hanging overhead. They were playing straight pool to a hundred fifty points for time and five bucks a game in Ames pool hall on the second floor of a nondescript building on 44th Street just east of Broadway. It was afternoon, and only four of the tables were in use. The big room was dim except where the hanging globes with the metal shades brightened the green surfaces of the tables. Dust motes and ancient cigarette smoke swirled through the light.

Orso's jacket hung on the back of a chair. His shirtsleeves were rolled up to protect the cuffs from chalk dust, and he had tucked his tie into his shirtfront to keep it from dragging on the table. His pistol, a .38 Detective Special with the three-inch barrel, showed on his belt, but he was known at Ames, and no one took notice. "Freed sent a check every month for Stanley's apartment on East Fifty-first Street just off Third. Ninety-eight bucks a month. Like clockwork." He missed the nine and stepped aside as Cassidy chalked his cue and studied the balls that were left on the table.

"What else did you learn about Stanley?" Cassidy asked.

Orso went to sit in one of the wooden chairs by the window with his cue upright between his thighs and read from a small notebook he took from his shirt pocket. "Stanley works decorating windows for Lord &

Taylor, and according to Stanley's boss, Freddie, Stanley does marvelous work, absolutely marvelous. Freddie thinks he has divine taste, absolutely divine, and his color sense is fabulous, absolutely fabulous. But when you talk to him a bit more, and lean on him just a little, Freddie admits that Stanley is something of a hustler, and that there are suspicions that Stanley is not always completely honest in his dealings and may, just may, have taken a kickback or two from suppliers."

Cassidy sank the twelve long and pulled the cue ball back for an easy eight in the side pocket. He slid the counters while he surveyed the table. "Where are Stanley and his divine taste now?"

"Stanley took his divine taste and his fabulous color sense to a convention in Chicago and he will be back in time for work on Monday. I called the hotel and left a message for him to call me at the squad."

"Marvelous." Cassidy sank the ten.

At the next table a tall, thin Negro called Jersey Red was hustling a white uniformed navy bosun who'd probably been hot at his local hall in some southern state and thought that might carry him in the big city. Red had won the first game close and lost the second on an unlikely scratch, won the third close, and now they were on their fourth and the stakes had climbed each game as the bosun gained confidence.

"How'd you do with the other guy?" Orso asked.

"Perry Werth. A place over on West Eighty-fourth. The neighbor hasn't seen them for a couple of days, and from what I gather, she keeps her eye out."

"Them?"

"He's married. One kid."

"Married? No shit? How does that work, a fairy married and having a kid?"

"I don't know. Maybe he's the guy pulling the strings, the one who's running the others."

"Where does he work?"

"His neighbor says he's a salesman but doesn't know the company. He's on the road a lot. She's going to call me when Werth shows up again." Cassidy ran the last three balls and slid the counters over. "Game. Another?"

"Nah, I've got to go." Orso rolled down his sleeves and slipped into his jacket. "I guess we're waiting till Stanley and Perry show up." He took out his wallet and put ten dollars on the felt. "Are you going to go back and ask the general if he knows them too?"

"Sure, when I get pictures of them. I admire a man who can lie with a perfectly straight face. I like to watch an expert work." Cassidy collected his shoulder rig from under his jacket on one of the chairs by the window. As he put on the harness, the bosun's voice rose in anger at the next table.

"I'm not paying you, man. You hustled me. I'm not paying."

"A bet's a bet," Red said. "You'd have taken my money if you won."

"Yeah, as if I could win. I ain't paying no nigger hustler." The man's raised voice stilled the games at other tables, and men turned to watch.

"Fifty dollars." Red unscrewed his split cue. He laid the more delicate tip end on the table and held the heavier butt casually by his side.

"Fuck you, fifty dollars. I'll pay the time. That's it." The bosun was a big man. He had a couple of inches and thirty pounds on Red.

"That's it?"

"Yeah. That's it."

"Okay." Red brought the heavy butt of the cue up and over and hit the bosun on the top of the head. The man bounced off the table and dropped facedown on the floor without a move to break his fall. A trickle of blood showed on the crown of his crew-cut head. Red bent over and took the man's wallet from his back pocket. He removed some bills and held them up for Cassidy and Orso. "Fifty dollars. What he owes." He put the money in his pocket, dropped the wallet by the unconscious man, picked up the other piece of his cue, nodded at Cassidy and Orso, and left.

"You ever play him?" Orso asked.

"Red? No. He's too good for me."

The man on the floor groaned. They stepped around him and went downstairs and out into the beginning of rush hour.

"Buy you a drink," Orso offered.

"No, thanks. I've got a couple of things to do and then I'm going to go meet Dylan."

"How's that going?"

"Jesus, Tony, I think I'm sunk."

"Run while you can."

"Too late."

"You give her keys to the apartment?"

"Yes."

"Give a broad the keys, the next thing you know you're standing up in front of some monsignor doing the death-till-you-part thing. I could shoot you now and save you some trouble." Orso slapped him on the shoulder.

"I'll see you tomorrow." He raised a hand, and a taxi darted across a couple of lanes and pulled to the curb to pick him up.

• • •

Cassidy spotted the man with ginger hair waiting in a doorway down the block when he and Orso left Ames. He stepped out to follow as Cassidy turned toward Times Square and the subway station. He picked him up again when he stopped to buy cigarettes at the superette on Broadway, and the man was up the block showing a strong interest in the new records in the window of Sam Goody's. Cassidy studied him while he tore the cellophane from the pack of Luckies. The man wore a light blue seersucker suit, a yellow button-down shirt, and a paisley tie, not the costume Cassidy would have chosen for a shadow job. He looked up and saw Cassidy watching him and seemed unperturbed that he had been discovered. When Cassidy started south again, the man followed.

The man rode the far end of the rush-hour-packed subway car. He looked around with bright curiosity at his fellow riders, the polyglot, multihued population of New York, and Cassidy wondered if he had ever been on the subway before. He followed Cassidy up out of the 12th Street exit and down Hudson Street. Cassidy went into the White Horse and ordered a beer and took it to a table by the window. The man came in a minute later. He ordered a gin and tonic and carried it over to Cassidy's table. He sat down and took a sip of the drink and sighed. "Ah, that's good." He offered his hand across the table. "My name's Crofoot."

Cassidy ignored the hand.

Crofoot pulled it back without embarrassment. "To me, the gin and tonic is the true sign of spring. It's not something you drink in the cold months, but when those first warm days come and you have that first gin and tonic. Ah. The lime, the quinine, the cold, clear bite of the gin. It's a promise of summer and wonderful things to come." He raised his glass to Cassidy and took another sip with evident pleasure. "So, Detective Cassidy, how was your trip to New Jersey? Interesting, huh? Dead men walking. Resurrected toddlers. What do you make of all that?"

"Who are you?"

"Why does someone appropriate a dead child's name?"

"To build a new identity."

"Right." He saluted Cassidy with his glass. "And who does that? Better, who needs to do that and knows how?"

Cassidy recognized the easy arrogance of someone whose position in the world allowed him to not give a damn what other people thought. "You're not FBI. Your clothes are too good, and you don't have an agent's nervy thing of always wondering if Hoover's watching him, and you don't have their earnest look of true believers. Not a cop. A spook."

Crofoot smiled.

"CIA."

"Why not?"

"Who was Alex Ingram?"

"Alex Ingram was a KGB sleeper agent. Do you know what a sleeper agent is?"

"Tell me."

"He's someone the KBG infiltrated to this country undercover who then does nothing but establish a strong identity and history here, a legend that makes him look like any other citizen, and then he sleeps until he's awakened for whatever job his control has for him. Alex Ingram came in as a child probably before the war when there were waves of refugees from all over Europe. We think he was nine or ten when he got here. He grew up as American as apple pie, except for the fact that whoever brought him up made sure he stayed a good Commie so that when the time came he could do his all for Mother Russia."

"And the time is now? What was his mission? What was he doing before someone killed him?"

"We thought you might be able to enlighten us."

"No. You already know what he was doing. You just want to see how much I know."

Crofoot smiled. "The NYPD seems to be hiring a brighter brand of cop these days. So what do you know?"

"It's blackmail. Ingram gets men in bed with other men and takes pictures. The targets are important—politicians, military, maybe successful businessmen with families, social position, people with major influence. If it comes out that they're fairies, they're going to lose everything."

"Do you know who the targets are?" Crofoot asked.

"No. Do you?"

"No." Crofoot leaned back a little and touched his nose. It was the tell of a lie. "What did you find in Ingram's locker at the theater?"

"Nothing."

Crofoot studied Cassidy to see if he was lying. "I don't mean to insult you, Detective Cassidy, but there are matters here that are beyond your scope. I need to know if you found anything."

"Nothing. What do you know about a guy named Victor Amado?" Cassidy asked.

"You mean the late Victor Amado." Crofoot was showing that his lines into the police department were current.

"Was he a Commie too?"

"No. We had people checking his background the moment we learned he was someone Ingram knew. They were both rehearsing your father's play, but it went back farther than that. Ingram and Amado shared an apartment for a couple of months two years ago. But his background checks out. His parents are still alive. They've been living in the same place for thirty years, a little town in Connecticut up near Bridgeport. The father makes false teeth. There are plenty of people who knew him since he was a kid. You want the file on him, I'll have it sent over."

"The FBI probably wants the photos for Hoover's famous files. Why do you want them?" Cassidy asked.

"It's a KGB operation. Our brief is intelligence and counterintelligence."

"Not in this country. You guys are limited to overseas."

"Wouldn't it be nice if the world was that simple and neat. The FBI is good at what they do, bank robbers, car thieves, public enemy number six, but this is a little out of their field of expertise. We've been asked to step in and help."

"By J. Edgar?"

"No, by someone higher up the chain than Mr. Hoover. Until we know who the targets are, we cannot evaluate the threat."

"Uh-huh. Where am I in this?"

"We think you can help. You're a smart cop. Everybody I've talked to says so."

"What can I do that the CIA can't do?"

"Don't be coy. Murder is police business. You're better equipped for it than we are. Find Ingram's killer. We'll take it from there."

"I'm off the case. You want to talk to Detectives Bonner and Newly."

"We have some influence. We could get you back on the case."

"No, thank you."

"You're working it anyway. Why not do it for us?"

Cassidy drank some of his beer and waited for the offer he knew was coming.

"Your father's sitting in an immigration holding cell waiting for his hearing. And you know how that hearing's going to end? They're going to ship him back to Russia. We can help with that."

"Put him on the street and we'll talk."

"Oh, I don't think it can work that way. One hand has to wash the other."

"You came to me, because you're getting nowhere and you think I've got something. You're right. I do. Get my father out and I'll tell you what I've learned."

"We'll eventually roll this up with or without your help. It may take longer, by which time your father will be knocking the rust off his Russian grammar."

Cassidy finished his beer and stood up. "See you around."

Crofoot remained unruffled. "Detective Cassidy, you think you know what's going on. It's much more complicated than you imagine."

"That's all right. I've been confused most of my life. I'm used to it." He started for the door. There was something Crofoot had said in passing that was important. He needed to get someplace where he could think to see if he could reconstruct the conversation and spot it.

"Interesting woman, Dylan McCue." Cassidy kept going. "A wonderful coincidence that she ended up in an apartment in your building a couple of days after you began investigating Ingram's murder." Cassidy came back to the table and gripped the back of a chair and stared at Crofoot. Cassidy said nothing. His chest ached.

"Sit down. We have a lot to talk about."

27

Leah and her stepmother, Megan Cassidy, got out of a taxi at Lexington
and 44th Street. They walked through Grand Central Station oblivious to
the commuters hurrying toward the trains, oblivious to the giant Kodak
color photo above the east balcony that showed spring in Yosemite Val-
ley, oblivious to the mural of the stars on the domed ceiling. Leah carried
a small overnight bag that held an old flannel nightgown, slippers, her
makeup, a hairbrush and comb, a package of Kotex, a pint of brandy, and
a small bottle of codeine tablets her husband had been given after he broke
his arm playing touch football in the park. They went out onto 42nd Street.

"Are you okay?" Megan asked.

"Yes. I'm fine." Leah's jaw was set.

"What will you tell Mark if there are any"—she hesitated—"problems?"

"That I'm having female troubles. He won't want to know any more."

They entered the Commodore Hotel and went purposefully through
the lobby to the elevators. Megan had booked a room on the sixth floor,
and she had the key in her hand, but that was not where they were going.
It was a precaution, a small price paid for legitimacy in case anyone asked
them where they were going. The guilty flee where no one pursues.

They rode up past six without speaking and got off at the eleventh
floor and walked down the corridor to room 1109.

"You're sure?"

"I'm sure."

A gray-haired woman with a severe, pinched face answered the door
and led them down the short corridor to the bedroom. She wore a black
dress with a white lace collar and looked like a small-town librarian who
would not tolerate talking in the reading room. The doctor was a short,

pudgy man in his midforties who had tried to add seriousness to a cherub's face by growing a thick mustache. He had red-rimmed eyes like a rabbit. He had removed his suit jacket and had rolled up the sleeves to his white dress shirt. He nodded to Megan and Leah, unsure which was his client.

"I'm Leah—"

He interrupted. "No, no, please, I don't need to know your name. It's better that way."

There was a large empty suitcase on the luggage rack near the window. The bed had been stripped, and the covers and spread were folded on a chair. The mattress had been covered with a plastic sheet and an old cotton blanket from the suitcase. The doctor's instruments were laid out on a towel on the bureau top: dilators, curettes, speculum. A box of large gauze pads was open on a table near the bed next to a bottle of disinfectant.

Leah looked at the plastic-covered bed and then at the cold metal lined up on the towel. She looked at Megan with wide eyes and a face drained and white. Megan nodded toward the door, but Leah shook her head and turned to the doctor. "All right."

"Mrs. Grant will help you prepare."

The woman in the black dress led Leah to the bathroom.

"Do you have the money?" the doctor asked.

"Yes." Megan removed an envelope from her purse and handed it to him. He opened it and counted the money carefully, nodded, and put the envelope in a pocket of his jacket that hung near the door.

"Will you be with her afterward?"

"Yes."

"Is she allergic to penicillin?"

"No."

He handed her a small bottle of pills. "She should take two a day until all the pills are gone. A precaution against infection. One in the morning and one in the evening until they're gone. That's important."

"All right."

"She can expect some bleeding, some cramps. This is normal. If the bleeding is excessive, if she bleeds through a pad an hour, take her to a hospital. Tell them about the procedure. Do not try to conceal it. If she is bleeding excessively, it's important they know she recently underwent a D and C. Do not call me."

"All right."

"Just in case, that's all. Just in case. I was . . . I am a good doctor."

Leah came out of the bathroom wearing her old flannel nightgown. Her hair was tied back severely and her face was pale and stiff. She walked to the bed and lay down on her back, and the plastic crackled under her. A few moments later Mrs. Grant came out of the bathroom.

"If you'd like, you may wait in the bathroom," the doctor told Megan.

"No. I'll stay here." She moved to the bed and took Leah's hand.

• • •

"Vandalism, pure and simple. I can't believe anyone thought he was going to make a buck doing this. Just the urge to destroy." Jerry Kulin's voice was thick with outrage, and it echoed in the marble hall of the James Farley Post Office on Eighth Avenue.

Cassidy could see that someone had wrecked a dozen of the brass-and-glass post office box doors in the bank of thousands that pierced the marble wall. Box 1289, the box to which Ingram's driver's license had been sent, was one of them. Its door hung by one hinge.

"I mean, what the hell did he think he'd find, an envelope full of money? A postcard from Grandma's more likely. Someone's Social Security check if he's real lucky, and how's he going to cash that?" Kulin was a post office supervisor, and he took the destruction personally.

"Did anyone see anything?"

"Yeah. A guy with a big hammer. Bang, bang, bang, bang. He whacked a whole bunch of boxes, then went back and grabbed what was inside."

"What did he look like?"

"Six different people gave me six different descriptions."

Cassidy thought of the hammers in Ribera's studio. "Big? Maybe a beard?"

"Not big. No. No one said big. No one said a beard. Medium height. He wore a hat."

"Could it have been a woman?"

"A woman? You ever seen a woman strong enough to do that?"

"Yes." Had he said anything to Dylan about Ingram's mailbox? That night in Bickford's when the drunk kid was singing to his date. Did he? He couldn't remember. If what Crofoot told him was true, she was involved. In what? In whatever led to Ingram's death and what came afterward. So everything she told him was a lie. No. Not everything. Some things were true. Weren't they? No. Everything was a lie.

NIGHT LIFE ··· 215

• • •

Bud Franklin came out of the squad room toilet buttoning his fly. The phone on his desk rang, and he limped to it and caught it on the fourth ring. "Franklin, Vice." He leaned his butt against the desk and massaged his left leg with his free hand. He knew it was the bone that hurt, not the muscle, but he kneaded it anyway hoping for relief that would not come without pills.

"Bud, it's Willa. I've got something for you. It could be good."

He met her at O'Hara's. It was early and the joint was nearly empty. He picked up a beer and a shot and carried it back to the table where Willa Grant chewed the cherry from a double Manhattan. She still wore the black dress with a white lace collar that made her look like a small-town librarian.

"Still limping," she said.

"Yeah. So what?"

"I'm just saying."

"I'm always going to be limping. You fall out a three-story window, you end up limping."

"Fall? Thrown is what I heard."

"You could get yourself a smack in the mouth without working too much harder, Willa. What've you got?"

"The doc did a procedure up at the Commodore today. You told me to let you know when I saw anything good, so here I am."

"Yeah?"

"Not a hooker, not a college girl, none of the usual. This one was classy. You could tell when she came in. A rich bitch. You said, keep your eye out for a real score. This could be one. I figured you might get some leverage on her, an abortion and all, so I went into her purse when she was in the next room. I copied down her name and address. Park Avenue." She pushed a piece of paper across the table.

Franklin read it. " 'Mrs. Mark C. Buckman. Seven forty Park.' Okay. Could be her husband doesn't know. Could be she doesn't want him to know. I'll check her out." He put the paper in his pocket and shoved a bill at Willa.

"Ten bucks? That's it?"

"If it pans out, you'll get more. First I've got to find out who she is."

28

It took Cassidy half an hour to search Dylan's apartment, and what he did not find worried him as much as what he did. He did not find any letters, photographs, or mementos of a past. He did find a blue steel automatic in her bedside table. There was a shell in the chamber, and the safety was off. He racked the shell out and ejected the clip. The top round had a hole drilled in the point of the slug. It was a hollow point, designed to expand quickly when it hit flesh, to tear a terrible hole, to make a mortal wound. A comfort to have close by on a dark night. He put it back where he found it and went out into the day.

• • •

Orso was playing slapsies with Benny the Dip outside of John's Pizzeria on Bleecker Street. Orso was proud of his quick hands, but Benny was the best pickpocket in the boroughs, a man who once dipped the wallets of the three parole board members after they believed his solemn pledges of reform and put him back on the street. His hands were quick enough to snatch flies out of the air. They rested palms down on Orso's hands. The game was simple. If Orso could slap the back of one of Benny's hands, he remained the slapper. If he missed, they reversed positions and Benny became the slapper until he missed.

"How're you doing, Cassidy?" Benny asked. Orso took advantage of the distraction, but when he slapped, Benny's hand was gone, and all he got was his own palm.

Benny put his hands out palms up and smiled. "My turn."

"Shit." Orso put his hands on Benny's, and as they came to rest, Benny struck right over left, hitting the back of Orso's hand with a crack that made Cassidy wince. "Hey, I wasn't ready," Orso complained.

"Are you ready now?"

"Yeah."

Crack. The same right over left, and the back of Orso's hand reddened. Orso tried watching Benny's eyes and then tried watching Benny's hands, but neither strategy worked. Slap, crack, slap, slap, crack, one hand over to the other, both hands up and over to slap both of Orso's, until both of Orso's hands were red. Orso would not quit. A schoolyard game played with grown-up stubbornness.

"Okay, Benny. I need him in one piece."

"Sure." Benny let his hands fall. Orso faked a punch at him, and Benny flinched. Orso smiled, an inch of honor regained.

"Benny, stay off the Stem for a while. You dipped a deputy mayor outside the Winter Garden the other night. He wants us to bring some heat."

"Sure, Cassidy. I got other places I can work."

"Why don't you take a break for a week or so?"

"Are you kidding me? I've got two kids. Do you know what it costs to buy shoes these days? They're out of them a couple of months later. Do you know what it costs to feed boys? Take a break, my ass. I wish there were two of me."

Orso and Cassidy went into John's so Orso could get a slice. John Sasso did not sell slices to the general public, but Orso was special. The slice turned into two slices. He folded the first lengthwise and held it away so the oil wouldn't get on his jacket and took half of it in one bite. Cassidy smoked a cigarette and watched the people passing the plate-glass window.

Orso wiped his mouth and fingers on bunched napkins. "Fast, man. He is fast."

"When was the last time you beat him?"

"Fifth grade."

"Give it up."

"I can beat him. I've just got to think on it a bit."

"I need you to do something for me. A tail job. You're going to need a couple of extra people. I don't want him to know it's happening." He told him about Ribera and the studio in the building on Prince Street.

"What's up with him?"

"He's tied to Ingram, but I don't know how." A half-truth. Ribera was tied to Dylan, and he wanted to know what that meant. And he didn't want to tell Orso that he'd been played for a sucker. Pride. Anger.

"I'll check it out. Hey, by the way, that broad Rhonda you were banging last year, works for the *Post*, she called the squad room. Said she needed to talk to you."

Cassidy shut himself into a phone booth on the corner of Seventh Avenue, dropped a dime, and dialed the *Post*'s switchboard. A series of clicks and then, "Rhonda Raskin."

"It's Michael, Rhonda. You called."

"General Wilson Caldwell."

"Who?"

"Don't do that, Mike. General Wilson Caldwell lived on the sixth floor of that apartment house you wanted me to case. It's the name I mentioned when the Feds interrupted our drink at the Plaza. What's your interest? What'd he do?"

"I have no interest in General Caldwell." This lie would be a small weight in the balance sending him to hell.

"Uh-uh. It's too great a coincidence. Give."

"I don't know what you're talking about. What coincidence?"

"It came in over the wire an hour ago. Caldwell shot himself. So give."

"I'm still working the case. I don't know where he connects. I don't know why he did it. When I have the story, you'll have the story."

"Pinkie swear, Cassidy. Pinkie swear."

"I know. I know."

• • •

Cassidy found Skinner in his morgue office with his feet on the desk. He was reading a Parke-Bernet auction catalog. "Hey, Cassidy, how are you doing? Jesus, I wish I were rich. You know what they want for a seventeenth-century desk over there at Parke-Bernet? Forty thousand dollars. For a piece of furniture. I had the money, I'd buy it in a minute. Beautiful." He reluctantly put the catalog aside. "What are you here to bust my chops about?"

"General Wilson Caldwell. One thirty-three East Sixty-fourth."

"Oh, yeah."

"Cause of death?"

"Lost half his brain matter out the back of his head."

"Suicide?"

"Absolutely. Gun in the mouth. Hand on the gun. Locked apartment."

• • •

There were two squad cars in front of 133. Cassidy recognized the patrol-man leaning against the fender of one of them. "Hackmayer, right?"

"Yeah. How you doing, Detective?"

Cassidy nodded at the building. "General Caldwell?"

"Yeah."

"Who's catching?"

"The Pig and The Nig . . . Sorry . . . Detectives Bonner and Newly, and some suit from the FBI. You going up?"

"No." He'd be as welcome as a nun at a bachelor party. He walked to-ward Park Avenue. Caldwell dead with his gun in his mouth. Did he do that to him? Was he the push that sent him over the edge?

29

A uniformed doorman with the bearing of an admiral opened 740 Park Avenue's brass-bound door and said, "Good morning, Mrs. Buckman."

"Good morning, Patrick," Leah said, and went out into the sunshine. She walked east on 71st Street, unaware that Bud Franklin limped behind her cursing her fast pace. She went to her dressmaker's shop on 75th between Second and First Avenues and spent an hour choosing fabrics and cuts for two dresses and two suits for the fall. Franklin watched from the other side of the street. When he realized she would be awhile, he took a stool at the end of the counter in a coffee shop and nursed two cups of coffee and a Danish.

Leah left the dress shop and stopped at the fruit stand on the corner of First Avenue. She bought a bag of plums and a bag of peaches and bit into one of the plums as she stepped back out into the sunshine. A fat man in a rumpled tan cotton suit was leaning on a car at the curb. He pushed away from it and limped toward her. "Mrs. Buckman? I need to talk to you for a minute." He showed her a leather case with a badge and ID.

"Has something happened to my brother?"

"Not that I know of."

"He's a cop too. Are you a friend of his?"

"We know each other."

"What do you want to talk to me about?"

"Mrs. Buckman, you had an operation last week, right?"

Leah said nothing, but she could feel her face tighten and her heart surge.

"An illegal abortion, right?"

"No. I don't know what you're talking about."

"Yes, you do. The Commodore Hotel. Room eleven oh nine. You came with some other broad. She carried the money. Shall I tell you what you wore? How much it cost?"

"What do you want?"

He put a hand on her elbow to steer her up the block. "Let's take a little walk, and we'll discuss it."

• • •

"Cassidy?"

"Yes." He cradled the phone against his shoulder while he lit a cigarette.

"Al Skinner here. What are you, these days, Typhoid Mary? Half the stiffs I get in connect to you. We've got a guy on a slab here who's got your business card in his pocket. I thought you might want to come take a look. They pulled him out of Potter's."

"That's me you hear coming down the hall."

Near the lower end of Manhattan, the East River makes a sharp bend between the Williamsburg and Manhattan Bridges. On an ebb tide an eddy in the bend picks up anything loose coming downriver afloat or submerged and sweeps it into a stretch of backwater on the Brooklyn side. The backwater is called Wallabout Bay on the charts but is known as Potter's Field to the cops who pick up the drowned bodies there. People who drown in the winter often stay down until spring raises the water temperature and the gases form and the bodies rise. The first month that happens is usually April, and so, as punishment for their transgressions, members of the New York Police Department who have fucked up in small ways are sent once a week to check Potter's Field. On that particular day, the three men who drew the duty were lucky. The body they found bumping against the bank in the oily water amid the garbage and bits of wood, soaked paper, soggy boxes, and orange peels was not a gas-filled floater-bloater up from the depths but a fresh corpse that had been in the water for only a couple of days.

Eddie Freed, the lawyer, lay naked on a gurney in the Bellevue morgue. His skin was pale and mottled. His jaw was slack, and his dead eyes were rolled up as if trying to see the dark-rimmed bullet hole in the middle of his forehead.

"Do you know who he is?" Skinner asked. "He wasn't carrying a wallet."

"Yeah. Eddie Freed, a two-bit lawyer."

"Why's he carrying your card?"

"I went to ask him some questions the other day. It looks like he lied to me, the stupid bastard. Being half smart got him killed. How long was he in the water?"

"Not long. A couple of days at the outside."

Cassidy leaned to look at the wound in Freed's forehead. "What do you think, a twenty-two?"

"Uh-uh. I'd say a thirty-two from the size of it." ·

"Do you mind?" Cassidy rolled Freed so he could see the back of his head. The man's flesh was cold and clammy. "No exit wound. You'd think a thirty-two would go through and through."

"Not always. And who knows? Maybe the shooter used a low load. Maybe a hollow point."

The .32 in Dylan's drawer?

"Where's his stuff?"

Eddie Freed died without much in his pockets. He went into the river wearing the same suit he had worn when he met with Cassidy and Orso in his office. The suit had been hung on a hanger to dry, and the contents of his pockets had been spread out on old towels. There was a key ring with six keys, home and office, Cassidy guessed. A white cotton handkerchief, a sodden pack of cigarettes, a cheap knockoff of a Zippo, a small plastic case holding toothpicks, a black hard rubber comb, a Timex watch whose second hand still flicked around the dial like the ad promised, a Parker fountain pen, and one of the new ballpoint pens people were starting to use, a wallet. It held fourteen dollars and not much else, a few business cards, and a condom in a foil package.

•   •   •

The receptionist with the black, black hair looked up expectantly when Cassidy opened the office door. Her face fell when she recognized him. There was nobody else in the waiting room of Fitcher, Freed, and Alamek.

"Mr. Freed's not here." She dismissed him with a look and went back to her typing. She did not approve of him. He wondered how much she had heard when they were bullying Freed.

"No, I know that, Miss . . . ?"

"Gedge. Mrs. Gedge. Mrs. Arnold Gedge."

"Mrs. Gedge, actually I came to talk to one of the other partners, Mr. Alamek or Mr. Fitcher."

For a moment she looked confused.

"There are no other partners. Fitcher and Alamek are just names on the door. Mr. Freed thought it made the firm seem more substantial. Gave it more class. There's no point in waiting for him. He hasn't been in for a couple of days. I don't know when he'll be back. Leave your card and I'll have him call."

"Mrs. Gedge, Mr. Freed's dead." He had never found a good way to deliver that information. "Someone shot him. I'm sorry."

She slumped back in her chair and looked at Cassidy with wide eyes. "Shot him? Why would anyone shoot Mr. Freed?"

"I don't now. I'd like to find that out. I'm hoping you can help me. How well did you know him?"

"I've worked for him ever since he opened the office six years ago. He was a wonderful boss, always doing something extra, flowers sometimes, or an extra five dollars in the pay envelope if there had been a lot of work. Always wanted to know how I was, how Arnold was. That's Mr. Gedge."

"Any family?"

"He has a brother out in California. In Hollywood where they make the movies. He's an accountant with one of the studios. Oh, dear. I'm going to have to let him know, aren't I? Poor Mr. Freed. Why would anyone want to shoot him?"

"Was there a Mrs. Freed?"

"Well, there was. But she took off when he had the troubles. Packed her bags, cleaned out the bank account, and took off." Her voice was frosty.

"What troubles were those?"

Her face closed up, and her mouth set. "I really don't know. It was before he opened the office. None of my business, I'm sure." She crossed her arms over her chest as a barrier.

"Mrs. Gedge, he's dead, and nothing you tell me can hurt him. But the more I know, the better my chance of finding who killed him. You'd like that, wouldn't you?"

She nodded.

"I can tell that you were a good friend to him as well as a good employee. Help me find who killed him. Tell me what you know. What were the troubles you mentioned?"

She thought about it for a while. Cassidy lit a cigarette and waited. Finally she sighed and uncrossed her arms as if opening the gates. "Like I said, he was a good lawyer. He went to Harvard Law School. Top of the heap. Before he opened this office, he worked for one of those big white-shoe law firms up on Fifth Avenue. I can give you the name. He used to talk about it. Big offices with wood paneling and leather chairs. Lots of lawyers. Everything done first class. Coffee served in china. You know. Anyway, they fired him."

"What for?"

"They said he was a Communist."

"Did he fight it?"

"How could he fight it? He *was* a Communist."

"Did he belong to some organization that was on the attorney general's list?"

"You bet he did. He belonged to the American Communist Party. And he was proud of it. Never tried to hide it. But that big firm, they said they couldn't keep him on with him being a Communist and all." She stopped as if she had suddenly thought of something. "I shouldn't be telling you this. I could get in trouble for working for a Red."

"Not from me."

"He said the Communist Party was the only hope of the little man, you know. He said the deck was stacked against the lower classes. The rich get richer and they do it on the backs of the poor. I don't know much about history or politics, but that's what Mr. Freed believed, and he was a good man. He did a lot of pro bono work for people who needed help." She sniffled. "He was a good man." She found a handkerchief in her top drawer and blew her nose.

"Mrs. Gedge, did Mr. Freed call anyone or meet anyone after my partner and I left the other day?"

She dabbed her eyes dry. "Yes. He called someone and then he went right out. He didn't come back after that."

"Can you tell me who he called?" It had to be the man who was paying Ingram's rent.

"No. I didn't place the call. He did it himself from his desk."

"Did he do that often, place his own calls?"

"No. Almost never. I placed all his calls. He said it was more professional."

"I'd like to take a look through his office. I could get a warrant if you need me to do that."

"No, that's all right. You go ahead. What's the difference now, I guess?"

Cassidy sat in Freed's chair. He found Freed's calendar book on the desktop. He leafed through a couple of months but found nothing of interest. He poked through the drawers and found two mismatched leather gloves, a file of old tax returns, a well-thumbed copy of Karl Marx's *Das Kapital*, a pair of thin rubber overshoes, a box of #2 pencils with three pencils left, a bottle of black ink, a ream of typing paper, and a couple of yellow legal pads. In the top right-hand drawer he found Freed's checkbook. Freed paid himself erratically and what it added up to was less per month than what he paid Mrs. Gedge, whose first name turned out to be Emily. When he shoved the checkbook back in the drawer, he found a crumpled strip of paper covered with clear tape. He flattened it on the desk. A phone number with an Algonquin exchange. Cassidy pulled the phone to him and dialed the number. A man answered after the third ring. "Yes?"

There was something about the quality of the man's voice that made Cassidy hesitate.

"This is the Bell Telephone Company calling. We're checking to see if you've had any problems on your line."

"No."

"Is this Algonquin 7-5897?"

"Yes."

"To whom am I speaking, please?"

There was a click as the man hung up. Cassidy sat holding the phone for a moment. Only three one-word answers, but there was something about the voice. Had he heard it before? Where?

30

The only noise in the squad room came from a detective at a desk near the window stabbing out a report with two fingers on an old Underwood. There was a note on Cassidy's desk telling him to call Freddie Barron at a Trafalgar number. He did not recognize the name, but he dialed and lit a cigarette while the phone rang somewhere in the city.

"Mr. Barron's office."

"Mr. Barron, please."

"Who's calling, please?"

"Detective Michael Cassidy. I'm with the police department."

"Just a moment, please."

The phone receiver clunked against a desk, and he could hear the click of heels on a hard floor. Another extension picked up.

"Detective Cassidy?" The voice was soft and unfamiliar.

"Yes."

"This is Freddie Barron?" The questioning tone indicated he did not know if Cassidy would recognize him. Cassidy didn't.

"What can I do for you, Mr. Barron?"

"I'm Stanley Fisher's boss? At Lord & Taylor? Detective Orso, I believe was his name, asked me to call this number when Stanley returned from Chicago?"

Cassidy groped. "Oh, wait. Stanley Fisher. The window decorator."

"Window designer. Yes."

"Is he back?"

"Yes. That's why I called." There was an edge to Barron's voice, impatience at Cassidy's dimness.

"Is he in the store now?"

"Yes."

"I'll be there in fifteen minutes. Don't tell him I'm coming."

"Are we to worry about this? Has Stanley done something awful?"

"No, no. I just want to talk to him about something he might have seen. How will I find you?"

"Ask anyone on the main floor. They all know me."

Cassidy followed a tall, elegantly dressed saleswoman with upswept blond hair and a haughty manner. Her high heels clicked on the parquet, and her girdled butt under her calf-length silk skirt was as solid and unyielding as a sack of sand. Women crowded the store. They had money in their pockets these days and were still excited about spending it after the wartime austerity. They quested through the aisles, shopping with a peculiar avidity and focus, like bird dogs quartering a field in search of game. Faceless plastic mannequins posed on platforms dressed in the spring fashions of long, bright cotton skirts and blouses in jewel tones, wide-brimmed hats against the coming summer sun, and cotton gloves.

"You'll find him just over there by window four." She flicked a dark red fingernail to show him the direction and turned away as he said, "Thank you."

"Not at all," she said without interest and without looking back, and then she stilted away on long legs.

Freddie Barron had the square, solid build of a middle linebacker and a soft, round face. His voice was low and breathy. "He was here a moment ago. Judith, where did Stanley go?"

A woman in blue jeans and a man's white dress shirt was carefully placing a large papier-mâché swan on a mirror lake in a window that looked out on Fifth Avenue. A small crowd of people stood outside watching her work. She adjusted the swan, glanced over at Cassidy, and then spoke to Freddie. "He said he had to make a phone call." Her voice was annoyed.

"I'm sure he'll be right back."

"Not if there's work to be done."

Freddie raised his eyebrows at Cassidy and shrugged.

"Where's the phone he'd use? I'll go find him," Cassidy said.

"You go through that door over there marked Employees Only. There's a long corridor and a pay phone at the end just before the exit."

"Tell me what he looks like."

"Tall, slender, dark hair, about twenty-five or -six. He's wearing chocolate-colored light gabardine slacks and a divine lime green sports coat."

"He's going to be hard to miss."

"That's the point, I believe. Stanley doesn't want anyone to miss him."

Cassidy pushed through the door and went down the corridor. There was no one at the pay phone. He opened the exit door and looked out into a brick alley that led to 38th Street. Twenty yards away a man in chocolate trousers and a lime green jacket stood with his back turned at the alley mouth talking to someone Cassidy could not see. Cassidy stepped out, and the heavy metal fire door slammed shut behind him. Stanley Fisher turned at the sound, saw Cassidy, and then turned back to say something to the other person. He chopped one hand down in emphasis, and while Cassidy could not hear the words, the tone was angry.

The shots were loud, flat cracks, like two boards banging together. Fisher stumbled back and went down, and his head bounced on the pavement. Cassidy dug his gun from under his arm. The man at the end of the alley raised his gun. Cassidy snapped a shot at him but knew it went wide. The man fired. Cassidy crashed down behind a stack of garbage cans. Shots blew brick chips from the wall above him. His breath came hard and his heart jumped in his chest. He gathered himself, took a deep breath, and lunged out from cover, gun up and ready, but the alley mouth was empty except for the body on the ground. He snuck a quick look around the corner of the building. The sidewalk was deserted. He ran to the corner. Foot traffic was heavy along Fifth Avenue and he could see no one who might have been the gunman. People broke around him like water around a rock. Many of them stared at him curiously, and a few shied from him, and he realized he still carried his pistol in his hand. He holstered it and ran back to the alley.

Stanley Fisher groaned. Cassidy went down on one knee next to him. The green jacket and the white shirt under it were dark with blood. Fisher groaned again and opened his eyes. "What happened?" His voice was as thin and pale as water.

"Who shot you, Stanley?"

"Shot me?"

"Who shot you?"

"No. No."

In the war Cassidy had seen men stitched by bullets who survived, and others with flesh wounds who died, as if the minor puncture of their flesh made them so acutely aware of their mortal vulnerability that it sucked away their will to live. Stanley Fisher was slipping out. "Stanley, I'm a cop. Tell me who shot you. Alex Ingram's dead. So is Victor Amado. Who did it? Why is someone killing you guys? What happened? Tell me what happened."

Fisher tried to speak, coughed blood, and tried again.

"Say it again, Stanley. I didn't get it. Say it again." Cassidy leaned down close to the dying man's mouth and heard a whisper that came like smoke with his last breath.

• • •

Hours of filling out forms, writing reports, answering questions, the inevitable aftermath of a shooting involving an officer of the New York Police Department. Everything in triplicate banged out with four fingers on the old Smith Corona typewriter with the ancient ribbon. The first copy was dim. The last was a ghost of the report, and it would all disappear into filing cabinets, forgotten within days, lost forever, another dead man in an alley, another poor sap's story finished long before the ending he had written for himself.

"You fired one shot?" The Internal Affairs man looked at him with mild interest.

"Yes. One."

"Broke a side window in a forty-nine Buick Skylark. That's going to cost the city a couple of bucks."

Cassidy said nothing.

"Did you fire first, or did he?"

"I told you. He put two into Fisher's chest. He brought the gun up to shoot me. I fired a shot. He fired two."

"Right. So you fired first."

"No. He shot Fisher twice before I fired."

"Sure. Right. I've got it." He made a note on the form on his clipboard, turned his head away and failed to suppress a belch. "Sorry. Chili for lunch. I should know better."

"Are we done?"

"Yeah. Read this through and sign it." He offered Cassidy the clipboard.

Susdorf appeared next to the desk and took the clipboard before Cassidy could. "We'll take it from here, Lieutenant."

Cherry showed the I.A. lieutenant his badge. The lieutenant looked at the two FBI agents and at Cassidy. He looked at his clipboard in Susdorf's hand as if thinking about asking for it back. Then he nodded, stood up, and walked away.

Susdorf leafed through the report. Cherry shoved the gooseneck lamp out of the way and put a haunch on the corner of Cassidy's desk and grinned at him. Cassidy lit a cigarette and waited.

"Was he alive when you got to him?" Susdorf asked.

"Yes."

"What did he say?"

"Nothing."

"Nothing? Did you ask him who shot him?"

"I asked."

Susdorf waited for more. "Well, what did he say?"

"Nothing. He was gone. A couple of breaths and that was it."

"It says here"—he waved the report—"you were there to talk to this, uh, Fisher, about the Ingram case. You're off the Ingram case. Bonner and Newly are on the Ingram case. You want to explain?"

"Fisher's boss called me. He had my number from when Orso and I were working the case. Bonner and Newly weren't in the house when he called. I figured I might as well go down and talk to him. If he had a lead, I'd pass it on to Bonner and Newly."

"Yeah? And?"

"Somebody shot him. The lead's dead."

"You know, Cassidy, I get the feeling you're trying to play us. If I find out you're keeping stuff back on this case, I'm going to jam you up. This is a matter of national security. You do not fuck with it. Your father's already in the shit, but I'll turn your whole family inside out, your sister, her husband, your brother, his wife if I have to. Do you know what happens when the FBI begins asking questions about people, asking about their loyalty, how they conduct business, who their friends are? Do you know what happens? Suddenly they don't have the life they think they had. Their friends tend to disappear. Business opportunities evaporate. Your brother works for a TV network. A TV license is a federal license. Do you get my drift?"

Orso, drawn by the angry tone, came to lean on Cassidy's desk. "What's going on, Mike?"

"You, butt out," Cherry said.

"Go fuck yourself. This is my squad room."

Cherry was one of those men who always teetered on the edge of anger. It took little to push him over. He stood up, fists clenched. Blood rose in his face.

"Careful, Tony," Cassidy said. "He's an FBI agent, and Mr. Hoover's boys are a rough-and-ready bunch of accountants and lawyers."

Susdorf slapped the clipboard down on the desk with a bang. "All right. All right. Paul," he said to Cherry, "would you mind giving me a minute with Detective Cassidy? Detective Orso, may I ask the same of you?"

Orso winked at Cassidy and went off toward the coffeepot. Cherry kicked a chair out of his way as he left the squad room.

Susdorf pulled up a chair and sat down facing Cassidy. He scrubbed his face with his hand and sighed. "I don't understand you, Detective Cassidy. I don't understand you at all."

31

"I don't much understand you either. Of course, I don't give a shit. This business of understanding people is way overrated. Live and let live, I say. Still, what part of you was giving Agent Susdorf so much trouble?" Orso accepted his martini from Al and took an appreciative sip. "Mother's milk." He raised the glass to the after-work crowd thronging the bar at Toots Shor's. "God, I love this place. And some people say there isn't a heaven."

"He was disappointed in my lack of commitment and trust. We are at war with a godless system that wants to destroy our way of life. We should all be working for the common cause of freedom and democracy, and he doesn't feel that I am giving my all."

"Are you shitting me?"

"He wanted to know if I was a friend of Joe Stalin's and if I wanted Stalin's people to be running this country."

"Isn't Stalin dead?"

"Yeah, but his people, Tony. His people."

"And the country's going to fall because you did what?"

"I have been holding back on the Ingram case."

"Shame on you. So what'd you tell him?"

"Nothing."

"More than he deserves."

"When he was asking me questions, he forgot to ask the one he should have thought of first. How was Stanley Fisher connected to Alex Ingram? Why didn't he ask?"

" 'Cause he already knew?"

"Right."

"So what does that mean?"

"It means they're hiding things from us. They know things that we don't know, and trust doesn't run two ways."

"Yeah. Too bad Fisher didn't say something before he died."

"He did."

Orso started, and some martini sloshed from his glass. "What did he say?" He licked the gin from his wrist.

"Sweet shine."

"What?"

"He said it twice. There was something before and then he said, 'Shine. Sweet shine.' And then there was something at the end like 'ear' or 'mere.' I asked him again, but he was going. That was it."

"Great. Clears up everything."

"The man died saying it. It has to mean something."

"Sweet shine?"

"He said it twice."

•   •   •

Cassidy met Dylan for dinner at Minetta Tavern, where they had first eaten together.

They ordered, and Cassidy let Dylan talk while he watched her. Did she look different now that he knew what he knew? Did she act the same? Was it an act? She glanced up at him and smiled, and his heart squeezed in his chest.

"Is this boring you?"

"No."

She told him about the piece she was working on now, the replacement for the smashed sculpture. Part of it would be welded steel, and part would be forged bronze. They were using a foundry in Connecticut to pour the bronze. It was run by Basques from northern Spain who spoke a language that sounded like rocks cracking. It would represent a man breaking loose of earthly bounds. "At least that's what I think he said. Sometimes Ribera's English is a little strange."

Cassidy pushed his plate away and lit a cigarette.

"What's wrong, Michael?"

"Nothing."

"You haven't said a word."

"I was happy to listen to you."

"Did something happen?"

"No. Nothing."

"Something at work?" She watched him with grave eyes.

"No."

"Really?"

"Really."

"You'd tell me, wouldn't you?"

"There's nothing to tell." He picked up the bottle to pour the last of the wine, but she put her hand over her glass.

"I have to go back to work."

"Oh. All right."

"We're going to be working all night. That's how he is when he gets toward the end of something." She took a drag from his cigarette and gave it back. "I don't know when we'll finish. I think I'll sleep at my place."

"All right."

She shook her head as if it was not the answer she wanted. She got up and came around and kissed him and said, "I'll see you tomorrow."

He watched her walk away, straight backed, head held high, aware of the men watching her, and unconcerned. He sensed how much he was losing and wondered whether betrayal was always the reward for caring.

• • •

That night the dream he had had in the hospital came again. *He was on a dark street. Someplace familiar. Featureless buildings, but someplace he walked often. He knew it but did not recognize it. He was scared. Why was he scared? Something waited for him ahead in the darkness. There was a darker darkness ahead of him where something waited. He wanted to stop, but he kept walking. Victor Amado stood on the sidewalk ahead of him and told him to go back. Why was Amado telling him to go back? He kept walking. Amado disappeared. Now he was at the point of danger. Now. Turn around. It's here. Turn around!*

Cassidy woke gasping for breath. He got out of bed and went into the bathroom and splashed cold water on his face to wash away the last of sleep, to wake completely from the dream. He went into the living room and lit a cigarette and looked out across the dark river. It was a dream. Just a dream. It was the second time he'd had it.

In the distance, a train loaded with dressed carcasses rumbled along the elevated track leading into the meatpacking district and then stopped with a metal squeal of brakes. Crofoot had asked if Cassidy had found anything in Ingram's locker at the theater dressing room. How had he known that Cassidy had searched the locker? Nobody had been there but Victor Amado. Is that why Amado was in the dream? What was he warning Cassidy about? Amado had been tortured to death. By Crofoot? Maybe. Or by someone he knew. Susdorf hid that he knew of the relationship between Ingram and Fisher. Everyone was lying to him. His mind spun through the details, but he could get no grip. Ingram had died by mistake under torture, and what he had hidden had not been found. Amado was tortured to find it, tortured with a knife while Ingram's torturer had used pliers. Fisher had simply been executed. Two different torturers were looking for what Ingram hid, but someone else was cleaning up the loose ends of an operation. Whoever it was wasn't interested in whether Stanley Fisher knew where Ingram's photographs were. He just wanted him dead. And what about Perry Werth, the salesman? Where the hell was he?

He turned on the lamp and moved it so it threw light on the gray cold-water pipe that ran to the ceiling in the corner of the room. Two days ago he had brought the coin he found in Victor Amado's locker down from where he had hidden it in the squad room and had taped it there to the pipe with gray tape, and even knowing where it was he could not see it and had to feel for it. He scraped the tape loose with a fingernail and pulled it free and held it close to the light to examine it. It remained what it had always been—a common fifty-cent piece, indistinguishable from the millions like it in pockets and purses all over the country. He flicked it with his thumb, and it spun up into the air and then dropped to his open palm. He flipped it again, higher. It spun up in the light toward the high ceiling. As it fell, a boat horn blew on the river, and for a moment Cassidy took his eye off the coin. It hit his hand, bounced, ticked the table, fell to the floor, and rattled under the easy chair near the window.

"Shit."

He got down on his belly and reached deep under the chair and found it way at the back. It felt different. One edge of the coin felt thicker than the other. He held it to the light. Was one edge higher?

"Jesus." His heart raced.

He carried the coin into the kitchen and turned on the bright light over the counter and found a small paring knife. He stuck the tip in the crack where the two sides were separating and twisted, and the coin came apart. One side flipped away, rolled on the counter, and then fell over and rocked to a stop. The coin was hollow. The side in Cassidy's hand held a tiny piece of film. Cassidy tipped the coin toward the light, but he could make out nothing on the film. He put the coin down and protected it with an over-turned coffee cup and went to the bathroom to find the tweezers Gwen had left. He found a magnifying glass in a desk drawer.

He uncovered the hollow coin and teased up one edge of the film square with the knife point until he could grip it with the tweezers. He lifted it out. There was another square of film beneath it. He held the film up to the light and looked at it through the magnifier, but he still could not make out the image. He carefully put the film on the counter and pried up the next piece. There was another under it. There were five in all, five tiny pieces of film for which four men had died.

32

"Cassidy, it's six o'clock in the morning." The door opened as far as the safety chain would let it.

"I need a favor, Howie."

"Come back in a couple of hours."

"It's important."

"Yeah, yeah. Without it the world goes up in a mushroom cloud."

"Howie, what's going on? Who is it?" A woman's querulous voice from a distant bedroom.

"Mike Cassidy. He needs a favor. Go back to sleep, Marnie."

"Tell him to go to hell."

"Go to hell. Come on in. I'm awake now anyway."

Cassidy stepped past Howie Lodin into the basement apartment of a brownstone on West 4th. Lodin was a short, wide man in his thirties in a shabby blue cotton robe over striped pajamas. His hair was afly from sleep. He closed the door and led Cassidy down the hall to a small studio. The walls were covered with black-and-white photographs of New York City street scenes: a couple kissing in front of a movie theater advertising *The Big Heat*; a woman in a fur coat and high heels dancing with a man in a diaper and top hat on New Year's Eve; a street fair, garlanded with strings of lights, crowded with booths, dense with people, the Feast of San Gennaro in Little Italy; a dead man in a gutter leaking dark blood, one arm flung up on the pavement, his hat resting against his face; pigeons covering the statue of William Tecumseh Sherman at the south end of Central Park; laughing cops leading a sullen, handcuffed prisoner into a station house. There were a number of cameras on shelves near the window that looked out on a scruffy patch of garden.

Lodin took a cigarette from a box on the desk and lit it with a kitchen match scraped on the radiator. He coughed up morning phlegm and scratched his chest where his pajama top was unbuttoned. "Whatever it is, it'll have to wait till I have coffee. I'm shit for brains till then. You want some?"

"Sure." Cassidy followed him into the kitchen.

After the second strong and bitter cup, Lodin lit another cigarette, coughed, spat into the sink, and said, "What do you need?"

From somewhere at the back of the house Marnie's voice called, "Are you spitting in the sink? Howie, are you?"

"No," he yelled back, and raised his eyebrows to Cassidy as if to say, *What are you going to do?* Then he quietly turned on the tap for a moment.

Cassidy took an envelope from his pocket and slipped one of the squares of film onto the zinc top of the kitchen table. Lodin bent to look, the cigarette dangling from the corner of his mouth.

"Microfilm," he said. "Huh." He bent closer.

"What?"

"You mind if I take a closer look?"

"Go ahead."

Lodin went out of the room and came back with tweezers and a hand-held viewer. He slipped the square of microfilm into a slot and held the viewer up to the window light. "Huh."

"Come on."

"Color."

"So?"

"Unusual. Mostly you use microfilm to archive stuff, papers, historic documents, newspapers, store it for years, a couple of hundred, even. You don't use color for that. Color degrades easier than black-and-white, so if you're archiving, you use black-and-white."

"What do you use color for?"

"Well, if color is important to the image, like with a painting or something like that, an interior, and you don't care if the image lasts a hundred years, then you take it with color micro, but even if you don't care if it lasts, you've got to store it correctly. Too much heat, and the image degrades fast. My guess is this guy left it on a radiator or something."

"What do you mean?" Cassidy's voice was sharp.

"Well, I can see that it was color, and I can see that there were images, but it's all a blur now. See for yourself." He passed the viewer to Cassidy.

Cassidy held it to the light. There were streaks of color, shapeless forms, but nothing identifiable. "Shit." Ingram must have hidden the coin near a heat source in the theater wall behind his locker.

"I've got something that'll give us a bigger image in my studio. Maybe you can see something with it."

Lodin projected the image on a patch of bare wall. It was bigger but no clearer.

"Jesus . . ."

"Bad, huh."

"I was hoping . . . I've been chasing something. I thought this was going to clear it up. Is there any way to get the images back?"

"We can try developing them. We can do some things in the darkroom, dodging, burning, maybe clarify some stuff that's just mud in the viewer."

Cassidy hesitated. "I don't know."

"What's the deal? You said these were important."

"Yeah."

"So? Let's go. How many negs have you got?"

"Five."

"Come on. It'll take no time."

"Howie, there's a problem."

"Yeah, there's a problem. Someone screwed up the negs, but we'll get something."

"No. Look, four people have been killed over what's on these negatives. Knowing about them is dangerous. I don't want to put you in that position."

"So what are you going to do? You've got to see them, right? Are you going to take them to the police lab?"

"I can't do that. I don't have anyone I could trust over there."

"Well, then?"

"Is there some way I could do it myself? You teach me. You tell me what to do. You don't see the pictures."

"No. You fuck up the negatives, they're gone. And there's no way to teach you in the next hour what it took me fifteen years to learn. You want to get images off these negs, you're going to have to let me try."

"I don't know what we're going to find, but you can't tell Marnie."

"Okay."

"If anyone finds out, they'll come after you."

"I heard you. I understand. Now do you want to do this or not?"

"Yes. If you're sure."

The darkroom was in a converted pantry off the kitchen. Howie talked while he worked. "During the war, we used microfilm to ship images, you know, to save space and weight. Like V-mail. You must've gotten V-mail. They take a picture of the letter over here, send it over there as micro-film, then turn it back into a printed letter over there. And of course the spies, the Resistance, they all used that stuff. Little cameras you could hide. You reduce the image to a microdot, stick it under the stamp on a post-card, and send it off to your Aunt Fanny with an innocent note like, 'Weather is here, wish you were beautiful.' Only Aunt Fanny is a guy in a safe house somewhere and he knows the score. He retrieves the micro-dot, and now he's got the plans for the Hitler bunker." He pulled an eight-by-ten print from the chemical bath. "There. Okay. Let's take a look." He hung it on a line with clothespins at two of the corners, turned on the light, and they moved in. "Shit. That's not much, is it?" The print was a blur of indistinct colors. "Okay. I've got some ideas. Yeah, yeah, yeah. Okay. Go sit down. Don't hover. Let me work."

In the end there was a stack of discarded prints on a table near the en-larger, and the best print from each negative hung on the line. Cassidy's hopes had dwindled bit by bit as Howie had handed each of the first four prints to him to hang up. They still showed indistinct shapes. Some of the shapes could be recognized as a table or chair, or the bright glow of a lamp, but there was no indication of where they were. There were darker shapes that were people, but they were featureless, unidentifiable.

Howie pinned up the last print and stepped aside so Cassidy could see. There was something in Howie's face that made his hopes rise again. Then he saw the print.

"Holy shit."

"Yeah," Howie said.

"Howie—" He started the warning, but Howie stopped him.

"I know. I know. I'm not stupid. I won't say anything. Who'd be-lieve it?"

"Not even Marnie."

"No. Tell Marnie, I might as well put it on the radio."

They went back into the studio to wait while the prints dried.

"He had to have some sort of camera that no one would notice, right? Something small that he could palm."

"Or something that no one would look at twice. Here, I'll show you. I've got a few things I liberated during the war."

Lodin opened a drawer under the shelves of cameras and took out a shoe box held shut by tape. He cleared a space on the desk for it, slit the tape with a box cutter, took off the top, and arranged the little cameras in a row.

"This one's a Minox, made by the Krauts." He put his finger on an aluminum rectangle about three inches long and an inch wide. A metal cord attached at the butt end, and along the cord at intervals were beads of brass. Lodin picked it up. "You hold one of the beads on the paper you're copying and pull the cord tight and you know exactly how many centimeters the lens is from the text. Perfect focus every time." He put the Minox down and picked up a matchbox. "British. The lens isn't much, but if you're given a quick search, all you're carrying is a matchbox." He picked up a cigarette lighter and showed how the bottom slid aside to expose the lens. "Russian. The Russians liked to copy American stuff, but they always screwed it up a little. Here, look at this." He held the lighter out for Cassidy and pointed at the manufacture's logo, RONSON. It was spelled RONSUN.

Where had Cassidy seen one like it before?

"Hey, Cassidy." Marnie Lodin leaned against the doorjamb and rubbed her eyes. She wore the twin to her husband's robe. She had a tough street urchin's face, and her black curls sprung from her head as if electrified. "Six o'clock on a Saturday morning. Jesus."

"Sorry, Marnie."

"Yeah, yeah. You want to stay for breakfast? I promised Howie buttermilk pancakes."

"Thanks. I've got to go."

"Maple syrup. Bacon."

"Another time. Thanks."

"Just so long as it's not six o'clock on the weekend. What've you guys been doing, developing?"

"Yes."

"Can I see them?"

"No."

"Did you pay the man?"

"Marnie, come on." Lodin shook his head in embarrassment. "Cassidy's a friend."

"Not the point. He came to you 'cause you're a pro. Pros get paid. Right, Mike?"

"Absolutely."

"Okay, then."

Cassidy put a twenty-dollar bill in her hand. "Sorry about waking you up, Marnie."

"Hey, what the hell. Who cares?" She kissed him on the cheek and patted his butt as he left with the prints and negatives in an envelope.

• • •

Weak bulbs in overhead fixtures dimly lighted the precinct evidence room. The room smelled of dust, disinfectant, and decay. Long wire racks that reached nearly to the ceiling held brown cardboard boxes labeled with case names, numbers, and dates. Some of them went back thirty years, memorials to cases never brought to trial, to justice avoided, to fugitives in the wind.

"Jorgenson said you were down here," Orso said. "What's up? You were lucky you caught me. I was headed for Coney when you called. I figured to eat a couple of red hots, drink a few beers in the sun, and then introduce myself to a bathing beauty and let nature take its course."

"At least I saved her from that."

Cassidy pulled the Alex Ingram case box off a shelf and spread its contents on the wooden table under a dangling bare bulb. He pulled Ingram's clothes from their heavy paper envelopes. The trousers and underwear were stiff with blood dried the color of rust. He pinched the seams and felt the shoulder padding of the jacket.

"What are we looking for?" Orso asked.

"I don't know. Anything. When we looked before, it was just a murder. It's something else now."

"Are you going to tell me about it, or do I have to guess?"

"He had a cigarette lighter. See if you can find it." Cassidy found Ingram's wallet and checked the compartments to see if he might have hidden more film there. There was nothing. The hundred and seventy-five dollars had disappeared into some cop's pocket.

"Here it is." Orso held up the gold lighter.

"Take a close look at it. Tell me what you find."

Cassidy replaced the contents of the box while Orso turned the lighter over under the light. "It's a lighter. A Ronson. Gold. Nice lighter. What am I looking for?"

"How'd they spell Ronson?"

Orso looked. "Hey, what the hell? 'S-U-N.'"

Cassidy took the lighter and slid the base aside to reveal the lens. "It's a camera, a Russian-made spy camera."

"What are you saying? Ingram was a Russian spy? Come on." He saw Cassidy's face. "Okay. Why not? But isn't that out of our league?"

"Nothing's out of our league. We're New York's Finest."

Two uniformed patrolmen entered the room talking about a Yankees–Red Sox spring-training game in Florida. One of them said, "How're you doing, Detectives?" as they went past Orso and Cassidy and looked for something on a shelf near the end of the aisle.

"Let's go," Cassidy said.

They walked to a hole-in-the-wall on 48th Street and ate thick Cuban sandwiches stuffed with roast pig, ham, melted cheese, pickles, and mustard, and drank bottles of dark Cuban beer.

Cassidy told Orso about finding the microfilm. He did not tell Orso Howie's name, and Orso did not ask. He told him that the first negatives were blurs and that he had been sure the last one would be worthless too. Orso stopped eating to listen.

"You want me to go on?"

"Don't fuck with me, Mike."

"The last one came out okay."

"Are you going to show it to me?"

"As soon as we've finished lunch."

"We're finished." Orso threw money on the table.

They went into the men's room and locked the door.

Orso held the print up and turned it to the light. "Well, I'll be . . . Four guys dead because of this."

"No. Four guys dead because of what people *think* is on the film. What have we got? One image. No idea of where it was taken, no corroboration of who else was there. But they don't know that. They think that everything is clear, who, where, when, and what happened."

"So what do you want to do, turn this stuff in?"

"To who?"

"We could give them to the lieutenant, let him take the heat."

"If we turn them in to the department, Costello, the Feds, the CIA all know about it in five minutes. Any leverage I've got to help my father is gone. I have to find out where this was taken, when it happened, and who was there. If you want out, stay out, I understand. No one will know you saw this." He put the print back in the envelope.

"Forget about it. If I was the guy sent to clean this up, I'd do me just to be sure. Partners and all, who knows what you might have shown me or told me? I'm in. What else do I have to do with my time?"

33

The late Eddie Freed sent rent checks for Perry Werth's apartment on West 84th Street between Columbus and Amsterdam. It was a postwar of no distinction built of pale yellow brick already going gray under New York grime. The window frames were aluminum, the miracle metal that showed up everywhere from airplanes to toothbrush holders. The acid in the air had pitted them with dark specks. Unlocked glass doors led to an outer lobby with a panel of buzzers on one wall. Another set of locked glass doors led to a small charmless inner lobby with a bronzed mirror, a leather bench with aluminum legs, and two elevators with a sand-filled column ashtray between them.

There were six apartments to a floor. Perry Werth lived in 8D. Orso jabbed the buzzer. He was about to ring again when the intercom hummed for a moment and then a metallic voice asked, "Yes? Who is it?"

"Police. Detectives Orso and Cassidy, Mr. Werth. We need to talk to you," Orso said into the intercom.

There was silence for a moment. "What about?"

Orso rolled his eyes at Cassidy. "Mr. Werth, we can do this over the intercom for all the neighborhood to hear. Or we can do it down at the station. Or we can do it in your apartment, comfortable and private. Your choice."

A longer silence, and then, "All right. Come on up. I'm in eight D." The door buzzed, the latch clicked, and Cassidy pushed the door open.

Orso and Cassidy crossed the lobby and got in the elevator. A man came in through the lobby door just before it closed and hurried toward the elevator. "Hold the door, will you?" He was in his early thirties, a trim, compact man with dark hair cut short in the military manner. He wore black trousers, a gray shirt, and a black windbreaker. Cassidy noticed that he wore thin leather gloves though it was not cold out. Orso pushed 8. "Floor?"

"Seven," Fraker said.

Just before he stepped into the elevator, he had recognized the cop he had pinned with his flashlight in Ingram's apartment. His heart jumped, but it was too late to stop, and then he realized that the cop had never seen his face during the fight in the dark, and when the lights came on, Fraker had been headed toward the door. The big cop pushed 7 and the door closed. Fraker stepped to the back wall. His right hand found the knife in his pocket. His heart slowed. They don't have a fucking clue. I could kill them both before they knew what hit them. Christ, it would be easy. A backhand slash across the big man's throat. A half turn to punch the knife into the other one's neck. What was his name? Cassidy, Crofoot said. Punch it into Cassidy's neck, or, if he had started to react to the big one's cut throat, into his chest, the bigger target. In and out. In and out. In and out. Hit him hard and fast before he could react. He'd be dead standing there. Then turn back to the big one to see if he needed more. The thought of their surprise, of how easy it would be, made him smile. But the elevator would be like a slaughterhouse. There'd be blood all over, all over him. And then he'd have to go deal with Werth, and that would take time, time enough for someone to find the bodies. And no one had told him to kill the cop, so, too bad. It would have been interesting. But he had a problem now. He was there to talk to Werth, and they were headed for Werth's apartment, no other reason for these two cops to be going to the eighth floor in this building. Rethink.

Cassidy saw the man smile and wondered what private pleasure he had thought of.

"Spring's finally here, it looks like," the man said. "It's great to be alive." He smiled again.

"Yes, it is," Cassidy said.

The doors opened on 7 and the man stepped out. "See you," he said with an inflection that made it sound to Cassidy more like a statement than the usual casual good-bye.

The doors closed, and the elevator lurched up.

Fraker ran for the stairwell and took the stairs two at a time to the eighth floor. He cracked the door there and watched Cassidy and his partner get off the elevator and walk down the hall to 8D. The big one rang the bell.

He could not see who opened the door a moment later, but he heard a man's voice say, "Come in, please."

Fraker stepped out into the corridor. The apartment next to 8D, 8E, was opposite the door to the stairwell. He crossed quickly and rang the doorbell. A moment later he heard footsteps approaching. A woman's voice asked, "Who is it?"

"Superintendent, ma'am. We're trying to check the source of a leak. It'll only take a minute."

"Oh, dear. Yes, of course. Hold on, please."

He heard her unlock two locks. She opened the door. She was a pleasant-looking gray-haired woman in a housedress and slippers. She held a feather duster in one hand.

"Please come in. A leak? Oh, dear. Please excuse the mess." Her gesture took in the neat living room.

"This'll only take a minute," Fraker said. He kicked the door shut and shot his hands out and grabbed her by the throat and squeezed. She dropped the feather duster and pulled at his wrists with her two hands. He felt the cartilage in her throat compress and then crush. Her feet kicked feebly and one of her slippers flew off. He held her off with rigid arms and watched carefully to see if he could tell the moment when life left and death came. He had watched Victor Amado in the same way but had been unable to catch the moment, and he had wondered if the pain of the torture had masked it. Her face reddened, her eyes bulged, and her mouth hung open. Her grip on his wrists slackened and then fell away. Her knees buckled, and he held her up by his hands on her throat until she stopped moving. He lowered her body to the carpet. He had seen nothing, no moment of change in her, just alive and then dead. He pushed aside his disappointment and moved quickly across to the wall her apartment shared with Perry Werth's.

The building had been cheaply made during the postwar construction boom, and the contractor had cut corners wherever he could. The walls were thin and poorly insulated, and when Fraker pressed his ear to the wall he could hear the rumble of voices next door. He caught words and phrases, but much of what was said was lost. He hurried to the kitchen and came back with a glass of thin and delicate crystal. He pressed the open end to the wall and his ear to the base of the glass. Yes, that was better.

· · ·

Perry Werth was a tall, dark-haired, good-looking man in his late twenties, a few years older than Ingram and Amado. He wore charcoal gray light flannel trousers and a blue-and-white-striped button-down shirt open at the collar with the sleeves rolled. He led Cassidy and Orso down the short hall and into the small living room, offered them the chairs at either end of the coffee table, and sat down on the sofa. He took a cigarette from a pack of Kools on the coffee table and lit it. From where he sat, Cassidy could see a suitcase on the bed in the room next door.

Werth noticed his look. "I just got back this morning. I've been on the road for a week. My wife's at work, but I can make some coffee if you like."

"No, thanks," Cassidy said.

There was a silver-framed photograph on an end table that showed Perry Werth and a young woman standing on a dock somewhere with their arms around each other's waists. A small boy stood against their legs and smiled up at the camera.

"What is this about?"

"Alex Ingram, Victor Amado, Stanley Fisher."

"I'm afraid I don't know those names. Who are they?"

"You mean who were they, because now they're dead."

"Dead? I don't understand." His face paled and he took a short, abrupt pull on the cigarette.

"Two of them were tortured. Fisher was shot."

"What? Wait, Officer, why are you telling me this? I don't know these men. What has this got to do with me? Good God, tortured, shot?"

Cassidy looked at Orso. Orso shrugged. "We've seen the photographs," Cassidy bluffed. "We know you were there with them. We want to know who set it up, who knew about it."

"I don't know what you're talking about. What photographs? Taken where? Of what?" Werth stubbed the cigarette out half smoked and lit another.

"They're all dead, Mr. Werth. We think Ingram was killed by someone who tortured him to get the pictures. Amado too. But Stanley Fisher was shot. Whoever did that didn't give a damn about the pictures. He just wanted Fisher dead. So someone's cleaning up, and now you're the only loose end. He's going to come looking for you. We can protect you, but you have to help us out."

"I'm sorry. You're telling me horrible things about these men, but I don't know them. I don't know who they are. I don't know why you're talking to me."

"We know you were there."

"No. It's somebody else. It's someone who looks like me."

"Hey, how come your rent's paid by a two-bit lawyer downtown named Freed?" Orso asked.

"My rent?" Werth showed his surprise but recovered quickly. "That's a private arrangement that has nothing to do with you or what you're talking about, and I am disappointed that Mr. Freed betrayed an attorney-client privilege."

"Yeah? Imagine Freed's disappointment when someone shot him in the face."

"Freed's dead?" That shook him. "I don't know what to say. This is a nightmare."

"Fuck him, Mike. He doesn't want our help. Let's get out of here."

"Hold on, Tony. Come on, Mr. Werth, be smart about this. We don't care who you are or what you've done. We don't give a damn about your private life. We just need to get these people off the street. You can help us."

Werth shook his head. "Sorry." His face was set.

• • •

Fraker heard the door to the apartment next door close as the two cops left. He heard the elevator arrive and go back down. He waited to make sure they were not coming back, then he stepped over the woman's body and left the apartment and went down the stairs to the lobby. He looked through the glass doors to make sure the cops were gone, and then went out toward Amsterdam Avenue to find a phone. He'd better talk to Crofoot and find out if he should still go talk to Perry.

• • •

"What do you think?" Orso asked. They were walking south in the sun along the wall next to Central Park across the street from the Museum of Natural History. Two yellow school buses were in front of the museum and harried teachers were trying to bring order to a seething mass of schoolboys giddy with sunshine and freedom from their desks.

"I'd like to get a dump on his phone. I bet he called someone the minute we left, and I'd love to know who it was."

"Not a chance. We're off the case. No one's going to pull phone records for us."

"He's lying," Cassidy said. "He's scared and he's still lying. He's married. He's got a kid. He's got a good job. That all goes away if they find out he's turning queer tricks."

"Yeah, but his friends are getting killed."

"Maybe that doesn't scare him as much."

• • •

Fraker found an unbroken phone in a booth on the corner of Amsterdam and 83rd. He called Crofoot, but there was no answer. He went across the street and ate a hamburger with a cherry Coke and went back to the phone booth and tried again. Crofoot answered on the second ring.

"Yes."

"I was on my way to see Werth. I didn't get there. Two cops were going up to see him. Cassidy and his partner, a big wop."

"Tell me something I want to hear."

"I got into the apartment next door. The place is built like crap. I listened through the wall. I didn't get it all. Sometimes they were too quiet, but I'll tell you one thing: Cassidy has the photographs."

"You heard him say that?" Crofoot's voice rose with excitement.

"Yeah, I heard him."

"What else? Did he show them to Werth?"

"No. I don't think so. If he did, I didn't pick it up."

"How long were they in there?"

"Ten, fifteen minutes. I don't know."

"How much did you hear?"

"Maybe half."

"Go see Werth. Find out everything they said. Call me when you're done."

"Right."

"Wait. Bring him to the house on Thirty-fourth. We might need some uninterrupted time with him."

"Okay."

Fraker walked back to 84th Street. He watched the apartment building from outside until he saw the elevator indicator light show the car arriving at the lobby. He took a ring of keys from his pocket and waited until a boy wearing a baseball uniform and carrying an equipment bag bolted from the elevator and slammed out through the front doors. Fraker met him in the small outer lobby, the keys conspicuous in his hand as if he was about to put them in the lock. He said, "Thanks," to the boy and went in before the inner door closed.

Fraker took the elevator to the eighth floor. When the door opened, a man waiting there started to enter and then stepped back to allow Fraker out. He nodded the way neighbors do when they meet in the hall, went in, and the door closed behind him.

Fraker stood outside Perry Werth's apartment and listened. There was no sound from inside. He rang the doorbell and waited. No footsteps approached. No one called out. He rang the bell again. Silence. He examined the lock and then took a thin stiff piece of celluloid from his jacket pocket and slipped it between the doorjamb and the tongue of the lock. Get this done fast before someone comes home and finds the dead woman next door.

He pushed the door open and went in. The runner in the short entry hall deadened his footsteps as he went to the living room.

Perry Werth sat in a chair near the window. His blue-and-white-striped shirt was dark with blood. Someone had shot him once in the chest and once between the eyes. The smell of cordite still hung in the air.

Fraker went back to the front door, opened it a crack, and listened. When he heard nothing, he went out quickly and shut the door, crossed to the stairwell, and ran down the seven flights. The lobby was empty. He went out onto the street, but the man who had gotten into the elevator was not there. Which way, west or east? He ran to the end of the block and looked along Columbus Avenue. The sidewalks were crowded. If the man was there, he was just another fish in the school.

What did he look like? Medium height, medium build, an even-featured face of no distinction, brown hair, unmemorable clothes. Glasses? Maybe. A man you would pass on the street without remarking. He could be standing twenty feet away and Fraker would not recognize him. Very cool. Walk in. Shoot Werth. Walk out. Nod to Fraker as they passed at the elevator as if they might be neighbors. No muss, no fuss. You had to admire that.

34

Cassidy awoke in the night and knew someone was in the room. His gun was on the bureau fifteen feet away. The closest weapon to hand was the heavy iron lamp on the bedside table. There was movement near the door and the soft pad of a foot on the rug. He kept his breathing steady and slow. *I'm asleep. I don't know you're there. I'm asleep.* His right hand was outside the covers, and he eased it toward the lamp. Whoever was in the room took another step. Cassidy lay still. A figure was silhouetted for a moment against the lighter grid of the window, and Cassidy let his breath out with a rush.

"Are you awake?"

"Yes."

"I was trying to be quiet." Dylan slipped into bed and pressed against him. She was naked. "I didn't want to wake you."

"You didn't. I was awake," he lied.

She hooked a leg over his waist and reached her arm across and put her palm flat on his chest and pulled closer. Her body was hot against him.

"Are you sure I didn't wake you?"

"I don't know. I just woke up, and there you were."

"Magic. Maybe you dreamed me up." She ran her hand down his chest and over his belly. "An erotic dream."

"Hmm. Not yet."

"Give me a minute. I just got here."

He could not help smiling. He did not know where she had been or why she had gone, but he was happy she was here. Tomorrow would take care of itself.

• • •

In the morning she was up before he was, and he found her in the kitchen.

"Hi. I woke up starving. I'm making eggs and bacon." Her smile was bright, but her eyes were wary. "Sit down and I'll feed you in a couple of minutes. The coffee's ready."

He sat at the counter and watched while she poured a mug of coffee. She knew he was watching, and it made her edgy. When she handed him the mug, it ticked the edge of the counter and coffee slopped over the rim. "Sorry. Clumsy." She mopped the spill with a dishcloth.

"It's okay." He sipped the coffee. The phone rang on the table between the two windows. He answered it in the middle of the third ring.

"Hello."

"It's me," Orso said.

"What's up?"

"I picked up that guy, Ribera, about half an hour ago. I've got Hanratty and Thomaselli working it with me. He put us over some jumps, did a nifty in the Fourteenth Street subway station, on and off a train, but we're still on him."

"Where are you?"

"Union Square. He's in that coffee shop on the corner, the one where they put the peppers in the hash browns. Looks like he's settled in for a while. Makes me hungry to watch him. What do you want me to do?"

"Yeah, stick with that. See where it goes."

"Huh? Oh, I got it. She's there."

"That's it."

"Okay. Check your messages at the house. I'll check mine. I'll let you know where he goes to ground."

"Later." He hung up.

"Who was that?"

"Tony Orso."

"Is it something important? Do you have to go?"

"No. An old case. A guy who used to rob up around Times Square. He used to work for Con Ed. Tony's over there checking to see if he's back with them. You'd be surprised at how many guys just drift back into their old patterns. They do the crime, they run for a minute, then they come back and it's as if they want to get caught."

"Nobody wants to get caught."

She turned back to the stove and banged the frying pans around like they were enemies.

"Don't watch me. I don't like being watched while I cook."

"Sure."

She clattered plates and silverware onto the counter, dumped eggs and bacon onto the plates, and shoved Cassidy's across. She watched him take his first bite and then sat opposite him with the counter between them and ate as if starved. She finished before he did and pushed her plate aside. She leaned forward with her palms flat on the countertop as if to brace herself.

"You're angry at me."

"No, I'm not."

"I don't have to tell you where I'm going."

"No, you don't."

"I don't have to say when I'll be back."

"No." That's what she thought it was?

"I don't explain. I do what I want."

"Okay."

"If you can't take it . . ."

"I can take it." He finished eating while she struggled with it.

"I'm not much good with this. Not much practice, I guess." Her voice was softer.

"Good with what?"

"With this. Being with someone."

"Are you?"

"What?"

"With me?"

"Yes." She looked stricken.

"You do fine."

"I can't help who I am."

"Have you heard me complain?"

She looked at him carefully to read his face. She started to say something more, and then stopped and shook her head. "I've got to go. I told Ribera I'd be in early. We've got a lot to do today."

"He's waiting for you at the studio?"

"Yes."

"Why don't I walk over with you? I'd like to say hello to him, see what he's doing."

"No. Not today. We're doing something really complicated. I have to think about it while I walk. I need to concentrate."

A small test she failed.

"Are you sure? I won't say a word. I'll just carry your schoolbooks."

She forced a smile. "Another day. Okay?"

A moment later the door closed, and she was gone.

• • •

By the time Cassidy got to the roof, Dylan was starting down the block. There was almost no foot traffic this far west, so he knew he could not follow her on the street without being spotted. From up here he had a clear view, and it was unlikely that she would look up. He had lived on this block for more than four years, and as far as he could remember, the buildings were separated from each other only by air shafts. How wide were the shafts? Not wide, he thought, but he had never studied it. He was about to find out.

Cassidy jogged east. The parapet of his building was higher than the one of the building next door, and the air shaft between them was eight feet wide, an easy jump. He crossed the next roof, dodging radio antennas and clotheslines. The next building was attached to the one he was on, and he went up and over the parapets and then ran to the street side and looked down. Dylan was walking slowly. He was ahead by twenty yards.

The gap to the next building was wider, ten feet, maybe more, enough to make him cautious. He checked his run-up for pebbles, guy wires, torn roofing, anything that could trip him. He tested the parapet for loose bricks and studied the landing area of the other side to see if he could spot other dangers. All right. Go. Ten, eleven feet. Nothing at all. If you were jumping it on the sidewalk you wouldn't even think about it.

Don't look down.

He stepped away, rocked back and forth, and then took off. He had to chop his stride at the end to hit the ledge with his lead foot, and he went out over the six-story gap with his arms windmilling.

His left foot landed at the far edge of the parapet, and the momentum carried him forward onto the roof and he took two lunging steps for balance, lost it, and started to go down. He tucked his left shoulder under and let the momentum roll him to his feet. He came up with his hands raised defensively. They slammed against the door of a rooftop shed and stopped his rush. He waited there for a moment until his heart stopped tripping and then walked across the roof and looked across at the last building on the block.

The gap was about twelve feet, not much more than the one he had just jumped, but the far parapet was three feet higher. He was pretty sure he could jump the twelve feet, but not the twelve feet and the added three feet of height. He looked over the parapet to the alley below and contemplated how far a man of his size might bounce. The door he had banged into led to stairs down from the roof. It was sheathed in metal. There was no exterior keyhole, and a square of steel extended out from the door to cover the crack between the door and the jamb. He was locked out. If he went back a building he might have better luck with the stairs, but by that time Dylan would be at the corner and he would not know which way she turned. Okay. Let it go. Wait for another opportunity. Tomorrow. The next day. This wasn't over yet.

He found a wooden ladder lying on the tar beside the shed. Was it long enough? He dragged it to the air shaft. A length of rope was knotted to a rung near one end. He braced the other end against a standpipe and used the rope to pull the ladder upright, then walked it to the parapet and let the far end fall. It bounced twice on the ledge of the next building and then settled. He pushed it out until there was about two feet of overlap at either end. It was long enough. Was it strong enough? It was not a new ladder, but the rails looked solid, and none of the rungs was broken. How much weight could a ladder support? Plenty, right? There were guys who weighed a hundred pounds more than he did who used ladders. *Just go. Don't think about it. Go.*

He stepped up on the parapet, got down on all fours, and crawled out on the ladder. He kept his weight on the rails and went forward one rung at a time. *Don't look down. Look up. Look at the far end of the ladder. It's not so far away. Okay, right hand forward, left hand forward. Now right knee forward, left knee forward. Do it again. That wasn't so bad.* The rungs dug into his knees. Right forward, left forward. Again. Hot air rose from the alley floor. *Don't think about how far down it is. Just do it again, right, left, right, left. Halfway there now. No problem.*

The far end of the ladder shifted on the parapet. He heard the scrape of wood on brick and felt the shift. The ladder moved backward about an inch.

Jesus.

Shut up. Ignore it. Keep going.

Right hand, left hand, right knee, left knee. The ladder shifted again. The high end slipped toward the drop. That was more than an inch. Okay. *Don't panic. Slow and smooth. Careful, careful. Easy.* But it did not matter how careful he was, every time he moved forward, the ladder slipped. What if he retreated? *That's it. Go back.* He went back one rung. The ladder slipped. *Stop. It's too far to go back. Go forward. How many rungs left to reach the end? Six. About six feet. Six feet is nothing.* How much of the ladder was still left on the parapet? About a foot, and he was losing at least a couple of inches every time he moved. The math was against him. He wasn't going to make it.

What if he moved forward two rungs at a time? Use the same caution and care. One hand and then the other. One knee and then the other. Slip, scrape. How much of the ladder was left on the parapet? *Don't think about that. There's nothing to do about that. Just go. Four feet more to go. Reach out. Do it again. Move the knees up. That's it. Did the ladder move? Yes. But not as much. Breathe. Breathe.* He looked up. The ends of the ladder rails were rounded. The last straight inch of each rail was still on the ledge of the parapet. One inch, and then the curve, and when the curve got to the edge, the ladder would fall.

Two feet to go. Reach for it with your hands. Don't worry about the knees. Reach. Keep balanced. Don't rock the ladder. Rocking the ladder makes it slip. Reach. Do it now. Not for the ladder rail, reach for the brick. The brick won't move. The fingers of his right hand felt the rough grit of the bricks of the roof ledge. *Okay. Reach with the other. Shit. Shit. Stop. Stop.* Just the small shift of weight moved the ladder. *Come on. Go. You have to do it. Go. You can't stay here for the rest of your life. The rest of your life? How long? Reach for it.* His left hand touched the brick. He inched both hands farther onto the ledge. *Okay, take some weight off the ladder. Now, move your knees. First the right one . . .*

The ladder slipped off the ledge and fell away from under him.

One moment it was there. The next it was gone. All his weight went to his hands on the ledge. His feet swung in and banged the building as the ladder fell away and clattered down the air shaft crashing against first one wall and then the other. He hung there with his weight dragging on his hands, with the edge of the parapet digging in. *Move. Move.* He pulled himself up and got one elbow and then the other on the brick surface and heaved himself higher. He got a leg onto the ledge, levered himself up and over, and rolled off the other side to lie on the soft tar of the roof looking up at the sky. When he caught his breath and his heart slowed, he got up and went to the stairs.

● ● ●

Dylan crossed Washington Street headed east. Cassidy watched her from the shadows of a truck that rumbled coal down a chute into the basement of the corner house. Halfway up the block, Dylan turned abruptly and walked back to the corner. Cassidy moved around the truck to keep it between them. She turned north at the corner and walked up the block and then stopped and stooped to retie her shoelace while she checked her back trail. Then she turned south again. Checking for tails.

Good technique for a girl from a small Pennsylvania town, he thought bitterly.

She kept going south, turned the corner, and went east on West 11th Street. Cassidy took the chance that she was really headed east now and ran along Bank Street to Greenwich Avenue. He stood at the corner and watched until she appeared a block south. She looked back along 11th Street and saw nothing that alarmed her. She raised a hand, and a taxi slewed across the street and stopped for her. The door slammed and the cab started up and Cassidy stepped into a doorway and watched it go north. As it passed, he pulled the cab number.

A cab was stopped at a red light two blocks away. When the light changed, Cassidy raised his hand and the cab pulled to the curb. The driver was a young man with two days' growth of beard and a Brooklyn Dodgers hat.

"There's a Checker headed north on Greenwich. Number 3B202. There's a sawbuck in it if you find it and follow it."

"You're kiddin'." The cigarette in his mouth bobbed when he spoke.

Cassidy dangled his shield where the driver could see it.

"Okay, you're not kiddin'. Let's go."

They picked up Dylan's cab as it waited at a red light to make a right at 14th Street. He could see her head in the rear window as she turned to light a cigarette. The light changed. Dylan's cab went east along 14th. The traffic was light.

"Don't get too close," Cassidy warned his driver.

"Hey, don't worry. I'm all over this. I've been waitin' for someone to get in and say follow that car since I took up hackin'."

Dylan's cab pulled to the curb at the subway station at Seventh Avenue.

"I better drop you here, or she'll make you," Cassidy's driver said as he pulled to the curb thirty yards back.

Cassidy dropped money over the seat back and got out, and lost himself in the crowd on the street. Ahead of him, Dylan went down the stairs into the subway station.

Cassidy followed her down the stairs behind a group of workmen dressed in stained white overalls. She was going through a turnstile when he reached the lobby. He followed her to the IRT line headed uptown on Seventh and let her go along the platform while he sifted into a group of people waiting for the train. A puff of warm electric air announced the train, and moments later the uptown local rattled and squealed into the station. Dylan got on. He remembered what Orso had said about Ribera's dodge in the subway, and so he hung by the door. Across the platform, the uptown express shrieked to a stop. The doors of the local started to close. Dylan came out of the car and darted toward the express. Other people ran for the faster train, and Cassidy went with them. He got in the car behind Dylan's and found a place among the straphangers where he could watch her through the connecting door without being seen. The train swayed and rocked its way north, and the people standing swayed and rocked with it, and through the gaps in the moving people Cassidy could see the copper shine of Dylan's hair. She stared straight ahead at the window in front of her and passing lights flashed on her face. Once she turned toward the glass that separated them, and Cassidy turned away and let the motion of the train pull him behind the bulk of a tall Orthodox Jew wearing a black fedora. When he looked again, she was staring out the window.

At Penn Station, she waited till the last moment and then got off as the doors closed, but Cassidy was ready for that and he stepped off behind two women carrying shopping bags from Barneys. He let Dylan take a lead and followed her through the vaulted waiting room of the train station and out onto Seventh Avenue.

She must have been sure she had shaken any possible tail, because she walked east along 34th Street without looking back. Cassidy crossed to the north side of the street and tracked her. She wore charcoal gray trousers of some thin material and a blue cotton shirt open at the throat that set off her red hair, and she walked with a free swinging stride, and men stopped on the sidewalk and turned to watch her go. One man spoke to her, and she laughed and threw a reply over her shoulder and kept going.

Dylan went north on Lexington Avenue. Between 38th and 39th, she stopped and looked around. Then she quickly entered a shop in the middle of the block.

It was the camera store run by the man named Apfel where Cassidy had taken the envelope he had found in Alex Ingram's dressing room locker. Apfel, the voice on the phone he had called from the lawyer Freed's office.

A moment after Dylan entered, Apfel appeared behind the glass door. He locked it, flipped around an OPEN sign so it read CLOSED, and pulled a shade down over the glass.

Cassidy found a greasy spoon halfway up the block and took a booth at the window that gave him a clear view of the front door of the camera shop across the street. He ordered coffee and settled in for the wait. Two men were sitting at the counter ripping each other the way men do who have been friends for a long time. They were in their twenties. One was rail thin, black haired, with a narrow, bony nose and a pointed chin, and the other was heavy, red faced, thick handed, and as bald as an egg. From their madras jackets, khaki trousers, and polished loafers, they were young executives on a break from one of the nearby book publishers or ad agencies.

Cassidy tuned out their genial insults and thought about Apfel in his camera shop. The photographs. How had Ingram been so careless that he'd ruined them?

He took the prints Howie Lodin had made from his inside pocket, put the clear photo back, spread the blurred prints in front of him, and examined them in the sunlight that fell through the window. What was this? A table? And this glow? A lighted lamp? This could be a window with city lights behind it, but where was it taken? This was a man, or maybe a woman. And this—another man? woman?—also unidentifiable. There was something in one of the photos that pricked his memory. A silvery rounded mass that reflected light. He had seen something like that recently. What the hell was it? And where had he seen it?

A bell behind him tinkled as someone opened the door to the diner, and a warm breeze blew in for a moment before the door closed. The man who had entered walked past him on the way to the counter.

"Orso."

Orso turned. "Hey, what the hell?" Orso slid into the booth.

"Ribera?" He gestured to the camera store across the street.

"Jesus, he took us through it. We lost Thomaselli in the subway, but

Hanratty and I stuck with him to Third and Thirty-eighth. Halfway up the block he ducks down an alley. We can't follow him there, 'cause the alley dead ends, so I cruise by and see him duck into a door. I figure it's the back door of one of the shops over here on Lex, so I run around to see if he comes out, which I don't think he did."

"He's in the camera shop."

"How do you know?"

"Because that's where Dylan went."

"Dylan?"

"I followed her up here. She's meeting Ribera and a guy named Apfel who runs the shop."

"Okay. Tell me about it."

"Apfel supplied the camera in the cigarette lighter. Apfel developed the photographs. When I went in there with the envelope I found in Ingram's locker, he was very interested in any negatives that might have been in it. Ingram stole them to go into business for himself."

"Do you think Apfel's the guy who tortured Ingram?"

"I do."

"Who is he?"

"A Russian agent."

"And Dylan?"

"Yeah."

"What are you going to do?"

"I'm going to burn her down."

The thin man at the counter said, "I've got to get back to the office. Coca-Cola is counting on me. I'll see you, Chrome Dome." He slapped his friend on the back and stood up.

"Hold on." Cassidy got up and went to the man paying at the register. "What did you just call your friend?"

"What?"

"What'd you call him?" Cassidy's intensity made the other man step back.

"I don't know. What do you want? I called him, what, Chrome Dome. What the hell?" The man held his hands up defensively.

"Chrome Dome. Right. Thanks."

"Jesus, man, what's wrong with you?" He backed to the door, keeping his eye on Cassidy, and then went out fast.

The woman behind the register, the counterman, and Chrome Dome watched Cassidy warily. New York. People go off the rails all the time. Be prepared to jump.

Orso drank his coffee, unperturbed. "What was all that about?"

"I'm going up to the Waldorf."

"Sure. Go ahead, don't tell me why. I don't have to know. What do you want me to do?"

"Wait here. Take whoever comes out the front first. Hanratty can pick up whoever comes out the back."

"Okay. You all right?"

"I'm fine." Cassidy lied, his rage at Dylan humming just below the surface.

He found a phone booth on the corner of 40th, closed the door against the traffic noise, and dropped a nickel in the slot.

The phone was answered on the third ring. "Yes?"

"Let me talk to Frank."

"Nobody here by that name."

"Tell him Mike Cassidy's calling." He heard the receiver clunk on a tabletop. Footsteps retreated. Moments later someone picked up a different receiver.

"Michael, how are you?"

"Great. Perfect."

"What can I do for you?"

"Do you guys do the linen service for the Waldorf?"

"We're involved, so to speak."

"I want to ask some questions people won't want to answer. I'm going to talk to a guy named Sorino who runs the service staff."

"Is this about the thing we talked about?" Costello was always circumspect. He was sure the FBI and the police tapped his phones.

"Yes."

"Sorino, huh? I'll call someone. Give me half an hour."

• • •

Cassidy entered the Waldorf through the revolving door on Lexington Avenue. He found the unmarked door and went down the iron staircases to the subbasement. A waiter pushed a service cart along the corridor. On it was a vase with a single rose, place settings for two, and a chromed warming dome over whatever had been ordered for lunch just like the one he had seen when he first came to the Waldorf tracking Ingram.

The blurred shiny mass in one of the photos. "Chrome Dome," from the ad man. The Waldorf.

Cassidy went into Sorino's office without knocking. Sorino was behind his desk running sums on an adding machine. He did not look up when Cassidy entered.

Costello's man, Packer, leaned against a wall near the door in his black suit and black hat. He nodded at Cassidy and drew so hard on his cigarette that the burning paper crackled.

"The boss thought I should come, make sure you got what you wanted."

To make sure Costello got what he wanted.

"Mr. Sorino, I'd like to see the books on the Towers for December–January."

Sorino typed numbers into the adding machine, pulled the lever, looked at the results with satisfaction and then at Cassidy with distaste. He opened a drawer, retrieved a ledger, and slid it across the desk without a word. Then he went back to his numbers to distance himself from the proceedings.

The book was leather-bound and stamped in gold with the Waldorf logo. Cassidy opened it flat and leafed back to New Year's Eve.

Sorino had told him that Ingram did not show up for work on New Year's Eve, but the room service waiter had seen Ingram in the Towers elevator with three or four other men dressed for a party. Where had they been going?

He could feel Packer watching him as he ran his finger down the page. The answer jumped out at him halfway down. The notations in the book were for services ordered for the apartments in the Waldorf Towers on New Year's Eve. There was an order for a suite on the thirty-seventh floor: twelve bottles of Louis Roederer champagne, two bottles of Johnny Walker Black Label scotch, two bottles of Jack Daniel's whiskey, two bottles of Beefeater gin, two bottles of Hennessy VSOP cognac, ice and mixers, six platters of assorted hors d'oeuvres including a pound of Beluga caviar. It was specified that the caviar was to be Iranian, not Russian. The order was to be delivered by six o'clock. No service staff was to enter the suite after six o'clock unless called for. That demand was underlined.

"Tell me about Suite thirty-seven oh three."

Sorino put down his pen with a weary sigh. "That suite is on a four-year lease to Mr. Junius Schine."

"Who is he?"

"Mr. Schine is a gentleman from California. He is in the hotel business, which is why, I suspect, he appreciates the service and the privacy he receives at the Waldorf."

"Is he any relation to the David Schine who works for Senator McCarthy's committee?"

"I believe he is David Schine's father."

Stanley Fisher's last words hadn't been "sweet shine." He had been trying to tell Cassidy where he and Ingram and the others were on New Year's Eve: Schine's suite. "Schine . . . suite . . . Schine." The last gasps of a dying man. And the word that had sounded like "ear" or "mere"? A fragment of New Year's Eve.

Cassidy closed the ledger and pushed it back across the desk. Sorino stopped his calculations and slipped the book into the bottom drawer.

"I need the passkey for the Tower suites," Cassidy said.

Sorino shook his head. "No, no, no. I agreed to this, but, no, not that. That is completely unacceptable. We have very important guests in the Towers. I cannot have you wandering about, poking your nose in wherever you want."

Packer pushed away from the wall. "Hey, come on, pal, you don't want to be like that." He said it mildly, but Sorino looked at him and read something in his face. He took a ring of keys from another drawer. There were three keys on the ring, each marked with a piece of colored tape.

Sorino handed them to Cassidy. "The yellow one. This is highly irregular. I don't like it at all. If we had not been threatened with a disruption of crucial services that would paralyze the hotel, I would not have agreed to any of this."

"Noted."

"I will hold you responsible."

"Good idea." Cassidy turned to Packer. "Wait here. I'll be back."

"In a pig's eye. Frank says stick with you."

Cassidy shrugged and led the way out of the office. A waiter pushed a service cart of dirty dishes down the corridor toward them.

"What's up?" Packer walked at Cassidy's shoulder. "What did you find in the book?"

The waiter banged the double doors of the kitchen open with the end of the cart and disappeared.

Cassidy slammed his right elbow into Packer's stomach. The man grunted in pain and surprise and folded. One hand came up to hold his stomach, and the other scratched at his coat to get at the gun under his arm. Cassidy punched him hard in the side of his neck. He bounced against the wall and sagged. Cassidy hit him on the point of the jaw and Packer sprawled face-first on the floor. Cassidy grabbed a handful of the unconscious man's jacket collar and dragged him down the corridor to a service closet. He pulled him in and left him propped against the back wall, legs splayed, among the mops and buckets.

• • •

Cassidy unlocked the door to the Schine suite with the passkey and went in. A short, mirrored hall led to a large living room furnished with big overstuffed chairs and sofas and good replicas of antique tables. Gold-framed landscapes of California hung on the walls. There was a photograph of Roy Cohn, David Schine, and Senator McCarthy on a table behind one of the sofas where you would be sure to see it when you entered the room. There were dark blue curtains at the north-facing windows. They had made dark blurs in the background of Ingram's photograph. He studied the room, memorizing the paintings and where they hung, the shapes of the sofas and chairs and the color of their upholstery, the placement of the tables and what ornaments and ashtrays they held. If what he had in mind was going to work, he needed to remember the room.

The living room gave on to a dining room, which led to a small kitchen, and a pantry stocked with nuts, bottled olives, boxes of crackers, and other cocktail snacks. The refrigerator held mixers, a pitcher of orange juice, half a lemon, a piece of something that might once have been pâté but was now curled leather, and a bottle of champagne.

There were two bedrooms off the living room. Neither had been recently used.

The closet in the bigger one held two suits, three sports coats, a number of trousers, an overcoat, and an army uniform with a name tag reading SCHINE pinned above the breast pocket.

Cassidy prowled the living room, opening and closing the drawers in the tables. He found nothing of interest besides ten identical pamphlets in a drawer in a tallboy near the dining room. They were bound in dark maroon cloth and were titled "Definition of Communism." The author was G. David Schine. Cassidy lit a cigarette and sat in an overstuffed chair and threw one leg over its arm while he read. The pamphlet was only six pages long. The writing was stiff and clumsy, and the thoughts were muddy.

Schine had confused Marx with Lenin. He had confused Trotsky with Stalin. The Republic was in good hands.

He took the prints from his pocket and studied them as he walked around the room. That dark blur with the brightness next to it was this chair and this lamp. The tall shape next to it in black-and-white was a man in a dinner jacket and white shirt. Another stood near the rectangle of a window. That table and that lamp. The bright silver of the warming dome covering a service cart. The figure in red, blurred in this picture, between the blurs of two men in dinner jackets. Ghosts and shapes, nothing that would stand up in court, but he knew the photographs had been taken in this room on New Year's Eve.

He left the suite and rode down in the elevator with just the elevator man. The doors opened at the Tower lobby. Roy Cohn waited to get on. He was with a good-looking young man with a soft face and curly hair. They were leaning toward each other talking with their heads close together. The young man turned to whisper something in Cohn's ear that made Cohn laugh. When he looked up, he saw Cassidy, and his face froze.

"What are you doing here?"

"General MacArthur asked me to stop by to tell him where he went wrong in Korea."

Blood rose in Cohn's face. "You don't learn, do you? I explained how things work, but you didn't listen. Do you think your father's the only person I can reach? Well, now, now you'll see."

Cassidy grabbed Cohn by his jacket and jerked him into the elevator.

The elevator man said, "Hey," in alarm.

Cassidy showed him his badge and said, "Get out." He swung Cohn around and shoved him to the back of the car and closed the door on the startled faces of the elevator man and Cohn's friend. He pushed the lever and rode the elevator up half a floor and then stopped it.

Cohn watched him warily from the corner of the car. His shoulders were hunched in defense, and he had his hands up. "You're in trouble."

"Careful, little man. I've got a bad temper and a thirty-eight pistol."

"Are you threatening me?"

"Absolutely. If you come anywhere near me or mine again, I will hunt you down and shoot you. Is that clear?"

Cohn stared at Cassidy and said nothing.

Cassidy took a step toward him. "Is that clear?"

Cohn's mouth worked for a moment and then he nodded.

Cassidy ran the elevator down to the lobby and opened the door. Cohn darted past him and out through the revolving door to 49th Street. His friend threw Cassidy a puzzled glance and went after him.

Cassidy stepped out of the car and smiled at the elevator man. "It runs nice. Good on the straightaways and the curves." He went out onto 49th Street feeling better about his day.

35

Dylan was sitting in a chair near the window when he came into the apartment. There was a book open in her lap, but the apartment was dark now, so she must have been there for a long time.

"How was your day?" he asked as he went to the kitchen to make a drink. *Stay casual. Feel it out. The ground underfoot is treacherous.*

"Fine. How was yours?"

"Great." He held up the bottle of Jack Daniel's, but she shook her head.

"How's the project going? Is Ribera destroying or creating today?"

"Is this how we're going to do it? Start with lies? You know I didn't go to Ribera's this morning."

He said nothing. It was her lead. His heart raced.

"I saw you come out of the diner across from the camera store. I was looking out the window. You followed me. I don't how, but you did."

"The rooftops."

"Ah." A wry smile. "Smart. I thought if you tried to follow me down the block I would see you, and if you couldn't follow me down the block you would have no way of knowing where I went. Imagine my shock."

"Imagine mine."

"Yes." She shook her head in regret.

He walked around the counter and into the living room. She lifted the book from her lap and put her hand on the automatic it concealed. "Mike, please. Far enough."

He settled into a chair across the room and took a slug of bourbon. Some of the tension went out of her, and she took her hand off the gun.

"I thought I was careful, but I knew you were onto me."

"Someone told me you weren't all you pretended to be."

"Who?" She saw him hesitate. "What does it matter?"

"A man named Crofoot."

"CIA."

"You know him."

"We try to keep track of the people who can hurt us."

"Who are you, exactly?" He held up a hand to stop her from speaking. "Don't do the business about Aliquippa, Pennsylvania, and your dead mother, and the old guy who taught you how to weld."

"Does it matter?"

"I don't know. Maybe. I'd like to hear it."

"Okay. Not Alquippa, but I was born in a town like it and not far away. My parents lost their business in the Depression. The bank foreclosed on the house. They took what little money they had left and moved my brother and me to Russia. They believed in what was happening there. They'd lost faith in America. They weren't the only ones. There were a lot of American families where we lived. We believed there could be a better future for working people."

"How's that working out?"

She ignored his sneer. "Every experiment has problems in the beginning. America, the ideal of freedom, every man created equal. Almost two hundred years later, and Negroes are little better than slaves."

"Where did all this take place, Moscow?"

"No, Molotov. Near the Ural mountains. That's where I learned to weld. There was an old man, and he taught me in a tank factory during the war. They used children in the tight places where a grown person couldn't fit."

"Did you know Ingram there?"

"No. I never met Ingram. We were in different cells."

"Who killed him?"

"What difference does it make?"

"It's what I do."

"You'll never get him."

"Then it doesn't matter. You might as well tell me."

She thought about it and then shrugged. "You know him as Apfel. He developed the photographs everybody wants so much. Ingram stole the negatives. Apfel went to retrieve them. Ingram refused to give them back. He said he had buyers who would make him rich. He offered to share with Apfel."

"But Apfel was too good a Communist to accept a bribe."

"He's a believer. Like you, he'll do what he has to do if he believes he's right."

He let that one go. "He killed Ingram, even if he didn't mean to. He killed Fisher and Werth and Freed just to clean up loose ends."

"And you wouldn't? You threw a man out a window without stopping to think if he would live or die."

Cassidy started to tell her that Franklin deserved it, but he knew that was the thin excuse everybody wrapped around a dirty move. He stood up abruptly, and she put her hand on the gun in her lap. He went into the kitchen and made another drink. "Sure you don't want one?"

"I do. Will you make me a martini the way I like it?"

He brought her the drink.

"Thank you." She took it with her right hand, and he could have taken the gun then, but she would not talk if he had the gun. She smiled up at him as if she knew what he was thinking.

He went back to his chair across the room.

"Tell me about Ribera."

"What about him?"

"Is he part of it? Is he part of your cell?"

"No. He is what he is, a wonderful artist."

"No sympathy for the downtrodden worker? No affection for the workers' paradise?" *IMPOSSIBLE*

She ignored his sarcasm. "Of course he has sympathy. He thinks. If you think, how can you not have sympathy? I needed work that gave me a flexible schedule. I needed someone who would not question me. Someone he admires put in a word for me." *FOR OPPRESSION?*

"Did he know Apfel?"

She hesitated. "Yes. But not like that. He needed photographs taken of some of his work for a catalog. I introduced him to Apfel. He's a good photographer. It's his cover, but he's good at it. And I needed an excuse to talk to him, to go to his shop."

That was the first lie he was sure of. She did not know that Orso had followed Ribera to the camera store, and how hard Ribera had worked to make sure that didn't happen. Not the behavior of an innocent artist. How many lies had he not seen?

"What's in the photographs that makes them so important to the KGB?"

"You should know. You have them."

"I do?"

"Yes. You told Perry Werth. He told Apfel."

"Before Apfel shot him."

"Yes."

"And you're here to get them."

"Yes."

"What if I told you they don't exist?"

"I know they exist. Apfel developed them. He saw them. Ingram stole the negatives and destroyed the prints so that he would have the only copies."

"They won't do you any good."

"Of course they will; the man can't continue if they come out. They'll give us leverage."

"It's not what I meant. I'll show you." He started to reach for his inside pocket.

She picked up the gun. "Mike, don't."

"It's all right. I'll do this slowly. My gun's on the left. The photos are on the right."

"Be very careful."

He slowly drew the envelope from his inside pocket with two fingers and showed it to her.

He got up and crossed the room, holding the envelope out.

"All right."

He flipped it out and it landed on the floor at her feet. "Step back."

He went back to his chair and picked up his drink.

She put the gun on the arm of her chair and reached for the envelope and opened it and looked at the photographs. She looked at Cassidy, puzzled. "What are these?" She fanned the four prints he had given her. The fifth, the only clear one, was still in his pocket. "Ingram's photographs. Printed from his negatives."

"I don't understand."

"He hid the negatives in his locker at the theater where he was dancing. He had them taped to the back wall. The locker was metal, and it was up against a steam pipe. The heat destroyed the negatives."

"I don't believe you."

"Yes, you do."

"I want the negatives."

"Fine."

She held up the prints again. "There should be five. Apfel said Ingram stole five negatives."

"The one closest to the pipe melted. There was no image at all. I threw it away."

"We have experts. Perhaps they could raise something you didn't."

"I don't think so. The guy I used is the best. Do you think I'd take them to an amateur knowing how many people have died for them?"

She looked down at the prints, and then looked at him blankly. He started to speak, but she held up her hand. "I have to think." She got up with the gun in one hand and the prints in the other and went to stand by the window.

She leaned against the window frame with her weight on one leg and her hip cocked. She had put the prints on the windowsill, and now she worried her thumbnail with her teeth the way he had seen her do often when she was thinking. Her head was down, and her face was in profile, serious and beautiful, and he wanted to cross the room and take her in his arms and tell her not to worry. *Get a grip. She's a Russian spy with a .32 automatic, and you want to go comfort her?*

"How did you know I was onto you?"

"What?"

"You said you knew I was onto you. How did you know?"

She turned away from the window to look at him and he saw her come back from wherever she had been. "Something changed in your lovemaking. You were holding back."

"*I* was holding back? I don't even know your real name."

"That's different."

"Is it?"

"I never lied to you about how I feel."

"How do you feel?"

"Do you really have to ask?"

"Yes."

She waited a long time. "I love you."

"Don't tell me that lie." She flinched. "You came after me because you thought I might have Ingram's photos. Are you going to tell me it was coincidence that you moved into an apartment here that's been vacant for months three days after Ingram died?" He could hear the bitterness in his voice.

"No. Of course not. They thought if I could get close to you, I might find out what you knew. They were worried after you went back to the apartment. They were afraid you had found the photographs."

"And that I was going into business for myself?"

"Yes."

"The capitalist urge?"

"Something like that."

"So they sent you."

"Yes."

"Pillow talk rather than torture. Smaller chance of a heart attack."

"It wasn't like that. I told you, I do what I want. Nobody makes me do something I don't want to do."

"Right. Sure. It was just a small sacrifice for the good of the workers' paradise. Fuck the cop. Get the photos. Long live the revolution. What a sucker I was. You searched the apartment, didn't you? I came in one day and things weren't quite right, but I ignored it. But that was you, wasn't it? Jesus. Blind him with pussy. That sure worked." He was angry that she had slipped the lock on his life so easily.

She flinched as if slapped but said nothing.

"And the night we went to Ribera's party, you didn't want me to go. Amado was there, and so was General Caldwell. Caldwell was a blackmail target. He was one of the men Ingram and Amado and the others roped in. You thought I might put it together. I wasn't that smart."

Her face set into harder lines. "Think what you like. I want the negatives."

"They're not here. They're in the squad room. If you want them, you'll have to go get them yourself. Or your masters will just have to be happy with the prints. And good luck to them."

"Please, Michael."

"That's it. That's all you get."

She thought about it for a moment. "All right." She gestured with the pistol. "Go to the counter."

He carried his drink to the counter that separated the kitchen from the living room. It was made of a long, heavy slab of black walnut supported by metal beams.

"I want you to handcuff yourself to the beam."

"Forget it."

"I need some time. Not much, but some. I'm not going to spend the rest of my life in an American prison. I'll do what I have to do."

He believed her. He took the cuffs from his belt and closed one around his left hand, then crouched and embraced the beam that braced the counter and closed the other cuff around his right. Dylan brought him a chair so he would not have to sit on the floor. She tested the cuffs and then felt in his pockets and found the keys and tossed them across the room.

"I'm sorry." Her voice had tears in it.

He said nothing.

She was about to say something else, but she shook her head, touched his face, and walked out without looking back. He heard the door to her apartment open and close, and then a few minutes later he heard it open and close again, and then her footsteps going down the stairs.

He pushed the chair aside and got his shoulder under the slab and heaved up. It did not move. He pushed until his legs ached. He tried dropping down and slamming up, but that just hurt his shoulder. He looked under the counter. The beam was fixed to the bottom of the wood by four hex bolts with slotted tops. He grasped one between his index finger and thumb and tried to turn it, but it was in tight and did not move. *Think.*

He pushed his belly in toward his hands and undid his belt buckle and pulled the belt free. The buckle was steel and the edge of it fit into the hex bolt slot, but he could not turn it. Leverage. That word again. *Leverage will set you free.*

He pulled his arms to the top of the beam and raised his head above the level of the counter. A knife lay next to the plate of butter left out at breakfast. He pulled the cuffs up as far as they would go on the bracket and pushed himself up as far as he could on the counter. The cuffs bit into his wrists. He reached out with his chin and touched the knife handle.

Careful. Get it. Get it. Don't push it away. Gently.

He pulled the knife toward the edge of the counter. It caught on a crack and slipped out from under his chin. He got it back, wiggled it. It moved. When he got it close to the edge, he stopped.

Don't drop it on the floor. If you drop it on the floor, you'll never get it back. He pushed it around with his chin so the blade stuck out beyond the counter edge.

Okay. Take it easy.

Carefully he picked it up with his teeth, slid back onto the chair, and leaned in under the counter to transfer the knife to his hands. He slid the belt buckle edge back into the bolt slot and pushed the knife through the buckle. He held the buckle in the slot with one hand, and levered the knife with the other.

Nothing happened.

He took the knife out of the buckle and scraped at the paint around the head of the bolt until he had scraped it clean. Then he put the buckle back in the slot and the knife back in the buckle and pulled. The bolt suddenly gave, and he nearly dropped the buckle and knife.

It took him more than half an hour to scrape the three other bolt heads free and to unscrew them. He put his shoulder under the counter slab to hold it, pulled the top of the bracket free of the wood, and slipped the cuffs over the top. The he pushed the bracket back in place to keep the counter end from falling and crossed quickly to the phone and dialed the number Crofoot had given him. It was answered on the fourth ring.

"Yes?"

"Cassidy. There are three of them in the cell, two besides the McCue woman. A sculptor named Carlos Ribera and a photographer and camera store owner named Rudi Apfel."

"He took the pictures?"

"No. Ingram took them. Apfel developed them."

"Does she have them?"

"No."

"How can you be sure?"

Cassidy realized his mistake. "I can't be sure. I asked her. She said no. I believed her."

"Uh-huh. Addresses?"

Cassidy gave them to him.

"What happened?"

Cassidy told him.

"How long has she been gone?"

"About forty-five minutes."

"Shit."

• • •

Crofoot was at Ribera's studio when Cassidy got there. Three young men in gray coveralls were cataloging the studio's contents. Cassidy found Crofoot in the bedroom looking at the painting of the woman on the beach.

"I thought it was a photograph at first."

"So did I."

"Will you look at that. It looks like she's about to step out of the painting. I swear to god I'm getting a boner. She's more alive than my wife." Crofoot took a last look at the painting and turned away with a sigh and led Cassidy back into the big room.

"What did you find at the camera store?" Cassidy asked.

"The fire department. He torched the place."

"What happens now?"

"Not much we can do. It's a joke to talk about sealing the borders even if we had the manpower or the jurisdiction, which we don't. Hell, you can walk across into Canada in a hundred different spots in New England. We'll put some people out at Idlewild, but I don't think they're going to be that stupid."

"Did you know about Ribera?"

"No. So that's a bonus, thanks to you. Interesting that they've got a Cuban working for the KGB. We've got some assets working in Havana. They'll keep a lookout for him."

"Apfel killed Ingram. And he killed Werth and Fisher to clean up loose ends. But he wasn't the man in Ingram's apartment when I went back, and he wasn't the guy who tortured and killed Amado."

"How can you be sure?"

"Amado was tortured in a different way. That's one thing. And the guy I wrestled with in Ingram's apartment was right-handed. I saw him sap down the super, Donovan. Definitely used his right hand. Apfel's left-handed."

"Ah. Interesting. Any ideas?"

"Either the Feds or you."

"Me? Please."

"Someone who works for you."

"You have a lurid idea of what we do. By the way, just curious, but why did you call me and not the FBI? You know it's their jurisdiction. They've got a lot of people they could have thrown at this. Not that they could catch clap in a whorehouse. I'm not complaining, mind you. I'm just curious."

"Fuck them. They piss me off. And you were the one who let me in on the Dylan woman." He told Crofoot what he thought he would believe, but he had a better reason, something he could not tell the CIA.

"Fair enough. I guess we're just going to have to assume these photos went to the grave with Ingram." He watched Cassidy brightly.

"I guess."

"Right, then. Well, thanks for the effort. It's going to be a long war, and losing a minor skirmish like this one isn't going to make a hell of a difference." He waved at the men searching the room. "Besides, who knows? We may turn up a nugget or two here. And we'll want to talk to you again. Debrief you. Everything she said that you remember. There'll be something there she let slip."

"Sure. Call me."

"Oh, we will."

Crofoot watched Cassidy get into the elevator. He waved as the doors closed. Why had Cassidy lied about the pictures? To be fair, he hadn't really lied. He just hadn't admitted that he had them, but Fraker had heard him tell Werth that he had them. It wasn't money. Cassidy had money. No need for blackmail. What was it, then? Power? Maybe. Everyone wanted power. What kind did Cassidy want? It would require some thought.

• • •

When Cassidy got back to his apartment, the phone was ringing, and for a moment he thought it might be Dylan, and his heart rose, and as he went to answer it, he wondered at his own delusions.

It was Leah.

"Michael?"

"Yes."

"I'm in trouble."

36

Cassidy found Brian in his new office on the sixth floor of the ABC head-quarters building. The curtains were drawn to darken the room. Brian, in shirtsleeves, leaned close to a kinescope to study the grainy images on the small screen. He looked up when Cassidy came in.

"I'll be right with you."

"Take your time."

Most TV newsmen had their ego walls, photographs of important people they had met and interviewed, ramrod generals in medal-weighted uniforms, puffed-up senators, movie stars with perfect smiles, jocks holding bats or balls, or leaning forward with their fists raised. Brian had only pictures of family: Marcy, dark and petite, and the girls on a boat on Long Island Sound; the girls sitting together wearing party dresses and looks of solemn good behavior; Marcy laughing at the camera; Leah on her wedding day; Michael in uniform looking young and wary just before he shipped overseas; formal portraits of their parents, publicity shots of Tom Cassidy, society page shots of Joan at this ball or that opening; pictures of Michael and Brian as teenagers in baseball gear playing at Randall's Island.

Brian offered love easily, without thought or restraint. Leah accepted it the same way, as if it was her due. Cassidy could do neither and envied their ease.

"Hey, I'm glad to see you." Brian came around the desk and grabbed him around the shoulders with one arm and hugged him. "Did you have any trouble finding the new office?"

"No, but I got a couple of funny looks when I mentioned your name. Everything all right here?"

"Yeah. Sure. Not perfect, but okay. You know how it is. People hear Dad's in jail, they hear what for, they begin looking at you sideways. A lot of people are scared, good people, smart people. They're afraid your troubles are going to slop over on them. Suddenly they want to keep a distance. I'm not the first guy they call for a drink after work."

"Are you going to be all right?"

"My boss is a good man, and he hates what's going on with McCarthy and all that. That's why he wants to film the hearings. He thinks the public's smart enough to sniff out the bastard if they just see him at work." He moved to a bar setup against the wall. "I'm pretty much done here for the day. Let's have a drink. Daniel's?"

"Sure."

Brian handed him a tumbler with bourbon and a couple of ice cubes. "What can I do for you?"

"I need an address."

"Why don't you look it up in the telephone book?"

"It's not one I'd find in the telephone book."

"Whose address?" Brian asked.

Cassidy told him.

"Jesus, Mike."

"Do you have it?"

"I know where I can get it." Brian waited, hoping, Cassidy knew, that he would tell him to forget it.

"Good."

"Are you sure you want this?"

"I'm sure."

"Okay. Goddamn it. Hold on. It's in my files someplace. We did a story on him last year. I'll find it. Jesus." It took a few minutes. He wrote the information on a scratch pad and handed it to Cassidy. "Be careful, okay?" Cassidy was headed out-of-bounds and Brian knew there was nothing he could do to stop him.

In the morning, Cassidy rented a two-year-old Ford from the taxi garage on Hudson Street. He took it out through the Holland Tunnel and rammed it south on the newly completed New Jersey Turnpike.

Leah's problem had to wait. He told her to pay Franklin, knowing that he would be back for more, but the first payment would buy time, and Cassidy needed time. The world was closing down on him. Leah and Franklin. His father about to be deported. And Dylan. He did not know which he felt more, anger or sadness, but whatever it was made him ache.

The farther he drove, the flimsier his plan seemed, but it was all he had.

37

The houses on 30th Place in Washington, D.C., were set back on deep lawns and were shielded from each other by broad yards and mature trees. The house Cassidy wanted was a brick two-story with a small portico at the front door held up by narrow white columns. It was solid and unpretentious, a house where a successful middle manager of a large company, or a civil servant of a high pay grade might raise a family. There were no lights behind the windows, no bicycles on the lawn, none of the untidy signs of family life, because there was no family waiting here.

Cassidy parked down the block and watched the house. He thought it might be guarded, but there were no cars with watchers on the street, no discreet loiterers. There was no obvious alarm box, no wires coming from the house other than telephone and electricity.

Was it going to be that easy?

At three o'clock, a light went on over the front door, and a few minutes later a middle-aged woman carrying a large purse came out, locked the door, and walked down the block toward the bus stop. The housekeeper. He watched her until her bus came and she got on.

A service alley ran behind the houses on the block. Cassidy counted in from the corner and found that the backyard of the house was separated from the alley by a sturdy wooden fence. It was too high to see over. The door in the fence was locked. The windows in the second story of the house across the alley reflected sunlight, and there was no way to tell if someone watched him. The lock was new and it resisted the tickling of his picks. A car slowed at the end of the alley and then went on. The tips of the picks felt for the tumblers. A rattle of garbage cans jerked Cassidy's head around. A hundred yards down the alley, a housemaid slapped the top back on a can and went into the yard of her house without looking in his direction. He turned back to the lock. Moments later, he felt it yield.

Mature trees shaded the yard, and the fences on either side were high, but the second-floor windows of the neighboring houses had good views. He walked quickly with purpose and hoped that anyone watching would assume he had legitimate reasons to be there. He slipped the lock on the French doors on a patio with white wrought-iron furniture and went into a living room crowded with tables and breakfronts cluttered with ceramic cows and milkmaids, vases holding artificial flowers. The portrait of a strong-faced, gray-haired woman over the mantel looked down at him in stern disapproval. The furniture was heavy and dark in the style of an older generation, and it was pushed back so that there was a cleared space in the middle of the room.

Cassidy went upstairs and began his search.

• • •

At dusk, Cassidy heard the car stop outside the house. He walked to the window on the second-floor landing and looked out at the street. A limousine was parked in front. The driver got out and walked around and opened the passenger door and held it while two men got out. Cassidy heard car doors close as he walked to the top of the stairs and looked down into the living room. The front door opened, and he could hear them in the hall.

One of them said, "How about a drink, Eddie?"

"A drink would be fine." They came into the living room. The shorter one was reading a note. "Mrs. Jenkins left a shepherd's pie in the warming oven."

"Very nice. I think we have some Birds Eye peas in the freezer. Would you like me to heat them up?"

"Wonderful. Yes, peas, please, Clyde." They both smiled at the childish rhyme.

Clyde went into the kitchen and came out a few moments later carrying two ice-filled highball glasses. He went to the bar and poured Johnny Walker Black Label over the ice and added water from a silver pitcher and gave one of the drinks to Eddie. They clinked glasses.

"Cheers," Clyde said.

"Chin chin."

They held each other's eyes as they took the first long, satisfying swallows.

Cassidy started to go down the stairs, but something held him back. He sat down in the darkness on the top step and watched.

"Say," Clyde said, "what do you think about a little music, and then we'll go in and eat Mrs. Jenkins's wonderful shepherd's pie before it dries out in the oven."

"Music? Sure. A little music. I'd like that."

Clyde found a Tommy Dorsey Band record in the pile and slipped it on the turntable. He dropped the needle on the first cut and held out his arms. Eddie stepped into them, his left hand raised to take Clyde's right. His right arm went around Clyde's waist. Clyde put his left hand on Eddie's right shoulder and waited. When Eddie felt the beat, he led them into a brisk fox-trot in the cleared center of the room, and as the music came to an end, managed to dip Clyde without dropping him.

Cassidy came down the stairs as the record ended and the needle buzzed in the last grooves. When they straightened, they both saw him at the same time and froze, Tolson's hand still on Hoover's shoulder, Hoover's arm still around Tolson's waist.

Tolson took a step forward to put himself between Hoover and Cassidy. "Who the hell let you in here? If you bring a message from the Bureau, you wait outside. Did Mrs. Jenkins let you in? She knows better."

"I'm not from the Bureau."

"You're not from the Bureau? Who are you?" Hoover looked confused, as if he could not get his mind around the idea that someone could and would invade his house. No matter who they were when they started their careers, Tolson and Hoover were now men who saw the world through the windows of limousines and expensive restaurants, from box seats and country club terraces. They were so swaddled in their power and privilege, so insulated by deference and obedience that they had lost all sense of their own vulnerability.

Tolson started toward Cassidy with a hand raised in threat.

"Don't," Cassidy said.

Tolson was angry, but there was enough steel in Cassidy's voice to check him, and he veered toward the phone.

"My name is Cassidy, Mr. Hoover. Michael Cassidy."

"That tells me nothing."

It told Tolson something. He stopped next to the table that held the phone. His hand rested on the receiver, but he did not pick it up.

"I'm a New York cop."

"Yes? And? What are you doing in my house?"

Tolson lifted the receiver. "He was the detective originally assigned to the Ingram killing."

"Yes? And? You were taken off the case. What do you mean by coming here? What's going on here? Mr. Tolson, I want this man removed."

"I'll call the Bureau," Tolson said. "They'll have someone here in ten minutes."

"You don't want anyone else here for this."

Tolson dialed.

"Let's talk about last New Year's Eve."

Tolson looked at him for a moment and put down the phone.

38

Hoover sat in a wingback chair with his feet planted squarely on the floor and his hands on his thighs and watched Cassidy without expression. He had recovered from his initial shock. Cassidy knew he was used to command, to hard decisions. Now he waited for what would come. He would deal with it when he saw the shape of it.

Tolson took a seat at the end of the sofa near Hoover. His face and neck were stiff with the anger he could not slough off, and his hands clenched into fists and then opened again and again.

"Let's talk about the party in the Schine suite at the Waldorf Towers on New Year's Eve."

He took out the red dress he carried rolled up under his arm, unrolled it and held it high for a moment so they could see it, and then spread it on the floor so that it would always be in their sight while they talked.

Hoover's expression did not change, but he took a deep breath and let it out slowly. "You have broken into my house, and you have searched it, and now you show me a dress that belonged to my mother, which I keep in her memory. Please explain this outrage." His voice was low, but the last word came out in a rasp that showed his strain.

Cassidy got up and crossed the room and took the print from his inside pocket and dropped it on the coffee table where both men could see it. "And it fits you so well. Did you have it altered, or are you truly your mother's son?" The photograph showed J. Edgar Hoover in the red dress holding a glass of champagne high and with a lipsticked smile on his face. His eyes had been heavily made up. His cheeks were rouged, and he was crowned with a curled blond wig. He had one arm around Victor Amado's waist. Perry Werth stood near them, smiling.

Hoover pushed the photograph away from him with one finger. "A forgery. Not hard to do. Any competent photo lab could have made this."

"Shall we talk about the other ones? Shall I describe to you what they show? Perry Werth, Victor Amado, Stanley Fisher. There are, of course, no pictures of Alex Ingram. He was taking them with a camera concealed in his cigarette lighter." Cassidy took the fake Ronson from his pocket, pulled it apart to show the inner workings, and put it on the table next to the photograph. "Shall we talk about the action under the big painting of California? Or what happened in the bedroom next door?" This was the moment when it could all fall apart. He was counting on Hoover's memory to paint the pictures the blurred photographs did not show. He had the geography of the Schine suite, and the vague blurs that represented the men there, but he had no real idea of what had happened there. All he could hope for was that Hoover's guilt and his fear of exposure would fill in the blanks.

There was a long silence. Hoover's head was down as he stared at the photograph and the lighter on the table. Then he raised his head and looked at Cassidy, and his face was stone.

"Are you a Communist, Detective Cassidy?" Hoover's voice was low and tight with anger.

"Oh, for christ's sake."

"Well, if you are not, you are certainly working to advance the Communist agenda, the Communist campaign to destroy this country, to undermine its institutions, to destroy its leaders. We're at war. I've read your file. You know what that means. You've been there. There are times when we have to put aside the niceties. There are times that require the strongest measures, because without those measures, we will lose the war. Do you know what happens to the losers? All you have to do is look at what has happened in Poland and Hungary and Czechoslovakia. The losers are stood up against the wall and shot. Don't you understand that the FBI is the strongest bulwark we have against this insidious invasion?" He flicked the photograph with a fingernail. "These are lies, manufactured lies. They have set out to destroy me, because they know that I *am* the FBI in the eyes of many good Americans."

"The FBI, without jurisdiction, interfered with a New York Police Department homicide investigation. FBI agents searched my apartment without a warrant. They searched my sister's apartment, my brother's apartment, my father's and stepmother's apartment without warrants. The

FBI helped jail my father and condemned him to deportation without a hearing. The FBI put pressure on an independent news agency to fire my brother, all of which was designed to make sure that if I found these photographs, I would come running to you. The FBI's concern in all this was to pull your ass out of a fire of your own making. And you call yourself a defender of American institutions? You're awfully damn kind to yourself. Five men were killed for these photographs. Five men had everything that they had or ever would have stolen from them to protect your reputation."

Tolson slapped the table, and Ingram's Ronson jumped. "Your father lied on his citizenship application. He lied."

"Yes, he did. We all have our secrets, don't we? Most of us don't kill to keep them hidden."

"No FBI agent has killed anyone in this operation."

"The men died because of these pictures."

"What do you want, Detective Cassidy?"

Cassidy crossed to the bar in the corner and poured himself a large bourbon. If you break into a man's house and threaten him with blackmail, drinking his liquor without permission seemed a minor transgression. Hoover and Tolson watched him while he tasted the whiskey. He let them wait while he lit a cigarette.

"I want my father released from custody and all records expunged. I want a public apology to him from Roy Cohn."

"We have no control over what Mr. Cohn does or says."

"Cohn offered to get my father out if I delivered the photos to him." He might as well throw poison down that well while he had the chance.

"I see." Hoover did not seem surprised.

"Remind him what you've got in your files. See if that persuades him."

"What do I get in return?"

"The photographs and the negatives."

"How can I be sure you won't keep copies?"

"You can't. I'll give you my word."

"Not very reassuring."

"It's the best I can do."

"On the other hand, I am a very powerful man, as you remarked. With a word from me, your father goes to Russia, your brother and sister and their spouses are subject to very intrusive and very thorough investigations for possible ties to Communist organizations, possible criminal activities. All of which we will find. Their tax returns will be scrutinized.

They will spend a great deal of time in court or in lawyers' offices until they are bankrupted. Until they're destroyed. And then they'll go to jail."

"Yes. I know. You hold a lot of cards, and I hold a few. But I'm a simple guy. If I can't have what I want, I'll have revenge. If my father goes to Russia, I'll get the photographs to every newspaper, magazine, and TV station in the country. You'll spend the rest of your life as Mary, the G-man with lousy legs in his mummy's red dress."

39

The headlights of the rented Ford drilled a tunnel through the night and pulled him north toward New York. Insects, awakened to life by spring, flew down the shafts of light and died on the windshield.

Tolson, not Hoover, had made the calls. Hoover picked up the dress from where Cassidy had left it on the floor, folded it carefully, and carried it upstairs. He did not come down again.

Cassidy agreed to meet Tolson at the New York FBI office at Foley Square late in the afternoon the next day to turn over the negatives. It would take that long to complete the paperwork that would expunge Tom Cassidy's record and restore his citizenship, but he would be released immediately to Cassidy whenever Cassidy presented himself at the immigration lockup. There had been no handshakes to seal the deal, just a curt nod from Tolson and the distant footfalls of Hoover overhead.

Cassidy had made enemies for life and he wondered when, inevitably, they would decide to eliminate him.

It was after one in the morning when Cassidy got to Brooklyn. The only other vehicle he saw was a black delivery van that passed him a few blocks from the Department of Immigration's detention center. In the flare of his headlights he saw two men in the front seat.

Cassidy parked the Ford at the chain-link fence in front of the detention center, showed his badge to the gatekeeper, and crossed the open yard to the metal door with its heavy glass window. He rang the bell and waited and then gave in to the impatience that had been eating at him all night and rang again and beat on the door with the flat of his hand. Dim yellow light shone through the smudged glass. A door opened at the far end of the corridor, and a fat man in a gray uniform shuffled slowly toward him dangling a ring of keys. He stopped behind the glass and raised his eyebrows in question. Cassidy showed the man his badge. The guard yawned massively, fumbled with his keys, and opened the door.

"Yeah?" The guard let him in and closed the door.

"I've come to pick up Thomas Cassidy."

"Who?"

"Cassidy. Thomas Cassidy. You got a call from Washington about him."

"I didn't get no call." Cassidy followed him down the corridor toward the open door. "Maybe upstairs they got a call, but I didn't get no call."

"Who's upstairs?"

"Rabinov, the fuckhead, that's who's upstairs. Lazy bastard. Think he'd lift a finger to do any work? Perkins, do this. Perkins, do that. Fucking guy wouldn't have the job 'cept his uncle's a fucking city councilman. Maybe he got a call. How would I know? You think he tells me anything? But it's too late anyway."

"Too late for what? What's too late?"

"They come and got him."

Cassidy grabbed the man's arm and jerked him around. "Who came and got who?"

The guard pulled his arm free and raised a hand in defense. "Hey, easy, man. The Russkis. A couple of the Russkis came and got Cassidy. They always pick 'em up after midnight. One of them told me once, they pick 'em up in the middle of the night 'cause guys don't fight if you wake them up in the middle of the night. Scares the shit out of them. They just give it up. I guess they've had a lot of practice over there, is what I heard."

The black van with the two men in the front seat.

"He was supposed to be released to me. Washington called."

"Like I said, they didn't call me. I got a deport order, release to the Russkis. The Russkis got a pickup order. That's how it works. You got a problem, take it up with Rabinov, like I said. And good luck to you with that."

Cassidy ran up the stairs to a corridor of office doors. Light shone through the pebbled glass of one at the end. Cassidy knocked. No answer. He opened the door and went in. A uniformed man was asleep, head down on the desk. His bald spot gleamed in the light from the gooseneck desk lamp. A bottle of rye stood open at his elbow. There wasn't much left in it, and the glass next to it was empty. The man snored, and when he breathed out, it lifted the edge of a piece of paper a few inches from his slack mouth.

Cassidy kicked the chair out from under the man. His face banged against the side of the desk and he awoke with a cry. His hand scrabbled toward the holstered gun on his hip. Cassidy kicked him lightly and said, "Don't." He righted the chair and then hauled Rabinov up by his collar and dumped him back in it.

The paper the man had been breathing on was a scrawled note telling Perkins to not release Tom Cassidy to the Russians and to hold him for release to Michael Cassidy, NYPD. Something that might have been Rabinov's signature was scrawled across the bottom.

"Who are you?"

Cassidy showed him the paper. "You got a call from Washington telling you to release Tom Cassidy to me. Why didn't that happen?"

Rabinov scrubbed his face with his hand and looked with longing at the whiskey bottle. Cassidy slapped him with the paper to refocus him.

"Not my job," he whined. "I called that son of a bitch Perkins to come up and get the message. He never showed. I called him three times. It's not my fault." He reached for the bottle.

Cassidy moved it. "Did you tell him not to release Tom Cassidy? Did you tell him on the phone?"

"He's got to have it in writing. I wrote it. He didn't come get it. It's not my fault. I'm following the rules, but the lazy son of a bitch won't come up the stairs. You know why? He wants my job. He's trying to get me in trouble, but I've got it in writing right here. He just didn't come get it. So fuck him."

"How do you rescind the order? How do you get him back?"

"Get him back? Get who back? Cassidy? I don't know. I never had to get nobody back. If they turned in a pickup order and took the release, they've got him legal."

"Call someone and find out."

"Call who?"

"Call your supervisor."

"Call Captain Winsick at two in the morning? Are you kidding?"

Cassidy grabbed Rabinov's hair and banged his face onto the desk. He lifted his head. "Call him." He let go of Rabinov's hair and wiped the oil off his hand on the man's jacket.

Rabinov picked up the phone and dialed. He rubbed the red patch where his forehead had met the desk while he waited a long time for the phone to be answered. The waiting made him nervous. He licked his lips, looked from the bottle to Cassidy, and drummed his fingers on the desk. Cassidy pushed the glass and bottle close, and Rabinov poured an inch of liquor into the glass and then into himself.

Captain Winsick answered the phone in a way that made Rabinov flinch. "Yes, sir. I know it's late, sir. I'm sorry, sir. It's just that we've got a problem over here. No, sir. No, sir. They're all locked in. No problem there. It's, uh, I've got a New York cop here who was supposed to pick up Cassidy, Thomas. Orders from Washington. Release to him. Problem is, we got a foul-up. Perkins released Cassidy, Thomas, to the Russian pickup team before the hold order got to him, so anyway, like I said, we've got a problem and . . ."

Cassidy snatched the phone from Rabinov's hand. "Captain Winsick, this is Detective Michael Cassidy. I'm sorry we had to wake you, sir."

"You related to the detainee?" Winsick was annoyed but alert.

"He's my father."

"Yeah, well, look, I'm sorry about this, but I don't know what can be done. We had a deport order on your father. The Russians had a pickup. That's how the system works. It looks like the order from Washington came in too late. We're sorry about any confusion, but it's not our responsibility. Who sent the order?"

Rabinov poured himself another drink.

"Clyde Tolson at the FBI."

"Okay. That's FBI jurisdiction now. It's out of my hands. They'll have to take it up with the Russians." Winsick had a seasoned bureaucrat's knack for duck and cover.

"How would they move him out of the country?"

"Ship is what they usually do. Look, Cassidy, I'd like to help, but once they're no longer in my custody, there's nothing I can do."

Cassidy hung up the phone.

"You can go."

"What?"

"Get out. Take the bottle."

"Yeah. Sure. Okay." Rabinov grabbed the bottle and glass and hurried out. Cassidy closed the door and picked up the phone and dialed a number Tolson had given him.

A sleepy Tolson answered on the sixth ring.

"This is Cassidy. Your deal's falling apart."

40

It was three in the morning when Cassidy parked the Ford on Park Avenue. The city slept. He walked south two blocks, and the only car he saw was a taxi that slowed hopefully and then went on when he made no gesture. The lobbies of the big apartment buildings were lighted, and uniformed doormen dozed in leather chairs behind brass-fitted doors. He turned east and found Susdorf and Cherry sitting on the granite stoop of a town house. They both showed the resentful air of men who had been pulled from sleep. Susdorf nodded. Cherry sneered.

"It's down the block," Susdorf said. "But I don't think it's going to work."

"What'd Tolson tell you when he called?"

"Come out here. Wait for you to show up. Do what you want."

"Did you bring the papers I asked for?"

"Yeah." Susdorf tapped his breast pocket.

"Let's go."

Cherry flicked his cigarette against the door of the house so it showered sparks and left a small dark smudge on the glass, a mildly contemptuous act that made him smile. The three men walked in silence along the dark street to another large house with an impressive limestone façade, big iron-barred windows, carved gargoyles, and a set of broad marble steps leading to a massive door of black wrought iron and glass, the former home of a captain of industry, now the consulate for the Union of Soviet Socialist Republics.

Two uniformed New York cops stepped from the portico that shielded the lighted door. Cassidy had his ID out and showed them his badge, and they touched the brims of their hats and one said, "What can we do for you, Detective?"

"We need to go in."

"Sure. People are in and out all night. They've always got someone on the door. I don't know what the hell they're up to in and out like that. I had my way, the Commie bastards wouldn't be allowed in the country. Just ring the bell. Someone'll show up. I'll go up with you so they see everything's okay."

"Anybody come in tonight?"

"Not up in front here. The guys at the back said a van delivered down the alley back there. They didn't see what. We can't go down the alley, can't go past the front step. It's like that's all Russia, Russian territory." The cop rang the bell loud and long. "They don't like it when I ring long, but what the hell. How do I know whether they can hear it or not? Could be asleep for all I know." He grinned at his small poke at the enemy.

A stooped old man in a black suit shuffled across the marble lobby floor and stood behind the glass. Cassidy showed him his ID and badge. The old man took his time reading it and then slowly disengaged three locks securing the door, his small revenge on the cop. He pulled the door open and stepped back as Cassidy and the FBI agents entered. The old man gestured with his head toward a desk at the far side of the lobby. He shut the door and relocked it and shuffled away to sit in a chair in shadows by the wall.

There were three framed portraits on the wall behind the desk, Malenkov, Khrushchev, and Molotov. A faded patch showed where a much larger portrait of Stalin had hung, and the smaller ones had a sense of impermanency. Two would go, and one would become larger when the complicated process of succession played out.

The woman behind the desk was blocky and thick. Her hair was drawn back in a bun, and her stiff woolen uniform made her lumpy. Small dark eyes looked out of the dough of her face. She leaned her heavy breasts on the desktop and smoked a cigarette and, with a total lack of interest, watched Cassidy and the two FBI men approach.

"Help you?" She didn't mean it.

Cassidy put his badge on the desk in front of her. "I want to see your security officer."

The sight of the badge straightened her. The cigarette disappeared. She calculated. Their authority was one thing. The authority of the people behind the wall at her back was something else entirely. Which was riskier, to dismiss these men or to bother her superiors?

"A moment, please." She went back through a door that locked behind her.

"Let me have the papers," Cassidy said.

Susdorf took them from his inside pocket and passed them over. Cherry picked up a pen from the desktop, looked it over, and slipped it into his pocket. He lit a cigarette with a kitchen match scratched on the desk and dropped the match on the floor and watched it burn.

The door behind the desk opened. The blocky woman held it for two men, then she stepped back out of sight. The first man out was muscle, five foot ten, two hundred and twenty pounds, a head like a tree stump. He wore a square-cut gray suit that was a size too big. He had small, dark, watchful eyes. He took in the three men and then moved around the desk so that he flanked them. Cherry winked at Susdorf and turned to face the man.

The second man was tall and thin. He wore a dark blue suit that was too well cut to have been made in the workers' paradise and a white silk shirt open at the throat. His face was narrow and pale and his hair was the color of water. "I am Colonel Vasily Antipov. How may I help you?" He spoke with an English accent.

Cassidy and Susdorf slid their IDs toward him across the desktop. "Sorry to bother you at this time of night, but a detainee at the immigration detention center was released to your people by mistake," Cassidy said. "We've come to pick him up." He took the papers Susdorf had brought and put them on the desk. "These are release orders from the Department of Immigration and from the FBI."

Colonel Antipov examined the IDs and pushed them back across the desk. He picked up the papers and read them quickly, then put them down and pushed them back toward Cassidy. "I am afraid what you ask is impossible. Mr. Kasnavietski has been released to our custody in a legal manner. He has expressed a wish to be repatriated to the Motherland as quickly as possible. We will grant him that wish."

"I want to speak to him," Cassidy said.

"I am afraid that is impossible at the moment. He said he was having trouble sleeping. He has been given a sedative and is asleep."

"I'll wake him up. He'll want to see me."

"You're his son, I believe. He spoke of you."

"Yes."

"He said you might come look for him. He recognizes that his repatriation will be seen as a political and propaganda defeat by anti-Soviet elements in this country. He knows that pressure will be brought to bear to make him change his mind. He asked that we insulate him from that pressure and to tell you, specifically, that he is happy in his choice and that he hopes you will come visit him after he is settled."

"I'd like to hear that from him."

"I'm sorry, but that's impossible."

"I can have a hundred New York police officers here with a phone call." Bluff.

Antipov smiled. "Of course you can. Mr. Kasnavietski is on Soviet sovereign territory, as you know. We will defend that territory to the best of our ability. If you want to cause that kind of international incident, then so be it." Bluff called.

Antipov nodded to Cassidy and the FBI men, and turned to the door. It opened before he reached it, so Cassidy knew someone had watched them the entire time. Antipov and his gunsel disappeared, and the heavy woman came back out and leaned on the desk and watched them until they left.

• • •

The Anchor Inn was a seamen's dive on Albany Street half a block from the Hudson piers. The windows flanking the door were brass-framed portholes. Worn life rings hung on the walls, and a shelf on the back bar held dusty ship models. In a few hours it would be full of longshoremen coming off shift and having a couple of pops before heading home, but at four in the morning the place was empty except for a drunk passed out in one of the high-sided wooden booths, the bartender, a bullet-headed ex-pug with a fringe of gray hair above his ears, and an aging bottle blonde in a lime green skirt and yellow blouse who talked to him while she sat at the end of the bar nursing a bright scarlet drink with a slice of orange on the rim.

Cassidy and Cherry were in a booth at the back while Susdorf worked the phone that hung near the men's room. They were drinking coffee from heavy china mugs, and there were a couple of empty shot glasses on the table between them. Cassidy had not slept for nearly twenty-four hours, and his eyes were gritty with fatigue. His stomach was sour with too much coffee, and his mouth burned from too many cigarettes. He closed his eyes and leaned his head against the high wooden back of the booth and opened them again when Susdorf slid into the booth next to Cherry.

"The only Russian ship scheduled to sail this week is the *Bakunin* over at the Venezuela Line pier. We had our guy at Port Authority check the passenger manifest. There are five passengers listed. One was put on the list tonight." He checked his notepad. "Name of Theodor Kosev. He's listed as a consular official going home on medical leave. We checked the consulate list. It doesn't show a Theodor Kosev. T. K. We figure it's Tomas Kasnavietski."

"Good work."

"Yeah, well, every once in a while we manage to do something right even without the help of the NYPD."

Cassidy let it pass. "When does it sail?"

"She's loading right now. Due to cast off at seven. We've got a guy with the longshoreman crew loading her. Normal surveillance. We do it with all the Russian ships."

"I want to talk to him."

"We passed the word. He's coming."

"Have the other passengers boarded?"

"They got on last night after dinner. All present and accounted for, except for the mysterious Mr. Kosev."

The door to the bar opened and a man came in. He wore blue jeans and a work shirt, and a pair of heavy gloves was tucked into his back pocket. He said something to the bartender, who jerked his head toward the back. He picked up a chair along the way and put it at the end of the booth and sat down. His name was Hellman, and he was a blond, corn-fed Midwesterner with the bland, open face of an innocent, or a skilled, liar. Susdorf offered him a drink or coffee. He refused them.

"Thank you, sir. I don't use them." He looked around the table. "What do you want to know?"

"Have you ever seen the Russians bring someone to the ship who looks like he might be a prisoner, might not want to go?"

"Yeah. Sure. A couple of times. Different ships. Not this one, but still, yeah, I've seen them. I mean, I don't know for sure they were prisoners, but there was something about it."

"How do they do it?"

"A couple of times they brought them in an ambulance and took them up the gangplank on a stretcher. They were asleep, like they gave them something to knock them out. A couple of times they came in a car. Pull right up to the bottom of the gangplank. Two guys helping another guy, you know, and him nodding off, but he could walk with the two guys helping."

"Who owns the pier, us or them?"

"Venezuela Lines, actually."

"Yeah, but whose territory is it?"

"Ours," Susdorf said. "United States territory. The ship? That's theirs. Once he's on the ship, he's in Russia."

"So we take him on the pier between the car or the ambulance and the gangplank. I'm betting it's an ambulance. They know we want him. They'll have him knocked out." Cassidy lit another cigarette he did not want. He had to do something with his hands.

"Jesus, I don't know. I mean, what's our excuse?" Susdorf complained.

"A broken taillight on the ambulance, loitering with intent, interference with an officer, spitting on the sidewalk. We take my father and argue about it afterward."

"I better call Mr. Tolson."

"Mr. Tolson doesn't want to know. He wants to be able to deny he had anything to do with it. Once we get my father, it's over. Then it's politics. Mr. Tolson's good at politics. Let him do what he's good at."

"Fucking Russkis. Let's just do it. I'd love to stick it to them once." Cherry, an unlooked-for ally.

Susdorf did not like it. "Okay. But you're out front in this. The Bureau's backup. If things go wrong, we'll try to get you out, but we can't afford to be the primaries."

"I wouldn't want it any other way."

41

The SS *Bakunin* was a battered tramp freighter of about three thousand tons. Its black hull was a patchwork of rust chipped off and paint reapplied. The sodium loading lights on the pier made the white superstructure brilliant in the surrounding dark. Two tugs from Moran Towing, black hulls, dark red bridges, black funnels painted with a large white M, were butted up against the ship, one at the bow, one at the stern, waiting to herd her out into the stream.

The brightly lighted pier swarmed with longshoreman loading crates and bales into cargo nets with forklifts and muscle. A deck crane hooked the nets and swung them up and over the ship's rail and lowered them into the hold. Occasionally longshoremen rode the outside of the net to work the unloading. Winches squealed, forklifts rumbled and clanged, and the men shouted instructions and warnings over the mechanics. Cassidy could smell the diesel from the forklifts and the salt of the tidal river from where he watched in the pier foreman's office, a glassed-in cube under the pier's high metal roof. Susdorf and Cherry waited in the shadows at the back of the office. The foreman, a big Polack named Kolwitz, had looked at Cassidy's badge and then shrugged and gone back to his paperwork. "As long as you don't shoot one of my guys." Cassidy wasn't the first lawman to watch a Russian ship loading.

Three big men in raincoats and fedoras stood near the bottom of the gangplank smoking cigarettes and talking to each other. Cassidy watched a Russian crewman come down from the ship and swing wide to avoid them.

"Who are the heavies by the gangplank?"

"Amtorg officials," Kolwitz said.

"What's that?"

"American Trading Corporation. They do the buying and selling, American goods for Russia, Russian stuff for here. It's a Russian outfit."

Cassidy gestured to Susdorf, who came and stood at his shoulder and looked out at the three men.

"The Soviets use Amtorg as a cover for some of their operatives. The one in the middle is named Ipatiev. We have him ID'd as a colonel in the KGB. He worked with the occupation forces in Vienna under that name in 1947. The other two are low-level hoods traveling under work names."

"Does he usually pull this duty? Watching a ship load at oh dark hundred?"

Kolwitz raised up from his seat to look out the window. "The middle one? Never seen him before. The other two, yeah."

"He's here to make sure there's no hiccup getting my father on board."

Cassidy checked his watch. Six o'clock, an hour until the ship cast off.

Ten minutes later a taxi stopped a few yards from the gangplank. The three hoods put their heads together and then turned and watched the cab. The white lights overhead cast the interior of the cab in shadow, and it was impossible to tell how many people were inside.

"I'm going out," Cassidy said. "If it's my father, I'm taking him before they get up the gangplank." He went to the office door and eased the knob.

"Go easy, Cassidy. Just take it slow. We don't need an international incident over this."

"Sure."

Fifty feet to the cab. It would take him five seconds at the most to cover it. Another twenty feet from the cab to the gangplank. They'd be moving slowly if Tom Cassidy had been sedated. He had enough time. Why hadn't they pulled right up to the gangplank? He opened the door and stepped into the shadows of a steel pillar that supported the pier's shed roof. He took his gun out from under his arm and held it down along his leg.

One of the cab doors opened. A man got out. He turned and reached back into the dark interior to help someone. From where he stood, Cassidy saw a man inside the cab throw an arm over the first man's shoulder. There was a struggle. The first man pulled back, dragging the second man with him while a third followed from inside and put his arm around the second man's waist to support him.

Cassidy moved, his gun in one hand, his badge in the other. *Play it straight. Show them the badge. The voice of authority. That'll freeze them*

for a moment until he was close. Then, if he had to, show them the gun.
That's when it could all go bad. That's the moment when they'd give it
up or start to fight. Five of them, the two from the cab, and the three Amtorg men. Bad odds. Who do you take first? Ipatiev, the KGB colonel.
Would he have a gun? Probably. They'd look to him for the lead. If he
made a move, they'd go with it. If he moves, shoot him.

He was ten steps from the pillar when the three men began to sing in
Russian. They staggered a few steps from the cab, then stopped and shouted
something. They took a few more steps toward the ship and paused to elab-
orately bow to the Amtorg men at the gangway, who watched them im-
passively. Then they staggered up the incline to the deck.

Drunken crewmen at the end of liberty.

Cassidy took a few deep breaths and rolled his shoulders to shed the
tension. He holstered the gun and turned back to the office. Susdorf looked
at him and shrugged. He went back to his place at the window.

They waited.

Ten minutes later a small flatbed truck drove onto the pier and pulled
up near the gangplank. It carried a single crate. Six longshoremen man-
handled the crate off the back of the truck and laid it on a cargo net. The
winch on the *Bakunin* ground to life. The cable tightened. The net and
crate rose, swung in over the rail, and disappeared into the hold.

The pile of crates and bales on the pier diminished until there was
little more than a net full left.

Twenty to seven.

A six-year-old Chevrolet sedan pulled onto the pier and parked in the
shade of the shed roof. The man who got out wore a canvas jacket, gabardine pants, and rubber-soled work boots. His face was shaded by an old
fedora. He carried a worn leather briefcase and walked toward the ship
with a rolling gate as if matching the toss of a deck.

"Who's that?"

Kolwitz looked up from his desk. "Damon Hodge, the harbor pilot."

Hodge nodded to the Amtorg men and went up onto the ship and disappeared behind the deck rail. Moments later he reappeared climbing
the ladder to the bridge.

Six forty-five.

"They can't get him from the consulate to here by seven."

"A ship's not a train," Kolwitz said. "Sometimes they leave as late as
an hour."

"Call your guys watching the consulate," Cassidy said to Susdorf. "Find out if they've seen anyone leave."

"They could be caught in traffic," Susdorf said.

"At six thirty in the morning? Call."

Cassidy lit his fortieth cigarette of the day. It burned his mouth and throat, and he stubbed it out. He scrubbed his face with the flat of his hand, but it did nothing to chase his tiredness. He could hear Susdorf on the phone behind him. Through the window he could see the three Amtorg men talking. The leader, Ipatiev, nodded to his men and turned and walked away from the gangplank.

"No one left the consulate," Susdorf said.

"No one? Nothing?"

"A truck went out from the back."

"What was in it?"

Susdorf asked into the phone. "A crate. A driver."

"Nothing else?"

"No."

Ipatiev got into a car at the end of the pier and drove away. The other two Amtorg thugs leaned against the gangplank and lit cigarettes, relaxed now that the boss was gone.

If he was there to supervise Tom Cassidy's arrival, why had he left?

Longshoremen loaded the last of the crates into a cargo net.

Cassidy shucked his jacket and threw it toward a chair. He snatched a canvas windbreaker off a hook near the door and scooped a pair of work gloves and a cargo hook from the windowsill. "He's already aboard. They brought him in the crate." Then he was out the door and running.

The winch whined. The cable tightened. The last cargo net rose from the pier. Cassidy reached it as it cleared. He stuck a foot through one of the net openings and grabbed a handhold and rose with it.

One of the longshoreman said, "Hey," but he did not look back. He watched the Amtorg men as he rose. They glanced up at him, assumed he was a worker, and went back to their conversation. The net went up until it was twenty feet above the dock, and then it swung in over the deck toward the black rectangle of the open hold.

Cassidy rode the last load down and stepped to the deck as the net went slack over the crates it held. The hold smelled of coal smoke, fresh-cut pine from the crates piled two stories high, and the swamp of bilges. Work lights in cages ran the length of the overhead, leaving the alleys through the cargo stacks packed in shadow. The steel walls sent a constant murmur as water brushed the hull.

Russian crewmen looked curiously at Cassidy as they unhooked the cable. They saw the windbreaker and the gloves and cargo hook and accepted him as a longshoreman. One of them pointed up toward the deck and said, "You go now. We go. Ship go," and made a gesture with his hands to show the ship sailing.

Cassidy nodded and stepped away as the men dragged the net aside and swarmed the crates it had carried. Near a bulkhead door, he found the single crate that had been brought on the flatbed. One end had been pulled off and left on the steel deck. The crate was empty. Heavy staples held canvas straps that had been used to steady its cargo. There were black marks on the wood floor. The rubber wheels of a gurney, Cassidy thought. Some of the crewmen watched him. Their faces were closed and sullen now. They did not like him examining the crate that had carried a prisoner on board. The one who had spoken before jerked a hand toward the deck overhead and shouted, "Go. Go." Tom Cassidy had refused to speak Russian to his children while they were growing up. It was the language of his past, not his future, and his American children would never need it. Cassidy needed it now; he did not even know the word for father.

"Where's the man they brought in this?"

"No man here. You go." They lived where questions brought trouble, where if you raised your head, someone was sure to hammer it down. Better just to do your work, to see and hear nothing. He was trouble, and they wanted no part of him.

Cassidy stepped through the bulkhead door and climbed metal stairs that zigzagged up past metal grid landings to the deck. He stepped out into the new day as four crewmen shipped the gangplank and lashed it to the inside of the rail. A glance at the shed roof of the pier showed him that the ship was moving slowly out from land. A blast of the bridge horn was answered at the bow and the stern by hoots from tugs. The deck under his feet throbbed with the beat of the engines, and he could hear the suck and wash of water at the stern as the screws churned.

Crewmen on deck whispered together and watched him, and he stepped quickly through an open door into the ship's castle before they could confront him. They would tell an officer he was aboard. There would be a search. He would have to find his father before they found him.

Cassidy had traveled to war in a ship not much different from this one.

He knew the castle held the living quarters and control centers of the ship. On this deck and the deck above he would find a mess hall for the crew, a galley, a wardroom for the officers, cabins for the officers and passengers, and probably a small dispensary. Above that would be the bridge with the navigator's station, the radio room, and a captain's day cabin behind the bridge. The deckhands would bunk forward in the forecastle. A long corridor ran toward the stern, and halfway down it two short corridors cut to the port and starboard sides. The galley, wardroom, and mess hall were forward of the short corridors. All three were empty. The crew was making the ship ready for sea. Breakfast would have been served before the loading started, and lunch was still hours off. Cassidy stopped at the corridor intersection. The door to the starboard side was open at the end of the short hall, and Cassidy saw the end of the pier slide by as the tugs backed the ship out into the stream.

The first door opened into the captain's cabin. It smelled of tobacco smoke and was big enough to hold a bunk, a desk and desk chair, a leather sofa, and a matching leather armchair, green, faded, and cracked with age. There was a rack of pipes and a canister of tobacco on the desk, and a small bookcase was pinned to one wall. Wooden slats held the books in against the roll of the ship. An oilskin jacket and a gold-braided hat hung on the back of the door. The next two cabins were officers' quarters, smaller than the captain's but with the same well-lived-in look. Cassidy was wasting time. Unlocked doors would not lead him where he wanted to go. His father, even sedated, would be behind a locked one.

A speaker fixed high on one of the corridor walls crackled and then spoke: "Here Captain Versikov speaks. An American longshoreman is on the ship in mistake. Please to come to the bridge and will go to shore with pilot when pilot disembarks. Longshoreman, please to come to the bridge." The speaker crackled again and then went silent. When he did not appear on the bridge in the next few minutes, they would come looking for him.

The last three cabins on that deck were unlocked and unoccupied.

Cassidy went up a narrow stairway to the next deck. The second door he tried was locked. He reached in his pocket for his lock picks and realized that he had left his jacket in the pier office, that he was wearing someone else's windbreaker. The doorframe was steel, and the door fitted tightly to it. The ship worked and creaked in the river current, and he could hear nothing through the door.

"Longshoreman. American longshoreman. Please come to bridge. Come to bridge at once." The speaker crackled and went silent.

In a tool closet at the end of the corridor, Cassidy found a three-foot-long pry bar. He took it back and jammed the claw in between the wood of the door and the steel of the frame and levered back hard. The wood crushed under it, and he pushed the claw in deeper and wrenched the bar again, and the door gave with a loud splintering of wood. He pushed it open and found himself in the ship's dispensary. Glass-fronted wooden cabinets held medical equipment. A wooden chest of drawers was bolted to one wall. The cabin was high enough above the water so that it had two square windows rather than portholes. The buildings at the lower end of Manhattan slid by as the ship slipped downriver.

Tom Cassidy was strapped to an examining table screwed to the floor in the middle of the cabin. Cassidy tossed the pry bar aside and went to him and undid the straps.

His father was in a sedated sleep still dressed in the detention center jumpsuit. His breathing was regular and his pulse was slow but strong. His skin was almost colorless in the morning light, and the stubble on his face was gray in places, a sign of age that surprised Cassidy. His father, with whom he had so often butted heads, who could ignite his anger with a flick, was shrunken, diminished, helpless.

"Dad. Dad. Wake up." Cassidy shook his father's shoulder, but there was no response. He did not know how he was going to get Tom Cassidy's two-hundred-plus pounds off the ship, but he knew he could not carry him. He had to wake him.

He retrieved the pry bar and broke open the locked pharmaceutical drawers. Most of the drugs were marked in Cyrillic and he could not read them, but he did find ammonia ampoules from an American company, and in another drawer he found a package of small brown waxed envelopes that held Benzedrine tablets from an army medical kit like the one he had been issued during the war. He filled a glass at the small copper sink in the corner of the cabin and carried everything back to the examining table. He snapped an ammonia capsule under his father's nose, and his father groaned and rolled his head away. He broke another, and the sharp vapor cut the sedative and his father rolled his head again and said, "No."

"Wake up. Come on, Dad. Wake up." Cassidy got an arm under his father's shoulders and levered him to a sitting position. He heard a shout from somewhere outside, and heavy feet ran on the deck above him. The search had started. "You have to wake up." He leaned his father against his shoulder to hold him up and ripped open one of the envelopes and took out two of the familiar pills. "Open your mouth. Open your mouth." Tom Cassidy's jaw went slack. He put one of the pills on his father's tongue and poured in water from the glass, and then tipped him back so the water washed the pill down, and his father swallowed reflexively. Cassidy swallowed the other pill himself with the rest of the water. He had been awake too long, and he needed the jolt. He shoved his father's legs off the table. "Come on, get up. You have to get up. You have to walk."

"What? What are you doing?" His father's voice slurred and mumbled.

"Get up. Walk." Cassidy pulled one of his father's arms over his shoulder and put an arm around his father's waist and dragged him off the table. For a moment he had to take all Tom Cassidy's weight, and his knees buckled, and then something in the older man's brain clicked, and he took a step. "Keep walking." They staggered the length of the cabin.

"Michael?"

"Yes, Dad. Me."

"What?"

"You're on a Russian ship. We have to get off. You have to wake up. I can't do it alone. Walk. Walk." They stumbled to the opposite side and turned.

Pounding feet on the deck outside. Two men ran past the windows. One of them glanced in, but Cassidy and his father were in the corner, unseen.

They staggered back and forth the length of the cabin. His father mumbled sometimes in English and sometimes in Russian. Cassidy felt the hot wire of the amphetamine working his nerves and knew it must be working in his father too. The older man took more of his weight and his steps were surer.

"Let me stop. Let me rest." He leaned against the examining table.

"What do you remember?"

Tom Cassidy shook his head to clear it. "I don't know. I was asleep. Two men came in with the guard. They spoke to me in Russian. At first I thought it was a dream. One of them gave me a shot. They got me out of bed and I could do nothing. I remember walking out of my cell with them, and then, I don't know."

"Let's walk."

"No. Let me rest a minute longer. Did you give me something? My head feels funny."

"Benzedrine to knock off the sedative they gave you."

"Ah. And how are we going to get off this ship? Have you thought of that?"

"They have to drop the pilot. If we can hide until then, we can get off when he goes."

"Do they know you're on board?"

"They think I'm a longshoreman who stayed on by mistake. They've used the loudspeakers to tell me to report to the bridge."

"And when you don't, they'll look for you."

"They're already looking."

Tom Cassidy looked around vaguely. "I can't think. You'll have to tell me what to do."

"We've got to get out of this cabin. I had to break open the door. It won't close all the way, and the wood's damaged. Someone will notice."

Tom Cassidy stood. He lurched, and his son reached out to steady him. "I'm all right. I'm fine. Let's go."

Cassidy listened at the gap at the broken door. He heard nothing in the corridor. He nodded, and when his father moved up next to him, he opened the door.

Dylan stood in the doorway of the cabin across the corridor. She held the .32 automatic from her bedside table in a steady hand.

42

"I knew it was you when they said there was a longshoreman on board by mistake. How does a longshoreman make that mistake? They load the last load. They blow the whistle. They make announcements, 'Everybody ashore who's going ashore,' and he's getting on? No one's that careless."

They were in Dylan's cabin across from the dispensary. She had locked the door and the gun was still in her hand. His gun was under his shoulder and the borrowed windbreaker was zipped up, and he knew there was no way he could get it out before she shot him.

"Then I thought, no, not careless. Someone who won't let go. You knew your father was here. You had to come for him."

"I take it you two know each other." Tom Cassidy was lying on the bunk.

Cassidy leaned against the wall near the small window that gave out on the deck. Dylan had shut the curtains, but when he glanced through the gap, he saw a Staten Island ferry passing toward Manhattan. They were moving downriver to the sea. "Yes."

His father heard something in his voice. "Ah, like that, huh?"

"I thought so, but I wasn't getting all the information."

"If you didn't know how I felt about you, you weren't paying attention."

"Your whole life's a lie from Aliquippa, Pennsylvania, on up, and I fell for it. You were on the job the whole time. You fucked me to get the photographs. No other reason. What a sucker I was."

Their anger brought them close together. The gun in Dylan's hand dangled. Cassidy snatched it. Dylan pivoted and drove her free elbow into his neck. His hand went numb and the gun fell. As he went down, he reached out and swept her feet out from under her. She kicked him in the head, rolled over, and found the gun.

She got to her feet, the gun steady on Cassidy. "Get up against the wall. Put your hands in your pockets."

Fuck it, he thought. Let her shoot. A little thirty-two like that, it won't stop me. The rage talking.

"Don't, Michael. Please." The gun was rock steady. "Lean your forehead against the wall and back your feet out." He did as he was told. "More. Cross your ankles." Much of his weight was on his forehead, and with his hands in his pockets and his ankles crossed there was no way to move fast. Part of his brain, unoccupied with anger, admired her technique. He felt the cold barrel of the gun against the base of his skull. She reached around and unzipped his windbreaker and lifted his gun from its holster. She backed away. "All right. Stand up."

He turned. She was at the door. For a moment she looked as if she wanted to say something. Then she shook her head, unlocked the door, went out, and relocked the door from the outside.

"That went well," Tom Cassidy said.

Cassidy crouched to look at the keyhole. She had left the key in the outside at a half turn so it could not be dislodged. He checked the window. It did not open, and it was made of thick glass to withstand the occasional high sea. He did not think he could break it.

Cassidy prowled the cabin looking for a weak spot, but he found none.

"I always wondered what she would be like, the one you fell for. I expected she would be strong. I did not expect Russian."

"She was born in America."

"What does that have to do with anything? I was born in Russia and I am American. She was born in America and she is Russian. Maybe something in your blood that calls out to that."

"Something in my dick." He was looking for a weapon. He tested the chair to see if he could break off a leg, but it was made of welded metal.

"Don't be a child. You're angry. But that anger does not come from your dick, Michael. It comes from your heart. And I am glad to see it. I was afraid you were going to drift coolly through life uncommitted."

Cassidy looked at his father in surprise. Did he know him so little or so well? "Let's talk about this later. We have to decide what we're going to do."

"I've already decided."

The door opened. Rudi Apfel came in first. He was as Cassidy remembered him, colorless, featureless, except for the black automatic he held in one hand. Dylan came in behind him.

"Detective Cassidy. I did not expect to see you again, but I'm happy you're here. You gave some photographs to Miss McCue. I'd like the real ones."

Cassidy glanced at Dylan. She was holding herself stiffly.

"Those are the real ones."

"Please. I developed those photographs. I saw them. They were perfect. Every detail was clear. I trained Ingram. He knew how to shoot pictures. He'd done it before."

"You should have trained him not to store microfilm negatives near something hot. He had them hidden in a locker backstage where he was dancing. The locker was up against a steam pipe. Those were prints from those negatives."

"You're lying. First of all, Ingram stole five negatives. You only gave her four prints. She, of course, was taken in. Women have their uses in our business, but sometimes they let emotion govern thought. It is one of the weaknesses of the sex."

"She got what I had. Maybe Ingram figured out he only had one good one so he hid that someplace else."

"No. You have them. Tell me where they are. I'll have someone retrieve them. If you do this, things will go better for you when you get to Russia."

"Did you kill Ingram?"

"What does it matter now?"

"Did you?"

"He died. It was inconvenient. He was stubborn when he should have been helpful."

"And Stanley Fisher in the alley outside Lord & Taylor? Perry Werth?"
Apfel shrugged. "Loose ends."

"And Victor Amado?"

"No."

"Who, then?"

"I don't know."

"I'm not going to Russia," Tom Cassidy said.

They turned to look at him. He was standing by the bunk.

Apfel barked at him in Russian.

"I do not speak Russian," Tom Cassidy said.

Apfel barked again.

"I do not speak Russian. I have forgotten all my Russian. I have put it behind me. I almost died getting out of Russia. I will die before I go back."

"I will kill your son. And then I will have you sedated. You will go back to Russia. And you will make a great noise about how happy you are to be back in the Motherland, how you loathed everything about America." He swung his gun toward the detective. "You two have to make some choices. The photographs. I can use the radio, patch to a phone, have someone pick them up in fifteen minutes. Your father, who does not want to go home, can be released on the pilot boat."

"There are no photographs."

"Well, then—"

Dylan stepped over to Apfel, put the barrel of her gun against his skull, and shot him. His head jerked. His eyes bulged. His knees gave, and he crumpled. The gun bounced away from his slack hand. *OH COME ON.*

Cassidy's ears rang from the shot. The cabin stank of cordite. Apfel lay on the floor, his ruined head leaking thick dark blood. *JUST NOT READ*

"Hurry," Dylan said. "The pilot's boat should be alongside. Hurry."

Cassidy stooped to pick up Apfel's gun.

"Leave the gun. It won't work if you take the gun."

"What do you mean?"

"Leave the gun and go."

"You're coming."

"No."

"Dylan."

"No."

Cassidy gestured to the body on the floor. "You have to."

"No. I can't."

"I can protect you."

"Just go."

"Come with me."

"No. If I come, one day you'll wake up and look at me and wonder. You'll want to know where I've been. You'll wonder why I'm late, or who I've been with. You'll start hearing lies where there are no lies."

"You can't go back to Russia. You killed a KGB officer. They won't let that go."

"Apfel failed. His mission blew up. He was careless. His own opera-
tive went into business for himself. They don't like failure. The best he
could hope for was some leniency because he brought back your father.
Maybe they would decide the propaganda offset his failure. Maybe not. I
will tell them that I discovered that he decided to defect, that he made a
deal with you, a member of the New York Police Department. He would
help you get your father ashore, and you would get him asylum. They'll
understand that. They always fear that their operatives will be seduced
by America. I discovered the plot. I shot him. You overpowered me and
escaped."

"They'll never believe that."

"Yes, they will. It's how they think. Now hit me."

"Hit you?"

"Yes. How did you overpower me, with a kiss?" Did she smile?

"Do as she says, and do it fast. Someone will have heard the shot." His
father's voice was cold, and when he looked at him he saw the iron of the
teenager who walked out of Russia surfacing through the well-fed New
York businessman. "Make it good. If they don't believe her, they'll kill
her."

He punched her hard near an eye and cut her, and then hit her again as
she sagged, splitting her lip. She went down hard and moaned in pain,
and he started to bend to her. "Go," she said. His father grabbed his arm,
and they went out into the corridor and down it to the door to the deck.

The ship's horn blasted above them. It was answered by the toot of a
motor launch as it pulled away from the ship's side. Cassidy could see the
pilot standing, legs apart, on the launch's deck.

• • •

"Come on." As they started down the ladder to the main deck, one of the
Amtorg thugs swung around the bottom and started up. He saw the Cassidys and reached for the gun under his coat. Cassidy went down the stairs
fast and kicked him in the face, and the man fell back to the deck. Cassidy jumped the last few stairs and kicked him in the head.

The pilot boat was fifty yards from the ship, and no one on it was
looking back.

Someone shouted from the bridge. The second Amtorg man put his
hands on the rails of the ladder on the bridge deck and slid down without
touching his feet to the steps.

Red cork life rings hung on brackets at the rail. Cassidy jerked two out of their brackets and gave one to his father. "We'll have to jump."

Tom Cassidy nodded. His eyes were bright and he seemed to be enjoying himself, and not for the first time the vagrant thought, *Who is this man?* slipped across Cassidy's mind.

Cassidy opened the gate in the rail. The water was twenty feet down. He could hear the Amtorg man's running feet and the shouts of crewmen. Someone fired a shot, and the bullet whanged off the ship's rail. Tom Cassidy showed him a tight grin and then ran through the gate and into space.

Cassidy followed him. The fall seemed to take forever, and the water was a cold shock. The cork ring wrenched at his arms when he plunged under and then brought him quickly to the surface. The black iron cliff of the ship's hull flowed past. He spun to look for his father and saw him clinging to the other life ring ten yards away. He thrashed and kicked toward him while he shouted. "Dad. Dad. Kick away from the ship. Get away from the ship." A wave slapped him in the face and he choked.

His father kicked his life ring away from the passing ship and toward Cassidy. The rings bumped. Tom Cassidy coughed up water.

"Are you okay?" Cassidy asked. His father nodded and waved a hand, but he was gulping air and did not speak. The stern swung toward them as the ship ran on. Behind it the water churned white. "We have to get farther away. We have to get away from the propellers."

They kicked hard, dragged by their clothes, slapped back by the waves, blunted by the wind. The stern swung closer. The water around them foamed, and Cassidy could feel the thump of the props as they thrashed. The stern loomed high above them and Cassidy saw men on the rail looking down at them. The churning water sucked at him and hauled him down, and he hung on to the life ring and struggled against the pull.

His father went under and his life ring popped to the surface.

Cassidy let go of the life ring and dove. The water was white around him and he could not see. It threw him one way and then the other. He felt something solid below him and grabbed cloth. He fought toward the surface with his lungs burning. A current pushed them upward, and they popped out of water that thrashed as white as milk. His father was slack. His head lolled, his mouth hung open. Cassidy put his arms around him and squeezed hard. He did it again and again. He put his mouth to his father's and blew in hard and then squeezed. "Come on! Come on!" and heard his father take a shuddering breath. The stern of the ship slid past, and the men at the rail pointed to them. One of them pointed farther off, and Cassidy turned and saw the pilot's launch headed toward them, a white bow wave like a bone in its teeth.

43

Cassidy met Clyde Tolson late in the afternoon in the Federal Building at Foley Square. The office was sparsely furnished, with a large wooden desk, four wooden armchairs, a sagging sofa, and four standing ashtrays. The only decoration was a large photograph of J. Edgar Hoover looking like a bulldog with a bad stomach.

Susdorf and Cherry were in the outer office when Cassidy arrived. Susdorf nodded. Cherry pointed a finger like a gun and grinned and said, "Come on in, the water's fine." They were not invited when a steel-haired secretary in a severe gray dress showed him into the inner office. Clyde Tolson turned from a window that looked out into the harbor from which Cassidy had recently been fished.

"All right, let's get this done. Where are the photographs and the negatives?"

Cassidy took the envelope from his pocket and slid it onto the desk. Tolson picked it up and slit it open. "Is this all of them?"

"Yes."

"Any copies?"

"No."

Tolson examined the contents. He held the one clear print of Hoover in the red dress, heavily made up, smiling at Victor Amado like a deranged coquette.

"I don't think red is his color."

Tolson flushed. "Careful." He looked in the empty envelope. "Where are the other prints?"

"There are no other prints."

Tolson examined Cassidy for a lie. He picked up one of the negatives and held it to the light from the window and then put it down on the print. He picked up the next one and held it to the light and then turned it and tried it from a different angle. What he saw puzzled him. He picked up another and went through the same process, and then quickly looked at the last two. He took a viewer from the desk and put one of the negatives in and turned on the light while Cassidy waited for the explosion. What came was a mild, "What the hell?"

"Ingram had five microfilm negatives. He hid them in a locker in the theater where he was dancing. The locker was up against a steam pipe. Color microfilm is unstable. Heat destroys it. Only one of the negatives was good."

Tolson ran all the negatives through the viewer and then banged it down on the desk. "I don't believe you. You described the pictures to us in Washington. How did you know what was on them if the negatives were destroyed?"

"I took a chance. I made them up. I went to the Schine apartment in the Waldorf and studied it, and I made up four different scenes that could have happened anytime during that night. I had a picture of Hoover in the dress. I said Werth or Perry was here or there with him. How would anyone know whether Ingram photographed those particular moments or not? He believed it because he knew it was possible. I took the chance, because it was the only leverage I had to get my father out."

"You're playing a dangerous game, Cassidy."

"No game. I told you I would give you the negatives and the photographs I got from Ingram. You have them."

"Is this because you think we didn't hold up our end of the bargain? Things go wrong. You can't hold us responsible for what happened in the detention center. We did everything we could in good faith. We expunged your father's record. We reinstated his citizenship. He cannot be approached again on this matter, and this is what you do to us? This?" His anger rose as he spoke. He swept his hand at the desk and knocked the viewer to the floor without meaning to, and it smashed at his feet. "What do you expect to gain? Who do you think you are? Do you think you can blackmail the director? We're the FBI."

"I gave you my word. I kept my part of the bargain. You got your end of the deal. You got what Ingram had. Ask around. People will tell you I keep my word."

"I'm marking you, Cassidy. I'm marking you. You just made a bad enemy."

• • •

Orso pushed himself away from the newsstand in the lobby of the Federal Building when Cassidy came out of the elevator. "Well?"

"He doesn't believe me, but he's stuck. If I'm lying to him, I still have the photographs. If he goes after me, I'll use them."

They pushed out through the brass-bound doors into Foley Square. The sun was in the west and the day was still warm, and people were leaving the building early, releasing themselves to spring. A small group of protestors walked in a circle under the watchful eyes of six patrolmen and two mounted cops. They carried signs saying BAN THE BOMB, PEACE, JOE MCCARTHY IS A NAZI.

Nobody paid attention to them except the cops.

"He could have you killed."

"No. That's not the way they think. He and Hoover deal in conspiracy and lies. They think everyone does. Think of the files Hoover keeps. If he and Tolson were in my shoes, they would keep the evidence and make sure that if they got hit, the stuff would go to the newspapers. They're sure I've done the same. I'm okay for a while."

"What do you mean, a while?"

"They'll expect me to ask for things. They don't know what, but favors of some sort. It's how they'd use the power. It would prove to them that I have the photos. When I don't ask for anything, they'll begin to think I'm telling the truth. They'll wonder if they should take me out."

"So ask for something. Have them pull some strings, make me a lieutenant. Make sure they think you have the photos."

"Fuck 'em."

"Oh, okay. If you're going to hit me with philosophy, you have to buy the drinks."

• • •

The family agreed to meet for dinner at Sardi's in the booth under Tom Cassidy's caricature, Tom and Megan, Brian and Marcy, Leah and Mark, and Cassidy.

When Cassidy arrived, he found Brian in the lobby buying cigarettes from the coatcheck girl.

"Harry Gould had someone he knows look at the papers. He says they're bulletproof. They can't come back at Dad in any way. You want to tell me how you managed that?"

"Leverage."

Brian waited for more. "That's it? That's all you're going to tell me?"

"All I can tell you for now."

"So maybe the papers aren't so bulletproof."

"They're fine."

"So maybe you're not so bulletproof." He had a newsman's instinct for asking questions until he got the real answer.

"I'm okay."

Brian studied him. He did not believe him, but he believed he would get no more. "You'll tell me about it when you can?"

"I will."

There was champagne on the table and new bottles appeared before old ones were empty. Tom Cassidy refused to talk about the time he spent in the detention center. He dismissed it with a wave of his hand. It was past, unimportant, forgotten. He told of their escape from the Russian ship as if it had been an adventure, as if it was a lark to leap from a ship into the outer harbor with no understanding of how you would get ashore, of how long you could last in the cold water while the tide carried you out to sea. He did not talk about Apfel dead on the cabin floor, about Dylan left bleeding near the body. There was laughter, and relief, and an unspoken understanding that they were not to take what had happened seriously. It was over and done with. It was the past, and Tom Cassidy expected his family to look to the future.

Megan hugged Michael as they waited for a cab. "Thank you."

"You're welcome."

"Do you know what he said to me? He said, 'I knew he would come. I was never worried.'"

Then Tom Cassidy was there to take him in a bear hug and lift him from the ground. "When will you come to rehearsal? Soon. Soon. Just listen to the eleven o'clock. It's so close, and I know you'll see what needs to be done."

Megan smiled at Cassidy and shook her head.

"I'll come soon."

Brian put an arm around his shoulder and hugged him quickly and asked, "Are you sure you're okay?"

"I'm fine."

"All right, but if you want to talk, call me."

Leah was the last to leave. She had been vivid during dinner, the first to call for more champagne, the one who laughed loudest at their father's jokes, but now she was subdued and her face had a haunted look as she watched Mark walk down the block to find a cab.

She held on to the lapels of Cassidy's jacket with both hands and leaned her head against his chest, and he put one hand on her smooth black hair and felt the skull underneath. She spoke against his chest. "Franklin came by again today. I paid him. He said that next time it would have to be more."

"I'll take care of it."

"You've done enough. I don't want you to get in trouble."

"I won't get in trouble. I'll take care of it. Don't worry. It's done."

He watched their taxi until it turned the corner and then walked east toward the Street. He could not go back to the empty apartment yet. Maybe jazz would lift him. Maybe music would loosen the stone in his heart.

44

"Want some?" Fraker asked and pointed to his plate.

"No, thank you," Crofoot said and, because he had been brought up to show polite interest, he asked, "What is it?"

They were in a Belgian restaurant on West 28th Street that, as far as Crofoot could see, had nothing to recommend it. It was a long, dim room, and the walls were covered by badly painted murals of Spain inherited from the last restaurant that had failed in that space.

"Horse meat. Just about the only place in the city you can find good horse meat. I like it rare, real rare, what they call blue. And they fry the potatoes in lard."

"Ah." Crofoot had a flash of the roan gelding his mother rode on drag hunts near the country house in Tuxedo. It was late in the afternoon, and the restaurant was nearly empty, and they could talk without fear of being overheard. "Cassidy still has the photographs."

"Oh, yeah?" Fraker said as he stuffed a piece of purple meat into his mouth.

"The FBI ordered Thomas Cassidy's release from immigration detention, and when that fucked up, they helped Cassidy get his father off a Soviet ship. And they pulled some strings to get Tom Cassidy's record expunged and to recover his citizenship. Why would they do that unless Cassidy had leverage?"

"What do you want to do? Do you want me to go get them?"

Crofoot turned his head to avoid watching Fraker chew with his mouth open. "No. He won't have them where he can get them easily, and he won't give them up."

"So we're done."

"Not yet. Cassidy knows Hoover will kill him if he doesn't protect himself. The only way he can protect himself is by threatening to have the photographs published if he is killed."

"Sure. It's what you do."

"So kill him. When he dies, the photos will go to the press. It's not as good as having them ourselves, but when it happens, the president is going to have to rethink who controls the intelligence apparatus for the country. He's not going to leave it in the hands of a degenerate. Do it soon. Make it loud. Make it obvious. I don't want anyone to think it was an accident."

• • •

Cassidy spent the day in the squad room battering reports out of a typewriter. Apfel had killed Ingram by torturing him. Apfel had killed Werth and Perry. Apfel was dead, killed aboard a Russian ship that was now well beyond the territorial waters of the United States. No one in the department was very interested in how he died as long as Cassidy could assure him that he was dead. Victor Amado, though, was still a problem.

Lieutenant Tanner came out of his office carrying a copy of Cassidy's report on Amado. "What do you mean, 'assailant unknown'? You've got Apfel."

"He didn't do it."

"He tortured Ingram. He tortured Amado. He killed Fisher and Werth. He killed Amado. What's the problem?"

"He used a knife on Amado. Apfel didn't use a knife on Ingram. Apfel said he didn't do it. He had no reason to lie. It's not the same guy."

"Let's go see the captain."

They went upstairs to Captain Leonard's office. Leonard was a tall, spare gray-haired man in his late forties. He had a lantern jaw and big bony hands and a mild manner that could change in a moment to ice. There were copies of Cassidy's reports on Leonard's desk.

"Good reports, Cassidy. I wish more of the men in the department could write as clearly and concisely. A pleasure to read." He shuffled the reports together and squared their edges on the desktop. "Okay, we're going to close these cases. The Russian's the killer. He's dead."

"I think Amado's killer's a different guy. I think he's still out there."

"Who is he? What've you got?"

"I don't know who he is. I've got nothing."

"We're done with this. The Russian was using four fairies for black-mail. They're dead. He's dead. We don't know who their targets were, and we don't want to know. It's done. Am I clear?"

"Clear."

• • •

"Let's go over to Toots and get smashed. On me," Orso offered.

"Not tonight, thanks."

"Hey, you don't want to pass up an opportunity. You could get hit by a cab on the way home, your last thought'll be, shit I could've been get-ting drunk on Tony's nickel."

"I'll see you tomorrow."

"Let it go, Mike. Let it go."

• • •

Cassidy walked home in a light evening drizzle that turned the world gray to match his mood. He stopped at the grocery store on Greenwich Ave-nue and bought a six-pack of beer and one of the new frozen TV dinners that came in a compartmented aluminum tray, Salisbury steak, green beans, and mashed potatoes, the single man's salvation. Single man. The idea of the empty apartment and a frozen dinner almost made him turn back to find a well-lighted restaurant where people were having a good time. No. The hell with it. Other people having a good time was not what he wanted. Where was she? How fast was an old ship like the *Bakunin*? Eight knots? That would put her about five hundred miles out. Had they believed her story? Was she locked up or drinking vodka with the captain? Why did he care?

Fraker waited for Cassidy in the deep doorway of a warehouse down the block from Greenwich Street. The doorway was masked by a row of garbage cans and piles of empty cardboard boxes that had been left for the morning trash pickup, and he could keep a watch up the block through gaps in the pile. There was a streetlight up the block that made the shad-ows in the doorway even darker. How should he do it? He preferred the knife. He thought about that moment in the elevator in Werth's building when the urge to kill both cops had been strong. The knife slash across the throat of the big guy, and then turn and stab Cassidy, in and out, in and out, fast. He could do it now, but he wasn't sure it would send the message Crofoot wanted to send. A bullet in the head, and then a double tap, heart and head, to make sure. That was more the FBI style. It would have to be the gun. Too bad. The knife would be more fun.

He had been prepared to wait all evening for Cassidy to come home, but now he saw him stop under a streetlight on Greenwich waiting for traffic to clear. He eased the gun from the holster on his belt. Wait till Cassidy passed, then step out and put one in the back of his head. Say something? Make him turn so he knew it was coming? It was tempting. What should he eat afterward? Japanese? Raw fish. Crofoot would hate that, but he'd want a firsthand report, and Fraker loved twisting his dick.

Crofoot sat in a car parked farther down on Bank Street. There was a pistol on the seat next to him. He had watched Fraker enter the dark doorway of the warehouse across the street, and watched him pull the boxes around until he was well hidden. It was a good place for an ambush. He had always admired Fraker's efficiency. He just couldn't stand the man. Well, he'd be done with that tonight. He liked his little plan. A dead cop and his dead killer, a man with no identity. That should pull the newspapers out. Headline: Mysterious Cop Killer. Whoever had the photographs wouldn't hesitate to reveal them. He watched Cassidy cross Greenwich and start down the block toward where Fraker waited. He picked up the gun and put it in his lap. It wouldn't be long now. And then dinner at the Palm. A martini, shrimp cocktail, a steak and baked potato, and maybe some creamed spinach. Reward for a job well done.

· · ·

Cassidy pulled his jacket tighter and turned up the collar and buttoned the top button against the rain. Somewhere on the river a foghorn moaned. He had the nagging feeling that there was something he should know, something he should remember. What? Nothing important, right? If it were important, he would remember it. He shifted the grocery bag from the crook of his left arm to his right. It was heavy. Heavy? There was something about the heaviness of the bag in his arm, something he should remember about that. Ahead of him, the street was dark. It seemed darker than usual, familiar yet different.

A hot wash of dread.

What was he scared of? What was he supposed to know?

Fraker took a deep breath and let it out. Twenty more feet and Cassidy would be here. Five seconds. A breath. Let it out. The doorway was deep and Fraker was wearing dark clothes, but the moment when Cassidy walked past him would be the time of danger. The lizard brain where the ancient animal lives in us often felt danger when the other senses were blind. He checked the safety with his thumb. He knew it was off, but he was a careful man. Another breath. Let it out. Cassidy's footsteps were loud now. He was close.

Cassidy slowed. The quality of the darkness. The slowness of his movements. The weight on his arm. The feeling of dread. Where had he seen this? Where?

The dream he had in the hospital. The dream came back to him like memory. Where was Amado? In the dream he had been standing down the block telling Cassidy to go back. Cassidy kept walking. It was here that Amado disappeared, here that the dread peaked. Whatever would happen would happen right here. *Turn around. Turn around.*

He turned, and as he did, a man stepped out of the darkness of the warehouse door. He had a gun in his hand and it was pointed at Cassidy's face. Cassidy instinctively jerked his hand up as if that would stop a bullet, and the gun cracked. The bullet punched through the six-pack of beer, slammed into the frozen TV dinner, and stopped in the ice-hard steak. Cassidy dropped the bag and drove forward into the gunman before he could shoot again.

Fraker had watched Cassidy pass. He stepped out. *Why was Cassidy turning? Why was he facing him?* He fired and then Cassidy plowed into him, knocking him back against the row of garbage cans that banged and clattered as they fell among them. *He shot him in the face. Why was he alive?*

Cassidy drove with his legs and smashed the man back into the garbage cans and the brick wall. He drove a fist toward the man's face, hit something soft, and heard the man grunt. Something hard slammed his head. The gun. He grabbed for it and got a hand on it, and then the gun went off and a bullet burned across his side. He head-butted the man and wrenched at the gun and it came loose and skittered away across the cement. They crashed over the garbage cans and the force of the fall knocked them apart, and Cassidy crabbed away and got to his feet. He dug for his gun, but his jacket was buttoned to the throat, and before he could get to it the man was on his feet, and Cassidy heard a snick of metal on metal. A knife. He had heard that sound before in Ingram's apartment just before the searcher there cut him. He tore at his jacket, but the cloth was wet, and the buttons would not give, and now the man was coming at him in a balanced shuffle with the knife out in front. Cassidy took a step back and stumbled over a garbage can and went down hard, and the man came at him fast.

Cassidy rolled away and found the top of the can and brought it around to use as a shield as the man made his first cut, and the knife blade scraped across the metal, and Cassidy shoved himself backward along the pavement, hoping to get enough separation to stand. The attacker came after him again, the knife flickering in front. Cassidy raised the metal top, and the man kicked it out of his hand, and it clattered away on the sidewalk. Cassidy's back was against one of the boxes, and he pulled it around and shoved it at his attacker's feet.

Fraker kicked the box aside, but by that time Cassidy was on his feet. Fraker moved forward, following the knife blade.

Cassidy worked at his jacket buttons and got the top one free and started on the second. It was bound in the wet cloth. His attacker came in fast. The blade flicked left and right, left and right, and then it came straight at Cassidy's gut, and he turned away from it, and as the blade passed, he snatched the man's sleeve and pulled, and the man came forward off balance. Cassidy grabbed him by the coat and used his momentum to run him into the brick wall of the warehouse. He hit face-first, but it was not hard enough, and he turned and slashed at Cassidy and ripped a long gash along his arm. Cassidy kicked a garbage can at him, and when he dodged, he followed and punched him in the face, and the man slashed again and ripped the front of Cassidy's jacket without cutting him. The force of the thrust turned the man off balance again, and Cassidy kicked him hard in the thigh and turned him more and then grabbed the back of the man's jacket in both hands and ran his face into the brick wall.

The attacker bounced and pulled from his hands and then went down on the sidewalk with his neck at a strange angle. Cassidy kicked him in the kidneys, but the man did not flinch. He felt for a pulse; there was none. He rolled him over faceup into the light. He had seen him before but could not remember where. The rain sifted down on him, plastering his hair to his skull. His body shook and his hands twitched as the adrenaline burned away. Who was this guy? Why had he tried to kill him?

Crofoot watched Cassidy walk by the doorway and suddenly spin around as Fraker stepped out with the gun to kill him. Fraker fired, but Cassidy didn't fall. He saw Fraker go down for the last time. From the way Cassidy turned his back on him, he knew Fraker was dead. Now what? Could this still work? Fraker dead. Cassidy dead. That was the plan. Nothing much had changed. Cassidy was supposed to die first. Now he'd die second.

Cassidy bent down to pick up his hat. He heard a car door open, and when he looked up, Crofoot was running through the rain toward him with a gun in his hand. Crofoot fired and the bullet splashed off the pavement inches from Cassidy's foot. Cassidy dropped and rolled, and another shot sparked his face with cement chips.

Crofoot stopped running and dropped into a shooter's crouch ten feet away to steady his aim. No way was he going to miss this one.

Cassidy felt something hard under his side. Fraker's gun. He rolled, snatched up the gun, and shot Crofoot twice in the chest. Crofoot dropped his gun and sat down in the gutter water. Cassidy walked to him, the gun ready. Crofoot pressed both hands to his chest. When he looked up at Cassidy, rain dripped from his chin.

"Damn it," he said in a forlorn voice. "This wasn't supposed to happen." Then he toppled over on his side. The gutter water built up against his body and then flowed around it and ran toward the river stained with blood.

Cassidy went through his attacker's pocket and found a wallet with thirty-eight dollars, a condom in a foil packet, and a driver's license from West Virginia that identified him as Edmond Fraker. He put it back in the dead man's jacket. He found Crofoot's gun and put it in his hand and wiped Fraker's gun clean of his prints and wrapped Fraker's hand around it. Someone would find the bodies in the morning, the garbagemen or people coming to work in the warehouse. What would the Homicide detectives make of this, bullets from Fraker's gun in Crofoot, and Fraker with a broken neck?

Who was Edmond Fraker? The guy who searched Ingram's apartment, that was certain. Where had he seen him before? Had he been alone? No, with Orso. A close space. An elevator. Fraker was the man who had gotten in the elevator when they went up to talk to Perry Werth. He got out at the floor below, but now it was clear that he had been on his way to Werth's, but he had recognized Cassidy. How? Not from Ingram's. They had fought in darkness. Someone had pointed him out. It had to be Crofoot. Why did Crofoot want him dead? The photos. Like everyone else, Crofoot thought he had the photos and that if he was killed they would be exposed.

In his apartment, he poured bourbon over ice and carried it into the bathroom and stripped off his jacket and shirt. The bullet had burned across his ribs above the scar from the knife wound from Ingram's apartment. It had stopped bleeding. The slice on his arm was shallow and long, and he poured iodine into it, hissing at the burn, and then pulled the edges together and taped it. He took a long pull of the bourbon and looked at himself in the mirror. For a man who was supposed to be dead, he looked remarkably well.

He got dressed and put a raincoat on and walked to a newsstand on Hudson and bought a couple of packs of Luckies and then went to an Italian restaurant on Bleecker and ate dinner and drank half a bottle of decent Barolo. He made sure to talk to the owner and the bartender. He walked back to West Street along Perry and then north to Bank Street to his apartment to avoid passing the place where Crofoot and Fraker lay. Someone might have found them already, and if the cops were there he would have to stop, and he wanted some distance before anyone asked him any questions.

· · ·

In the morning, the sky was gray. A light rain fell, and the river was the color of slate. Cassidy's doorbell rang while he was drinking his first cup of coffee. Orso's voice squawked on the intercom. Cassidy buzzed him in.

"Coffee?"

"Yeah. Coffee's good." Orso stirred two teaspoons of sugar into his mug. "It's still raining."

"Yeah. The radio says it's going to rain all day. But it's warm. It must be seventy already."

"Uh-huh. Spring is really here."

"Are you going in today?"

"Sure. Why wouldn't I go in?"

"I don't know. Just asking."

They were silent for a moment. "Do you want to tell me why you're here? It's a little off your traffic pattern."

"There's a crew from the Sixth Precinct working a double homicide up the block. I just wanted to check and make sure it wasn't you." He watched Cassidy closely.

"Up this block? Who got hit?"

"They don't know. A couple of guys. One's ID says Edmond Fraker. The other's name is Crofoot. Crofoot's the CIA guy, isn't he?"

"Yeah. How'd they get it?"

"It looks like Fraker shot Crofoot. Crofoot had a gun too, and it's been fired, but Fraker's got a broken neck."

"That's a weird one," Cassidy said. Orso looked at him strangely but said nothing.

When Cassidy and Orso reached the crime scene, the techs were just loading the bodies into the meat wagon.

"Hey, Cassidy, did you hear anything last night?" Detective Dickens was a sandy-haired middleweight in a plastic raincoat with a clear plastic cover on his fedora.

"Like what?"

"Gunshots. One of the deceased had a gun in his hand, a thirty-two. If the clip was full when he started, he fired it four times, hit the other guy twice."

"I didn't hear anything. When did it happen?"

"Around seven thirty, near as we can figure."

"I was having dinner about then on Bleecker, that Italian joint, Bella Luna."

"Okay. Thanks."

Orso and Cassidy caught a cab at the corner. Orso gave the driver the address of the precinct and lit a cigarette. "I took a look at the guy."

"Yeah?"

"Hard to tell. His face was kind of bashed in. I think whoever did it ran him into the wall."

"Uh-huh."

"I think he was the guy who got into the elevator with us when we were going up to talk to Perry Werth."

"Yeah, I remember that guy. You think it was him, huh?"

"Mike, is there anything I should know?"

"No. Nothing you should know."

• • •

Cassidy was interviewing a tourist from Pennsylvania who had been robbed at knifepoint by three teenage punks while he waited for a bus on Eighth Avenue when Tanner came out of his office and gestured that he wanted to see him.

"I'll be right back, Mr. Colquitt. We'll finish this up." He went into Tanner's office.

"What've you got?" Cassidy asked.

"The guys who were killed a couple of days ago, the guys on your block?" Tanner lit a cigar.

"Yeah?"

"I got a call from Skinner at the morgue. He says the knife they found with the Fraker guy matched wounds on Amado."

Cassidy nodded and said nothing.

"So you were right, which is good in some ways, because it shows what hot shits I've got working for me, but is not so good in others, because it means Captain Leonard has to go tell all those guys above him that he was maybe a little quick clearing all those murders with Apfel as the fall guy."

"Too bad."

"Yeah. Here's the funny part. You know the two IDs the dead guys were carrying? Well, one of them, the West Virginia license, dead ends. The name on that one, Fraker, that particular Fraker died thirty years ago at the age of four. The other, Crofoot, turns out to be legit. An address in Washington, D.C. We ask the D.C. cops to go by and say hello. Ten minutes after they get to the house, while they're talking to the missus, a big-time lawyer and a couple of very quiet, very cool guys show up. Phone calls come from on high, and the cops are told to go way back and sit down. What do you think of that?"

"FBI?"

"No. I talked to a lieutenant down there. He says, no. The CIA is what he thinks."

"And?"

"And that's the end of it."

But it wasn't. There was one more thing.

45

It rained for the third night in a row. At midnight Cassidy stood in the shelter of an awning on 11th Street just west of Fifth Avenue and watched a brownstone across the street. The door opened and three middle-aged men came out laughing and talking loudly. They stopped at the bottom of the stoop to raise umbrellas, slapped each other on the back, and then two went east toward Fifth, and the other went west.

Cassidy crossed and rang the brownstone's doorbell. A small door behind a grille opened and someone looked out at him. Three locks clashed and the door opened. A tall, good-looking Negro woman in a pink silk dress held the door so Cassidy could enter.

"Good evening, Officer." She shut the door behind him.

The front hall was decorated with heavy Oriental carpets, a plush sofa from another era, and a large mirror with a carved gold frame. A carpeted staircase led to the upper floors. At the end of the hall, an arched doorway opened on the parlor where there was a bar and groupings of comfortable leather chairs and sofas where sports could wait and look over the girls before choosing one or two and going upstairs.

"Is he still here?"

"Oh, yes." Her voice was resigned. She shrugged and her breasts moved under the cloth.

"Where?"

"Third floor, back room." She handed him a key, turned, and swayed away down the hall on six-inch heels.

Cassidy went up the stairs.

The thick runner in the upstairs hall deadened his footsteps. He stopped outside a door. From the other side came the smack of flesh on flesh and then a muffled cry of pain. He put the key in the lock, eased the latch, and opened the door.

Franklin had a woman crouched on the bed so he could thrust into her from behind. Every time he did, he slapped her hard on the side of the face or the thigh or buttock. She had taken a mouthful of pillow to stifle her cries. Her body was red from the blows.

"Okay," Cassidy said.

Franklin jerked around. His dick stuck up at an angle. His face went slack in surprise and he bolted toward the chair where his pants hung with his gun on the belt. Cassidy kicked the chair away and slapped him open-handed, and Franklin stumbled against the end of the bed.

"You spoke to my sister."

"It was a mistake. I didn't know it was her until after."

"No more."

"No. Swear to God." His eyes calculated the distance to the overturned chair and gun.

Cassidy wondered what kind of god Franklin would swear to. The woman stood near the bed, clutching a robe. "You might want to get out of here."

She fled through the open door.

Franklin saw a chance and went for the gun. He had his hand on it when Cassidy kicked him in the ass as hard as he could. Franklin went over the fallen chair, and the gun spun away. Cassidy reached him as he rolled over and hauled him to his feet. He slapped him again and then grabbed two fistfuls of Franklin's gut and lifted. Franklin went up on his tiptoes, whistling in pain.

"Don't do it again. Jesus, don't do it. Not again. Don't."

Cassidy walked him backward across the room until the back of Franklin's legs hit the windowsill. Then he threw him out the window.

• • •

That night he dreamed of walking by a tropical sea, deep blue-green. Waves beat against slabs of stone and spray blew high over a stone wall. Cassidy walked a broad, unfamiliar pavement. A car stopped in the distance and someone got out and started toward him. At first he did not know who it was and then he knew it was Dylan, changed somehow but still Dylan, beautiful, vivid, alive. When she got close, she smiled and said something he could not hear. He started toward her. She waited, smiling, but he did not get closer to her. He kept walking, but he could not close the distance. Dream geography, dream reality. Again she said something he could not hear. She waved and Cassidy ran toward her, but he could not close the distance.

When he woke, he was standing by the window looking out at the river with no memory of how he got there. The rain had stopped, and the day was clear and bright. The dream lingered—Dylan on a tropical shore and Cassidy running toward her.

It filled him with hope.